ADVANCE PRAISE FOR

BRIDE OF THE BUDDHA

"A remarkable and riveting love story—I literally could not put this book down—told in luminous and mindfully crafted prose. By reimagining the Buddha's disciple Ananda as Yasodhara, the wife Siddhartha abandoned in order to seek the Way, McHugh offers a story equally poised between transcendence and simple humanity. The reading became for me a meditation and an invitation to examine the Buddha's teaching in a new light. Highly recommended for anyone interested in living a more awakened life." — Mobi Warren, translator of Thich Nhat Hanh's *Old Path White Clouds: Walking in the Footsteps of the Buddha*

"For the most part, the women who support and inspire great men remain anonymous. We have Barbara McHugh to thank for bringing Yasodhara out of the shadows. Making use of historical texts, oral traditions, and a vivid imagination, she has created a portrait of the bride of Buddha and the world in which he lived. Crisp, charming, and unforgettable." — Sam Keen, author of *Fire in the Belly* and *Your Mythic Journey*

"From the first page to the last, the tale of this feisty bride and seeker held my heart. Yasodhara/Ananda repeatedly risks the hell realms out of love for others and a passion for justice. In her scrupulous honesty with herself about her own faults, she is often blind to her own goodness, but her sometime husband, aka the Buddha, sees her more clearly and tenderly. As someone who has found Buddhism baffling, I was deeply informed and moved by Barbara McHugh's brilliant imagining of Yasodhara's life." — Elizabeth Cunningham, author of *The Passion of Mary Magdalen*

"How wonderful to have the feminine written back into the Buddhist tradition. Where the Pali Canon leaves women out on the periphery, denied their place in the meditation grounds (and therefore denied a path to enlightenment), Barbara McHugh's imaginative placement of Yasodhara as Ananda, the historical Buddha's right hand 'wo/man,' is timely and welcome. As the narrative aligns so closely to the Pali texts, it is truly delightful to imagine Yasodhara / Ananda helping the female sangha become established. I shall happily consider this course of herstory from now on." — Ruth Phypers, author of "Dragon King's Daughter and Women, Meditative Practice and the Path to Enlightenment in Mahayana Buddhism," University of London, School of Oriental and African Studies

"In prose that glides like poetry, McHugh weaves the bold story of a remarkable woman. Transported to a period when women were meant to be vessels only for breeding and serving, we follow her perilous spiritual journey to enlightenment. So much of women's truth has been lost to history, but McHugh lifts the veil to reveal Yasodhara, the Buddha's wife." — Dorothy Edwards, author of *Langston's Moon*

"*Bride of the Buddha* is a masterfully woven story of love and a yearning for freedom, both societal and spiritual; a relationship that changes and grows with time; and a quest beyond the home on the path of the homeless that develops into a shared awakening. This evocatively written and moving story offers us a perspective that is not easily available to us of a girl who is searching within herself and in relationship to others as she grows from an inquisitive, sensitive, and playful child and sister to a rebellious daughter, a dutiful wife, a loving mother, a sincere seeker, a builder of the Sangha, a mindful attendant, and the relayer of teachings and practices that still ring true to us. Barbara McHugh's skill in telling a moving and gripping narrative; transmuting characters into each other; and weaving in facts with fiction, teachings with tales kept me engaged and wanting to know what happened next. I very much enjoyed reading the book and will definitely recommend it to others." — Shantum Seth, founder of BuddhaPath Pilgrimages

"A daring reimagining of the life of Yasodhara, wife of the Buddha and mother of the infant Rahula, left by Siddhartha so he could pursue enlightenment. As a young girl, Yasodhara is determined to engage in a spiritual quest in the midst of a suffocating patriarchal culture. It is all the more shocking, therefore, when Yasodhara infiltrates the Buddha's Sangha as the young monk Ananda and plays his pivotal role in the life of the Buddha. At the heart of Yasodhara's spiritual seeking is an unshakable love that fiercely defends her husband and son, women, and young seekers, and eventually expands to include the entire Sangha and the preservation of what the Buddha taught. I finished this novel with a yearning for this story to be true." — Wendy Egyoku Nakao, Abbot Emeritus of Zen Center of Los Angeles and coauthor of *The Book of Householder Koans*

"In the tradition of alternate-reality novels, Barbara McHugh spins a creative tale of intrigue and family drama as she reimagines aspects of the story of the Buddha. It is engaging and inventive, and very enjoyable." — Phillip Moffitt, author of *Dancing with Life: Buddhist Insights for Finding Meaning and Joy in the Face of Suffering*

"A rare and captivating story, set in India some 2,600 years ago, that explores who the Buddha might have been as a husband, father, and supremely enlightened being as seen from the point of view of Yasodhara, the beautiful wife he abandoned. Barbara McHugh skillfully weaves documentation of the historical lives of the Buddha, his family members, and his disciples as known from the earliest Pali texts, together with vividly imagined fictional events and characters, and the result is a gripping page-turner that deftly explores and illuminates important questions in contemporary Buddhism: the ordination of women, renunciation, ethics, the role of faith, gender, and the difficult challenges one inevitably has to face on the path to liberation. A literary delight that will be widely enjoyed by seekers of all stripes." — Meg Gawler, author of "Voices of Early Buddhist Nuns," Graduate Theological Union, University of California, Berkeley

"In deft prose, Barbara McHugh creates the voice of Buddha's wife as a protofeminist in a profoundly patriarchal culture. Yasodhara journeys from being the Buddha's profoundly sensual spouse to becoming his valued spiritual companion and attendant, Ananda, credibly disguised as a man. *Bride of the Buddha* is first a story, not a philosophical discourse, a reimagining, not a retelling of Yasodhara's story, that even a nonBuddhist can appreciate." — Carol L. Gloor, author of *Giving Death the Raspberries*

"*Bride of the Buddha* transports us to the years after Prince Siddhartha leaves his wife, Yasodhara, to seek his Dharma and become the Buddha. In this extraordinary imagining of Yasodhara's own journey to awakening, you'll feel you are with her every step of the way." — James N. Frey, novelist, writing teacher, and author of *How to Write a Damn Good Novel: A Step-by-Step No-Nonsense Guide to Dramatic Storytelling*

"As the wife of Siddhartha, the man who would be Buddha, Yasodhara sees her husband's heart and sacrifices her marriage to his quest for enlightenment, and then has to face hard truths to pursue her own spiritual authenticity. *Bride of the Buddha* is a riveting tale of the nature of suffering and the journey to wisdom. Magically written, McHugh creates a world of mystic hope and earthly promise that leaves us looking more deeply into our own hearts." — Tess Collins, author of *Shadow Mountain*

"In this unique and gripping novel of a historical figure relegated to the shadows by her famous husband, Yasodhara forges her own path, sacrificing her position and privilege to undertake a perilous quest for enlightenment. *Bride of the Buddha* educates, illuminates, and captivates as it brings us into a legendary world." — Max Tomlinson, author of *Sendero*

"In an ambitious and brilliantly conceived historical novel that is both spiritual inspiration and heart-stopping entertainment, Barbara McHugh, a lifelong student of Buddhism and an accomplished teacher of poetry, brings these gifts together in a novel with characters so well-realized that readers will be drawn into their quest and make it their own." — John Martel, author of *The Alternate*

Bride
OF THE
BUDDHA

A Novel

Barbara McHugh

Monkfish Book Publishing Company
Rhinebeck, New York

Paperback ISBN: 978-1-948626-23-1
eBook ISBN: 978-1-948626-24-8

Library of Congress Cataloging-in-Publication Data

Names: McHugh, Barbara, author.
Title: Bride of the Buddha : a novel / Barbara McHugh.
Description: Rhinebeck, New York : Monkfish Book Publishing Company, [2021]
Identifiers: LCCN 2020048462 (print) | LCCN 2020048463 (ebook) | ISBN
  9781948626231 (paperback) | ISBN 9781948626248 (ebook)
Subjects: LCSH: Yaśodharā (Wife of Gautama Buddha)--Fiction. | Gautama
  Buddha--Fiction. | GSAFD: Biographical fiction.
Classification: LCC PS3613.C53316 B75 2021 (print) | LCC PS3613.C53316
  (ebook) | DDC 813/.6--dc23
LC record available at https://lccn.loc.gov/2020048462
LC ebook record available at https://lccn.loc.gov/2020048463

Front cover design by Lisa Carta
Front cover painting: "Hotoke" by LuAnn Ostergaard
Book design by Colin Rolfe

Monkfish Book Publishing Company
22 East Market Street, Suite 304
Rhinebeck, NY 12572
(845) 876-4861
monkfishpublishing.com

FOR BILL

"Those who refuse to give credence to the tradition until a diary kept by Ananda has been found, duly authenticated by the authorities of Rajagrha and Vaisali, will have long to wait."

—ERICH FRAUWALLNER (1898–1974),
Austrian pioneer in the field of Buddhist studies*

* Erich Frauwallner, "The Historical Data We Possess on the Person and the Doctrine of the Buddha," *East and West 7* (4), 1957: 309–312. Quoted in David Drewes, "The Idea of the Historical Buddha," *Journal of the International Association of Buddhist Studies* 40, 2017: 16.

PROLOGUE

"I won't leave without your blessing," Siddhartha whispered so softly I wasn't sure he wanted me to hear. He stood in the carved rosewood doorway of our bed chamber, and in the deepening silence of my refusal, I pulled Rahula closer, praying that our two-day-old son would feel only the beating of my heart and not the bitterness that filled it.

"You don't need my blessing. Just go. Find your Dharma."

My young husband, who would one day be called the Buddha, didn't move. He stood in the darkness, across the room from our wedding bed, and I lay on my side with my back to him, staring out the window at a moon waning to a diamond-white crescent. A single star, sharp as betrayal, was poised beside it. It was just before dawn.

Rahula stirred against my collarbone, a small shifting warmth under the cool silk coverlet. My husband had named him Rahula, the common word for "bond." But it also meant "fetter."

"Yasi," Siddhartha said, "if you ask me to stay, I will."

I looked at him, still standing in the doorway, but he was only a silhouette, his clear eyes and the tender curve of his lips already fading in my memory. Perhaps if I'd seen his face and it had revealed a change, I would have begged him to stay. But in recent months, his look of sadness and revulsion at the sight of my mortal flesh and all the suffering it implied had lodged in my soul, and now I could think of nothing but that look.

"I won't change your plans," I said. "You're right to cast off your illusions. I only wish you'd done it before we married." I gazed at the rising crescent moon, which was soon to be effaced by morning sunlight. Already there was a green smear in the eastern sky.

My husband spoke one last time. "I promise if I find the truth, I'll bring it home to you and Rahula."

I doubted his words. A minute went by, then another. Finally, the breeze shifted and the crickets resumed their refrain. Siddhartha had left, as I knew he would. He was taking the journey I'd once intended for myself.

Supposedly, the moon was full the night he left. Supposedly, I slept through it all. My version of these events will not be the one told to future generations. I was all but banished from that story. It's the price I had to pay for the life I chose.

Book One

YASODHARA

hen I was ten and my sister Deepa was seven, we
met the dog-duty ascetic. We'd endured needle-
work and hair-plaiting lessons followed by endless
instruction on preparing pujas, offerings to the gods. Now we were
lolling about in the shade of the mango tree outside the kitchen
of our teak residence—palatial by village standards, three stories
high—which housed my father's family and the families of two of
his brothers. It had rained earlier; puddles flashed and steamed in
the sunshine, and the air was scented with cumin, greenery, and a
faint drift of dung. The moist heat weighed us down, and we were
hoping a wandering holy man would come along to distract us. If
we were lucky, we'd hear stories of distant western lands populated
with blue-black demons made of smoke; purple-scaled mermen
with arms and chests as pink as raw fish; and spherical people who
had two faces, four hands, four feet, and two sets of sex organs—
so complete in themselves they never had to marry or search for
enemies to vanquish. Holy men tended to come around mealtimes,
and Cook, with her jowly grin and brown midriff bulging over her
green-striped sari, would direct the more respectable ones to my
father's pavilion and feed the others leftover rice or lentils. Our

mother, Pamita—"Ama" to us—was upstairs in the women's quarters attempting to predict the future from grains of sand and preparing our older sisters for marriage.

At long last, we saw a holy man in the distance, shambling on all fours between the millet fields, sniffing at puddles and growling. At first, I thought he was an oversized monkey, then I noticed his long gray hair, matted and clotted with mud, all but covering his down-turned face. He was also naked.

"How ugly he is!" I nudged my sister.

Deepa looked as though she was about to cry, her round little face stretching into an enormous sorrow. She loved to trick us into worrying about her; then she'd burst out laughing. "Yasi, look at his doodle!" She covered her mouth, knowing that her laughter was impertinent. But the audacity of the man's nakedness—and of the gods for inventing it—captivated us, and we both started laughing.

"Yasi! Deepa! Stop it!" Cook stood in the kitchen doorway, her thinning gray-streaked hair pulled into a single braid like mine and Deepa's, her scalp glistening in the heat. "He's a dog-duty ascetic, and he deserves your respect."

"And why?" I demanded.

"Yes," Deepa said. "He's *hideous*." The man ignored us, skulking around the clearing, howling under his breath.

"Don't look at him," Cook insisted. "Come inside."

"You can't tell me what to do." Spoiled, I took advantage of my position as the daughter of the village oligarch.

Cook snorted. "I'll tell your mother."

Deepa did her about-to-cry performance again, then laughed. "But you won't," she said, patting Cook's brown slab of an arm. "You're our friend." Cook liked to listen to the wanderers' stories, too, and her duty to supervise us while Ama was with our sisters gave her an excuse.

We needed to stay on Cook's good side, so I appealed to her authority. "Why should I respect such a filthy man?" I wrinkled my nose at a waft of his odor, considerably ranker than a dog's.

"He's degrading his body to purify his soul," Cook explained, wiping her curry-stained hands on her sari.

"That's ridiculous," I said. I knew Cook felt the same as we did. Our family followed the old ways, sacrificing to household deities to keep the universe going, then joining our ancestors above the clouds or under the hills—or wherever—then returning to earth, and on and on. My father entertained these wanderers, mainly to hear gossip that might help him marry off his daughters or advance the fortunes of my brother, Jagdish.

Cook had her eye on the ascetic, who continued sniffing around the bushes. "The dog-duty wanderer believes that when his soul gets pure enough, he'll enter a state of absorption and never be bothered again with life on earth. If he's right, someday he'll be barking among the stars."

"Well, then," I addressed Deepa, my hilarity rising again. "Let's purify our souls. Arf! Arf!"

"Arf!" Deepa said, and we both got down on all fours.

"I pray you won't be reborn as dogs," said Cook.

"But I like dogs!" said Deepa.

Cook disappeared into the kitchen and returned with a clay bowl full of pan scrapings—chicken bones, stale chapatis, and assorted greasy lumps—and flopped the whole mess on the dirt not far from the dog-duty man. He lunged for it, gobbling it up like a canine, and shambled off into the forest.

Deepa and I were still on all fours. "We didn't get our share!" I complained, and Cook suppressed a laugh.

"Your souls aren't pure enough," she retorted, and went back to the kitchen, which by now swarmed with her daughters and grand-children grinding spices and sifting stones from heaps of orange and ocher lentils.

I gave Deepa a look. Our dog imitations were about to ripen into a full-blown enactment.

"Let's take off our clothes!" Deepa said, already tugging at her red-and-yellow-dotted shift.

"We'll get into trouble."

"You're a scaredy mouse—squeak, squeak! You're not a dog at all! Dogs will laugh at you!"

"I don't care what the dogs think," I said, "but I do care about Ama finding out." Our mother could confine us to the dreaded women's quarters.

"Ama has to understand, we're purifying our souls." Deepa grinned. "And it's so hot today!"

True, the heat had not let up, and my thick black braid, flopping like a dead squirrel on my back, weighed me down. The shining pud-dles beckoned, reflecting the infinities of a cool, blue sky. Besides, I couldn't let my little sister get the better of me.

"Wuff, arf, wolf, glumph!" I yanked off my own shift and tossed it against the mango tree. Deepa followed suit, barking and howling and laughing. We headed for the puddles. "Doggy needs to cool off! Arf!"

The deliciously cool ooze of the water swept us into a splatter-ing and laughing frenzy. The calf-deep puddles erupted into gray clouds around our bare feet; black mud spangled our honey-col-ored bellies and butts. "More!" I shouted. "More purity!" I was up to my knees and elbows in muddy water and could feel the grit of it between my teeth. "Roll like a dog!" I ordered Deepa, as I threw myself down into the gray slop. "Arf!"

Half a dozen kitchen children had gathered around to cheer us on. "Clean up your souls!" I said. "Leave your bodies in the mud!"

Suddenly, I was flying through the air backwards, my head nearly wrenched off my neck. *Slam!* The back of my skull hit up against something hard. It was Jagdish's chest.

"Yasodhara!" he shouted. "Cover your shame!" Clutching my braid, he yanked me out of the puddle. My scalp stung, feeling like he'd pulled out half my hair.

Deepa was crying, but I willed myself not to. The kitchen children vanished.

My brother was fifteen, as tall as our father, and his voice had the resonant depth of early manhood. He dragged me by my wrist, the back of my skull throbbing, my ears ringing as though my head had been invaded by locusts. Deepa trailed along, whimpering.

Jagdish pushed us toward our heap of garments—"Pick these up!"—then pushed us behind jasmine bushes big enough to conceal us from passersby. "What if someone saw you acting like little whores! You've darkened our father's good name."

"Whores don't roll in the mud," I muttered, having no idea what they did do. My anger, which would remain a problem for much of my life, was working hard to replace the shame, pain, and fear, and almost succeeded. "We're purifying our souls," I told him in my haughtiest voice. "We'll be dancing in the *deva* realms while the demons torture you in hell."

"You stand right there, or hell you'll pay." My brother's handsome face flamed with a fury that overwhelmed mine. Deepa and I huddled together in the bushes.

In the time it would take a mango to drop from a tree, Jagdish sprinted to the cistern and back, and before we knew it, a torrent of water crashed over Deepa and me, knocking us to our knees.

Gasping, I shook my head to clear it, trying to figure out how to get back at him.

"Please don't tell on us," Deepa said in her best baby-sister voice.

Jagdish sighed, handing us rags to dry off, his anger seemingly spent, or perhaps Deepa had won him over. Most likely, as I would learn one day, Jagdish simply didn't want to make unnecessary enemies—even powerless ones—because he already had too many, starting with his grown-up male cousins who ruled over him. "Put your clothes on and come with me," he said. "I won't tell Ama how you disgraced yourself, but I'm going to tell her about the dog-duty charlatan. You shouldn't be down here listening to these crazies. You should be with your sisters, learning to purify your body, not what you think is your soul."

"But—" I tried to plead with him.

The fierce glitter in his brown eyes stopped me. With the side of a finger, he rubbed the developing cleft in his chin. It was a habit he had, edging his fingernail in that cleft, as if trying to deepen it. "I said I wouldn't tell. If I did, you'd be locked in the women's quarters until the day you marry."

The threat was clear, so as he marched us up the stairs to our mother's domain, I was grateful things weren't worse. As long as he didn't tell about our naked adventure, Ama would probably confine us for a week or so, and then, preoccupied as ever with our older sisters, release us to our own devices.

The teakwood women's quarters were gloomy as always, despite the carved shutters letting in jiggles of sunlight over the patterned red and green tapestries affixed to the dark walls. Once inside, I sat

8

cross-legged, sullenly spinning cotton into thread, wrinkling my nose at the jasmine perfume and the unending gossip of my mother, aunts, sisters, and cousins' wives. Their stories were mostly tales of childbirth deaths, disappointing marriages, and the dismal and frightening present age, with the old gods drifting away or deigning to speak to only a few priests and prophets.

"Dog-duty man was right," I told my mother as Deepa and I wound dreary balls of undyed thread. It was our second day in captivity, and our elder sisters and other female relatives were out making offerings at the village temple. We sat in the smallest room, devoted to the spindles and spinning wheels, barely able to accommodate the three of us. "When I die, I want to go to the land of eternal bliss and stop riding the stupid samsara wheel lifetime after lifetime."

Ama slapped her forehead. "And what land is that? Did he tell you there's some land out there?"

"No, he didn't talk at all, Ama. He was a *dog*," I said, happy for her ignorance, which I could now correct. "Cook said he would end up in eternal bliss."

"She was toying with you." Ama smoothed her sari, which was teal with a bright orange border. She was beautiful, with symmetrical features, a torrent of shining black hair, and glimmery brown eyes with the classic fish shape craved by all women. She also had a precision of movement, as though every gesture had been taught to her by the gods. But her voice was severe. "The only bliss comes from following Mitra's rules and playing our roles as best we can, trusting in the *Rta* and the devas to guide us. They will reward us with bounty and joy." Her words sounded wooden, as if belonging to some dead aunt.

"You don't seem happy," I said. "All you do is worry about your daughters not marrying into the right clan and whether you put the right number of millet grains in the offering fire. You hardly go outside these rooms. Maybe the gods are leaving because they're bored."

"Don't you speak to me that way." Ama plucked the misshapen thread ball out of my hand and threw it down like a dead rat. "I'd be perfectly happy to live in harmony with the divine order—except that human filth like the dog-duty ascetic and the so-called holy men your father invites to his table are driving the devas away."

"I like the wanderers," I said. "They have more fun than you do, even the dog-duty man."

Deepa chimed in. "I'm going to be a dog-duty when I grow up."

Ama glared, and Deepa screwed up her face as if about to cry, then burst out laughing, as always. "I will!" She glanced at me for support. I did a poor imitation of a righteous frown.

"Enough," Ama said. "I hope none of the gods are listening." She glanced down where she'd tossed my thread ball on the floor. "What a mess," she said. "I have to rewind the whole thing."

She stood up in a swoosh of blue and orange. "You will stay here the rest of the day and meditate on your proper position in this earthly realm." She strode over to the windows. The room, though small, was a corner one, and its two windows let in enough light for spinning. Now Ama closed the shutters. "I don't want to hear giggling or even talking in here. You must learn decorum." She stood at the door, speaking in her borrowed voice. "A woman's gift to men and devas is her beauty, which requires silence. Beauty gets lost in chatter." The door closed behind her, followed by the rattle of the latch. We were locked in.

The closed-up room was stuffy and darker than ever, the shutters' carved filigrees allowing only the tiniest glimpse of flickering green mango leaves, as doves cooed and mynahs whistled amid the wretchedly joyful laughter of the children outside. Monsoon season would soon be upon us—who knew how many more days of sunshine we'd have before being confined to these rooms even more?

"I can't stand it," I whispered and creaked open a shutter as quietly as possible. A branch of the tallest mango tree extended to within a finger's length of the window. But how strong was it?

Deepa crowded close to me. "Are you going to climb out?"

I was having second thoughts. "Maybe we should try the door latch first."

"Ama will hear us. But if we go out the window, we can climb back up the tree and get back before she even knows we're gone."

Trying to steady my breath, I looked out again at the leaves, slick in the afternoon sun, the branches heavy with fruit, bunches of mangos dangling from single stems as if arranged by the devas to make harvesting easy. The baby mangoes, green with the faintest hint of rouge, had a while before they'd ripen, which meant they wouldn't fall and attract attention.

No one was around. "I'll go first," I said, asserting my big-sisterhood once again.

I leaned out the window, my heart suddenly faltering, suspended over the abyss between the window and the ground three stories below. Still, the main branch was thicker than my thigh and sloped gradually down to the trunk, where other branches sprouted into a convenient ladder nearly all the way to the ground. Slowly, I leaned as far as I could out the window and grasped the branch. It was steady. I looked out above the trees at the land of freedom beyond, the hills of new grass rippling silver in the wind, glossy white clouds tumbling in the blue northeast, everything freshened and sweetened by the first monsoon rains. How I wanted to get out into this glorious day! I took a deep breath, and after the stuffiness of the spinning room, the breeze filled me with the confidence of air-devas skittering through the sky. In a single motion, I grabbed hold of the branch and swung myself around so I could shimmy down to the trunk. My shift had ridden up awkwardly, but there was no one to see. "It's your turn," I said in a loud whisper. "But don't grab the stems, they won't hold your weight."

"I'm lighter than you."

"Just don't!"

Framed by the window, Deepa's round face puckered with terror, and all at once the beautiful free landscape in front of me contracted into my own fear, and all I could see was the ground far, far below, the clay soil trampled and packed hard as stone. I regretted ever having thought of this cockamamy plan.

Then Deepa broke into one of her wide grins. "I'm a bird!" she whispered. "Yesterday I was a dog; now I'm a bird."

"That's not funny," I said. For once, her terrified-child act had failed to amuse me. I wrapped my legs around the branch and held out my arms. "Be careful," I said.

She fell into my arms, the front of her first, clawing hands and a wild-eyed face and heavier than I expected, the branch swaying, my heart pounding through every part of my body. "Hold on!" I said, still taking care to whisper. I had to let go of her with one arm or fall myself. With my other arm I clutched her hot, squirming little body as the branch continued to sway. My arm ached. Shiny mango leaves pitched to the ground.

"I'm all right," she said in a gasp. "You can let go."

"Maybe we shouldn't do this," I said. "I could hoist you back up."

"No! Let go! Don't be a squeaky-mouse."

I let loose of her and started climbing down the branch, keeping my eyes on my hands to avoid the twigs. I'd almost reached the trunk when the branch jerked upward.

I stared at the emptiness where my sister had been, my heart paralyzed, the world rocking back and forth so violently I feared it would break apart. Had Deepa jumped back inside the window? She'd had an excellent hold, I knew that for sure. She must have gone back inside.

Far below lay a broken puppet staring up at me, wearing Deepa's red and yellow shift.

Without knowing it, I'd started screaming her name over and over and over. A crowd of women from the kitchen and loin-cloth-clad men from the fields appeared from all directions, swarming over the small figure on the ground, hiding it from my view, but not before I noticed the green mangos scattered around it. I had warned her! I wrapped my arms and legs around the branch I lay on, still howling as if only the tree could save my sister, reaching down with its branches and sweeping her back up. Then I saw my mother hurrying toward the crowd. Her scream split the air, swallowing my voice and every one of my thoughts. All I could do was hang onto the branch. I didn't even see our two maids until they grabbed my shoulders and hauled me back into the dark room.

I lost all sense of time. Surely, not enough of it had passed since we'd climbed out the window for anything bad to happen. Surely I could climb back inside the moment just before we decided to escape and everything would be fine!

My mother burst into the room. "What have you done? You killed my baby!"

"No! I wanted her to go back..." I stared up at Ama, unable to say anything more, and then I fell backwards into moonless, starless night.

I awoke in Ama's arms; she was crushing me against her and weeping. "It's not your fault, it's mine. I never should have locked you in."

But I would never be able to pry her blaming words from my heart.

Over the next day, time jumbled even more. I lost the order of things. Night seemed to come and go, with everyone praying in the main altar room and the priest and the doctor conferring in rumbling, muted voices. Then I was back in the sewing room, still calling Deepa's name; then night returned in a different form, full of chants and incantations, and through it all my mother and sisters kept weeping. At other times all sound fled from the earth.

Finally, the next morning Ama wrapped me in a white sari so tightly that it hurt my hips and belly. She and my sisters were dressed likewise. Voices murmured around me, sounds without form. Someone offered me milk-rice pudding, but I turned my head away. I dwelled in my own silence, and a thought was struggling to emerge from it, like someone in danger of drowning.

My sister wasn't dead.

She couldn't have died, the branch was too thick and steady. And when she climbed out the window, I had held onto her. Perhaps she had fallen, but surely not far enough to kill her. She'd just been knocked out. When I had this thought, it became clear that I'd known it all along. Then I remembered I'd seen her—when? Sometime late yesterday or last night. She'd been lying on a plank behind our home altar, bouquets of lilies and heaps of plumeria all around her, the onyx statues of Mitra and the little household gods staring out over the praying mourners. But Deepa was just sleeping, just knocked out, wrapped in a white sheet. She didn't look dead, not like my aunt or my grandfathers with their closed eyes sunken like dried-out puddles and not like my baby cousin, his skin gray and his skull wrinkled like an overripe plum. And not like the accident-mangled or sickness-ravaged children and adults I'd caught glimpses of through the years.

Hands were pushing me out our front entrance into blinding sunlight. Twenty or thirty women in white saris had gathered under the trees, along with an equal number of men in *lungis*, mostly white. The women were keening, and my mother occupied the center of the group, her long hair tangled down her back, her voice raw and hoarse. The old priest, dressed in a white *dhoti*, stood just outside the group, and now he started walking, holding up an incense burner, filling the air with choking fumes. My father, Suppabuddha, followed. The adults parted, and the sight of the cart with the wrapped-up body burned itself into my memory for all time. One of the male servants led a donkey to the front of the cart and hitched it up.

Deepa's face was covered. "She won't be able to breathe!" I dashed forward and threw myself on the cart, intent on tearing off the wrappings.

"Yasodara!" Jagdish lunged at me, almost throwing me to the ground. "Stop tormenting our mother! You're old enough to understand the difference between life and death." He clapped his hand over my mouth. "If you don't shut up, I'm locking you in the cellar. We're taking our sister to the charnel ground."

Another thing I'd known all along.

Still, I would have tried to pull my sister off the cart, but my brother held me fast. And I realized that if I really wanted to help Deepa, I would have to follow the procession so I'd know the route.

She didn't look dead. I clutched that thought to my heart like a cherished secret. I would come back that night and rescue her.

I'd only seen the charnel ground once and from a distance when we were on the road to visit our cousins in another village. It was on a long slope next to the river outside of town. Although we'd passed it well before the driest time of year, the grass on the slope seemed worn and faded, except for patches of lurid green grass that nourished itself on rot. From the road, we could make out a couple of face-down naked corpses and scattered white bones, but by far the worst sight was what appeared to be huge beasts, brown-black and heaving, five or six of them randomly positioned over the field.

It took me awhile to see that they were vultures in clumps so thick they appeared as single beings, flapping their multiple wings and plunging their slimy meat-colored heads to gulp down innards, the way I'd seen them consuming the occasional dead dog or rabbit. But never so many, and never like this.

Ama had ordered us to look away. She said that it was bad luck to gaze on such a sight, and that we were fortunate not to be passing the charnel ground at night, when roaming spirits hovered above, mourning their lost flesh and driving living beings mad with fright. At the time, I'd feared the vultures more than the ghosts, and now as I followed the cart with my sister, I was glad that by nightfall the birds would have all disappeared.

Our procession stopped even farther from the charnel ground than the road my family had taken before. As the priests and the cart with Deepa headed up the dirt road without us, I felt only desolation coupled with my ongoing guilt. I closed my eyes and reminded myself that I would soon see her again; for now I knew the way to get here.

*

The moon, three days past full, rose late, but well before midnight. I slept in the same room as my three older sisters, and now I had to wait for their steady breathing and little snores before I could start my journey. At least we weren't locked in from the outside, I thought, as I crept down the wooden stairs to the side entrance. The air was sour and weighed down with stale incense from the previous day, and when I opened the door, the fresh night atmosphere braced my spirit and pushed away my fear, at least for a while. The lopsided moon was big and yellow. Although its light was still weak, I didn't dare steal a lamp. The only thing I took with me was one of my own saris to wrap Deepa in so she wouldn't have to return home naked. I wore my dark blue day-shift, which would be easier to run in, if necessary.

The windless night, cool in contrast to the dead air inside our house, seemed to heat up as I made my way to the packed dirt road that went around our village, a cluster of twelve wooden dwellings and thirty straw-and-wattle huts. Only a half-dozen scattered lamps glimmered faltering yellow light; the entire village looked to be asleep. Not that I walked in silence; frogs and crickets clamored and dogs barked, echoing through fields of freshly sown millet, mist-gray in the light of the rising moon. I was glad for the creatures' noise; it would mask any sounds I might make.

As I walked along the empty road, my fear, which I tried to ignore, began to swell up, tightening my chest and making it hard to place one foot ahead of the other. I reminded myself I'd never seen a ghost (unlike almost everyone I knew), so I wasn't afraid of them. After all, these roving spirits never *did* anything. Still, anxiety sped up my mind, spinning off new problems. I had to face the possibility that Deepa really was dead, or that she'd died when they brought her to this terrible place. If so, I would have to beg her spirit to return to her body. I'd try to reason with it. What good was a spirit without a body? And if her soul was hurrying off to another life, did it really think it could find one better than Deepa's? We had a wealthy father, a loving mother, beautiful sisters, a houseful of servants, and—as much as I clashed with Jagdish—a brave older brother dedicated to protecting us. Deepa's spirit could end up inside a dog—especially since we'd played that foolish dog-duty game. What if our heedless play created bad karma, which forced Deepa into the animal realm?

By the time I approached my destination, the moon was shining in my face, making it impossible at first to make out the bodies and bones, except for dark patches and faint white shapes. The voices of the little night creatures echoed ominously in the stillness, but at least the vultures were gone. I increased my pace, as if I could leave my trepidation behind; then I hit a wall of stench that knocked me to my knees. The other times I'd seen the charnel ground it was from a distance, and it had been downwind. Tonight there was no wind at all.

I held my nose, but the smell leaked in, a combination of feces and decaying flesh, yet worse—it had an ultimacy about it as if it were the source of every foul odor in the world, warning me to run from it as far and as fast as possible. I staggered to my feet and forced myself forward. I had yet to arrive at the charnel grounds proper.

"Deepa!" I cried out, hoping she would come to me and we could both flee this wretched stench. But all I did was momentarily silence the crickets.

I kept walking, gagging with every step, so preoccupied with the odor that I didn't realize I'd reached the grounds until I almost walked into a bloated corpse, its huge, pale face inflated almost to bursting, the mouth a writhing ball of worms, black excrement for eyes. At this point, my body heaved, and the smell of my own vomit knifed up through my viscera. It actually provided relief from the smell of death, but not from the horror pounding through my veins as I stumbled up the slope, the sickening crunch of rotting bones under my feet. Now on the charnel hill, I could see well enough, and it was horrible! I had to get Deepa out of here, but where was she? I dodged an armless skeleton and another naked corpse, this one face down, arms and legs flung out at impossible angles as if the body had been tossed carelessly from above.

Where were the spirits? By now I was in the center of the field, the moonlight turning the corpses a glistening gray and the bones chalk-white. "Deepa!" I called out, again and again. I screamed when I almost stepped on what once had been a baby, its head little more than a mashed piece of fruit, its mouth an empty hole in the center of its face. Reflexively, I looked up; surely the spirit of such a little one would still be hovering above its body, unsure where to go.

Then I realized: there were no ghosts. No souls, only people who had turned into Things. These Things were far more awful than mere objects, more soulless than something that hadn't had a soul to begin with. They seemed to deny the very possibility of souls, not to mention life itself and the warmth and vibrancy of love. Far better to be haunted by armies of roving spirits, even demon spirits, than to have the image of these corpses settle in my heart. But now they had, forever.

A shapeless new fear lurched up inside me, one I couldn't articulate at the time and didn't want to in any case. Cold sweat sliming my body, I kept on. These Things were not Deepa. Deepa was alive and trapped here, and only I could save her. I broke into a run, pass-ing a heap of skulls, trying to make out her shape on the slanting moonlight ground. "Deepa!"

Then, praise be to the devas, I saw her familiar form, silver-pale in the moonlight, up the slope just two or three body-lengths away. The vultures hadn't touched her—why would they? She was alive, lying much as she had on the plank behind our altar. I started toward her, but a sudden sound made me stop.

My engrossment with the smell and the sight of the corpses, plus the bleat of the crickets, had prevented me from hearing the other noises all around me.

The sounds of feeding.

Wild dogs, a good thirty of them, had spread out over the field sin-gly and in groups, growling and gulping as they fought over the gore. I could see them clearly now, gaunt and ragged-eared, snarling and snapping with jagged rows of teeth polished white by moonlight and their greedy saliva. One of them was headed toward Deepa.

I broke into a run and reached her first, throwing my sari over her and snatching her up. She was heavy as stone, and oddly stiff—from fear, I told myself, but I had no time to think about this. Staggering under her weight, I backed away from the dog, which was almost as tall as I was, only to have another one join it. They crouched down, one black, one a scruffy gray in the moonlight, as if about to leap, their growls growing louder. I was terrified to turn away from them, which would in all likelihood prompt them to launch themselves on top of us. "Go away!" I shouted in the most fearsome voice I could manage.

Now two other dogs approached.

I slung Deepa around, holding her collapsing form up in front of me, pain clenching my arms. "Wake up!" I screamed. "We have to run, now!" Her weight was getting unbearable, and she didn't move. I turned her stiff body to face me. "Wake up!"

Then I saw her face, without expression, mouth half-open. Her eyes were also partway open, cold dull slits in the moonlight, as uncaring as gashes in stone. She was a Thing.

She couldn't be my sister.

The first dog jumped, landing on the corpse's back. If I didn't let the dog have it, he and all the others would tear me to shreds.

I dropped it and ran.

I didn't stop running until I was halfway home. Then I fell and lay face down in the middle of the road, sobbing into the dirt. All I could think of was the hollow shell of Deepa's absence, now filled only by the horrible image of her as a Thing. Then another image came to me, and the shapeless fear I'd first struggled against in the charnel field finally took form.

I, too, would someday be a Thing.

So would everyone I loved and everyone else, from the strongest warrior to the youngest baby.

No! I shouted into the night, and the village dogs erupted in barking. Reflexively, I filled with hatred, then I stopped. They, too, were going to turn into Things.

Why hadn't I seen anyone's spirit? Had they left the corpses to go live elsewhere? But what could spirits possibly be without bodies to give them form? I struggled to my feet and started walking, not caring if the dog clamor I'd caused woke up villagers who would drag me home to be punished. No matter if my mother locked me up in some room. With this newfound knowledge of death, it didn't matter where I ended up.

The dog racket died down, followed by the tiniest puppy yelp. I jolted to a stop, remembering that Deepa's spirit might be in a dog.

Was it possible?

That's what the wanderers were trying to find out.

At that moment, the only worthwhile pursuit seemed to be this search for spirit. Certainly, such a quest was the only thing that could make my grief bearable. Under the white misshapen moon, I knelt down and promised my sister that if at all possible I would find her soul so she could be with her family again and not have to travel though realms of *samsara*, lonely forever. I would look for the solution for all souls, for some way to save every being from the awfulness of death. As soon as I was old enough, I would go forth into homelessness and become a wanderer myself, uncovering the truth. I'd never marry, that went without saying.

2

*I*t was one thing for me to imagine going forth as a seeker and quite another to face my grieving family. Although Deepa was dead, I was the ghost in the weeks that followed, as I attempted to remain invisible while one of the worst monsoon seasons in years engulfed us, drenching the forests and pummeling the rooftops. Between downpours, pestilence-ridden white fogs crawled over the green-black hills, filling everyone with thoughts of death made worse by the dim haze of mosquitoes over the fields and a trickle of rot-smells from the nearby jungles. I was sure I haunted my mother, my presence reminding her of not only Deepa, but also my responsibility for how she had died. The last thing I wanted to do was inform Ama of my plans for a future that went against all she believed.

Ama continued to wear white—her hair tangled and her eyes bruised with sorrow—for a month. Then one day she appeared as her usual self, every gleaming hair in place, every fold in her sari the appointed width, every step and gesture precisely what it needed to be, no less and no more. She had decided that Deepa died because our family had been lax about offerings and sacrifices. Suddenly, double the usual number of chickens, goats, and tubloads of *ghee* went into our outdoor altar fire, and the priest appeared twice daily and stayed on and on, muttering prayers at our circle of black river stones flanked by a chunky carved granite statue of Bhaga, god of wealth and patron of marriage, and a polished curvaceous one of Adi Parashakti, the Divine Mother. To me, though, all gods now seemed no more than rocks and plants, like dolls who spoke only when I pretended they did. Yet I had no choice but to occupy myself by making florets out of palm leaves and other little sacrifices for the indoor altar fires, my fingers numb, my heart deep in the bottomless well of my loneliness.

The only hope for me was to ask the spiritual wanderers for advice and direction, but they were extremely rare, for the rains had turned the clay roads into mud rivers that sucked at my calves and slowed even the mightiest war horses to a stumbling crawl. Still, whenever the weather allowed, I'd crouch at the kitchen door, waiting. Midway through the season a holy man finally appeared, tall enough to pick his way through the mud quagmires. He was gaunt and naked, his withered body gray with pounded ash. His matted, dust-colored hair reached down to his knees.

I approached him with a banana leaf plate of rice mixed with *dahl*, which I hoped he would notice wasn't moldy or stale like most of what he probably received. He looked to be a table-scraps kind of holy man, not one my father would entertain. I gestured toward the heavy clumps of mangos, which I normally couldn't bear to look at, much less eat, since the accident, although they were now ripe as golden sunsets. "Take as many as you like."

He bowed his musty head in thanksgiving, his scant beard brushing his upper chest like tree moss. A smile broke through the many crevices on his face. "You have gained much merit, little princess," he said. Even though his legs were splattered with dried mud up to his emaciated thighs, and his manly parts were even more diminished and neglected-looking than the dog-duty ascetic's, he seemed gregarious, his smile settling happily into the ruin of his face. "Perhaps you would like some description of how the young ladies are dressing in the towns these days?"

"I would like to know how to find people's souls."

The man's smile vanished as completely as if I'd lifted up my shift and exposed myself. He looked down at his meal, which he had yet to devour. "Little princess, such topics are not for such as yourself to discuss."

"Why not? Souls belong to everyone."

"Of course. And if you fulfill your household duties on earth, you can hope to become a man in your next incarnation, where you can talk about the soul all you like." He tipped his banana leaf into his mouth, finishing off about half his food.

"I don't have time to wait for another life. My sister's soul is lost, and I need to find it. I need to find *her.*"

"So, you saw her ghost and wish to contact it. Simply pray to the devas, you needn't complicate your little mind with doctrine."

"I've never seen a ghost, nor any devas either. I'm beginning to think they're made up." I could recite all the fables by heart, but for absolutely no purpose as far as I could see.

The man gobbled up the remainder of his meal not looking at me, perhaps hoping I'd leave. Finally, he spoke. "I had no idea females could be inflicted with this strange blindness."

"I'm not blind! I see perfectly clearly."

"I'm not talking about ordinary blindness. But why do you think the gods are leaving? It's because men can't see or hear them. I've heard of some western lands whose prophets wander the deserts, imploring their gods to return, but these devoted worshipers perceive nothing."

My heart sped up. What was wrong with me? Or the whole world? "Tell me about this blindness."

The man regarded me with a kind of squinty fear. He tossed his slick-clean banana leaf into the underbrush. "Little princess, I have to leave. It's not appropriate for me to discuss such things with a female, let alone a child. It violates the ancient order and allows the devil Mara to sneak in, corrupting both our minds. Such a thing could cost us many incarnations."

Of course I knew about Mara, the god of death and the realm of the flesh, tempter and creator of ignorance—yet another unseen deva I was supposed to believe in. I wanted to shout that I cared nothing for devils or incarnations, just my sister, but I knew such an outburst would only work against me. "But I'm not an ordinary child, as you pointed out," I said. "And maybe if you teach me about the soul, you could cure my blindness. Surely, this would win you merit with the gods."

I willed my eyes to look as non-ordinary as possible, and stared into his, a wilderness of broken veins crawling around two shiny black disks. Something passed between us then, like a god or a spirit, whether I believed in it or not. I held my breath.

He brushed grains of rice out of his scraggly beard and straightened his spine, needing, I guessed, to assume the role of wise man, perhaps to protect himself against the blindness I embodied. "I'll tell you a few basic things, eternal truths the world has forgotten, for even the followers of the old ways live in an age of decline. They, too, have mostly forgotten that there is one eternal Soul and we are already united with it. But we must work hard to remember this, because the Soul is vast beyond pictures or words—a great mystery that periodically destroys Being itself, while remaining immortal over the great cycles of the universe." He lifted his face, as if to bask in his own speculation. "True remembering requires many physical and mental exercises, leading to abandonment of the body even while it remains alive."

"What exercises? Can you teach me?"

He shook his head. "Women, who are in love with their bodies, find such practices disagreeable, if they can do them at all." He smiled in a satisfied way, as if the enjoyment of his own wisdom had banished his discomfort with me. "And you, little princess, will soon be a very beautiful woman."

I recognized this denigrating flattery—I'd seen my father and other male relatives pour it over all sorts of women, from my mother to Cook. "I'm not a woman yet," I said, letting my anger show. "And I'm not in love with my body and I never will be. My family is over-stuffed with beautiful women, and I hate the idea of becoming one more of them."

"You'll change. And you will enjoy the change. Trust in the devas, even if you can't see them." He turned, as though to leave.

But I wouldn't let this arrogant so-called holy man brush me off that easily. "Maybe you really don't know the exercises," I said. "Maybe all you know are silly performances, like the animal-duty ascetics."

The man turned back toward me, his face a battlefield. Then he exhaled sharply as if acknowledging to something inside him that his pride had won and required to be appeased, even with a child. "Of course I know the exercises, which take many years to perfect. You must learn to still all thoughts by concentrating on a single object, like a lamp's flame or the breath. You must fast for days and remain awake for weeks. But you need to find teachers who will help you learn to do these things correctly, or the devas will punish you, whether you believe in them or not."

With that, he turned his back and, on his mud-splattered stilt legs, strode away.

At least he'd said "you."

Nevertheless, he'd left me with more questions than I'd begun with, and my encounters with other holy men over the next couple of years didn't help. They had all sorts of opinions. Some, similar to this first man, insisted that all beings were already happily ensconced in a common Soul, which for me seemed like a gigantic, bland pudding, expanding until it popped—inflating and exploding, over and over again. Others told me the Soul didn't exist at all—nor did anything else, because all is impermanent. Meanwhile, I had yet to broach the topic of "going forth" with my mother.

I was almost fourteen when an opportunity arose. By then my mother's prayers to big and small gods had changed from repentence to thanksgiving, for my father had married off my two elder sisters and had just arranged the most coveted match of all for my third sister, Kisa, who at sixteen had the reputation of being the most beautiful girl produced by our clan—never short on beauties—in generations. Kisa's looks were more an enhancement of perfection than anything unique: her eyes brighter and more expressive; her hair longer, thicker, and sleeker; her waist smaller; her fingers more tapered; her lips more full and curved; her cheekbones more exquisitely sculpted. Overall, these features, on the borderline of exaggeration, endowed her presence with such intensity that when she walked into a room it felt even to me as if she brought with her the realm of the devas, increasing the significance of everyone's life.

Young men, after setting eyes on her, had a way of improving their performances in athletic contests as well as fights, whether or not they had any chance to court her.

Most importantly, she had attracted the attention of Suddhodana Gotama, my mother's half-brother. Suddhodana was not only the richest member of our clan but also its current leader, elected by the elders. Although Suddhodana's son, Siddhartha Gotama, didn't seem eager for marriage any time soon—preferring to spend his nights with musicians and dancing girls and his days with feasting and sporting events—my sister's beauty apparently had persuaded him to settle down. Our family ignored the rumor that he was spoiled beyond redemption—the result of a vision, shortly before Siddhartha's birth, that the gods supposedly had presented to his father. Suddhodana's mystical experience—full of revolving wheels of fire, streams of rainbow devas, and other celestial excesses—had announced that his unborn son's destiny was either that of a world-turning monarch or some kind of ultimate holy man. To prevent his son from ever considering the latter option, Suddhodana had made sure his son enjoyed earthly life to the maximum degree.

I could think of nothing worse than marriage to such a man.

But it was my sister, not I, who was the bride in question, and my mother was both ecstatic and exhausted with the prospect of preparing for such a grand wedding. I hoped to use both her reactions to my advantage. One day we were alone in the women's quarters folding altar cloths and pillow coverings, my sister having gone off with her many cousins to the market to price bangles. The grated windows were open wide, letting in light and the sweetness of the forest. Outside, fat clouds nudged each other in the eastern sky, far from the afternoon sun. It was another monsoon season, but much milder than the one after Deepa died.

"You've borne the burden of marrying off so many daughters," I said. "Not to mention all those dowries. I hate to think of putting you through this again."

"Burden?" Ama looked perplexed, then smiled and patted my hand. "Yasi, this is our life as the devas have ordained."

"But maybe the devas have ordained something different for me, to ease your burden. Perhaps I could go forth as a seeker."

"Yasodhara!" My mother's dumfounded gasp and exhale made her earrings jingle wildly. "Has your mind been deranged by demons?"

"Ama, I have to confess something. I've never seen a demon, or a deva either. I've heard talk of a certain blindness that some people have. According to some of the seekers, the only way to cure this blindness is to go forth and find the right teachers to train one's mind." This, granted, was a loose interpretation of what they'd actually said.

"My child. What you speak of is not blindness, it's the devas' despair over our degenerate age, which these self-appointed seekers themselves have caused. If you want to see gods and spirits, you need to perform the correct prayers and carry out your duties, and most of all you must listen. Do you think I am always in the company of the gods? No, I must beg them to come to me, and then listen with all my heart and soul. We no longer live in the times of your great-grandmother. The devas sang to her constantly." My mother suddenly looked older, and I noticed for the first time that grief and accumulating years had dulled her hair (but only to the shine of ordinary women half her age), and imprinted the faintest of mushroom-colored crescents under her perfect brown eyes. "My grandmother lived her whole life inside their songs."

I wondered if that was true, or if it was just another story about the past, full of prodigious beings and titanic gods who nobody had actually ever seen. "But I've listened for these voices," I said. "The seekers taught me how to still my mind so my thoughts wouldn't block the way. And I've tried to do my household duties, and I've prayed, but I've yet to see or hear anything except a tingling in my ears." I didn't add that the tingling sometimes opened into a vastness that seemed to expand my spirit far beyond my small concerns—even my worries about Deepa's soul—a state I wasn't sure I wanted. "I need to find if somewhere there's a teacher who can cure me."

"But to go out all alone on the road!"

"Some women do," I said.

"Very few, and those women are old. As a young girl, you would be attacked and left to die—or sold into slavery."

"Times are different now. There are more women seekers, I think."

"That's how much you know! In this darkening age, things are getting worse for women, not better. Men have started calling themselves not only kings but emperors, whose soldiers regard females as spoils of war. In the cities we're bought and sold like pet monkeys. And not far from here, I've heard that we can't even own property anymore. If our husbands die, we are slaves to our sons."

"All the more reason to go forth and defy these changes."

"Haven't you heard me at all? These changes mean far more danger to every young woman walking alone, let alone homeless ones."

"So? I could get attacked or a lion could eat me in the rice fields just outside our house. I'm not afraid. Besides, I'd take care to walk with other mendicants and only in the day."

My mother gazed at me silently. All at once she lunged toward me, her bangles ringing loud as prayer bells, and pulled at my hair, worn in a knob like a boy's, until it spilled out and cascaded down my shoulders and back. I gasped, too surprised to say anything as she plunged her hands into the whole mess and ran her fingers through it, easing out the major tangles and kinks. "Wait here." She got up and left for her private dressing chamber, two rooms away. When she returned she was carrying a mirror, unlike any I'd seen before. We had a small one of polished obsidian, but this one appeared to be silver. "I traded for this in honor of my daughters' marriages." She held it up to my face.

I had no choice but to look at the bright reflecting silver. There was my face, unsettlingly like Kisa's, with the same luminous features and emerging cheekbones, with darker eyes and a slightly sharper jaw. Curving eyelashes thick as feathers. I'd hardly glanced at my image before; I'd never even used the obsidian mirror. At most I'd glanced at myself in a pool or a ceramic bowl of clear water.

Ama kept holding up the silver mirror. "Do you want this beauty to shrivel away under some patched and malodorous mendicant's robe? Do you want to become an old woman, never knowing the joys that young womanhood has to offer? Never to lie with a man? Or to feel the love of a husband? Or to be celebrated in a wedding, surrounded by the love and joy of all your kin?"

The mirror image stared back at me, rose-hued lips curving with innocent sensuality, dark eyes shining and full of depths I didn't know I possessed, skin smoother than the silver that reflected it. A tiny thrill jolted my belly and spread through my chest, softening and brightening me inside and out. Yes, I was falling in love with myself. And what better way to fulfill this self-love than by marrying? Looking every day into the eyes of a living mirror, a husband radiating love and admiration for my beauty.

Except that in next to no time I'd be a droopy-nosed old woman mourning this beauty and knowing nothing beyond the vanity it engendered. And then I'd die and turn into a Thing. And I would have deserted Deepa.

Panic sent me stumbling backward.

"Ama, I can't stay here." I could barely speak.

My mother stared at me.

"I visited the charnel ground," I said. "I tried to rescue Deepa right after she died. I promised her spirit, even though I couldn't see it, that I would find her. And do whatever I could to make her happy."

"You visited the charnel ground? Oh, my dear baby, why? The dead are dead; you must have faith that their spirits are with the ancestors."

I shook my head. "I don't have that faith. And I promised! If not for me, she never would have climbed out on that branch! She would be alive!" I buried my head in my hands, my shoulders heaving with sobs.

My mother put her arms around me. "Dear, dear, Yasi. You can't blame only yourself. I locked you up, after all, and tempted you both."

She sat back up, looking over my head, staring out the window into the empty space where the mango tree had been, the one Deepa fell from, which Ama had ordered cut down shortly after. Finally, she spoke. "Perhaps to seek your own truth is your karma. And mine."

She waited as I slowly straightened, my whole body filling with hope. "But I don't want you wandering off like a crazy woman," she said. "There are groups of female mendicants. When you're ready, we can try to see if any of them are suitable for you to join. But you must promise me that until then you'll start acting like a graceful young lady and not an orphan beggar boy. I want you to learn to be a proper woman, with all the skills necessary to be a wife, so you can recognize your true karma when the time comes."

"Yes! Yes! I promise. Thank you, Ama."

Both of us stood up from our mats, brushing off our saris, preparing to go downstairs and dust the altars. We didn't hear my brother until he burst through the door.

"Ama! How could you allow such a thing, for my sister to go out as a beggar! I forbid it." Jagdish, now taller than Suppabudda, our father, and with broader shoulders, stood before us in a black lungi, his naked chest glistening, his head thrust back, hands on his hips. He looked so much like our father, with his cleft chin, long nose and penetrating eyes—lacking only his stiff gray mustache.

Ama took a step forward. "A son does not issue orders to his mother."

He raised his hand as if to strike her. I tensed. "You touch our mother," I said, "and you'll spend a thousand kalpas in hell."

Slowly, he lowered his hand, but he kept his eyes strictly on Ama. "Our uncle Suddhodana will never approve of my sister wandering the roads like some fanatical hag," he said. "Yasi will ruin the chances for Kisa's marriage."

My mother snorted, even smiling a little. "The marriage will have occurred long before the question of Yasi's destiny comes up."

"That doesn't matter. She'll be a laughingstock and bring shame to the family."

"Not true!" I said. "A lot of people think going forth is the noblest thing one can do. What if a few pompous old men like Siddhartha's father disapprove? What if some silly gossips laugh at me? But you don't care about our family. You just care about yourself and how your self-important friends might see you."

Jagdish continued to address only Ama. "How can you let her

defy me? Yasi is not you! She's five years younger than I am!" He was blinking rapidly; you'd have thought I'd held him up with a bow and arrow. "She's probably doing all of this just to spite me."

"What!" I couldn't believe my brother was taking my actions so personally. "You are the most conceited person I've ever met."

Ama smacked her hands together. "Enough! Both of you. The question of Yasi's going forth won't even come up for several years. Meanwhile, we must all meditate on our karma and hope that the devas will give us direction." Her voice was a heavy knife, cutting through our anger and pride. "And that includes you, Jagdish. It's not seemly for young men to listen in on women's conversations."

My brother's complexion deepened with shame, and I realized how important it was for him always to perform perfectly; in that way he resembled our mother. "I had not intended—"

"But you committed the act," Ama said. "Now go. And let there be peace between the two of you."

Silently, Jagdish left the room.

Once he was gone, Ama turned to me. "Don't be too hard on your brother. Your father has always taken him too seriously, while your sisters don't take him seriously enough." She leaned over and picked up the silver mirror, polishing it on the edge of her sari. "You haven't been around your sisters and Jagdish enough to know how they've mocked and teased him over the years, even while your father wants to set him up as Siddhartha's mighty general and heir to some throne yet to be devised. These conflicts have created an imbalance in your brother—if you want to speak of blindness, he's an example. He can't always distinguish between his idealism and his pride."

"That's true," I said. "He often mistakes himself for a god."

Ama's small smile was almost mischievous. "You've never seen a god," she said. "So how would you know?"

Over the following weeks, I noticed that Kisa and Jagdish seemed to be always quarreling, especially after competing for Siddhartha's attention on his family visits. Jagdish definitely had dreams of being his second-in-command. "He's marrying me, not you!" I overheard Kisa say. They stood at our iron-bolted entrance door, having just bid farewell to the visitors. My brother and sister were oblivious to my presence, which was understandable. I was a fixture by now, stationing myself as often as I could on the path in front of our house, hoping against hope for some female holy wanderer to happen by, full of advice for a fellow aspirant.

Kisa snorted at our brother and gave a little shake to her head with its glittering array of intricate black braids embellishing a gleaming bun at the nape of her neck. "Don't think for one moment that you're joining my household after the wedding."

"That choice will be your husband's, not yours."

Kisa only laughed, her perfect white teeth flashing in the sunshine. "How could you ever think that a future husband of mine would risk angering me for the sake of a dolt with barnyard breath and the wit of a dung beetle? You bore him as much as you do me."

Jadish stood for a moment, quivering, although from rage or shock or hurt I couldn't tell. His reply seemed to crawl ominously from his throat. "You overestimate your influence, which you'll learn soon enough after you marry."

Kisa laughed all the more. "We'll see."

"If you don't behave properly," Jagdish said, his voice smoothing while his ominous tone remained, "the devas might not let you marry at all."

I thought little of these exchanges. I was too busy helping my parents prepare for the grandest wedding they could afford. We planned to harvest all our marigolds and hibiscus and purchase more from traders; we also would bring in extra cooks to help set up the banquet and prepare the spices. My father employed his brother-in-law's goldsmith to refine the precious metal and hammer out bangles and earrings, along with vases, platters, and other dowry gifts. Some of these were displayed at the family visits where my sister had finally met the nonpareil Siddhartha. He visited three times that season, accompanied by his father and the aunt who had raised him after his mother died shortly after his birth. This aunt, named Pajapati, supposedly doted on him even more than his father did. I hardly noticed her, my future enemy and ally, as everyone sat on newly dyed straw mats and our best patterned cushions—with Suddhodana, Kisa's future father-in-law, occupying the largest one, woven with gold thread. I was given the task of demurely handing out almonds to the group, which now included my two eldest sisters and their husbands; I had to prove to Ama that I knew how to make myself attractive, braiding my hair neither too tight nor too loose and wearing a sari folded to perfectly display my navel, an important part of a woman's appearance, as it represented the center of the universe. The purple and gold cloth of my garment also set off my new gold necklaces and earrings. In this way, I showed off my personal wealth as well as my sparkling beauty to prospective husbands.

I thanked whatever powers ruled the universe that Siddhartha had no brothers.

As for Siddhartha himself, I made a point of never looking at him. I noticed only that he was clean-shaven, unlike my father and uncle, whose mustaches occupied their faces like extended raptors' wings. Otherwise, Siddhartha resembled the other men at these gatherings, wearing an ankle-length formal *paridhana* pleated in front and an *uttariya* thrown over his shoulder. He also wore the standard princely gold earrings and his thick hair in a high knot that to me seemed prouder than those of the others, except for another cousin, Devadatta—yes, *that* Devadatta, who became an object of such controversy in later years. At this point, he was just another relative, albeit one who seemed intent on outdoing his cousin Siddhartha in every respect. My brother, four or five years younger than these cousins, followed Devadatta around as much as he could, joining in the boring conversations—mostly about the grandness of Suddhodana's establishment and the many projects that Siddhartha had undertaken to improve it, not only designing new mansions but also installing pleasure parks, including an artificial lake for fishing, boating, and growing lotuses. Did he have no notion at all that these pleasures led only to death?

Not that I could raise such an issue. To avoid seeming rude and also to keep my promise to my mother, I occupied myself with my eldest sister Chandra's year-old baby—a son, which my parents hoped indicated the ability of our disproportionately female family to produce male heirs. I held him while Chandra flashed her eyes and bangles, eager to be noticed in the ways she had before vanishing into the role of married woman.

Looking back at myself then, so critical of others' pride and arrogance—I certainly managed to overlook my own! Still, my snooty attitude helped me achieve my goal of avoiding attention. Although I wasn't overtly sullen—Ama would have chastised me for that—I wasn't the kind of girl Siddhartha would recommend to his male friends and cousins. I said nothing, showed no enthusiasm, and always kept my head turned away. As for the young men

I met at pre-wedding parties and dances—including the pompous Devadatta—I became adept at scaring them off with conversational gambits such as, "What do you think comprises the universe? Does all emerge from fire, or is it water? Do the gods perish or not? Or are they some conjurer's trick?" Of course I did this out of Ama's earshot.

The young men would suddenly remember they had elderly aunts to attend to and hurry off.

The wedding was scheduled for one and a half months after the monsoon, and I congratulated myself that I had kept my promise to Ama while avoiding attracting any suitors, although of course at any time some family could swoop down and mark me as suitable for their son. Still, it hadn't happened, and I allowed myself to hope that once Kisa was married, I could again bring up the topic of my going forth.

But as my mother would have said, the gods had their own plans.

The monsoon had ended, but on the night that everything changed, the moonless sky offered no more light than during the storms. I was dead asleep on my cot in the room I shared with my sister when something woke me into a greater darkness. Had Kisa moaned? I thought, she must be having a nightmare about being married—no wonder! Then she moaned again, this time followed by a strangled shriek.

"Kisa?" I whispered. "Are you all right?"

She didn't reply.

In absolute darkness she crashed to the floor, gulping in air with broken yelps, her skull and heels pounding the planks. "Kisa!" I shouted, grappling toward her heaving shape and clutching the knobs of her shoulders as I kicked open the bedroom door to let in torchlight from the outer courtyard. All at once she vomited loudly, the throat-clawing smell filling the room along with my corresponding nausea and fear. "Ama, help!" I screamed. "Something's terribly wrong with Kisa!"

Then came the lamps and clamor: Ama, servants, someone shouting an order to send a runner for the doctor, women screaming, my sister's yelping and moaning, more shouts, and a storm of thudding footsteps down hallways. In the light, her skin was ocher as if her blood had turned to yellow dye, her eyes orange crescents cast back into her head. She was so close to being a Thing, moved not by her own will but by some alien force. Amid the pandemonium of priests, doctors, relatives, and panicked servants, I struggled to keep the blackness behind my eyes from taking over as I applied damp cloths to her brow and gave her over to the doctor. Kisa's paroxysms were ebbing to a far more awful stillness. I held my mother in my arms, and she neither sobbed nor screamed but rocked back and forth silently. It was another instance in which time seemed jumbled. Dawn arrived as a shock. My sister Kisa was dead.

Apparently, a poisonous mushroom had been overlooked in the harvest of ordinary brown mushrooms. The two varieties were almost indistinguishable, although the lethal one was rare in this part of the land. We had all eaten the mushroom dish, but only Kisa had consumed the poison one.

The procession to the charnel ground was far larger than Deepa's. It overspilled the road with hundreds of white-clad mourners, the crowd swelled by Suddhodana and most of his household, with the exception of Siddhartha. Suddhodana had forbidden his son to come, saying that his status, now of former fiancé, was unclear.

(Here was another reason for me to dislike Siddhartha: I was sure that the real reason for his absence was that he couldn't be bothered with such unpleasantness.) Anyway, but for its increased size, the procession was almost identical to the last one: led by the same elderly priest, accompanied by gongs, chants, cuckoo cries and monkey shrieks, clouds of choking incense, and the heavy tramp of grief. I followed not far behind the bier. Although I didn't feel Kisa's death as profoundly as I had that of Deepa, who'd shared my childhood, I mourned my spirited elder sister, her cleverness and passion, and I suffered the same sense of irretrievable loss as at my little sister's funeral. Even the weather was similar, the day sunny and innocent as we made our slow despairing way between the green, monsoon-fed fields toward the territory of death.

Only my parents had changed.

My father, who had headed Deepa's procession in a manner properly grave and stiff, now trailed near the end of Kisa's, leaving Jagdish to handle Suddhodana up front. Father straggled along with my surviving sisters and their families, displaying little of his usual upright dignity, clutching alternately at his elbows and cheeks and swinging his head around like an abused donkey looking for someone to rescue him. He'd paid far more of his own fortune for this aborted wedding than he could ever expect to recover. No doubt that was part of his distress.

My mother, on the other hand, had turned herself into stone, at the molten center of which was a rage with the power to demolish all in its path. She wore her same white mourning sari, but had yanked her hair back into an angry bunch, as though she were forbidding every part of herself to choose grief over fury. She marched behind my sister's bier, not once looking at the priest. Since Kisa died, she had refused to go anywhere near our house altar, and the night before the funeral procession someone had toppled the deva statues in our banana grove. I strongly suspected it was Ama.

As the march continued, I drifted through the crowd, back and forth between my parents, fearing something bad was about to happen. More than halfway to our destination, my father noticed Cook and her family behind him, a dozen children and adults all wearing white and weeping copiously. "How dare you walk here!" he shouted. "I should have all of you driven into the jungle!" He had already dismissed the mushroom gatherers, even those who were relatives. "I should have you put to death!"

"I checked those mushrooms three times!" Cook stood tall, her belly quivering above its white wrap. "I sampled them at all stages of the dish."

My mother appeared, her face unmoving, her eyes shooting flame. "Husband, you will not speak to our cook in such a way. She's innocent of all charges. I checked those mushrooms as well. The fault belongs to our wretched gods, who hurl us to our doom as a matter of sport."

My father stared at her. "Woman, it is you who are speaking out of turn. You should be on your knees praying for forgiveness for such blasphemy."

Shockingly, my mother turned her head and spat at my father's feet. "I've prayed enough to compensate for a thousand blasphemies. I've followed every one of the devas' pointless rules, blistered my fingers making offerings, and served them up perfectly good dishes we could have used for our own table or at least given to the poor. And look what they dished out to us in return! It was they who hid the poison mushroom among the others—or else temporarily blinded us all, including the mushroom gatherers, to its presence.

I curse all devas! I only want that they join me in the hell they've created."

My father, I guessed, was stunned into silence, fearing his wife's impending madness. I didn't blame him. I was desperate to help Ama, but there was little I could do in this crowd. I headed toward her, thinking at least to put my arm around her—or to try.

Iron fingers bit into my arm, whirling me around. I knew even before I saw his clenched face that it was Jagdish yanking me aside, his grip making my arm tingle with pain as the crowd passed by. My anger was mixed with concern. Why had he abandoned his duty as head of the procession?

Still holding on to me, he nodded at the mourners. "Let them pass." He waited until the last of them were out of earshot. "You know how much Father has invested in this wedding. He will never have this opportunity again to ensure that we have control over our own estate for the next generation. At best, our family will become vassals to our uncle."

He drilled his eyes into me. "Only you can save us."

Could this be? Had my brother finally accepted my holy path? "I give you my most sacred promise that I will not rest until I learn how all our souls can be saved from the darkness of ignorance."

"What?! Stupid girl! This has nothing to do with your absurd fantasy of becoming a beggar. I'm talking about the family fortune."

I swallowed my hurt. "Then what—"

"Suddhodana and his son have noticed your resemblance to Kisa. True, you're taller and thinner, but at times I've seen Siddhartha gazing at you."

I yanked my arm from his grip, hardly able to believe what he was implying. "Are you saying I take Kisa's place? That I marry that pampered peacock who couldn't even take a day off from his fan dancers and trained elephants to grieve our beloved sister? I intend never to marry, but if I did, I'd choose a pack of rabid dogs over him."

Jagdish played calm. "Don't be selfish, Yasi. Think of Ama. She may not survive this loss. She hasn't had anything to eat or drink since it happened."

This sobered me, but not enough to accede to Jagdish's outrageous demand. "You talk about replacing Kisa the way we might buy a goat to fill out the herd. The prospect of such a thing would make Ama worse."

The tendons twitched in my brother's jaw, but he kept his voice steady. "You're letting your own concerns cloud your vision."

"What about *your* concerns? It seems the person with the most to lose is you—your opportunity to become Suddhodana's second son."

Jagdish brought his fist to his forehead. "I can't deny I'll lose a lot."

It was then I remembered the argument he'd had with Kisa, and a forbidden thought exploded inside me. Jagdish also had the most to gain. He'd lost a hated sister who mocked him and thwarted his ambitions, and now he saw a way to avert the disgrace of his other sister going forth as a wanderer. "Brother," I asked, "what do you think caused Kisa's death?"

The outrage in his eyes and hung-open jaw almost completely allayed my suspicions. "I have no idea. Perhaps the gods saw fit to take her. Perhaps they were offended by your plans—which defied them."

"You wanted her dead."

Tears sprang into my brother's eyes. "How can you say that? It's my duty to protect my sisters! Are you accusing me? What would that do to our parents? To Ama?"

"I haven't accused you of anything." I felt the breath sucked out of me. What had I been thinking? Even if there were any remote chance my accusation was true, I had no way of proving it. Voicing my suspicions would only shatter our family.

My brother's tears glossed his cheeks. If he was lying, I feared he was lying to himself as well. "Please, Yasi," he said. "I beg you. For Ama's sake. Offer to take Kisa's place. Only you can lift our mother out of hell."

What if my mother went mad or died of grief? I could never go forth into the holy life knowing I failed to prevent her death when I had the chance. I, who had contributed to her madness by my part in the death of her youngest child.

"I'll go to Ama with the suggestion. If, *and only if,* the prospect of my marriage to Siddhartha will truly move her, bring her back to life, will I go through with it."

"You need to approach her very soon, before Suddhodana starts looking for other candidates."

"Jagdish! This is our sister's funeral, not a matchmakers' conference! I refuse to talk about this anymore today."

Far in front of us, the crowd had stopped at the entry to the charnel ground. From here I could see the shapes of the gobbling vultures in the bright sun, even as a flock of parrots flew overhead, green as springtime. Jagdish took my arm. "I know what this is costing you," he said, "even though I never approved of your plan. But you'll benefit far more by your noble sacrifice."

It would be many years before I revisited my suspicions about poisoning.

That night, I brought a lamp and a gourd of water to the little weaving room where Ama had retired after the funeral. She lay, a dirty white mound curled on the floor in the room's far corner. The wooden storm windows and filigree blinds were bolted shut, and the room smelled of stale sweat and dark, female despair. I leaned over her. "Ama, you must drink something," I said.

Her voice was muffled. "A dead woman doesn't have to drink anything. Go away, child. Your mother has already left this world."

I was surprised by the intensity of my hurt. "So, then, you're going to desert your family because you're piqued at the gods."

She turned, crouching as if to slap away my gourd and lamp and drive me out the door. "You're fortunate to be blind to the devas. Better never to have seen them than to hate them as I do."

Her appearance shocked me. Her hair, a black mire, would take weeks to untangle, but the dull red tracks down her cheeks—she must have clawed them—and the voided-out expression in her eyes made me fear my Ama's spirit had fled her body, even while she lived. Jagdish was right. To abandon her now would be to condemn her to countless lifetimes of darkness, gods or no gods. "Don't hate the devas, Ama. It will only hurt you." My words sounded as feeble as dead petals fluttering to the floor.

She looked away. "Just go," she said.

I don't know where my next words came from. Perhaps from the gods themselves, perhaps from my own unacknowledged soul, not that of a seeker but a schemer. "Ama, our gods were jealous. They knew you would leave them for the more powerful ones worshiped by Suddhodana. By killing Kisa, they thought they could stop you."

"They've succeeded."

"Don't let them. If you want to punish them, make them bow to Suddhodana's gods. Find a new priest. Don't send yourself to hell!"

"It's too late. Suddhodana is no longer interested in our family."

I felt suspended in some strange floating numbness. "I could replace Kisa."

Ama said nothing.

"Please," I said. "You yourself acknowledged how much I resemble my sister. It would benefit all parts of the family, including Suddhodana, to have this wedding."

My mother gasped, suddenly remembering the real reason for her rage. "Our beautiful Kisa!" She broke down sobbing, and I could only watch as grief finally overtook anger. Finally, she turned toward me, supporting herself with her arms, her ruined hair hanging down on either side of her shoulders. "She's lost forever."

I swallowed. "I can live her life. I can honor her beauty. My actions and my children will be dedicated to her. She will live through me."

Ama sat up, leaning against the plank wall, breathing hard as if she'd summoned her spirit either to return to her body or to offer these final words before leaving it forever. "You plan to go forth. I don't want you to ruin your life, child. One life is enough."

"I no longer believe that going forth is my karma," I said, torn apart by my own grief, not for my sister but for my lost future. Yet I was moved to know that Ama still cared about my plans. "We could arrange a meeting with my uncle and cousin for as soon as the mourning period ends."

Ama patted at her hair, calmer now. "You did little to endear yourself to them, I fear."

"I can change that. Let me try."

Ama gazed at my face, lit by the little oil lamp; I could feel its heat. "I would be happy not to let your beauty go to waste," she said.

I opened the windows, and the night flooded in, a cool breeze and the yowls of a catfight below. "All I want to do is make you happy."

For I was certain that happiness was no longer a possibility for me.

A month later I stood with my parents in our main receiving room, with its patterned bolsters and cushions leaning against the teakwood walls, greeting Suddhodana. The weather had cooled; we all wore paridanhas with shawls, no longer white. My garment was midnight blue, worn with a gold cloth belt and earrings and bangles to match, an outfit intended to convey seriousness without being too somber. I now had to convince everyone that I looked forward to an event that filled me with dread: marriage to my coddled, worldly cousin Siddhartha, who had yet to arrive.

"You may sit," Suddhodana said, as if the three of us were servants or children, and we seated ourselves on the floor, not knowing why my prospective father-in-law wanted to meet with us alone. He glanced approvingly at the platform altar, now dedicated to Durga, the Vedic goddess. There was no statue, only a simple conch shell and a half-bloomed red lotus. Ama wasn't ready to overdo her new devotions. That seemed to be fine with Suddhodana, whose relationship to the gods apparently was a matter of keeping them at bay and paying them off when necessary.

Seating himself on our fattest pillow, he turned his attention to me. Compatible with the severity of his granite gray mustache, his long jaw was lean and his brown eyes watchful, those of an older brother needing to make sure none of his younger siblings were plotting against him. Next to him, my own father looked like a good imitation of a Sakyan leader, but an imitation, with a jaw consciously thrust forward to compensate for its narrowness.

Suddhodana spoke: "My priests and diviners have agreed that the gods have given us your younger daughter as a gift."

My parents nodded and smiled vaguely; I could hear my father attempt to swallow his sigh of relief. I tried to smile as well, hoping my despair passed for a mixture of shyness and ongoing sisterly grief. As for the divine support for my marriage, I couldn't help wonder how much Suddhodana had bribed his priests to tell him what he wanted. It was clear that both our families stood to profit from this switch.

Suddhodana's upper lip tightened a notch. "However, we are left with one question."

The room seemed to shrink.

Suddhodana wasn't smiling. "There are rumors your daughter has kept unsavory company."

"Cousin!" my father said. "Are you impugning Yasodhara's purity?"

Ama, still shaky after her ordeal, clutched her elbows. "That's not what he means, husband." My father's benign indifference toward my life had resulted in his complete ignorance of my interest in holy wanderers.

"Well then, what?" My father flashed his eyes at me, as if my mother had kept me in hiding my whole life and now was about to unveil some gross deformity.

Suddhodana folded his arms. "I am not speaking of the purity of her body, brother, but rather of her soul."

Ama's eyes were cast on the floor, as if she expected me to speak for myself.

It was then I was tempted. Ama had resumed eating and presiding over household life, although not yet with her former vigor; still, it was possible she no longer needed me to keep my promise. I glanced over at her, but she wouldn't look back at me. Did she feel guilty about my sacrifice? Was she giving me an out?

What if I just confessed outright that I was hardly the kind of worldly wife suitable for the temporal monarch Siddhartha was destined to be?

"Our family gets its share of spiritual seekers," I began. "I couldn't help meeting a few of them." I hesitated. Now was when I was expected to laugh off my spiritual concerns and say that all I cared about were the visitors' comical looks and stories of exotic places. Could I bring myself to speak such a lie? Surely telling the truth instead was justified, considering that my dedication to the holy life would benefit my family's ultimate karma far more than the extra geese, cattle herds, and outbuildings a marriage to the son of Suddhodana would bring. Perhaps if I said nothing more, my mother would speak, either to condemn me to this marriage or to rescue me.

No one spoke.

I couldn't lie, I decided. I prepared to confess who I truly was.

Just then the outside door opened and in rushed Siddhartha. "Father, I couldn't wait any longer," he said in a breathless voice, "to look into Yasodhara's eyes."

It was his face that undid me. I could go on about symmetry; the strong yet refined bone structure; the searching brown eyes lit from within; the full lips curving with sensitivity, yet firm enough to show strength of character; and all the other components of male perfection—but it was something else that melted my heart. His face, with its skin like concentrated honey, combined intelligence with a glowing innocence—something that even at fifteen I recognized. He also seemed to radiate a concern for all the world that I almost had to call love. And currently this love was directed at me.

Transfixed, I found myself believing, if not in devas, in their realm, where this man and I would live as divine mirrors of each other, reflecting each other's beauty, celebrating our natural glory and offering it like star showers to the living and the dead. Already, it seemed we were in love with each other—and ourselves—and this love was one and the same.

Yet just a moment ago I had been convinced I could not and should not lie, and I had always despised personal vanity. Something inside me went tight. Had I believed in Mara, I might have wondered whether he was using Siddhartha to tempt me away from my true calling. "Why didn't you come to Kisa's funeral?" I asked him. "Did your father really forbid you?"

"Yasodhara!" my mother warned.

"He did," Siddhartha said. His eyes beckoned me back into the exquisite universe of his gaze. "And I allowed him to, because I don't believe that humans should dwell on death. I believe we honor the dead by serving life, and therefore I want to cherish your sister by serving you as long as I live. I promise to be the best husband I can be. This act I shall dedicate to Kisa, but I will belong to you and you alone."

Essentially the same thing I had said to my mother. Only he meant it. And now I wanted to mean it, too.

Suddhodana cleared his throat. "We need to clear up this matter of your daughter consorting with vagrant holy men. My son cannot be distracted from his destiny by the pointless speculations of spiritual riffraff whose only purpose is to help Mara make mischief and disturb the divine order."

Siddhartha broke his gaze from mine and looked mystified. Apparently, he had not heard the rumors about my wishes to go forth.

At that point, all I wanted to do was return to that mutual gaze between Siddhartha and me that had swept the clutter of my earthly life into its own heaven. Surely, I could learn about souls in some other way than by living as a celibate wanderer.

Forgive me, Deepa, I thought I heard my true self whisper. A self to be locked away in the proud palace of my heart.

I looked over at my future father-in-law. "As a child, I listened to the silly tales of beggars who stopped at our door," I said. "But I stopped listening to them years ago. I have dedicated my life not only to Kisa but also to my youngest sister Deepa. I plan to serve as a wife in their names. Should I have other than sons, I shall name my children after them."

My future husband's smile filled my entire body with incandescence. "Father, we will marry," he said.

I lowered my eyes, those of a devoted wife-to-be.

I can make no excuses for myself, but when I think back on what won me over, I can only point again to Siddhartha's innocence. It had not only surprised me that a grown man could possess such a thing, but also in itself it was so beautiful that I wanted more than simply to preserve it. In my vague, fifteen-year-old way, I wanted to inhabit it, believing in the promise I had made to his father the same way he had believed in his promise to me. And for a time, I did.

3

*I*n these later years of my life, I've seen how the gossips and pundits distorted the truth about Siddhartha and me. I suppose many people want to fit us into a preconceived idea. (Kisa, of course, is never mentioned outside of a persistent rumor that Siddhatha took her as a second wife!) In the most popular depiction, Siddhartha was only sixteen when he married me, and I was little more than the prettiest of the crowd of girls and women who temporarily blinded him to life's suffering. Nonsense. He was twenty-six; he had known women, and what he wanted when he met me was a far deeper love. Our life was never one of decadence, where Siddhartha enjoyed his orgies and I sat around contriving ever new ways to titillate him—and where my father-in-law was perfectly content to wait thirteen years for me to bear him a grandson. As if Suddhodana would have allowed his son to endure a barren wife for so long! Such an idea is preposterous. Most likely our first years together have been distorted because few want to believe that even a profound and committed love is not enough to stop one from going forth to relieve the suffering of life's dualities. But that is what Siddhartha did.

*

So what was our story? Had my husband died before I got pregnant or had we somehow lived to an innocent old age, I might have remembered those first three years of our marriage as a series of seamless moments of wonder and love, starting with our wedding. I wore a sari of scarlet and gold silk, material I'd received from my future in-laws as a gift, silk being almost unknown in our province. A rare Chinese fabric, it whispered to itself and reflected and mutated light in a way I'd never seen before. It seemed yet another manifestation of the deva realm I had entered, like the wedding procession to my husband's home. He and I rode on a painted elephant high above the celebrants, with a view of soft green forested hills and glimmering blue lakes filled with lotuses like floating rainbows. Everywhere, nature's beauty was accentuated by bridges and pavilions Siddhartha had designed and built, garden paradises we now would share.

My new husband introduced me to so much, beginning with my own body. After everyone's endless vows, the spangled processions, the feasts of curries and crisp spiced meats on mounds of saffron-suffused rice accompanied by sweets of every kind—not to mention vessel after vessel of bright, transparent wine—we finally entered the marriage chamber. In front of the high rosewood bed— carved with images of vines and fanciful blossoms and shimmering with silk spreads like luxurious multicolored seas—my husband stripped off his garments.

I was shaken out of my trance. Was this big glistening penis actually going to force its way into me? Of course, I had been prepared for this as part of my education since childhood, and I had long ago accepted that I would feel some physical pain. But now I was remembering the holy men's talk of celibacy, how it was a way of guarding one's true Being, which otherwise would be squandered and washed away in the tide of desire. And if a man's soul could be lost, how much more so a woman's? I wasn't ready to be changed into a completely sexual entity, much less a mother, my questing soul forever subordinated to my animal role.

My husband's voice was gentle. "What's the matter?"

"Nothing," I said, pressing my elbows against my ribs. I was still in my wedding sari.

"No, something is wrong, I can tell." He reached down and picked up his upper scarf, which he wound around his waist.

All I could see in his eyes was sadness, not the anger I might have expected. "Isn't it better to be celibate?"

I explained to him the theories of the holy men and confessed that I'd once considered going forth on a quest to discover the soul's true nature.

"Souls!" Siddhartha laughed in his innocent way. "What can we know of them, really? They're just ideas floating in the future or past. All we have is the present, where our bodies are, and our love." The scarf around his waist stirred, and now he reached for my shoulder. "All I know is that I love you more than the devas, Yasi."

"I've never seen a deva," I said, suddenly needing to reveal this.

My husband's grin spread across his face as if I'd told a marvelous joke. "You don't need to! You're more beautiful than any of them!"

"So you don't believe in devas?" I dared to hope that he shared my peculiar blindness.

He kept on smiling, although with a bit of strain, I feared, because of the delay I was causing. "I don't worry about devas," he said, without anger or righteousness. "Best they stay in their realm and visit only on holidays."

"But what about our souls? Do you believe they live in the deva realm?"

"So what if they do or don't? I live in the earthly realm. Yasodhara, you are so much more than some ghost of a soul." He leaned toward me, his eyes tender in spite of a touch of exasperation, and I could feel his warmth, smell his salty scent, and a sweet weakness pulled at my belly. But I told myself I needed to resist, because suddenly I knew that here was my one opportunity for a life where I could gain some kind of knowledge—if not of souls or devas, at least of the world that Siddhartha seemed to think took precedence over them.

I touched his warm shoulder. "Only one thing," I said, my heart pounding—with fear and desire but also with determination. "I want to see this earthly realm for myself, and not spend all my time in the women's quarters."

He blinked. "You mean ride with me in my chariot? Help me inspect the property?"

"Yes." I held my breath. "And help out as well."

A funny little smile quirked up one side of his mouth, but his eyes lit up with wonder, as if he'd just heard a butterfly speak. "My father would never approve."

"He would. You're his precious only son. He grants you everything."

He laughed again, fresh as rain. "Why not?" he said.

"Why not, indeed! We love each other. So why wouldn't we want to be together?"

"All right," he said. "We'll do it." He took my hand, still on his shoulder, and gently placed it around his waist, where his scarf was in the process of drifting to the floor. My sari followed suit.

"But please, Yasi," he said in a breathless voice. "No more talk now of souls."

With his merest touch, the swells and curves of my flesh turned to silk, my senses uniting in surrender to his gentle hands encompassing my waist and thrilling their way to my breasts. I closed my eyes in a swoon of pleasure, all my doubts and speculations falling away like diaphanous shawls, useless in the moment's mounting heat. What could be more solid and real than our warm clutch as we fell upon the bed, my desire rising hot and urgent beneath him—my soul, whatever I might have thought it was, dissolving into a wild throbbing ecstasy—the pain of his entry opening me to a profound release of all my life's petty tensions, followed by blissful, oblivious peace.

I needed nothing else, I thought. I had yet to turn sixteen years old.

As Siddhartha had promised, we spent those early days inspecting the land, riding in a chariot driven by his wiry and dependable manservant Channa, steering Siddhartha's ivory-white war horse Kanthaka over the clay roads, hard as stone during the dry season—the worst heat a month away. Siddhartha's knowledge of all aspects of practical life astounded me—planting, plowing, carpentry, metallurgy, engineering (he'd even invented a roller to remove the seeds from cotton); his aim was to create a good life for all, no matter what class you belonged to. But he had definite ideas of what this life required.

One crystalline day, we'd stopped at a cluster of squat, orange-brick buildings next to a grove of lychee trees, where a half-dozen bricklayers in dhotis were enlarging the servants' quarters, seeming to ignore the worker sitting at the edge of the grove with his back against a tree. Siddhartha leapt out of the chariot, and I was expecting that he'd launch into some lecture to the foreman on some new method of stacking one brick on another. Already, I understood my husband was a great talker—he loved to teach and he also loved to learn, so he could teach some more. But not that day.

He approached the foreman, a mahogany-skinned giant about forty with ballooning calves and biceps, his dusty black hair tied up in a red rag. The air around him smelled of straw and sweat.

"What's this man doing here, Agrata?" Siddhartha asked him, nodding at the worker sitting under the tree. The narrow leaves pelted shadows across the man's leathery back.

The foreman wiped his forehead with the back of his wide wrist. "He'll be okay, Master."

"His eyes are watering," Siddhartha said. The man was breathing harshly as if in pain, but when he saw my husband, he blinked frantically and wavered to his feet. Sweat had slicked his thin gray hair against his head; one of his eyes had a pearly white cast, as if half his vision had lost itself in the realm of the dead.

Siddhartha kept his eyes on the foreman, making no move to approach the sick man. "He needs to go the hospital."

"We're short on workers today," Agrata said. "He was just taking a break."

Immediately, Siddhartha pulled up his lungi into a makeshift dhoti. "Channa, take the man, now." He nodded to the foreman. "I'll help you unload."

"But, Master, you can't perform the duties outside your *varna*—"

"Agrata, the sight of this unfortunate man will only upset your workers and sap their strength." Siddhartha was already bent over the wheelbarrow scooping up bricks, his back to the sick man.

My first impulse was to admire my husband for choosing

kindness over class duty, which had always seemed like just some more priestly mumbo-jumbo—especially the varna system, introduced by Suddhodana's newfangled gods, which unduly segregated the four social classes. Yet even in the midst of my admiration, some cold hand pulled aside a curtain in my heart as if to reveal a falseness where my Siddhartha was deliberately overlooking something important. But what? The worker was clearly ill, and certainly getting him to a doctor was the right thing to do. I shook off the feeling. "I'll go with Channa," I said. "I can help."

"No! You wait right here," he said to me over his shoulder. "I'll have Agrata's wife bring you some *lassi*."

I glanced over at the craggy-featured Channa, who shrugged in a knowing way, as if he was used to his master's behavior. I was mystified, and the feeling of falseness returned. "I'd like to go along," I said. "I've never seen a hospital."

Siddhartha straightened, his back to me. "And pray to the devas you never shall."

"But I want to. Perhaps I could help out there."

He thundered the bricks into the wheelbarrow, then strode over to me, placing his hands on my shoulders. For the first time since our marriage, I thought I saw his father's tight upper lip pressing against his teeth. "Yasi, it is our duty to keep sickness as separate as possible from health. We'll all have to face such things soon enough. There's no reason to be miserable in advance."

"But what about Channa? And all the people who have to care for the sick and the dead."

Siddhartha shifted from one foot to the other, sweat glittering under his clear eyes. "They have some karma, obviously. Even so, I believe in making it as easy as possible for them, with plenty of time to get away. No one healthy needs to live permanently anywhere near where they'll come in contact with pain and misery."

His discomfort made the day seem to gray over, despite the sun shining on. I remembered that first monsoon season after losing Deepa. "Sometimes I can't help but think of death," I said quietly.

"Those are precisely the times we need to leap back into the present!" He smiled then, but his eyes were the same as when he'd warned the foreman against being in the presence of a sick man. "You can do it, Yasi. You just have to fill yourself with appreciation for life."

"I'm not sure..."

In a flash, his smile spread over his entire face, his teeth a startling white, his innocence returning like the sun. He placed his arm around me. "Because we all can sing."

To my shock, my husband burst into a work song that all the men knew and I remembered from my childhood, praising the devas for muscle and lumber and the joys when the work was done. Now the whole grove rang with rich male voices. Once again, I felt swept up into the glory of the present moment, and when Agrata's wife arrived I remembered the women's part of the song, and the two of us joined in. Afterward, she served me spiced chai in a clay pot, and we watched our husbands work and sing. How wonderful, I told myself, that Siddhartha keeps up his spirits and those of everyone around him. The dark part of the moment, his refusal to look at the sick man, I folded away in my mind like a burial cloth I hoped I would never have to use. But I knew now never to ask my husband about his family's charnel ground. Later, Channa told me it was on the other side of an almost impenetrable jungle, and the road through the jungle, although kept clear, wound and twisted as if trying to hide from itself. From no part of Suddhodana's domain, not even the hilltops, could the charnel ground be seen.

Our blessed life continued for almost three years. I helped Siddhartha set up his paradises. It turned out I had a knack for designing gardens, using shrubbery to create interlocking chambers flooded with roses, lilies, and orchids. We also planned systems of pools and waterfalls, arranging rocks and planting trees so that reflected ripples trembled over them, reinventing sunlight and shadow alike. Our gardens and fish-filled ponds attracted throngs of birds: kingfishers, black-crested herons, golden loras, rose-ringed parakeets, and so many others—their darts of song and color sparkling through the air. All this beauty anchored everyone who passed through, rich and poor, deeply in the present—everything so new and astonishing. Who needed to quest after souls when the glory of the earth could enter one's heart and mind the way Siddhartha entered me? In these moments, everything was one.

Suddhodana and his wife Pajapati stayed benignly in the background, gently reminding us of our duty to produce a son. I looked forward to having children, although living in the present as I did, my future as a mother was little more than a thought that flitted through my mind like a bright hummingbird in a pleasant landscape. Besides, those first two years of my marriage were mostly devoted to being shown off. My in-laws held feasts and parties attended by most of the clan, my own parents celebrating their daughter's marital success and all the cousins wanting a glimpse of the ideal heir and his new wife. If they also wanted to gossip and compare, I remained oblivious as we rushed from one perfect moment to the next. In those days, I barely noticed the slivers of time in between, those dips in spirit when the pretty sights seemed to shrink into a vacuous landscape that hinted no perfect moment could ever be enough.

But these in-between times, minuscule as they were, could be relieved as easily as a bodily pain that comes from staying still too long. If we ran out of ideas, we had the gods, who, believed in or not, always gave us an excuse to celebrate. Every god had a repertoire of deeds to be commemorated with dancers and acrobats, trained doves and elephants, musicians with lutes and drums—all joining together to reenact the cosmic dramas. Here, too, was a time for paying particular attention to the poor. Siddhartha—with his father's halfhearted consent—made it a point that every festival not only had to include them in the communal feasts but also had to provide appropriate clothing and plenty of time off work to enjoy themselves.

I basked in the revelations of my husband's generosity; it was part of my overall joy. But joy, as I would learn in so many ways, is always impermanent.

One morning I awoke in our wedding bed with a queasy feeling, not totally unpleasant, for it was surrounded by a strange kind of excitement. Through the open windows I could hear the chuckling of parrots and the gargling of peacocks, as if full of enticing news, and as the sun rose the morning light seemed to expand the room, illumining the mahogany ceiling to a rich, warm gold. I took a breath of sweet morning air to calm my queasiness and suddenly had a sense, as of a message from long ago, that a new spirit had actually made its home inside me, a soul to share my body. I was going to give birth, and I had the thought, what if Deepa was being reborn in me? I found myself hoping for a daughter in spite of everyone else's expected desire for a son. Yet who was to say Deepa couldn't be reborn a boy?

I lay still, not wanting to wake my husband, wondering how to tell him.

I must have drifted back to sleep, because all of a sudden a hoarse male shout tore through the fabric of some pastel dream. I yelped and sat straight up, terrified we were being attacked.

"I had a nightmare," Siddhartha said. He was panting as if he'd run the length of his property and back.

I turned to him. His face was dark with a flush; his mouth gaped, his eyes dull with dismay.

"What was it?" I asked, my own heart galloping as if to catch up with his.

"Never mind."

I had the uneasy thought that he was still back in the dream, trying to convince himself he'd been mistaken about it. "Tell me," I said. "Please."

"I don't want to trouble you."

"You're troubling me now." I felt a shadow of foreboding. On this morning of all mornings, I hated to think my husband the victim of an inauspicious dream. "I feel that you're somewhere else."

He sat up, placing his forehead against his knees under the crimson coverlet. "I was trapped under a giant's corpse and couldn't get free."

"Well, the dream is over," I said, shaking off my superstitious thoughts. "And nothing more than an illusion to begin with."

He finally looked over at me, and this was the beginning of all the trouble, although I didn't recognize it at the time. "It was a woman's corpse," he said.

Then he sprang out of bed. "But you're right. There's no sense dwelling on illusions."

My belly remained clenched with unease. I decided to postpone telling him my news.

I let the next two weeks go by without revealing my pregnancy to anyone. Concealing my increasing nausea, I continued to go forth with my husband on his daily inspections, occasionally wandering off to vomit in the bushes while he conferred with this or that farmer or architect. I hoped to wait until I felt better to tell him about my condition. The last thing I wanted was for him to connect it with illness and banish me to the world of the sick.

We were planning yet another big festival, although not for several months, celebrating Durga's return of the buffalo demon's blood to the earth, a commemoration most people believed would incite her to keep the seasons going and bring the life-giving monsoon. It was an annual affair, but this year Siddhartha had decided on upping the number of military games and contests, he said, to thrill the maidens and distract young men like my brother and our cousin Devadatta, who might otherwise form raiding parties in the name of spreading our Sakyan happiness to territories beyond our traditional lands. These added games required clearing a large field near the edge of the property where stables and temporary housing needed to be built, and we visited the site daily.

One morning, I'd just left the dining room, where the servants were clearing away the collapsed rice *dosas* congealing on my plate, and I was waiting at the winter palace's tall oaken door on the lookout for Siddhartha's chariot, trying not to be nauseated by a choking smell of woodsmoke from the outside fires. The day was bright— too bright, I thought. The swallows dipping through the air around the almond trees made me dizzy. My stepmother-in-law took me gently by the arm.

"Is everything all right?" she asked, her tired brown eyes holding me in a dark study. She wore a plain beige paridhana, and the loose braid of her long coarse hair was gray as old rope.

I had spent the past two years being as cordial as I could to Pajapati. She was kind enough, with a keen intelligence in her eyes, but back then I cringed at her dogged devotion to her husband and adopted son. I thought she'd let her love for them drain off the sparkle of her own life, leaving her only a servant for her men's every need.

"I'm fine," I said.

"You haven't eaten these past mornings," she observed.

I knew she knew. "I just lack an appetite," I said. "I guess that's what happens."

"You haven't told Siddhartha." Her voice descended into severity, and I heard it as an accusation. She must envy me for being the center of attention, I thought.

"I haven't told anyone," I said a bit coldly, turning her accusation back on herself. "I'll tell Siddhartha today."

Her grip on my arm tightened. "You can't go out. You can't risk yourself anymore. It's time both you and my son entered the next phase of your life."

Suddenly I was ten years old and locked in the women's quarters—and subject to this disagreeable woman who wanted to dull me down to her level.

"I'm perfectly fine. And the air will do the baby good."

The two-wheeled chariot appeared on the road. I broke Pajapati's grip and ran toward it. "Don't worry!" I called out, as if we'd been exchanging harmless jokes.

I smiled up at my husband as he hoisted me to the seat next to him. I gave Channa a nudge. "Let's go!" I said in a reckless voice, and Channa, with his usual genial shrug, whipped Kanthaka into a canter.

Trees and fields flew by. At first I thought that my burst of energy had cleared my nausea, but I was soon overtaken by dizziness. The landscape slid into a green and yellow blur, and my viscera heaved inside me, threatening to liquefy. I grabbed Siddhartha's arm and shoulder, fighting a dull panic as we hit a bend in the road. I wanted to close my eyes against the image of being hurled out of the chariot, but that could well make the wooziness worse. I kept my eyes on the horse's churning white rump.

Finally, at the edge of the big gaming field we jolted to a stop. Shaking and clammy-handed, I allowed Channa to help me to the ground, hoping Siddhartha wasn't watching. I could hear little over the ringing in my ears, and the yellow field in front of me swarmed with black insects—no, they were men. By now my mind had slowed to a crawl, telling me how bad I felt.

That was the last thing I remembered before I flipped out of space and time altogether.

When I opened my eyes, the world had started over. I was peering into the dark, slick face of some indeterminate being—a demon, an animal, the god of death?—with lips drawn back over teeth so white they hurt my eyes.

In this new world, I felt no fear or anything else, not even numbness. I closed my eyes and opened them again, and I was looking into the eyes of an unknown man. Horror and revulsion had conquered his face.

Somewhere inside me, dark emotions I couldn't identify were gathering for an attack. I closed my eyes again.

"Yasi!" The strange man had put on a mask, that of my husband. "I thought you were dead!"

I stared up at him. I was lying on the stiff yellow grass, Siddhartha leaning over me, Channa standing in the background. "I just fainted," I said. "I'm going to have a baby."

"Darling! That's wonderful! You should have told me earlier!" But it was the mask speaking, not my husband. Then I had the thoughts: the demon had put on the stranger's mask and the stranger had put on my husband's mask. The dark emotions crashed through me.

I remembered Siddhartha's nightmare about the female corpse. I also remembered how he refused to look at the sick man, that he'd never mentioned the charnel ground the whole time I'd known him, and that he hadn't attended Kisa's funeral. Then an image came to me, how I must have looked when I passed out—my mouth hung open, my eyes rolling back into my head like empty porcelain spheres as I dropped to the ground like an unstrung puppet. Even now, saliva was drying at the corners of my mouth and on my chin. He'd seen me as a corpse.

I looked into Siddhartha's eyes, barely visible through the squint of the stranger, and I knew he was still looking at a dead body. All I could think of was the charnel ground: the torn-off arms and legs, the slimed-over skulls, the bashed-in baby. My sister, no longer a sister but a Thing.

Yet Siddhartha was gathering me up in his arms, stroking my tangled hair, and kissing me lightly on my cheekbone, where an ache surrounded by a sting told me a bruise was forming. I sucked in air and told myself I was just imagining things.

"We need to get you home," he said, lifting me into the chariot. "Do you need someone to ride with you? I can get one of the workers' wives to help."

"You're not—?" Desolation choked off my words.

"I'm needed here," he said.

For the next few months, I hardly saw Siddhartha at all. He was always thoughtful, always courteous, bringing me bouquets of roses and honeyed ginger to ease my nausea. He usually left these gifts at the women's quarters, where I was forced to "rest," enduring my mother-in-law's relentless kindness amid the company of Siddhartha's twelve-year-old half-sister and assorted cousins. I still slept in the marriage bed, but without Siddhartha, who spent his nights in the workers' barracks, claiming he didn't want to wake me when he went off at dawn.

We were never alone together. We appeared at ceremonies celebrating us, where we sprinkled ghee and dried petals into sacrificial fires to bring a healthy son into the world. These days Siddhartha seemed like the puppet, complete with varnished-on smile, jerky motions, and eyes painted to meet every gaze but mine. I had no idea what he was thinking, and my bewilderment grew. How could he just stop loving me because of one event, one I couldn't even help? I dreaded to hear that he had taken up with some concubine.

As often as I could—I wasn't a prisoner, not like later—I would take long walks, even as my belly grew, revisiting the sights of happier days. How different everything seemed now, although the spring greens thickened and deepened and the fat rhododendron buds exploded into bright punches of pink and scarlet, as they had for the past two years. But now the sweet grass and spring flowers failed to fill me with their joy. At best I felt them as a heavy solace; at worst a cruel charade, where everything remained as it was but excluded me. Over and over, my mind churned out the same thoughts: Would none of this had happened if I hadn't fainted?

Why had I foolishy insisted on going out that morning when I'd felt so sick? And what would happen to the child inside me without a father's love?

Then one afternoon, I came upon Siddhartha under the shadow of an enormous rain tree. He was wearing a workman's dhoti and sitting alone next to an artificial lily pond. Beyond the tree a field of cattle lowed; the air smelled of cow dung. My husband stared into the dark water paved over with slick black lily pads, nothing in bloom.

My heart gave a little hop of anticipation, but I realized this was an old reaction. The man in front of me had not come here to meet me, much less find me a welcome sight. Still, I had to ask the question that in one way or another he'd prevented me from asking ever since the beginning of my pregnancy. "Why are you ignoring me?"

The mask fashioned itself into a tentative smile. "How can you say that? I spend all my spare moments with you."

"Me and fifty others."

"I'm truly sorry," he said. "This Durga festival is taking up all of my time."

"That's why you're here, staring at the water bugs."

"I was just taking a break." Again, the contrived smile, with just the right amount of regret. "I'm afraid I didn't have time to find you to enjoy it with me."

"I'm here now." I stared into the artificial eyes, trying to see behind them.

He eyed my belly, by now a good-sized mound tugging at the front of my blue sari. "Yasi, you shouldn't be out here. You need to take better care of yourself." He stood. "I'll call Channa with the chariot. I need to get back to work."

He was going to leave me again. A feeling of utter helplessness made me sink to my knees in front of him. All this time, in all my mulling and second-guessing, I had avoided the simple, miserable truth—that I could no more make him love me than I could change the course of a river with my bare hands. "Just tell me what happened." My lips were quivering like a child's, and I felt tears welling up in my eyes. "Why don't you love me anymore? Do I disgust you that much?"

He sat down again, head against his knees as it had been after his nightmare, and for many moments he said nothing. Finally, he stirred. "It's not you, Yasi."

"Then, what? Some other woman?"

He shook his head. "For a long time I hoped that everything would change back, that I wouldn't have to hurt you more than I already have. Yasi, all I can think of is that we're all going to die."

"But you've always known that! You've always had the strength to keep your mind from sinking into these thoughts." A spark of rage ignited inside me. "You taught me how to do this as well." And to desert the holy life without a backward glance.

"I don't know what happened. The thoughts caught up with me. Now all I can think of is how everything dies, including love. How can a corpse love?"

The spark flared up. "What about souls? Didn't you love me beyond my body?"

"I thought so. But now—I've never understood how bodies and souls can be separated. And when I look around I picture everyone dead—I can't help myself—it's as if I live in a charnel ground." He still didn't look at me. "Yasi, I so want to love you!"

"But you don't," I said.

He clutched his bare shoulders. "I look back at our time together, and it's like all time—insubstantial as a clot of foam on a river. It dissolved even as we enjoyed it. We were always chasing after something new."

"So what? It was worth it! We always knew about impermanence! Why can't you get past this?" As I stared at his hunched-over form I saw him as I'd once feared he was, spoiled and weak. I also saw that his face, although freed from its artificial expression, no longer radiated the benevolent innocence I'd loved. "You used to care about things, about helping the world."

"I don't know what the world is anymore, beyond death. I'm afraid I just make everything worse by creating false paradises, which only raise expectations and in the end cause more suffering."

"That about sums up what you did to me," I said.

Suddenly, the being inside me gave me a kick. I was overwhelmed with tenderness, then rage. The little soul-body I was carrying didn't deserve such unhappy parents. "You deflected me from my path! You seduced me! Now what?" I knew I shouldn't blame him for my own decision, but I couldn't help myself. I wanted to hurt him as he had hurt me.

He was dry-eyed, despairing. "Yasi, I'm sorry."

Once again, I saw the world through his eyes. In his memory, our loving moments had been swallowed up by the in-between times of doubt and discontent, which had for whatever reason expanded to enormous proportions. The past that I cherished amounted to little more than a scattering of sequins in a vast desert.

He was as miserable as I was, and we were unable to comfort each other. This only fueled my anger. "You're of no use to me now," I said. "Now that you're so disillusioned with earthly life, you're fit only for the spiritual one. You should be the one to go forth. Find out what's what and forget your so-called duties to your father."

He buried his head in his hands, and I walked away, remembering the time when, to avoid thoughts of sickness, he had burst into song. Now singing was impossible, and all I heard was the bellowing of the cows.

The Durga festival was the last time I would appear in public before giving birth, and I had no desire to be there. The field, big enough for horse racing, contained an arena surrounded by tiered wooden benches occupied by hundreds of brightly clad Sakyans of all ages, cheering, laughing, and fanning themselves in the springtime heat. Cooking fires and food pavillions surrounded the field, and the early afternoon air was smoky with grilled lamb, trout, and venison. Everywhere, banners flapped, bells rang, and children dashed around, making me think sadly of Deepa and her ebullient spirit, the memory of which I had abandoned for Siddhartha. These days I hoped that my sister hadn't reincarnated inside me, for she would only share my loveless life. At least I hadn't burdened my family with my feelings. My parents, my sisters and their children—all at the festival—were overjoyed like almost everyone else that the clan was about to produce an heir, praying, of course, for a boy.

Only my mother seemed to notice that I wasn't steeped in happiness. Earlier that morning, she'd looked in my eyes. "I know," Ama said, "you want a daughter." I let her believe this was the only problem.

Siddhartha and I occupied a place of honor in the stands, front and center, surrounded by others of our generation, including my brother and my cousin Devadatta, who had prevailed in the wrestling and fencing contests. Four years ago—before I met him—Siddhartha had won every competition; this time he was begging off, saying that the younger warriors needed a chance. But I knew he had no more heart for any of this than I did. Not that we spoke of our feelings.

After that day under the rain tree, our pattern of never being alone together continued, and I made no more effort to break it.

As Devadatta and Jagdish took their seats, my husband congratulated them.

Devadatta glared at Siddhartha. "My victory means nothing, Cousin, as you have placed yourself above competition." Devadatta had yet another version of the Sakyan face, narrower, and with higher cheekbones. His black hair was tied back with a leather strip.

"I've done nothing of the sort." My husband smiled, keeping up his own facade of normality. "You're the unqualified winner."

Devadatta squinted at the spectators, his cheekbones crowding out his eyes. "Not according to them."

"Let it go, Cousin, I've lost all interest in anything to do with killing. You're the premier warrior, not I."

My brother, on the other side of Devadatta, stared at Siddhartha as if he had just surrendered Suddhodana's entire territory to the Kosalans. "How can you say such a thing? How can you abandon your gods? You were born to expand our uncle's domain."

In spite of all my recent disillusionments, I couldn't let this pass. "My husband has always preferred spreading happiness to spreading death. Let other clans ally with us when they see how we live in peace and prosperity. There are many ways to serve the deities, after all."

"Not for the warrior class," Devadatta said. He made a point of addressing my husband. "As you know."

"That's exactly right!" Jagdish's eagerness made me wince. "By risking death, warriors alone can honor the gods with the greatest virtue of all: selflessness."

"Risking death?" I said. "If women didn't risk death by giving birth, there'd be no warriors to risk anything. And as far as selflessness is concerned, most mothers could give lessons on it."

"Are you going to let your wife speak for you?" Jagdish switched his angry look to me, but he, too, addressed my husband. "Perhaps marriage has made you soft."

"Please don't bait me," Siddhartha said, his voice tinged with the weariness of an adult speaking to a child, even though Jagdish, at twenty-four, was only five years his junior. "The greatest virtue is conquest of the self, not of others. If you want to see selflessness, look to the holy men around you. And I don't mean the priests."

"Perhaps you should go forth," said Devadatta, tight-lipped.

"There are worse things to do," my husband said, looking straight ahead.

Another silly tale I've heard over the years is that Siddhartha had never known that sickness and death existed until, at age twenty-nine, he had Channa drive him outside the family compound so he could see what he'd missed. More nonsense, as you have already seen. My husband had been trained in war. He knew full well that his mother had died shortly after his birth, and he had witnessed the deaths of grandparents, cousins, and servants like everyone else. However, there's some truth to the story, in that Siddhartha's parents had kept him out of the presence of sickness and death as much as possible to the point of refusing any servant over the age of fifty to work in any of the residences. And of course, Suddhodana had moved the hospital and the charnel grounds out of sight soon after his birth. In the days after the Durga festival, Siddhartha had Channa take him to these places, where he spent many hours contemplating mortality.

One evening he entered our marriage chamber, but I knew by now it wasn't to take me in his arms. He stood at the door, the full moon bluing the hall behind him and blanking out his face. "You were right, Yasi," he said. "I should enter the holy life, and I want to do it."

I'm still not sure what possessed me back then, why I had so little sympathy for my husband. Perhaps I envied his freedom, but more likely I was bitter because it was he who had convinced me that the earthly life was all I needed. "Are you asking my permission?" I said, hearing the coldness in my voice. "Or do you need to be persuaded?"

My husband's silhouette shifted. "I'm not sure. I want to do my duty."

I felt my anger rising. "How dare you put this decision on me? But since you do, I want you to go. But I have a couple of stipulations. First, if you learn anything about how to meet with the souls of the dead, come back and tell me how to reach my sister."

"That's not what I'm looking for."

"Just promise me if you find out, you'll tell me. I sacrificed my own holy path for your love, which you now deny me."

He stepped into the lamplight, his eyes seeking mine. "I do love you, Yasi. I'd never have another woman."

I stared into the clear gaze I once trusted would cherish me forever. Now it seemed as impersonal as water. "Your love for me—as you yourself said—is the love of one corpse for another. Please go."

"I'm so sorry." With a rustle of his cotton garments, he knelt in the darkness. "If I survive, I'll return. This I promise you."

My bitterness remained, immobile as an anchor in a dried-up pond. "One other thing. Delay your departure until after you see your child. I want you to know exactly what you are leaving."

Siddhartha nodded, his face as grave as if he expected a stillbirth. "Please don't tell anyone until I'm gone."

And so, it came to pass.

4

There are many unofficial stories about how I spent the six years before my husband's enlightenment, some of which I occasionally wished were true—although not the tale that my pregnancy lasted the whole time! Many of the other rumors contain partial truths: my efforts as a seeker and the appearance of suitors during those times Suddhodana's spies lost track of his son. But for reasons that will eventually become clear, I'm just as glad for my scant presence in the overall story. Less for people to think about, less to suspect.

Some things I will reveal, however, as a way of deflecting obvious untruths. It's been bandied about that I had many suitors. I had one, of a sort. I also supposedly practiced austerities to parallel my husband's quest. Well, there's no way I could have starved myself and remained sleepless while nursing a baby or caring for him as a young child. But I did resume my search for my sister's soul by meditating and otherwise attempting to still my mind as much as I could. Not that I knew that much about meditation, only what the holy men of my childhood had said about sitting cross-legged and concentrating on my breath until my thoughts disintegrated in the silence surrounding them. In this stillness I looked into my son's eyes, so like his father's. They seemed to radiate their own light rather than merrily reflecting the light of the world, as Deepa's had. I concluded that my son Rahula couldn't be my baby sister's reincarnation. No matter, I loved him; he was truly my bond to the earth. Yet it wasn't easy.

At times I became another person, besotted with my son and his needs. Other times, alternating waves of grief and anger pounded through me, washing away my meditational calm and making me curse the day I ever became a mother having no choice but to live on and bring up my fatherless son. Yet I also had to admit that I'd participated in depriving Rahula of a father by suggesting Siddhartha leave in the first place—and with this thought all other feelings sank into a swamp of guilt.

The day after Siddhartha left, I was locked into the women's quarters, which had its own private courtyard complete with gardens, carved benches, ornamental fish ponds, and gilt-painted swings— where we were free to gossip, tell tales, and fuel each other's jealousy—all, I thought, to distract us from the fact of our captivity. We were about twenty in number—cousins, aunts, and their children— including Siddhartha's sweet-natured, thirteen-year-old half-sister, Nandi. Suddhodana's arrangement was somewhere in between what I'd experienced as a child and what I would later come to understand was a proper harem, where all the women existed to service a single male ruler. In the realm of Suddhodana, who was an elected head of our clan but not a king, the women's quarters were a repository not only for my father-in-law's wife and children but also for female relatives married or marriageable to other Sakyans.

To ameliorate the blame, self-blame, and overall despair of my days, which included loneliness, I tried to make friends. The women of the compound cared little for my stories memorized from holy men, but they came to me for advice on beautification—alas, despite my holy aspirations, my mother had trained me well. What with her surplus of daughters to marry off, she'd used her excellent memory to learn as much as possible about transforming oneself into a talisman with the power to stop men in their tracks, dislodge their sense of space and time, and delude them into craving after female beauty as something eternal. She'd taught her daughters everything she knew, including hundreds of recipes calling for everything from saffron to cow's urine to improve upon one's looks.

To my surprise, Pajapati approved of my strategy. "You can help your cousins distract themselves from their less healthy distractions, such as envy and hate." She was sitting in her usual corner, tucking back palm fronds into a flower-offering, and she glanced up at me, her yellowish eyelids free of kohl, and almost smiled. She knew all too well, I concluded, the consequences of living as pampered prisoners with little to do.

My loneliness eased once I became part of the women's society. Rahula thrived, making friends with the toddlers in the group, and I found myself happy to babble away to anyone who'd listen about his little quirks and fascinating (to me) habits, such as running around the garden and through every room pointing at objects. "What this?" he'd ask, "What that? What this called?" He clapped his hands at my answers, whether "golden necklace" or "chamber pot." During this time, I even came to appreciate gossip. It provided a way of making sense of life, not only for the women but for the men, as we wove them and each other into stories of loyalty and betrayal in ways that enlarged our lives, assigning them an importance rivaling those of the gods. But, unfortunately, stories require antagonists, which in our closed society meant one another. What helped me was my status as an object of pity; I let it be known that I grieved for the husband I'd failed to keep, and that I was resigned to virtual widowhood for the rest of my life.

But I needed to counter my guilt about encouraging primping. So I worked to realize what I considered my husband's true vision—improving the lives of everyone. I expanded my beautifying efforts beyond the women to the courtyard gardens, planting ornamental shrubs and introducing new varieties of orchids and hibiscus into the flower beds, set off by drifts of white alyssum and lakes of blue delphiniums. I also made sure that the servants could take advantage of what I had to offer, tailoring my cosmetic advice for them. If they couldn't afford saffron, they could substitute turmeric; without gold and jewels for their bangles and necklaces, they could use shells and beads to best effect. When the clanswomen objected to the time I spent on the servants, I reminded them that now these servants had the skills to help them with their own personal decoration. As I gained the women's trust, I even tried to explain how my husband's vision was for us all. In this way, I could make myself believe that in spite of everything he and I remained on the same path.

This effort was futile in almost every respect.

Suddhodana and his nephews—including my brother—were reversing many of my husband's efforts to minimize the difference between classes. And all over, not only in our region, the new religion was solidifying these differences, stating that to protest one's caste obligations would lead to a lower rebirth, perhaps even a hell realm. More and more, the lower castes became associated with vileness and filth, and even touching them required purifying oneself afterward with a ritual bath of milk. So far, our household hadn't adopted such practices, but I feared it was only a matter of time.

And I could do nothing, other than meditate and primp.

By now I was twenty-four and Rahula was almost six, and we hadn't any news of Siddhartha for over a year, not since he'd mastered the disciplines of Alâra Kâlâma and Uddaka Râmaputta, the two most esteemed sages in the land, and then turned down their offers to succeed them as the supreme master of their disciplines. Rumor was that he had become a strict ascetic, surviving on one mustard seed a day. I could only pray that these rumors were false. Suddhodana, though, apparently believed them, and I learned through Pajapati that he was thinking about declaring his son officially dead and marrying me off—choosing, of course, one of his nephews, who would provide his grandson with a father and himself with a son-in-law he could control.

Around that time, my brother paid me a visit. I dreaded to think he had a replacement for my husband in mind.

We met in a small anteroom adjacent to the compound. It was intended for brief formal encounters, and as such had no furniture other than a woolen carpet over bare tile. The room had a varnished wooden door, which could be closed for privacy, but just outside it stood a sword-carrying guard to prevent abductions—and the possibility of escape, for its third-story location meant that its two arched windows were not a factor. Outside them, shifting layers of thin white clouds drained the color from the land.

Jagdish had arrived before me. He stood in the room's exact center, arms folded, wearing a black lungi with a thin gold border and a matching uttariya over his shoulder. Since my confinement in the women's quarters, I'd seen him only from a distance, at festivals and other rituals as part of a group of young, unattached males who knew to keep their distance from the women, herded around like so many mares and fillies—you can only ride them if you pay the price. Up close, my brother looked older than I remembered, his chin cleft fully defined, his shoulders broader than Suddhodhana's. He was almost thirty and in his prime, sporting a bright black mustache almost identical to his uncle's.

"I need to talk to you about our cousin Devadatta," he said.

I braced myself. I knew he and Devadatta had taken on many of my husband's duties, and now I could only think that Jagdish had decided that I should marry Devadatta, or that my brother was acting under his—or Suddhodana's—orders. Of all the cousins, Devadatta, with his rigid class views and contempt for my husband's refusal to indulge in war games, was the last man I'd want to marry, had I wanted to remarry at all.

"I think I've done enough for our family," I said. "If you need to secure your position here, I'm sure you have the ability to do it without my help."

"What about your position? If you marry Devadatta, he'll do more than push me aside."

I blinked. Apparently, my brother had not come to urge me to marry our cousin, but the opposite. Of course. The two of them had to be rivals, and Jagdish feared that an alliance between me and our cousin would edge him out. I was on the point of opening my mouth to reassure him, but here was an unexpected opportunity. I cleared my throat. "Devadatta could be very helpful in the raising of my son," I said. "And now that my husband seems to have left for good, he's the most capable, not to say best looking, man on the land."

"Yasi, I can't believe you would consider that strutting opportunist. If you think you're a prisoner now, wait until you're married to him. He'll set up his own harem and lock you away."

"Nonsense," I said. "He needs the love of a woman to soften him.

There's a touch of sadness under his hard expression. I see it." This was a blatant lie. Devadatta's sadness, such as it was, came out of his failure to best his cousin Siddhartha, particularly when they both trained as warriors. His gaze belonged to a man who wanted to conquer my love for my husband and have it for himself. "I might even be able to influence him to keep you on."

Jagdish snorted. "Why are women so sentimental? I know the man. He'll trample us both."

I made a point of looking into his eyes, etched with rage and anxiety. "I'll take that risk. Devadatta is offering me love. If it turns out to be a disappointment, it will be no worse than my current life, the one that I have you to thank for."

"So," he said, "you're doing this to spite me."

He still took everything personally. "Not at all," I said.

"Then why? Have you no loyalty for your only brother?"

I hardened my gaze. "Loyalty to individual family members has never been anything you've pursued. Why should you expect it of me?"

But I'd gone on long enough. I folded my arms, in imitation of his favorite stance. "But if you truly want me to refuse to marry our cousin, I will do so only under certain conditions."

He jerked up his chin. "What conditions?"

"I want you to do all you can to implement what my husband would have wanted, had he remained focused on his worldly life. The houses he was constructing for the field workers were never completed. Have them up within the year. Dig the four wells that he promised to the village. Also, tell the priests they can no longer commandeer animals for sacrifices without compensating their owners, and make sure that not only do the farmers and servants get festival days off, but they are not saddled with extra duties that prevent them from working their own land."

"You can't expect me to destroy the natural order and defy the gods!"

"That's your interpretation, not mine."

The hatred in his face jolted me so much I almost lost my footing. "You should accept the request from a brother out of duty," he said. "Instead you scheme and manipulate to compensate for your female weakness. And for what purpose? To act out your inane fantasy that your husband will return and reward you for carrying out his will."

There was a grain of truth in his words, but mostly they brought me sorrow, for now I understood my brother. The flash of hatred in his eyes wasn't just for me; it was for all women, except perhaps our mother. Now I knew why he had chosen to remain unmarried, preferring courtesans and dancing girls to having to look the same woman in the face day after day. What a barren life he was doomed to live, and there was nothing I could do about it. "I've told you my conditions," I said.

"Suddhodana and Devadatta will never agree."

"Persuade them. Speaking of manipulation, I know you have skills in this area." I couldn't contain my sarcasm—I suppose I was angrier at my brother's hatefulness than I wanted to admit. "If you want to be a great leader, you'll need to practice."

Jagdish appeared to be considering my offer, staring out the window, where swallows swooped and knifed through the air. "You'd better hope I can persuade the priests to make the proper sacrifices."

"I'm sure that won't present a problem. Just don't be obvious when you pay them off."

"I'm surprised you're not more worried about your karma with all of this."

"I'll worry about mine; you can worry about yours."

"You've left me no choice."

I didn't reply. In spite of a niggling little satisfaction at besting my brother, I disliked resorting to blackmail. I also feared that his anger could sprout into vengeance. So be it, I told myself. I had managed to exercise the little power I had to help the servants.

As he turned to leave, he looked back at me. "You can't let Devadatta know about this conversation. You need to discourage him in some unrelated way."

"Don't worry. I'll do what I should have done a long time ago."

That night I cut off my hair; the next day I sewed myself a set of ocher robes. To assure the good will of everyone in the compound, I gave away my clothes and jewelry, trying not to play favorites, although I did reserve my best ruby earrings for my sixteen-year-old personal maid, Vasabhakhattiya, who'd been given to me when I arrived. Vasa had been loyal and friendly from the beginning, and her round face and bright laughing eyes reminded me of Deepa. I also gave her my silver mirror. If I never looked at my image, it had far less power over me, beautiful or hideous.

"But it doesn't seem right," she said, studying her face in the mirror, her lips naturally curved in the direction of a smile. "I don't deserve to look like a princess."

"You deserve it every bit as much as I do."

"But the gods..."

"The true gods will celebrate you," I said. "Just don't flaunt your gifts to the others."

"I would never," she said.

And she didn't, as far as I knew. But this didn't eventually matter, and one day I would long to beg her forgiveness, never having imagined how our karma would ripen.

I had yet to be seen by any of the men, but the next morning was the day before our full moon fast, a day when the women ate breakfast in the main dining room. I arrived just as the men were leaving. There were perhaps twenty-five of them, the clan leaders and their sons, including Jagdish and Devadatta, all clambering to their feet and kicking aside the cushions where they'd been seated around the varnished dining platform. Silver plates, utensils and drinking vessels lay scattered about as if by some restless wind—as usual, the men were eager to be off. The room smelled of woodsmoke and reheated dahl and rang with the laughter and shouts of men confident that their day of hunting, practicing warfare, and overseeing the lands would go according to their expectations and the will of their gods. Meanwhile, wives and servants were clearing away plates and consolidating bowls of rice and chickpeas to be served to the women, mostly on plain ceramic dishes, after the men had finished—a custom I had never questioned until recently and that for now was the least of my worries.

I felt Devadatta's gaze on the side of my neck. I glanced at him—his narrow face, jutting cheekbones, caustic eyes—and saw enough to understand his reaction. He was looking at me with more disgust than anger, as if he had been considering the purchase of some silver belt or dagger, only to find that his potential property had been dented and tarnished beyond repair. At least, I thought, he didn't seem to share my brother's active hatred of the female sex, but I had no time to feel relief over avoiding some angry encounter, because Suddhodana was striding toward me, his sword clanking

85

at his side. He glared at my hair and yellow robes. "Were it not for my wife, you'd be out on the street, begging or dying of the plague," he said. "You have three years. If my son hasn't come to his senses by then, you will leave this household. I'll bring up my grandson without you."

Sick with fear, I returned to my bare room, which seemed smaller and darker now that I'd gotten rid of the furniture but for one small chest and a stuffed cotton mattress on the floor. Suddhodana's threat seemed to vibrate in the air around me, as if it had followed me here, and it grew louder in my mind as I considered its implications. He had left me with no choice. If Siddhartha didn't return within the allotted time limit, I would have to track him down myself and lie, which meant stealing my own son. And if Siddhartha had permanently disappeared, it meant throwing myself on the mercy of some itinerant group of seekers—if such a group existed that would accept a woman and her child.

5

To prepare Rahula for our future life, I had to teach him how to meditate and how to climb. When the time came, I would descend using clotheslines, tying my son to me in a way that if he fell, it would only be as far as the rope between us. After everyone went to bed, I practiced my escape, hanging out the window in the darkness, eventually lowering myself to just above the rose bushes. I hated to think of landing in thorns, but I was glad my escape route didn't involve a mango tree. The memory of Deepa's wild-eyed face as she clung to the mango branches remained as immediate as it had been on the day of her funeral.

Encouraging Rahula to take up climbing was easy enough—he was a boy! At six, he'd already conquered every climbable tree in the lower courtyard—the jacarandas, the neem trees, and even the two big palms, which he'd shimmy up without a thought. Meditation was another matter.

I made a game of it. How long could he sit still? How long could he go without words coming into his head? Could he look at this one lemon for the count of one hundred without turning away? All during the dry season and into the hot season, we played these games, sitting cross-legged on the roof terrace among the half-tamed doves. At times I'd sneak in a comment or two that holy men were the best and truest warriors, because they learned to master themselves, the hardest task of all.

Then one morning on the terrace as I sat down for a before-breakfast session, Rahula tapped me on the knee. At first I thought he was just being affectionate. "You can sit with me if you want," I said. I smiled, allowing myself to enjoy the feeling of a day just starting out, with pink clouds unfurling through lavender skies, bird trills and warbles sailing through the bright clang of temple bells. Here was the one time of day that I could believe in the promise of Atman, the eternal soul, as a goal I could actually reach and not just some vague concept to wedge between myself and the fear of death. I closed my eyes.

I felt another tap. I opened my eyes to my son's brown-eyed gaze, a tiny pucker of disapproval between his eyebrows. "I don't want to do this," he said, meaning, to meditate.

"That's okay," I said trying to keep my predawn moment from disintegrating into annoyance. "Go off and play until breakfast. I need to sit here and learn to tame my emotions. Then I'll be happier all day long. And I'll be nicer to you too."

"I don't want you to do it either." There was something oddly sinister in his tone, especially for a six-year-old.

"Why not?"

Rahula bunched up the edge of his green dhoti. "You might go over to the enemy."

"What?! What enemy? What are you talking about?"

"Nobody."

"Then why did you say it?"

Rahula backed away from me. Then he spoke at double the usual speed. "Because-Father meditated-and-now-he's-with-them."

"With whom?"

"The king. He's going to join his army."

The morning crashed to a halt. Had my husband quit the holy life? Was he staying in the nearby Kosalan kingdom, not even bothering to let me know? I scrambled to my feet, reeling. "When did you hear this?"

Rahula stood in the doorway of the dim little room, shaking his head, holding on to the doorframe as if to some adult protector. "I can't remember."

I tried to steady my breath. A fine exemplar of meditation I was turning out to be. "I'm going to talk to your grandma."

In the flickering shade of a peepal tree, Pajapati sat on the tile floor in her usual corner of the courtyard, stripping leaves from the stems of white chrysanthemums piled at her feet. Their penetrating scent seemed to cool the morning air, already heating up, but the fragrance of flowers was not enough to soothe me.

"Rahula told me something very strange," I said, planting myself in front of her. "Something about Siddhartha joining King Pasenadi's army."

"Rumors and tall tales are always flittering around here." She continued stripping leaves. "Go tell Rahula that everything's fine. The last thing his father would do is join an army."

She had yet to meet my eye.

"Siddhartha is back, isn't he?" My voice bucked in my throat. I fought to steady it. "My uncle is keeping him away so Rahula won't meet him."

Pajapati glanced around, as if to make sure no one was listening. We were alone in the courtyard but for a pale yellow lizard behind her head, its waxlike little body clinging spread-eagled to the grayish trunk of the tree. "I happen to agree with Suddhodana. Rahula is too young to meet his father."

"Too young? He should have been with his father all along!"

"Not if his father's a recluse." She cast a look, somewhere between thoughtful and accusing, at my hair and robes.

"How can you say that? The spiritual quest is the noblest pursuit of all."

"You and I have different opinions about that, Yasi. Rahula needs to learn about human life as it is. He's too young to chase after some magical peace he'll never find." Her unpainted lips tightened around the words—revealing, I thought, a hidden bitterness that her life, for all its discipline and virtue, failed to satisfy her deepest self.

"You still blame me, don't you?" I said. "For my influence on Siddhartha."

"What does it matter, at this point? We've lost him."

I hated her attitude then, her resignation about everything. "How can you say that? What do you know about him? Or about the spiritual quest, for that matter?"

A rare anger flashed in Pajapati's face, surprising me. "Stop," she said. "I'll tell you what I know, but you can't tell Suddhodana I told you. Siddhartha is in fact staying with the king of Kosala."

"How did this come to be?" I stared at her. Kosala was our dangerously powerful neighbor to the south.

"My son, apparently, is his teacher," Pajapati said. "He's the kings's guest. He and his five hundred followers."

My knees almost gave way. "Five hundred?"

"He'd been on the brink of death, starving himself, when he had a vision. A year ago, he announced the turning of the Wheel of Dharma, and it's said that a thousand deities came streaming down from the Tusita heaven to hear his words. Since then, he's been traveling with a band of monks that keeps growing by the day."

"You've seen him! You visited him! How could you betray me?"

"No, I haven't seen him."

"But you're going to," I said. This was the only way Suddhodana could have persuaded her to stay silent. "The flowers," I said, glancing down at the chrysanthemums—an offering.

She nodded, more somber than guilty-looking. "Yes, I'll be allowed to hear him speak. But so what, really? I'll see him once— and who knows when or if again? He's a monk now, and he's given up his family."

There it was. What I'd longed for and dreaded. "Are you saying he's abandoned us forever? What proof do you have?"

"He could have come home months ago, but he didn't."

"He's staying away on purpose?" I couldn't believe it. "He promised he'd come back! He promised!" I felt like a child possessed by a rage that could escalate into hysteria.

Pajapati grasped my wrist. "I don't know how much he chose, and how much the men in our family have kept him away."

I snatched back my hand. "Why would they do that?"

"The thought of a Sakyan begging for food repels them. And that's how my son and his followers survive. And Sakyans have always looked down on Kosala, including their king, as little more than acorn farmers and fish gutters, even though compared to their army, ours is a dozen fifteen-year-olds with slingshots. Suddhodana is sending me to see Siddhartha alone, with only my personal maid and the charioteer to accompany me."

"But doesn't your husband want to see his own son?"

The anger had never entirely left Pajapati's face. "Your brother persuaded him that allowing Siddhartha to come here would endanger our property. Siddhartha has denounced the varna system. Our servants would be tempted to become his followers."

Jagdish! Would he never let up? Yet I was relieved to hear that Siddhartha had not abandoned his ideals. "I doubt our servants would choose celibacy," I said. "Can't you convince Suddhodana of that? At the very least, Siddhartha could pay us a personal visit. Then maybe I could persuade him to come home."

Pajapati gave me a one-sided smile, and a second glance at my hair and robe. "Too bad you abandoned so many of temptation's tools."

I glared at her. "Isn't letting me try worth possibly getting your son back?"

"But then there's your brother. He has a lot of power these days, Yasi. My husband's getting old."

The leaves of the peepal tree shivered in a stray gust of wind, and I watched the lizard skitter up the tree trunk and disappear. Some of Jagdish's power was because of me and how I'd manipulated him. Now I feared I'd have to do it again.

I looked back at Pajapati. "I think I know how to change his mind."

Jagdish and I met in the same anteroom as before. It was even darker than the last time: clouds in all shades of gray swarmed in the sky outside the narrow windows, heralding another monsoon season. My brother arrived after I did and immediately folded his arms and began tapping his foot, as if I were the late one. "I don't have much time," he said.

"I have one last favor to ask." I kept my voice gentle and free of spite.

"I've done everything you've requested." He swept his gaze over me and then focused on the storm brewing outside, as if my altered appearance was too awful to bear scrutiny. I saw myself through his eyes, my female figure lumped over by robes, my face unimproved by cosmetics or jewels, my shorn hair standing out from my head like black bunch grass. To him, my looks had a moral dimension, affronting the universal order. "I have no reason to grant you anything more," he said.

"Why not do so out of loyalty to your youngest surviving sister?" I let that question hang in the air, but I don't think my brother recognized the reference to our previous conversation. "I'm simply requesting a meeting with my husband—not only as a spiritual seeker but as the mother of his son."

Jagdish glanced at me, then looked away again. "When Siddhartha left, he abrogated his paternal rights. Suddhodana is now Rahula's guardian."

"Just let me see my husband," I said. "I need to know where I stand with him."

"Your former husband is not welcome here. Our clan has no more to do with him. I have decreed it."

"*You* decreed! What about our uncle? Has he died and no one informed me? It's hard to believe my relatives wanted to spare my fragile feelings." I admit, I was goading him.

But my brother remained calm. "Suddhodana appreciates my wisdom regarding Siddhartha," he said, his voice smooth as pearl. "I've witnessed Siddhartha's unwholesome influence on the lower varnas firsthand." Jagdish's gaze finally rested on me, level and triumphant. "After all, I've spent a lot of time with the servants and field labor overseeing your husband's projects—the ones you insisted I carry through. Now they have more houses and wells and free time—and it's still not enough for them. I've seen for myself that the only thing these so-called improvements have done is breed more discontent." The tiniest hint of a smirk tightened his upper lip. "Siddhartha's presence would only make things worse."

I let the anger charge through my body before I replied. "You'll have to tell Suddhodana that you've revised your wisdom on this matter. You might even find it wise to say that, in fact, Siddhartha's presence will improve the morale of all the varnas, upper and lower."

"What! What's wrong with you, Sister? I have no reason to poison my lips with such drivel. Now, if you'll excuse me, I've spent enough time here in this suffocating female atmosphere."

"Actually, you do have a reason to reconsider your view of the varnas, or at least change your reports to my father-in-law," I said, abandoning the hope that I wouldn't have to resort to blackmail again. "If I can't see my husband, I'll tell Devadatta exactly why I degraded my looks and took a vow of celibacy. Even as you yourself warned me—if he finds out that you were using me to undermine his power, he could well get Suddhodana to send you home."

"Devadatta wouldn't believe you."

"Why shouldn't he?" Now it was my turn to smirk. "All he really needs is the suggestion that you are a potential enemy, and he'll send you packing."

"I'll deny everything." His hand had traveled to the cleft in his chin; despite its maturity, he still had the habit of trying to deepen it with his thumbnail.

"Well, good luck explaining why we met in semisecret in this little room," I said. "Let's see now, twice? There are plenty of witnesses, including the lower-caste guards you despise so much. And who, by the way, despise you back." I shook my head. "Too bad, Brother, you used to be more skilled at not making unnecessary enemies."

"Which you were never any good at, at all." He pushed past me to the door.

An implied threat, but there was nothing I could do. "So you agree to talk to Suddhodana?"

He turned back in my direction, the desperate fire in his eyes surprising me. "Don't you even care about the honor of our clan? Don't you see that if we start treating everyone equally, the gods will desert us? And without them to reward and inspire the godlike among us, everyone will live identical vulgar lives—breeding and feeding, and little more."

Except for shallow, nonvirile pleasures such as watching sunsets, making music, and loving each other, I thought, but I wasn't going to let him drag me into one of his rants about warrior virtues forged on battlefields in wars often created mainly for that purpose. "You can convey Suddhodana's reply through Pajapati," I said, and he stamped out of the room.

I got my answer two days later. I was weeding the flower beds, trying to distract myself among rows of orchids, white tongues of petals and sepals framing their flame-patterned sex, the rows of blooms bobbing in the breeze. The courtyard was pleasant enough, fresh with recent rain, the puddles shrinking as they mirrored the bright morning sun. Rahula was out beyond the compound walls, playing with his friends in a ball court where the older boys often gathered. My seven-year-old son had more freedom than I did.

Pajapati approached from the other side of the courtyard, where she shared a suite of rooms that included a special entrance, seldom used, for Suddhodana. Although she wore her usual faded blue wrap, I almost didn't recognize her. She'd always carried her shoulders high and a little crooked, and her habitual walk was stiff, as if slowed by too many thoughts. Now she moved smoothly as a ship on a deep river. Her eyes and skin radiated a new light, and even her hair, drawn back into its ususal braid, seemed more lustrous. "Yasi," she said, her voice throaty with wonder. "I've seen him."

We'd been alone in the courtyard, but as if her words had the power to carry through walls, we were suddenly engulfed by almost the entire populace of the compound. Sparkling girls in their bright shifts, sober aunts in widow's white, smooth-haired wives in dark-hued paridhanas and shawls assailed us with overlapping questions, their children dancing and jittering around the group, chasing each other around the ginkgo trees, everyone talking at once. "Where?" "What was he like?" "Is he coming here?"

They must have been waiting for Pajapati's news all along.

My emotions were more turbulent than the crowd. Among other things, I was shocked at all this enthusiasm. "Tell us about your visit," I said to my mother-in-law, finding myself barely able to speak. As Pajapati prepared to answer, everyone went silent, which I feared revealed the pounding of my heart.

"He's done what I never imagined anyone could ever do, god or human," she said, her eyes aflame, as if to burn away the last of her lifelong cynicism. "He's here to show us—all of us, not just the Brahmins—the way out of pain."

"So," came the quaver of Pajapati's aunt, the eldest among us, "has he brought gods to help him? Do we need to make sacrifices?"

"I certainly hope not," I said, recovering my speech. I found myself annoyed with Pajapati's fawning attitude toward her son. What if my husband had turned into just another priest—or some charlatan beggar with power over gullible women?

"No, no," Pajapati said. "No sacrifices and no helper gods. To end suffering, he says, all you have to do is understand it for what it really is."

"Well, that sounds simple enough," I said. "Most of us, especially if we've given birth, know all too much about pain." I was surprised by the anger pushing itself forward through my emotional turmoil. He'd left me to languish for years in this spiritually stultifying atmosphere, and now he'd come home to bask in women's awe.

"What he teaches is not simple," Pajapati said. "This knowledge of suffering and its cause is nothing less than awakening from the cycles of life after life in this samsaric world. That's what he does—he teaches people to wake themselves up."

Waking myself up indeed, while my sister's soul could be languishing in hell. But why was I having such resentful thoughts? My husband had only done what I had urged him to, and his efforts to achieve liberation had almost cost him his life. I should be rejoicing in his enlightenment and eager to learn what he had to teach. Yet I found I didn't trust him. He who had waited so long to visit his family and who had failed to send any message this whole time. "And how does he propose to instruct us?" I asked cooly. "Are we supposed to take ourselves to the brink of starvation?"

"Not at all!" Pajapati said, a little breathless, suddenly sounding about sixteen. "He's found a middle way between denying the body and indulging it. Everyone can practice, beginning by living an ethical life, which results in calmness and clarity, which allows us to meditate and come to understand that the cause of our misery has always been our thirst for what can never bring lasting satisfaction. Once we truly know the pain that clinging to these desires brings, we simply let go. And our suffering is extinguished."

"And that's what Siddhartha has accomplished for himself," I said in a dead voice. He had achieved indifference to me, our son, and all we'd been together, because he had decided that we could never bring "lasting satisfaction."

Pajapati read my eyes. "It's not what you think, Yasi! You have to see him to understand. He's changed in a way I can't describe—the very air around him seems clearer. He's beyond an ordinary being, he's ... not even my son anymore, not in the old sense."

I could hardly bear to listen. I was halfway convinced that Pajapati's transformation was a form of derangement. "And how will ordinary householders have time for all this meditation?" I demanded. "Let alone the lower varnas."

For the first time, a shadow of discomfort flickered across Pajapati's face. "Well, of course, the best thing is to become a monk and give up the worldly life and all the temptations. But householders can start by making sure never to harm other beings, and even if they don't achieve complete liberation in this lifetime, they greatly improve their chances to achieve it in the next." She looked into my eyes, recovering herself. "But I can't speak for him. You must go, visit him for yourself." She smiled, her look of eagerness fully returned.

"Well, now, that's never really been an option, has it?" I was engulfed with fury—she got to meet with my husband before I did, and now she was luxuriating in her inside knowledge. "All these years, I haven't even been permitted to send a messenger to him! I've just had to sit back and pray for shreds of gossip to inform me whether he was living or dead."

"Please, Yasi, don't blame me for the men's rules. Your brother's, most of all!"

"I don't blame you," I said. But I did. I blamed all women, including myself, for our resignation, our complicity in what appeared to be an enslavement growing worse over time. "I should have run away," I said. "Let their arrows shoot me down on the road."

"Yasi." Pajapati gripped both my forearms. "You *can* see Siddhartha now. My husband will allow it. Your brother spoke with him, and now Suddhodana plans to build a pavilion for Siddhartha and his followers to visit after the rains. But you needn't wait until then. I know he'll give you permission to go at once."

"Permission," I said. "And do I have my husband's 'permission' to pay him a visit?" My anger turned back to its original object, my husband, who after promising to return, expected me to go groveling to him.

I looked around; all eyes were on me. I had to get out of there. "Send Siddhartha a message," I told Pajapati. "I wish him to come here and visit me alone."

The very next day the monsoons swept down on us in earnest, making travel impossible and giving Siddhartha an excuse to put off coming if he felt he needed one. Otherwise, life continued as usual but for the thrill of anticipation that seemed to penetrate every social class, even as I waited with alternating hope that my husband would eventually provide some magical explanation that made complete sense of my own sacrifice—and despair that such an explanation was impossible. I watched as Pajapati and the women attempted meditation and—much to my grudging gratification—made a point of treating the servants well, no longer slapping them for mistakes, making sure they were fed more than table scraps, and allowing them time off to visit relatives and linger over their meals. Yet none of my fellow inmates abandoned their golden bangles and elaborate hair arrangements; if anything, they labored all the more at their beauty routines. I feared they hoped to impress this great holy man they were soon to meet. I wondered, in my bitterness, if their techniques would work.

I made one vow: not to poison my son's mind against his father. At the very least, meditation had taught me over the years that hurt, anger, and envy were not dependable guides, and I wanted, above all, for my son to judge his father for himself. Meanwhile, I tried to teach Rahula what the holy men of my childhood and adolescence had told me about reuniting one's small soul with the Ultimate one, assuming that the practices my husband taught worked to that end—especially meditation, nonharming, and avoiding sensual excess, which for my son meant gulping down a third honey cake after dinner. I wanted to familiarize Rahula as much as possible with the spiritual disciplines before he met with his father. Only then would he be able to tell if his father was a hypocrite.

Finally, the rains abated and serious preparations for the visit began. Trees were felled on the property and in the outlying forests; the rain-swollen rivers floated them to the site of the future festivities where the pavilions and bunkhouses were to be built. Both of the main residences would house visiting royalty—including the Kolyan king, Pasenadi, so disdained by Suddhodana and all my male relatives for his so-called vulgarity—yet whose powerful army remained a territorial threat. Ironically, King Pasenadi seemed to believe that the Sakyan clan reflected my husband's attitudes of tolerance and peacefulness. To Suddhodana's horror, it was even rumored that he hoped one day to marry a Sakyan woman.

Pasenadi—another person who remains in my forgiveness meditations; I still ask his forgiveness each day. But I fear the dead cannot forgive.

After six weeks of cleaning, painting, and tying multiple ribbons around everything from poles to trees to elephants, the full moon approached, the day for Siddhartha's homecoming. (Here for once, the report of the moon's phase is accurate. No one, not even a spiritual revolutionary such as my husband, could ignore the importance of the full moon Uposatha ceremony, which had been practiced for as long as anyone could remember. Siddhartha timed his major Dharma talks accordingly.) My own preparations were minimal. I would wear my yellow robes, although by now they felt a little silly. What was I trying to prove, and to whom? I was still a member of Suddhodana's household, living as the wife of Siddhartha, who had yet to dismiss me formally from this position—and who had yet to grace me with a visit. He also had not invited me to join him on the path, and as the day of the gathering approached, I didn't have it in me to cut my hair again, which had grown to almost shoulder length over the past three months, let alone shave my head in the way of his followers. I couldn't identify my motivations for keeping my hair, and when reasons fluttered into my mind, I brushed them away, welding my attention to the task at hand, whether clearing the algae from the lotus ponds or reassuring my son that his father would forgive him for stepping on a beetle.

"I harmed a being!" he cried one foggy morning, bursting into our little room. In his open palm was the squashed black shield of the insect's back. "I didn't see him in the rain."

His look of terror shocked me. "Darling!" I said. "Everybody steps on beetles. What's important is that you're kind to your friends and to the servants."

"No! Grandmother says that one of Papa's most important rules is not to harm any beings, not even mosquitoes, or you'll go to a hell realm."

"I'm sure you heard her wrong, dearest." I could only hope so. I was not ready to think my husband's spiritual victory amounted to a kind of madness. "Or maybe Pajapati doesn't quite understand what your father means. Anyway, I'm sure your father loves you no matter what, and I'm sure he wouldn't want you to be upset over this. And you're definitely, definitely not going to anything approaching hell."

Rahula just stared down at his hand. "I caused harm to a being," he said softly, and went back outside.

What had Siddhartha become? I was trying not to think ill of him, even though he apparently wasn't planning to contact me at all. I would have to meet him formally, accompanied by the rest of the family.

Finally came the long-awaited lightning bolt, the announcement of my husband's arrival. He'd scheduled it two days before that of the other guests, so he could meet with his immediate family. And now Rahula and I—along with Suddhodana, Pajapati, and their two teenage children—awaited Siddhartha in a stateroom adjoining the grand banquet hall. The stateroom had the effect of generating both light and darkness. Silver- and gold-striped tapestries partly occluded the paired arched windows that normally opened to a view of the morning hills, while on the inside wall a five-tier arrangement of thirty oil lamps flickered, reflecting the tapestries' metallic fabric. Divans draped in red and purple lined the walls, but we were to stand to greet Siddhartha when he entered the room.

As I stood in my yellow robe, with my hair drawn up in a bun, I tried to ignore my frivolous worries about how I looked, which swarmed in my mind like a plague of gnats on a battlefield. Physically, I'd changed little from the day my husband and I met; my figure remained slim, and I still had those fine-cut Sakyan features that didn't require cosmetics to show them off. I gave my head a shake to clear it, which only returned me to my nervousness, which soon reached the point of wooziness. The smells of the impending banquet—the melange of fried chapatis and stewed vegetables—served only to increase my nausea. Suddhodana's voice seemed to fade in and out of my mind as he described the logistics of our meeting. Rahula was clinging tightly to my hand.

Suddhodana strode to the center of the room and signalled to his seventeen-year-old son, Nanda. I noticed how my father-in-law had aged over the past seven years—his nearly white mustache, the sagging flesh along his neck, the tentativeness in his gait. His voice, though, remained deep and powerful. "We men will stand to greet him and escort him to his dais. Nanda will kneel briefly, and I will bow my head, as a father should not kneel before his son, and give my formal greeting. The women and children will then approach, kneeling before him. He will speak whatever words he wishes, perhaps a short discourse on his Dharma. Then, once I have asked my own questions, Nanda and then the women may ask theirs, if he so permits."

All at once my nervousness exploded into outrage. I was being shunted aside as part of a group, when I was the guest of honor's wife! I was to grovel and kneel and ask questions only about whatever the great man felt like discussing, which I suspected wasn't going to be the abandonment of his wife and child. Oh, yes, I'd told him to leave, but he could have at least apprised me on the stages of his journey.

I walked to the center of the room and faced my father-in-law. I spoke loudly so all would hear, including Pajapati, who would transmit my message to Siddhartha if no one else would. "You may inform my husband that if he wishes to see me again in this lifetime, that he may meet me tomorrow in this room, where we will speak together alone." Next, I addressed Suddhodana. "Please send a guard to accompany me tomorrow to ensure propriety is maintained." I knew this was the only way he'd permit me to leave the women's compound on my own.

When Suddhodana hesitated, Pajapati spoke up. "Of course," she said, driving her gaze into her husband. He nodded at me, then looked away.

As gently as possible, I released Rahula's hand. "My darling," I said, "go to your father when he arrives and receive your inheritance."

Not looking at anyone, not even Rahula, I headed for the door.

Hours later, Rahula burst into my room, the one I still shared with him, with its little alcove for his bed. "Ama!"

It was already dark; I'd spent the day closed in here, sitting on my single cushion trying to meditate, not planning to leave until I returned to the stateroom to meet my husband—or not—the following morning. Rahula had spent the better part of the day with his father.

"I'm going to become a monk!" He was laughing with excitement.

I was jerked into alertness. "When you grow up, you can decide," I said in a measured voice, my heart hammering. With trembling hands I lit the oil lamp on the little table beside me. My son's small eager face wavered in the orange light.

"No! Today!" Rahula somersaulted across the room, bumping into my sleeping pallet. "And guess what! I'm not going to a bad realm for stepping on the beetle. The Tathagata says that—"

"Who?"

"The Tathagata—that's what I'm supposed to call Papa now! That's because he's both the one who has 'thus gone' and also 'thus come'!" Rahula smiled proudly, happy for the ability to teach his mother.

"Oh, so we're supposed to worship him now?"

A look of dismay flashed across my son's face, only to be banished by laughter, as if he'd just gotten the joke. "No, he's not a god! But he said I wouldn't go to a lower realm for killing the beetle, because I didn't intend to do it."

The room seemed to go still and the light became steady, if only for a moment. These days, many people talk about the importance of intention, but back then, motivation made no difference. Only action counted. It didn't matter how you felt about it, the karma was the same. So said the priests. There was even a sect of holy men who wore veils over their faces to prevent inhaling insects, to avoid killing them by accident. According to them, the most holy life one could lead was to starve to death.

Had my husband truly come upon something momentous? It seemed so simple, yet no one had thought about it before, that the rightness or wrongness of something depends on whether you intended to do it, your attitude toward it.

I couldn't let my personal resentment get in the way of seeing the truth.

But for my son to leave me and take on a life of abstinence at seven years old! Even his grandparents couldn't possibly approve of this.

"That's a very nice piece of wisdom," I said, "but tell me, what does your grandpa think of you ordaining?"

He looked away. "Please, please, tell him I can. Please!"

For once, my father-in-law was on my side. "I'm sorry, Rahula, but you are absolutely forbidden to even consider ordaining as a monk until you're at least eighteen."

Rahula burst into tears. "No! I want to be a monk now! I want to go with Papa! He has teachers for me and everything!" He threw himself against my bed, sobbing.

This was totally uncharacteristic of him. I took him gently by the shoulders. "Listen to me. I'm meeting with your father tomorrow. I think you're probably mistaken about exactly when you're supposed to ordain. Your father will inform me what you're to do. Meanwhile, it's time for bed."

My son, clinging to the bedcover, gave me a dubious look. I kissed his hot, wet cheek. "Truly," I said, "everything will work out fine."

By the time his breathing became regular, I had decided on my plan. If my husband didn't deign to meet me the next day—or if he insisted on ordaining my son—I would take Rahula to my mother's house, telling Suddhodana that the best way to prevent his son from stealing his grandson was to remove Rahula temporarily from the premises. At Ama's I would prepare him and me for a life on the road, never to return here again. Hopefully, there were female seekers remaining.

Tomorrow I would order Rahula to wait for me in our room, and I'd make sure the guards wouldn't let him out until I got back. Fortunately, what with all the guests milling around, every door in the women's compound was locked as well as guarded.

Yes, I was resorting to lies and deception. But I wouldn't let my life or the life of my son be stolen again.

After a sleepless night, I called for the guard, who accompanied me to the stateroom. I pushed through the heavy door, struggling to breathe through my nervousness, dreading the long wait, which would probably come to nothing. Then I saw the man who had been my husband, a silent silhouette in the dawn light.

He was seated on the dais, apparently meditating. He wore a simple monk's robe and his head was shaved. He seemed so still it was hard to believe he had ever been anywhere but where he sat now. I stood just inside the door until I was sure my bones would hold me up. Was it really him?

The room seemed chilly and cavernous, darker than the day before—not only because of the early hour but also because only two or three of the oil lamps were burning. I needed to see him better. Without saying anything, I rushed over to the eastern windows and pushed away the tapestry, letting in the predawn light and a wisp of breeze, dispelling the scent of the burning oil. Then I stood before him, a beating in my chest, as if my breath were struggling to escape. He opened his eyes. "Yasi," he said, his voice more resonant than I remembered. "I'm so glad to see you."

I felt a profound connection, then immediate doubt. In spite of his shaved head, he was still physically beautiful in the way he'd always been, although older and thinner. Yet something about him was not-Siddhartha. I don't mean to say the face before me was cynical or world-weary; on the contrary, it seemed to emanate a luminous kindness. Yet there was an impersonal quality to the expression in his clear eyes. With a shock I realized I wasn't sure if he was human. *Tathagata.*

"Are you some god wearing Siddhartha as a costume?" I asked. I, who had never given credence to divinity, was now fighting the kind of terror more suited to holy crazies and mumbling old priests.

He shook his head. "I've awakened from the dream that we take for life. That's what I've come back to tell you."

I closed my eyes and called my familiar emotions back, especially righteous anger. I placed firmly in my mind the vacillating and evasive man my husband had become during my pregnancy. "Why were you gone for so long?" I demanded. "For all these years, you didn't even let me know where you were."

"It's what I had to do." He spoke softly and deliberately, forming the silence that surrounded him. "The loneliness, the feeling that all was lost. As you yourself said, one of my most important teachers would be my own solitude. I had to go into that as deeply as I could."

"You make me sound like a spiritual exercise."

"I ask your forgiveness for any suffering I caused you."

"And when you returned? You've been back for months. You could have sent a message."

"But I did. You didn't receive it?"

Jagdish. My brother could very well have intercepted it.

Yet I wasn't sure I believed Siddhartha.

"I never received any word from you at all," I said. "Someone must have stopped it from reaching me."

"Then for that, also, I ask your forgiveness," he said. "Please believe me that I intended to meet with you long before now."

"Never mind," I snapped. I doubted that there was any way, at least not right now, he could prove whether he'd actually sent a message. "Just tell me this. Do you remember what you originally promised me? I want to know what happened to my sister's soul."

His compassionate expression remained unchanged. "I'm so sorry, Yasi, but all I teach is how to penetrate the true nature of suffering and, in that way, end it."

I clutched my elbows. "I don't care if I suffer. All I want is my sister. You promised!" My rage had taken on a new aspect, one of a child denied her childish dream.

My husband—my former husband—remained completely calm, but now with the kind of sympathy you show a child. "First, you need to tell me what you mean by her soul. Is it some image you have of her?"

"No, of course not." His question made me uncomfortable. All my thoughts of Deepa's soul included some picture in my memory. "It's not an image," I insisted. "It's her essence."

"But what's an essence? Wasn't her body, now the dust of dogs' bones, part of that essence?"

"I'm talking about her mind."

"Her thoughts? Which come and go? Which thoughts are truly hers? Which thoughts are *her*?"

I had no idea of Deepa's true nature. "Stop playing games with me! Her soul is her eternal consciousness!"

"And where could that consciousness be? One can't be conscious without being conscious *of* something, and the something that determines consciousness is always changing. And how is her consciousness different from everybody else's?"

"Are you saying my sister has no soul? That nobody has a self? That we're all nothing?" I stared at the man who had turned into my husband's ghost. "Is that why you threw our lives away? To learn that?"

My grief for those sun-washed times of my early marriage, which over the past few years I hadn't wanted to admit to, much less feel, now shook me to the core. "We were happy," I said, a knot tightening in my throat. "We had everything."

He looked into my eyes, his compassion just this side of sadness, yet his clarity was unnerving. "'Everything' never lasts," he said. "Even back then, with all our wealth and our projects, we were trying to escape that fact. In fact, almost all of our actions were for that very purpose. You know that. You once knew it better than I."

Something black and fearful opened up beneath me. "So it's true. My sister's soul—or mine, for that matter—doesn't exist. We die and that's that. Nothing matters at all."

He shook his head. "I'm just saying that the self can't be found in any of the places you can think to look. That you need to change the nature of your spiritual search."

I was having trouble keeping my focus, both visual and mental. I remembered what Pajapati had said of the Tathagata's teachings about craving and clinging as the cause of suffering, then what Rahula had said yesterday about the importance of intention when it came to good and evil. This man seated in front of me had to have awakened to some deep knowledge, which enabled him to have these revelations.

And perhaps he truly had tried to send a message to me, after all. Perhaps he really had wanted to see me.

"If I can't search for Deepa's soul, what do I search for?"

"The way things truly are. That's what's uncovered when we stop clutching at unreality."

The thought that a ground of truth existed comforted me. "How can I learn this?"

"You could start by coming to the talks I'm giving over the next couple of weeks. I'll make sure Suddhodana lets you attend."

"No, that's not enough! I've already been meditating. I want to learn all your practices."

"I'll explain some of them in the talks."

"No!" A sudden hope—the first I'd felt in a very long time—spiraled upward inside me. I now understood Rahula's urgency. "I want to join your order. And devote my life to the Dharma." I smiled into his clear eyes. "We can raise our son together."

My former husband's shoulders dropped, and I had the strange feeling that his body, which the Tathagata now occupied, was reacting out of its own memory of the past. He spoke softly. "Yasi, that's impossible."

"What do you mean? Surely you can talk Suddhodana into allowing me! Pajapati can help."

He shook his head. "Women can't join the order."

A new darkness fell over me, as if someone had slammed shut every door and window in the room. "Can't join? But all I've heard is that your Dharma is for everyone! That any member of any varna is welcome to ordain! And yet women can't?"

"I'm sorry."

"You're *sorry*? You've betrayed me! You went off on the journey that you stole from me and left me to a life of triviality! I waited for you, brought up our son, endured the arrogance of your male relatives, and now I can't even reap the benefits of what you've gained, except as crumbs tossed out every couple of years when you happen to be in the area. You've not only betrayed me, you've betrayed who you once were—someone who kept his promises."

His voice remained soft. "It's true," he said. "Siddhartha would have allowed it. But now I am one with the Dharma. With the eyes of Dharma I see that our society will never accept my teaching if women are allowed to live and travel with men in such a way. We're attempting something that's never been done before, gathering a *Sangha*, a community that will awaken on its own without priests or sacrifices but by its adherents banishing their own ignorance. The priests and the Brahmins will try to stop us in every way possible. The presence of women would give them a weapon to discredit us to the point of destruction."

I had the momentary thought that here was not any Tathagata or my former husband, but Mara himself, delighting in his clever excuses to exclude women—and me, in particular—from the truth.

"I don't believe you," I said. "You're not omniscient. You may have the eyes of Dharma, but they are in a human body. You've chosen to risk admitting pig farmers and vulture catchers, but women are to remain trapped in suffering. Because you see them as a 'weapon.'"

Through the windows, the sun had risen, backlighting him and concealing him in shadows. I stared at the spot where his face should have been. "You have nothing to teach me," I said. "And I won't let you take my child."

The blankness spoke. "You need to let him choose, Yasi. Suddhodana will train him as a warrior—is that what you want? And I'm his father."

"You're not his father," I said. I turned to leave. "You are the Tathagata, the one 'thus gone.'"

I realize how different my version of this event is from the one that later became popular, even though it was never acknowledged by the official Sangha. In the popular rendition, the Tathagata graciously came into my presence after I proved by my virtue to be worthy of this honor. The Blessed One then praised my patience and sacrifice, and I entered into a life of serving him and eventually attained liberation.

I'm touched by these efforts to restore my reputation, if only they were true! Although I'm just as glad for the falsity of some rumors, especially the one that I recently died. I can't die yet. I still have certain tasks to perform.

I returned to my room through the dining hall, where I hoped to encounter Suddhodana to inform him of my plan to take Rahula to my mother's—although I'd omit my subsequent plan for my son and me to go forth as spiritual seekers. The men were just sitting down to eat, the room rumbling and buzzing with more than the usual plans and boasts. Everyone seemed to be discussing the Dharma and its ramifications on the life of the Sakyans. To my mild surprise, I noticed two or three shaven heads in the crowd. Were these cousins planning to join the Order? Well, they can have it, I thought grimly, as I scanned the room for my father-in-law. Instead, I glimpsed my brother coming toward me. I ducked away. Although I imagined that all this celebration of Suddhodana's son was not to his liking and though his mood was probably as bleak as mine, he was the last person I wanted to talk to.

Too late. He'd seen me, and I was shocked by the smile on his face. "Good morning, Yasi," he said. "I suppose you've heard the news."

I shook my head, trying to look around him for my father-in-law.

He kept smiling. "Our beloved cousin Devadatta has decided to join your former husband's Sangha."

"Devadatta?" Jagdish had succeeded in bringing me up short. Of all people, Devadatta always struck me as the least likely to go forth. But on second thought, why not? He'd always been Siddhartha's rival, and now that his cousin had disdained the worldly life and succeeded wildly in the realm of spirit, it was logical for Devadatta to carry the rivalry into this arena.

For all my anger at my former husband, I felt a twinge of concern for him at the prospect of our cousin, so full of envy and competition, joining his Sangha. "Well, the Tathagata will have his hands full," I said, wanting to end the conversation.

"And so will I," Jagdish said, "now that I'll have to take on many of his duties."

I gave my brother a sharp look. Apparently, his whole purpose in speaking to me was to inform me that I no longer had the prospect of marrying Devadatta as a bargaining chip. But I wasn't rising to the bait. "I congratulate you, Brother. I wish you all success with your new responsibilities."

I could only hope that Jagdish would prove a mature leader now that he was without a contender. For there was nothing I could do if he didn't.

I spotted Suddhodana across the room and hurried toward him. I told him my plan and the need to keep Rahula away from his father until Rahula calmed down. "I'm afraid that if Rahula is permitted to see Siddhartha again, the monks will take him from us," I said. "At the very least they will turn him against you."

Suddhodana sighed. His eyes were murky and threaded with scarlet, and the circles under them had creased and deepened. "You have my permission," he said. "I'll assign a chariot and some guards to escort you." He gripped my hand, which he had never done before, and looked into my eyes. "I don't want to lose my grandson."

I steeled myself against his new softness, remembering my years of captivity. "I'll take good care of him," I said.

I hurried back to the compound. By now the sun was bright, and the day resounded with the shouts and bellows of farmers and their animials. The third-floor terrace was empty; most of the women were in the dining hall, directing the servants or waiting their turn to have breakfast. I hoped Rahula hadn't become restless. I'd told him to stay in our room until my return. I'd planned to be back before now.

I opened the door. I hadn't locked it. There was really nowhere he could have gone but the terrace, which had only one exit, presided over by a guard.

Inside our room, nothing was stirring, not even the dust motes in the sunbeams slanting on the varnished plank floor. Was my son still in bed? "Rahula!" I called. "Get up."

No answer. I checked the alcove. His blue-striped wool coverlet was neatly pulled over his empty little bed. "Rahula!" I shouted, trying not to panic. "Are you hiding?"

Still no response.

I ran out to the terrace, calling his name, pounding on doors to the women's rooms. I opened the door to the stairway and queried the guard. No one had seen him.

Terrified, I returned to our room. He had to be there, hiding somewhere. "Rahula!" I said, trying not to scream.

It was then I saw the chest, the small wooden one next to my pallet, gaping open. I'd kept my purloined clotheslines there, ever since I'd planned to escape with my son by climbing out the window.

The chest was empty, and now I saw the ropes, tied to the leg of his bed and flung out the window. Rahula, whom I'd taught to climb, had made use of them.

All I could think of was Deepa's body lying on the hard ground like a discarded doll.

I lunged toward the window, dreading beyond dread what I might see below.

A knotted double rope was swinging in the wind.

My son had left me to become a monk.

I fell to my knees and wept.

6

O f course, I tried to get him back. Still in tears, I ran back to the dining hall, hoping to enlist Suddhodana's aid, but by the time I approached him he'd turned to stone. "I should never have trusted you," he said. Jagdish, who knew me all too well, had already gotten to him, warning him that I most likely had no intention of returning Rahula to the compound. "Your brother wishes Rahula to live with the men and train as a warrior," Suddhodana said.

"You would let your nephew rule both your son and yourself?" My desperation had sharpened into cruelty, trying to shame him as an impotent old man.

"My grandson will not train as a warrior." The lines around Suddhodana's bleary eyes deepened with a reproach that at first I didn't wish to consider. "He'll remain in the monks' Sangha," he said, "where he will be protected."

I returned to my disheveled room, thinking that now at least my son wouldn't end up a warlord. Apparently, the Tathagata had influenced my father-in-law more than I'd known. Small comfort, I thought, as I pulled the ropes up from the window and plotted how to steal my son on my own. But as I glanced down, the memory of my terror when I'd imagined Rahula dead on the ground sent me reeling backwards. I remembered the reproach on Suddhodana's face, and his words that as a monk my son would be protected. And it was then I had the realization. My anger at Siddhartha and my whole situation had blinded me to how much I would be risking my seven-year-old by taking him with me on the road as a mendicant. He'd be far safer as a monk.

If I wanted to embark on a spiritual journey, I'd have to do it alone.

I could come back for him later, when I had my own truth to offer. This was much better than confronting his father now with anger or tears, which at best would upset Rahula and at worst make him see me as his enemy.

My decision was made.

Suddhodana, now that I no longer had a function in his court, was happy enough to provide me with an escort back to my parents' home. Hopefully, Ama could direct me to a group of female seekers, as she had suggested so many years ago. My mother—what with my two older sisters safely married and bearing yearly babies—had made an uneasy peace with her old goddess Adi-Parashakti, but the loss of Deepa and Kisa had left her faith permanently unmoored. As a result, she was more open these days, not only to wandering seekers but also to healers, diviners, and anyone else who might reassure her that her children's souls were safe. If anyone could help me find a spiritual teacher, she could.

Most of the week I spent with my family, I was alone or with Ama. As a disgraced wife who couldn't keep her husband or son, I wasn't popular with my aunts and cousins, not to mention my father. I stayed in the stuffy little weaving room helping Ama with the sewing and querying her. At first, she just shook her head, but after I pleaded, reminding her of my promise to Deepa's spirit, she finally remembered a holy woman who lived in the hills and supposedly communicated with the dead. Hopefully, this hill woman could help me uncover some truth about the soul that went beyond the Tathagata's list of what the soul is not. I could resume my original quest and track down my sister's true being, whatever it was. And this truth would form a part of what I would eventually offer to my son.

Ten days after relinquishing Rahula, there I was, staggering up the side of a hill, dodging the scraggly tendrils of a banyan tree as big as an emperor's palace. Ama had been willing—not overjoyed, for she was risking yet another daughter—to persuade one of her sons-in-law to carry me for three days in his oxcart, staying with relatives along the way, to the edge of the forest, a long day's walk from my destination. Since morning I'd been trudging along among stands of palm trees and banana plants, their leaves thick with yellow dust, until I'd crossed over a ridge into this deeper, wetter, darker jungle.

I fought my way through hundreds of aerial roots, the late afternoon sun trickling through leathery green leaves and cascading root-ropes that drooped and slithered over rocks and clawed their way into the earth; I feared if I didn't make it to the top of the ridge by nightfall, I'd lose the trail and end up hopelessly lost, if not devoured by wild animals. Finally, the trees gave way to shrubs and boulders, and I glimpsed some empty sky. The sun had just set.

At the ridge's high point, a small fire was burning. A lone woman squatted in front of it, thin to the point of emaciation. Her cheekbones stuck out like knuckles; her eyes, circled with creases, glittered bright black. She wore a ragged orange polka-dot dhoti and a filthy yellow band of cloth tied around her chest. Most unnervingly, affixed to the top of her head was the upper half of a wolf's head, including its ears, muzzle, and black polished stones for eyes.

Reflexively, I reached back and touched the satchel tied up in my scarf, which along with my nearly exhausted food supply contained two gold bangles and a sapphire ring—all that was left of my jewelry. Payment for services rendered if necessary. Or perhaps to spare my life.

She glanced up at me and smiled, but not in a particularly welcoming way. She could have been forty or eighty, and she could be downright mad. "Sakyan," she said, appraising me.

I nodded. "I've heard that you can communicate with the souls of the dead."

"Your people enslaved me," she said equably.

My fear mounted, along with a creeping guilt as if for some terrible wrong I'd committed and forgotten about. "I've never heard Sakyans doing such a thing. They must have been distant relations."

She shrugged, then gestured to the other side of the slope I'd come up. "The Gorge Serpent tribe purchased me from them."

"That tribe set you free?" I wished I knew where this conversation was going.

"They bought me to sacrifice to the Fierce Mother." She stirred the fire, which had dwindled to black-scummed embers.

Was she entertaining herself at my expense? What if what she was saying was true? Although I'd never taken the rumors about the hill tribes seriously before, I'd heard that the Sakyan clansmen who lived in this area justified raiding them because of the tribes' extreme savagery. "You survived," I said.

"No thanks to you Sakyans. The Gorge tribe set me free because after they strangled me and threw me in the fire, I went to the spirit realm instead of dying. The fire went out."

I had no idea how to reply. I reached back from my satchel and took out my jewelry. "I'm truly sorry for what my people—if that's who they were—did to you," I said. "All I want is to contact my sister's spirit and learn about the soul. I'll recompense you as best I can."

"And why do you think I can help you?"

"My mother heard from several travelers you supposedly guided into the spirit realm."

"Were they Sakyan travelers?"

"I don't know! No one I know captures people, let alone sells them to be sacrificed."

The woman reached over with a bare bony arm and picked up a gold bangle, which she twirled around her thumb as she talked. "And yet you have servants who clean up your natural filth and fix your meals."

"Forgive me for the life I've led. I knew nothing else." I had always been taught—and so had my husband—that servants were a part of life since the birth of the universe. "Please," I said. I'll do anything for your help. I could work for you."

She quirked a smile. "As a servant?" She glanced down at her ragged clothes, her skinny body. She patted her wolf-head. "I don't need people to feed and dress me."

"I could help you gather herbs, help you mix potions. You only have to tell me something once and I remember."

The woman let a few moments drift past and watched the fire, now flaring in sharp yellow flames. In the deepening twilight her wolf-head eyes glittered in harmony with her own. "To see your sister's spirit, you'll have to meet the god of death."

A chill ran through me. "I've never seen a god."

"Never seen a god? You've been looking in the wrong places. Helping you might be difficult."

I nodded toward the jewelry. "I'm giving you everything I own. And along with my accurate memory, I do have some experience with herbs." As cosmetics, anyway.

I thought I heard her chuckle. "I do my own herbs. But I could use somebody to haul buckets up from the river." She gestured to where the ridge dropped off to unknown depths, and my heart likewise plummeted.

"Don't worry," the woman said. "Thanks to me, the people down there don't sacrifice human beings anymore. Although I couldn't save you from Sakyan raids." She gave me the kind of conspiratorial look one might use on an escaped criminal. "Who knows? Your own people might sell you to the Gorge tribe and tempt them to start up their practice again."

I stared into the fire. I'd come this far. "I'll take the chance." I put off thinking about the buckets.

She stood up. "You can call me Stick Woman. And I'll call you the Fugitive Bride."

"I didn't run from my marriage," I said. My righteous anger, even here, pushed through my other emotions. "My husband left me to become a spiritual teacher and he seduced my son into joining him."

"So now you need to show him up."

Before I could object, she added, "That's understandable."

"I want to teach my child—," I said, wanting to put myself in a better light, but she raised her hand as if to discourage further discussion.

She nodded toward a heap of animal pelts, unidentifiable in the twilight. "You can use these for sleeping."

They smelled all too much of their former owners. I tried not to be revolted. She had almost taken my side against my husband and the Sakyan villains.

"Where do you sleep?" I asked.

"I'll show you tomorrow." She turned into the darkness, which suddenly became enormous.

"Wait," I quavered. I'd never spent a night alone in the forest, which had merged with the darkness into an infinite Unknown.

"Don't worry," she said. "As long as you stay in this fire circle, the wolves will protect you."

Unreassured, I nevertheless succumbed to exhaustion and slept through the night. I awoke to the muted crunch of footsteps too heavy for the skinny likes of Stick Woman. Fear lurched inside me. My eyes flew open to blinding sun and blank blue sky.

"Greetings." The man standing above me looked to be in his early to mid-twenties, a couple years younger than I. His butternut-colored face was flat and simple, his cheekbones broad, and his nose wide at the bridge in a rectangular shape. His lips curved to the brink of a smile, and his warm brown eyes seemed soft with a gratitude for his surroundings, which included me. A comforting face but for the multiple gold hoops rimming both his ears and the thick gold ring through his nostrils. He wore only a loincloth and his black hair was chopped off at the shoulders.

Still wary, I sat up, gathering the pelts around me, although the day was quickly growing warm.

Stick Woman emerged from the underbrush, carrying a dusty basket woven out of twigs. She wasn't wearing her wolf head, and her gray hair stuck out in all directions and scraggled down her back. Unlike the man, she wore no jewelry. She gestured in his direction, speaking in the same equable voice she had the night before. "This is Bahauk. He can speak your language, because your people enslaved him for six years."

How many more of these cheerfully indirect accusations would I have to endure? "I'm from a distant branch of the family," I said. "You can call me Yasi," I added in an effort to be friendly.

Bahauk was staring at me with his same benevolent expression but intensified enough to unnerve me. Then he glanced over at Stick Woman. "Is this the wife you promised me? She looks prettier than I expected."

"You'd marry a Sakyan?" Stick Woman appeared to be feigning surprise.

"Sure," the man said happily. Apparently, he didn't hold his former enslavement against me. Unless, of course, his people considered marriage as a form of punishment for the female sex.

Stick Woman kicked the fire into life with her bare feet, their soles polished black with grime. "Well, you can't marry her. She'd refuse to worship every one of your eighty-three gods. Not only because she's Sakyan, but also because she's blind to the spirit world. She's here so I can cure her blindness."

As Bahauk continued to stare at me, I realized that part of my discomfort came from a momentary urge to nuzzle his smooth broad chest. I hadn't felt such an urge since the days of my marriage, and certainly not for someone who struck me as a primitive savage. What was I becoming without the trappings of my aristocratic life to define me? I steadied the muscles of my face. "I'm here to find my sister's soul."

The man raised the gentle arcs of his black eyebrows. "Why here? Would she not be among the Sakyans?" His words were misshapen in the way of foreigners, but he was easier to understand than many of the distant clans who supposedly spoke my tongue. Perhaps I'd been wrong to label him primitive.

"Never mind where her sister's spirit is," Stick Woman said. "This woman has volunteered to haul water from the river."

I'd hoped she'd forgotten.

By now the sun had risen enough for me to see a trail pitching down a steep slope through jungle scrub, disappearing finally into a deep gorge, where a green silk ribbon of water was intermittently visible. The slope faced east, which meant most of my walk would be in the hot morning sun. A waft of something dead rose from the underbrush nearby. In the midst of the bird and monkey din, I thought I heard a snake hiss.

"I could get the water," Bahauk said.

Stick woman shook her head. "No, I need you here. To help with the herbs."

Anger reared up inside me; I jerked it back. She was testing my resolve, I told myself, or my courage. After all, she was a spiritual teacher.

Unless she was a vengeful old hag who delighted in tormenting the Sakyans who'd sold her to be killed.

"We'll have breakfast first," Stick Woman said as Bahauk disappeared into the forest, filling me with both disappointment and relief. "Dried rabbit and water."

I thought about offering up the last of my apricots, but I didn't. I rationalized that hauling buckets was enough recompense, and I'd need the nourishment myself, especially considering the trek I faced. I munched on a rabbit haunch, which splintered in my mouth. No wonder Stick Woman was so skinny.

After this all too brief meal, Stick Woman started off through a forest of scrub trees and I followed. On three sides of us, green ridges fell away into blue distances. Over the ridge on the fourth side, the sun was rising steadily, dazzling through twigs and leaves and directly into my eyes. I tried not to take the sun's behavior as a personal attack.

The old woman turned around and peered at me, as if I weren't supposed to be following her.

"You said you'd show me where you lived," I said.

"Where I sleep. I live everywhere."

I found this spiritual-sounding statement heartening. I'd begun fearing she wasn't the teacher Ama had told me about, the one who traveled in the unknown. "What do you mean?" I asked, in the tone of a respectful student.

"Everyone lives everywhere, even you."

"You mean because we're all facets of the Atman?"

By now we'd reached her hut, which was little more than a straw shelter, barely high enough to stand in. "You're thinking too much about atmans," she said. "And not enough about water." She pushed aside a faded blue rag of a curtain and disappeared. "Wait here," she said. In the space of a breath or two she emerged with two wooden buckets attached by ropes to a wooden yoke. "Here you are," she said. "You saw the trail from back at the fire. You should be able to make it to the river by mid-morning and be back by noon."

I heaved the contraption on my shoulders. It felt heavy even without water, and the yoke dug into my flesh; I could already feel the grooves forming, the tender skin of my shoulders flaking away. "How can I defend myself, alone on the trail?" I tried to make this sound like a reasonable query and not a whine.

"You can't, so you might as well not worry about it."

I stared at her. "Is this kind of test really necessary? Isn't there another way I can learn what I need to know?"

"You want to seek out the spirit. To do so, you may have to lose your body. Or at least take the risk." She looked at me with those black, crinkly eyes. In the morning sun, her creased skin looked varnished. "Do you think you can pay for wisdom with a couple of bangles?"

"I thought you could teach me meditation techniques. Which could include austerities," I added.

"Why waste my time when I need the water? Of course, had you offered up your apricots, I might have considered them as payment, but it's too late now. You'd better start. It's getting hotter with every heartbeat."

I felt small and selfish, then resentful. They were my apricots, after all, and she must have discovered them by snooping around my bag while I was sleeping. No matter, she'd shamed me, making me fear that a life of deprivation could reveal my true self as petty and spoiled, unworthy of my son. I started walking, telling myself that this chore was part of a benevolent plan to train me in patience and humility.

The trail started out rocky and dusty, the brush coming up only to my waist and offering no protection from the sun, heating up more and more as the air thickened with buzzing black flies that landed on my arms and the back of my neck and crawled up my legs and under my yellow robes, already sodden with sweat and rapidly turning the color of dust. My sandals, the kind worn by all the members of Suddhodana's female household for those rare occasions they needed foot protection, were deteriorating even more rapidly than my bleeding feet, still sore from yesterday. By the first switchback, stinging blisters competed with the heat, insects, and shoulder pain to dominate my awareness and blot out all thoughts of humility and patience. It didn't help that I stumbled every ten or so steps as I taught myself to balance the yoke.

Self-pity, which I thought I'd overcome after losing my husband, welled up in me. I swallowed it and swallowed it again as I staggered onward for what seemed like the whole morning, even though the sun was still staring mercilessly into my eyes. I tried to find things to be grateful for. Well, I'd yet to encounter signs of predatory animals or humans—or any humans, for that matter. Also, the flies, although tracking dung and decay-slime all over my body, didn't bite, and the trail was too dry for mosquitoes. Or so I thought until it dipped into a boggy grove where thousands were waiting, the atmosphere threaded with their high-pitched whines. I was soon seared with itching welts and sobbing with misery—who cared if I displayed my weakness? There was nobody here to judge me but myself. No Rahula to be upset by his mother's lack of self-control. The thought of my son made me sob all the more. By now I hardly cared if a tiger or a pack of wild dogs jumped me and ended my suffering, at least in the worldly realm. Surely, a hell realm wouldn't be worse.

Then, all at once, I entered a cool grove of huge sal trees, liquid birdsong, and the distant rush of water. I breathed in a smell of fresh greenery. I was almost at the river. I tried to focus on patience and humility.

The trees became smaller and closer together and the trail narrowed, forcing me to shove my way through underbrush of sharp green leaves and even sharper twigs. But the river roar was mounting, drowning out the birds and insects, filling me with hope and the anticipation of soothing water cascading over my seared and aching body. I caught a glimpse of dazzle between the trees. I pushed forward and finally stopped at the water's edge, my heart pummeling.

From where I stood, the green river was an immense shining serpent, sliding and heaving its unfathomable weight of water past me at a terrifying speed. Forget any gentle immersion into a refreshing bath; even if I knew how to swim, the current would hurl me downstream and over the falls thundering just around the bend. I glanced down at my feet, planted on a margin of mud the width of a hand span. I hardly had room to move, let alone take off the yoke and fill my buckets. Legs quivering with exhaustion, I leaned out over the water to get a sense of its depth.

The next thing I knew I was somersaulting through green translucence and pounding cold, the river booming in my ears and blocking my breath. I was plunged into shock, followed by total terror.

I was surely dead. I'd never see my son again.

Suddenly, I flew into white sunlight, slamming down on my back, then rolling over and over on rough sand. Choking and gasping, I heaved myself to my knees, terror still hammering inside me. What if I could never catch my breath? I coughed out globs of phlegm, gasped some more, and my mind came back to me.

That old woman had tried to murder me.

Of course! She wanted revenge on the Sakyans. She'd set me on this trail, knowing how dangerous it was, figuring I'd probably fall in the river and die. What I had taken for a holy woman was nothing but a gristly husk of cruelty and spite.

Meet the god of death, indeed.

But when I stood up, I noticed that the bushes parted to reveal a trail leading to this far safer bank than the one I'd fallen from. I couldn't exactly blame Stick Woman for my wrong turn. Still, the trail was dangerous, and I'd almost drowned.

By now it was almost noon. I was hungry, but when I reached for my sash I discovered the water had taken my apricots.

No, I told myself, I couldn't blame Stick Woman for this, much as I wanted to.

The trudge back up the ridge was worse than the way down, with the steep upward slope, my back bruises from the sand bar, the added weight of water on my back, and the ongoing dread that I'd spill it and have to return to the river. My consolation was that the numbness of exhaustion dulled my pains, mental as well as physical. At times, I marched in a trance, counting my steps. But I couldn't bear the prospect of making this trek again.

It must have been mid-afternoon when I staggered up to the fire circle. The fire was dead, and Stick Woman was squatting at its rim, doing nothing. "I thought you'd get here earlier," she said, pushing herself up between the brown garlic bulbs of her skinny knees and rising to her feet.

Panting, legs jittering, I put down the yoke and my shoulders flew to the heavens. Waves of release shuddered through me.

Stick Woman unhooked one of the buckets. To my horror, she lifted it up and tossed its water into the bushes. "Some spirits need appeasement," she said.

If only I could fling myself on top of this scraggly hell-being and pummel her ten fathoms into the earth! But I told myself that such a flagrant act as tossing away the water confirmed that this all was a test.

Stick woman eyed me. "You'd better do some meditating while you have the chance," she said. "It's too late for you to make another trip."

"Another...? I couldn't breathe.

"From now on, you'll be making two trips a day."

From now on? My jaw dropped.

She didn't change her expression. "You can always go home. You know the trail. I'll make sure the wolves protect you on your way down."

"I haven't seen a wolf yet," I said out of a defiance that didn't even make sense.

"Lucky you haven't, considering you don't believe in their god."

Or hers, I thought. But I still wasn't ready to give up on her. Except for Stick Woman, I had no way to achieve the kind of transformation that would allow me to return to my son as a teacher in my own right. I'd have to return to Ama's and live as a cast-off wife, an object of Ama's pity and my father's contempt, tending the altars of gods I couldn't believe in. But something else kept me here. Stick Woman had been right when she said I wanted to show my former husband up. Or at least not fail where he'd succeeded. If he could endure trials, so could I. "Where should I meditate?" I asked.

"Doesn't matter. Out of sight somewhere. Pick a tree and go sit under it." Stick Woman sat down at the dead fire and resumed staring into space.

For the next two weeks, this torture continued, with me still sleeping by the fire and hoping it wouldn't rain. I alternated between fury at Stick Woman's cruelty and determination to pass her tests, even if the only result was to show her she couldn't break me. Then one afternoon, after a midday rain that turned the trail up the ridge into a treacherous gray slick—where I had slipped and fallen a third of the way up and spilled the water, requiring a trip back down to the river—I reached what had to be my final conclusion concerning Stick Woman's intentions. She had dedicated her life to avenging herself against all Sakyans. By now I had ample evidence. First off, she wasn't depending on me to supply water; she usually threw away most of what I brought up, and she'd kept Bahauk away from me after he'd offered to help me. And all this time she'd given me no advice about meditation or any other spiritual discipline. Then something else occurred to me: the reason why her reputation as a healer had spread among the Sakyans was that she had fostered the rumors herself in order to lure in gullible Sakyans to torture. How could I have been so stupid as to have been taken in?

The late afternoon sun was breaking through the sludge of rain clouds when I heaved my exhausted body to the top of the trail. There sat Stick Woman, diddling by the fire as usual.

I threw down the buckets and charged toward her, picturing my hands around her throat. "You deceived me!"

Then, in a blinding silver flash, I was confronted by the god of death.

It had the most horrific face I'd ever seen—not so much the shape of the features but the ugliness of rage yanking down the lower lip and wrinkling the upper one, exposing a row of savage teeth, the slick red-brown face one huge deformity of malice. Worse than the rage was the arrogance in its big eyes, whose uncompromising glare blocked all possibility that light might penetrate it. It was a face that killed off all hope that any world existed beyond the one it reflected.

I jolted to a halt, but Mara kept coming to destroy me.

Then Mara disappeared, and I was facing Stick Woman. She held a silver mirror, twice the size of the one my mother had forced me to look into so many years before. Mara's face was mine. I'd worn it against everyone I blamed for my misery.

Yes, I'd been wronged but all the while dressed in finespun clothes, waited on by servants, and fed the choicest delicacies. I wore the face when I'd cursed Stick Woman, refused her my apricots, and dismissed Bahauk as a primitive savage. It was the mask of beauty twisted into self-righteousness, far worse than mere ugliness, for it condemned everyone, including me. My acts of blaming had closed off all chance of knowing the truth.

"You don't have to be the god of death," Stick Woman said calmly. "You just had to meet Him."

"Him?"

"Him, Her, It. Doesn't matter. Let it be."

I stared at her, the earth swaying under my feet. I felt the same way as when I'd almost drowned in the river, only this time I'd fallen out of the world altogether and into death's endless domain. Now I was back—or was I? "Where did you get that mirror?" I asked, my heart numb, my head still clogged with my earlier conclusions. A question formed on its own: Had she stolen this mirror from the Sakyans?

Stick Woman peered into my eyes as if scouring them out. "You don't have to keep grabbing onto those thoughts. Just let them fly away." She raised her skinny arms, flapping them. "Off with you, now! Shoo!"

I blinked, cast into a remarkable clarity, as if she'd wiped clean the atmosphere I'd been living in, one dulled by swarms of demons. I looked up at the late-afternoon, sunlit clouds spreading out their glossy plumage, filling an azure sky with splendor. The scrub trees beyond startled me with their delicacy and grace. I also noticed that someone had built me a small sleeping shelter, similar to Stick Woman's, not far from the fire.

"I know why I had to see Mara for myself," I said. "The god of death, inside and outside and both and neither. I know now that I need to change the nature of my quest."

Stick Woman brushed off her boney shoulders. "Don't think you're done hauling buckets."

So began my stay with Stick Woman. I still had to carry water from the river, but only once a day. And the trip seemed easier. Not only was I growing stronger, but the flies and mosquitoes by and large left me alone. When I mentioned this to Stick Woman, she said she'd asked them not to bother me, the way she'd done with larger animals already.

"You talk to insects?" I asked, while we were sitting at the fire circle late one day. The crust of cold ashes blended with the gray earth under whorls of pink sunset clouds.

"I visit the spirits, insects included."

"I thought only evil people were reborn as bugs."

"In your Sakyan world, perhaps. Here, the spirit is shared in the very air we breathe. You need to see yourself this way." She gave me a wicked smile. "You've already seen that Mara lives all over the place. So do you."

"Unlike Mara, I'm stuck in a body."

"You're not stuck in a body. You're stuck in your thoughts." She raised her hand and gestured out over the successions of ridges, fading from black to pale gray in the mist. "Look at things and listen to them," she said. "Don't just think them."

To this end, she had Bahauk take me to sacred sites where I could learn the languages of animals, trees, and rocks. At least these were things to hear and look at, unlike the invisible gods and spirits back home who lived in a hierarchy of heavens and visited mainly the priests. At times I almost understood what Stick Woman was getting at—feeling the jagged cry of an eagle in my throat or sharpening my gaze in the glittering eyes of a sand fox, I was looking and listening from their points of view, which could only enter me when my own viewpoint, no longer shored up by thoughts, fell away.

Not thinking was also the key to being with Bahauk, but for a different reason.

Although he'd never spoken of marriage after that one time, his eyes seemed to quicken every time he looked at me. More disturbing, I felt a quickening inside me. He had that kind, broad face, eager to see the best in everything, and his muscles rippled and his rich brown skin flashed in the sunshine when he heaved my buckets on his shoulders, which he was now allowed to do at times. He seemed happy to teach me and answer my questions, although some of his answers upset me, especially when he spoke of sacrifice. Every year, he explained, the Sun—angry that the Earth Mother had stolen some of his light for her children—demanded a sacrifice or he would refuse to let her soothe his burning rage with the monsoon. Bahauk's tribe had once had to sacrifice their own children, but Stick Woman had convinced the elders to replace the child with a white goat.

I confronted her about this. She was sitting by the fire, grinding up turmeric and mixing it with soapy water, which turned the spice a brilliant scarlet; she was planning to give it to a sick little girl later in the day. What I'd used as a simple cosmetic she made into a medicine whose sacred fiery color supposedly helped restore balance between the little girl and the rest of the universe. "Bahauk has a point," she said. "One way or another, sacrifice is the only way to save the world."

"I can't believe that." I tried not to say this in a righteous way.

Stick Woman went back to squeezing the ground-up spice into

the water. "You will. As long as you cling to your world, you'll sacrifice your dearest possessions to save it."

I thought of Rahula. "No," I said, and all of a sudden I wanted to cry. "I refuse to believe that sacrifice is the only choice."

"That's because you don't understand the world." A red foam rose in the bowl as the speed of her hands increased. "But one day you will."

I decided to let that pass for now and to concentrate on learning what she else had to teach me.

7

As the dry season progressed and the heat returned, Stick Woman taught me how to make medicinal pastes and potions out of aloe, pepper, turmeric, cardamom, and a host of other herbs, roots, and seeds. I memorized the stories and songs that went with each preparation, and with the spirit that each ingredient invoked. Not only did these spirits abide in earthly materials, they also occupied the spirit world, she maintained.

Yet I had learned nothing that helped me find the spirit of Deepa, and I mentioned this to Stick Woman one day at the beginning of the hot season when the two of us were sitting in the grass, breaking cinnamon twigs in the shade of a neem tree "That's because you haven't forgiven the tree," she said.

"The cinnamon tree?" What nonsense was this?

"No, that tree." She pointed up the hill to a lone mango tree I passed every day when I carried the buckets up from the river. Early on, I'd noticed it and ignored it, the way I usually did that species of tree, putting it out of my head.

"Why would I need to forgive a tree?"

"The way you act around it, it's clear you hold a serious grudge against it. Your grudge is Mara getting between you and your sister."

I felt a jolt. Had Stick Woman somehow known that Deepa had fallen out of a mango? I looked at the tree, which had nothing special about it. It bore no fruit; mangoes were out of season. I couldn't believe I had acted in any special way—what had she seen? It was just a tree. "My sister fell out of a mango tree, but not this one."

"Oh, no? Then why do you keep your distance from it and curse it in your heart?"

"I don't curse it. I just don't like to think about it."

"You need to sit under the tree and tell it you forgive it. And you need to mean your words."

"That's impossible." It was one thing to repeat the incantations Stick Woman taught me about herbs and a whole other thing to feel an emotion that depended on something entirely unreal. "This tree has nothing to do with my sister."

Stick Woman stood up abruptly. "Then you'll have to lie. Just go over there, sit, and offer the tree forgiveness until you can understand its point of view. You've learned that much here."

I supposed I could do this until it was obvious that my forgiveness had no effect. Then I would have proven she was wrong. "How long do I sit?"

"For as long as it takes."

Feeling foolish, I climbed the hill to the tree. I stood in front of it, clutching my upper arms until I realized how hot that posture was making me. I remained standing for what seemed like the passing of morning into afternoon, longing for the welcoming shade of the neem tree where I'd been sitting with Stick Woman. The mango tree did offer shade, but how could I accept it when I was so angry at it?

Yes, I *was* angry at the tree! I folded my arms again, pummeled by the thoughts of a ten-year-old. Why did the tree drop my sister to her death? It had deceived her, and me, pretending its branches were safe. The memories flooded back: the branch bouncing upward, Deepa in her yellow shift lying face-down on the hard clay. I sat down cross-legged in the hot sun and forced myself to look up through its shiny green leaves, seeing for the first time the tight little nubs of unripe fruit dangling in clusters from every branch.

How dare it bear fruit when my sister is dead?

The sun's heat bore into me, but I would rather enter a hell realm than accept the tree's shade. That tree had helped me murder my sister.

Yes, murder. I had enticed her to climb out the window, just as Ama had accused me of doing. I was no better than this tree. I deserved the hell realm, I deserved to be burned up by the sun.

Suddenly, there was a sharp hand clap behind me. "Tell Mara to leave, now!"

Stick Woman.

I blinked and my thoughts dissipated.

How could I have failed to recognize Mara, when he'd been putting all those thoughts into my head? The answer came to me. Because Mara had been with me in this way ever since my sister's death, delusion being one his major weapons. Now his face hovered in my mind, the way I'd seen it in the mirror. "Leave me," I said.

And he was gone. In his place was the tree, its little unripe fruits and its dancing shade. I sat under the branches of the mango tree, and immediately a cool breeze washed through me as the shadows fluttered over my skin. Just like when I was a child, playing in the mango grove with my sister.

How had I forgotten how much Deepa loved mangoes? I recalled those summer days when the golden windfall fruits all but obliterated the ground. We'd find the ripest ones, knead the rubbery skin with our thumbs, poke the skin with a stick, and then suck out the insides, the sweet juice dribbling down our necks. We'd laugh as Cook splashed a bucket of water over us, the only way to clean off the stickiness.

I looked up into the luminous green foliage, the little fruits quivering on their long individual stems. Without being able to explain, I saw how this mango tree was all mango trees, in that in some equally inexplicable way it shared my sister's spirit, that of the little goddess of mangoes. "I forgive you," I said to the tree. "And I beg you to forgive me."

Not long after, Stick Woman wandered over to where I was sitting. "Don't think you're done forgiving," she said.

As the hot season continued, I entered a trance of contentment, pierced from time to time by pangs of loneliness for my own people, especially my son, but full of hope that carrying water, gathering and preparing medicinal plants, and learning the songs and rituals to invoke the spirits would teach me what I needed to learn. Slowly, I made the acquaintance of some of the villagers, the ones who came to the ridge seeking Stick Woman's help. I set myself to learn their language with the help of Bahauk, but in spite of my skills at memorizing, it was difficult to master. The Gorge tribe had a single word to mean "white butterflies circle around the black rock," which could also be translated "the wing-wind of air reverses good and evil." There were also words that made no sense unless you were standing in a certain location.

Still, I learned simple communication, enough to laugh and joke with Bahauk as we went about our tasks. Yet as the monsoon approached, I realized I still knew almost nothing about the ceremonies Stick Woman performed with the villagers. When I asked her if I could witness one, she always refused, citing not only my ignorance of the language but also the tribe's suspicions of Sakyans. Maybe in a few years, she said, if I stayed that long.

But by then Rahula would have reached manhood, his memories of me faded, his views solidified into a wall that could separate us forever. I needed to speed up my education.

One of the herbs we gathered was a bright-green, spiky plant that Stick Woman used as the primary ingredient in what she called "spirit tea," and which she sometimes brewed and drank when she journeyed to the spirit world. She had never warned me or ordered me not to consume it, so I decided to try. I would never dream of stealing from her supply; the tall green bushes massed over several nearby slopes, exhaling their dizzying astringence in the damp heat.

I picked two arm-length bunches and dried them in my little shelter, not liking my secrecy but desperate for anything that might infuse me with a knowledge I could transfer to Rahula. I waited for one of the afternoons when Stick Woman headed down to the village as she did every few weeks for her ceremonies with other spirit guides or people who, for whatever reason, couldn't climb to the top of the ridge. As soon as she left, I brewed a small pot of tea over the fire. My plan was to let it cool and then drink it in the shade of the mango tree, out of the heat, then go meditate in a tiny palm grove a little way off the main trail.

Just as I was pouring the brew from the unfired clay pot into a smaller clay vessel, I heard a familiar heavy footfall.

Bahauk.

I took a gulp of air, permeated with the tea's astringent aroma. I knew he smelled it, too.

"She lets you do that?" he asked. He was smiling, but there was a groove of doubt between his eyes.

My one hope was to make Bahauk an accomplice.

I hoped it wasn't Mara who prompted my next words. "Would you like some?"

"It's only for sacred ceremonies."

"My intention is to meditate in the palm grove."

"I could tell on you," he said, sounding worried, the way a child might worry, about a host of impossible-to-imagine consequences, some of which he himself could bring about.

"You could," I said, "but I thought I could trust you." Aware of the slant of my cheekbones and my shining, thickly lashed eyes in a way I seldom was these days, I looked into his open face. "I didn't steal the plant from Stick Woman," I said. "It's my own supply."

The doubt groove smoothed and faded, but his eyes seemed darker, quieter, older. He sat down beside me, not touching me, but I could feel his heat. "I've had this tea," he said. "After you drink it, you shouldn't be alone."

A fear cut into me. "I ... I'm still..." and I used the word of his people for "celibate," a complex term that included one's vow to the spirit world, dedication to the sun, and an apology to the gods of marriage and fertility.

At the sound, however mangled, of his native language, he smiled with the amiable innocence that never left him for almost the entire time I knew him and reminded me ever so slightly of Siddhartha when we first were together. "You don't need to worry," Bahauk said. "When we go to the spirit world, we can leave our bodies behind."

We shared the tea and then made our way toward the coolest part of the forest. I walked ahead of Bahauk, his footsteps, as always, reassuring. With him, I never worried about tigers or leopards attacking from behind. He knew every animal's habits and predilections, not to mention all the subtle sounds they made moving through the forest. Truly, he occupied their points of view and in that way shared their souls.

We reached the palm grove, which consisted of perhaps twenty trees close enough together for their translucent, lime-colored leaves to arc above our heads, creating a temple dome filled with shimmering green light. Nearby, a spring composed melodies that swam up through the hush of the air as we sat cross-legged, facing just off to one side of each other. I plunged my attention into my breath, waiting for the air to breathe me. Then I'm not sure what happened. Suddenly, we were talking, but our speech seemed to be a form of breathing, of sharing spirit between us.

In that green, holy light, time loosened; we seemed to be still conversing, but perhaps we'd finished and were now just watching our thoughts. We had been speaking of our childhoods, of his father teaching him to swim and catch fish in the river, of my sister and me listening to the holy men tell their stories of the world. We also talked about our current lives, our favorite trees and trails and even Stick Woman and the unknown sources of her mysterious powers. It was strange. This reminder of her could have made me worry, but all I could feel was her benevolence, as if she had guided us to this very spot.

I had the feeling she was protecting us from sex.

By now the light seemed to saturate us, the outlines of our bodies dissolving and Bahauk's face disintegrating into innumerable grains of radiance, which seemed to reform into Siddhartha's face—not as the Tathagata but as his old self—and then the radiance orchestrated itself into the face of my beloved Rahula, who I saw through Deepa's eyes, feeling her heart beating in my chest. At that point, I was certain Bahauk was looking at my sister's face, even as the contours of our faces kept transforming themselves into a series of benevolent loved faces I couldn't identify, their spirits flowing through us like silent breezes, or perhaps we were flowing through the spirits of all those we'd loved or would ever love. And then it struck me that we were indeed in the spirit world. It seemed to include the realm of the gods, but not in the way I'd thought as a Sakyan bride, as a domain of beauty apart from others. We were at the center of the universe, deeper than any notion of aesthetic pleasure, and we had been here forever.

Then all went still; there was no more center, no more periphery. No "here," no "there," only peace. So this was eternity.

Except that I didn't have any such thoughts until I reentered the impossibility that I could only label time. It seemed inconceivable to be back inside time and space when they had so definitively—and retroactively—dissolved.

Yet here we were, and we had changed in some yet-to-be-determined way.

Bahauk and I continued to gaze at each other. I was still bathed in wonder at what had happened, but the wonder began to subside, replaced by a longing for bodily contact, as if the mingling of our spirits now required physical confirmation. Bahauk spoke. "In the spirit world we are husband and wife." He touched me gently on the forearm. A dark heat spread through my body.

I had the feeling of no longer being under Stick Woman's protection.

Without thinking, I reached out to him. "Celibate" in both of our languages seemed to have lost its meaning.

Almost as if I'd willed his hands to move, they slid their warmth up under my garments, igniting a passion that spiraled from the molten core of me. Here it was, the unbearable craving that for so many years I had denied.

The cause of all suffering is craving. The words came unwanted into my mind.

These were just words, I told myself, I had not truly tested them. Yet they stopped me long enough for doubt to enter. "I can't!" I gasped. "I have a son."

"Stick Woman told me," he said in his simple way. "He should live with you here."

I stared at him. I realized I'd thought about this before, not in words but in flickering images: Rahula climbing the banyan trees, learning to gather herbs, Bahauk teaching him to hunt.

"Yasi." His hands gripped my hips, as if to steady us both. "We must marry. If you need to, get the blessing of your monk husband."

His words stunned me. Even more shocking was that I felt myself considering the possibility. Yet it was my mind that was shocked, not my body or spirit.

"I can't ask such a thing from my husband if I'm pregnant with another man's child."

"I don't have to stay inside you." He smiled into my eyes. "The spirits of our children will just have to wait."

The cause of suffering is craving. Which I could quench, at least for now, if I dared.

We lay on our sides face to face, my head buried in his shoulder as the heat of our bodies rose and merged, and his hands grew more urgent, moving in gentle circles closer and closer to my deepest center of desire; it had been so long since I had been touched there. All at once he grasped it, and my earth-body exploded into a flood of stars. Then he was on top of me, and it was too late to stop.

At the very end, he flung himself off me, spilling our children's spirits into the earth.

By the time we roused ourselves and started up the trail to the fire site, it was twilight. I walked behind him, amazed at how late it was and wondering whether days or years had passed. Then I looked up and saw the wolf blocking my way.

I staggered backwards. The beast seemed to tower and sway above me, its black eyes reflecting some unknown light.

"So you decided to dream up your own world." It was Stick Woman, wearing her wolf head.

"I'm sorry, I..." I was flustered, guilty, and at the same time eager to tell her what had happened. "I think I was at the center...I think I was beyond all worlds."

"You think." Yet her voice had a maternal softness, something I never would have said about her before. I also knew she knew about me and Bahauk, and she hadn't out-and-out condemned me. "Well, my dear, you are going to have to be very careful. And I'm afraid you'll have to experience the consequences."

"I'm ready," I said, still full of confidence after my experience. It didn't occur to me at the time that such confidence could only come from Mara.

I planned my trip home for after the rains, giving myself time to plan and prepare how I would present myself to my husband and relatives. The monsoons were mild that year; I'll always remember the season as one of palatial clouds gliding through pale sapphire skies, which could well have housed Indra's empire, for all I knew—or Bahauk's sun god or my people's god Agni, also associated with fire. But it no longer seemed to matter that I couldn't discern the gods. All that mattered was my earthly life with Bahauk. Love was its own divine realm, and this was where I chose to live.

Yes, I had dwelled here with Siddhartha, but in a less honest way. In my former life, I had tended roses and hibiscus for the sake of beauty. These days I gathered pine nuts, gourds, melons, and lotus roots for the sake of survival—which meant the survival of love, far deeper than beauty. I also learned to identify and preserve wild herbs for food and medicine, storing this knowledge in my mind the way I'd once memorized the holy men's metaphysics. Overall, I was doing everything my servants did in my former life. This left me less time to strive for spiritual liberation, but at least I was liberated from the guilty conscience of the pampered upper class. Siddhartha talked of abolishing the varnas. I was living his truth. Also, I told myself, I was not hiding from death. After all, Bahauk and I were no spoiled young couple feted by loving relatives. Our every mutual look and touch was edged with a knowledge that we could be torn apart by our separate peoples—or by the beasts in the forest, for that matter. When I was with Siddhartha, living in the present meant trying not to think about dying. Now I savored each moment Bahauk and I had, because death could occur at any time.

Yet as the days passed, I couldn't deny that in between those precious moments lurked the same fear that had been with me ever since the charnal ground, and my love for Bahauk made this fear all the stronger. I couldn't bear the thought of losing him.

No matter, I told myself. This would be my spiritual practice. Learning to master this fear, as well as the other unpleasant emotions that love entailed, such as the jealousy that sometimes seized me at the thought of Bahauk in the arms of some black-eyed Gorge tribe girl. Or the faint sadness I felt when drinking the spirit tea again failed to yield any more mystical experiences beyond lovely blendings of sounds and color. At least we could always repeat sex (eventually, as we'd vowed to abstain until after I'd made my journey), although I knew from my marriage that repetition could make the craving worse or else wear it down to a disappointed emptiness, such as had happened on Siddhartha's part. But the key was appreciating the precious moments, no matter what they were. Because although the preciousness of the moments made fear worse, so fear made the moments more precious.

By now I was actively preparing for my journey. Stick Woman assisted me, although in a wooden way, as if going through the motions. Still, she'd given me a bolt of white cloth, bartered from traders some years back, so I could travel as a spiritual seeker. She also handed me a half-dozen packets of herbs, for myself or others, for healing or bribery. I thanked her.

"I hope you have reason to," she said. We were standing in the rocky overhang shelter we'd slept in since the beginning of the monsoon. "Your monk husband—what does he call himself, the Tathagata?—might have had more to teach you."

"He teaches how to end suffering," I said, folding the herb packets into a rag. "But I don't need to be happy all the time."

Then one cloudy morning, the Sakyans attacked.

Later, I learned it was my brother who engineered the invasion, raiding the tribe's sacred grove of sal trees for lumber. I awoke just before dawn to male shouting in the distance. Across from me, for we had separate straw beds, Bahauk leapt to his feet, and before I knew it, he was pounding down the trail, disappearing into the remains of the night.

I kicked aside deerskins, jerking myself into my clothes, the air under the rocky outcropping still dank and smoky. Stick Woman was standing in front of me, holding her wolf head. "You stay here. Only here can I guarantee your safety."

"Let me come with you."

"No. You'd endanger not only yourself but also Bahauk and possibly me."

She was right, of course. "Is there anything I can do?"

"You can wait," she said, "and pray to something or other."

Then she, too, was gone.

I closed my eyes to meditate, in hopes of clearing my mind enough to be of eventual use. Dawn must have come and gone; I opened my eyes to stony daylight. A hell-being was standing over me.

A bow and arrows were strapped across its flame-red chest, a knife tied to its waist. But far worse was its face, crowned by a conflagration of oiled black hair and striped with vermillion across the cheeks and forehead, the blood-hued diagonals repudiating every emotion except rage.

The wrathful being spoke. "The Sakyans have murdered the daughters of the Sun."

The voice belonged to Bahauk. As did the chest and arms I'd held against my flesh, the broad brow and cheekbones I had smoothed and caressed. With a jolt, I remembered how I'd once mistaken Siddhartha for a demon. It was happening again. I stared at Bahauk's face, desperate to find him behind the war paint. His warrior's eyes were narrowed, as if my brother's violent soul had taken the place of my lover's.

I understood what he was saying. Bahuak's people believed that the firstborn child of the Earth and the Sun was the ancient sal tree that grew in the center of their sacred grove. The sal trees formed a crucial link between heaven and earth, and the village had been entrusted from time immemorial to protect them. If anything happened to the trees, the bond between gods and humans would break, unless the village could make amends.

"Are you here to kill me?" My horror at his transformation was greater than any fear for my Sakyan life.

"Yasi, no. You're not a Sakyan anymore. But the Sun must be avenged."

"You can't!" I pleaded. "The Sakyans have horses and elephants. Their warriors outnumber you by hundreds."

"You would have me betray God?"

"What good would it do any of your gods, your dying in some Sakyan cow pasture?" I didn't dare say, "There are other sal trees," because his language had no equivalent for one sacred object replacing another and he wouldn't understand what I meant.

"If we have to die, we will. To condone this crime would be worse."

"I can't bear the thought of you dying. I love you." Even as I spoke them, the words seemed limp and pastel and my love trivial and selfish compared to his loyalty to his people.

Yet my words seemed to give him pause. "How could you love anyone who betrayed his God?"

"I love your true self, your soul. Your refusal to go out on a raid wouldn't change it." I reached out and touched the demon-painted cheek, perhaps to prove to myself I could do it, to prove that this manifestation of Mara had nothing to do with his soul.

Bahauk's fierce stance softened. "Yasi, my soul belongs to you. But without my people and without my gods it's nothing." And now a younger face emerged behind that of the warrior, a boy's face, with a boy's needs. "If I don't do this, I lose all hope that my kinsmen will ever accept me."

"What about you and me in the spirit world? Does that not mean anything to you now?" I, too, sounded younger, even to myself, my arguments collapsing into a simple need for love.

"Unless we avenge the Sun, he'll destroy the spirit world and cast my people into darkness."

"I can't believe that. The sun will go on shining."

He touched his painted chest. "Not here," he said. "Your sun is different from mine."

It was then I realized that I'd misunderstood Bahauk when he called our experience in the palm grove a marriage. I'd thought he shared my assumption that our sense of mystical oneness had made our differences of language and belief irrelevant, but he'd meant a far simpler, emotional coupling. And now I began to doubt my own interpretation of the event. Although I'd clearly felt an eternal union with Bauhuk and all of existence, I also remembered disappearing into many selves and then into no self at all, implications that I'd chosen not to think about. Perhaps I'd used my mystical experience to hide from death, all the while thinking I was facing it.

He placed his hands on my shoulders, and even now his touch was a comfort. "Please give me your blessing," he said. "If I do this, the Gorge people might accept you as well. We still may have a chance. Perhaps the Sakyans will respect our revenge."

Whoever respected a revenge taken on them? But I knew he wouldn't hear this reply. He needed to hope. "Don't kill people," I said. "Burn their shrines. Maybe then they might understand." Or at least they might not be motivated to go to extremes in retaliation. Also, I admitted to myself, I did not want to be the lover, let alone the wife, of a killer.

What did this say about his eternal soul? Or mine?

"For you, I'll try not to kill," he said. "But I cannot guarantee what others will do."

Once again, he ran off, not waiting for my blessing.

Stick Woman didn't return for three days. I didn't eat, I could barely make myself drink water from the cistern. When she finally arrived, it was past midnight in the dull light of the waning half-moon, the wayward lover/sister of the sun, according to the Gorge people. I hadn't dared light a fire.

She lifted off the wolf head, and in the weak light of the moon I saw her face, gaunt and wrinkled, and somehow ordinary, as though it could belong to anyone, including me in some possible future—a grief-stricken widow whose life had turned to ash.

It was then I knew Bahauk was dead.

"Only three men survived," she said. "The survivors fed the bodies of the others to the sun."

"That's impossible! I want to see him!" I said, once again a child in the charnel ground, desperate to believe what I knew could never be true.

She had a fist-sized cloth bag around her neck. She took it off and emptied its handful of ashes into the dead fire. "This is all that's left."

Sobbing, I threw myself on the ashes, smearing them over my face and arms. This time I wouldn't leave the person I loved alone, I would not let the dogs get this last remnant of him.

"You have to get out of here," she said, her voice kind but firm. "I can protect you for only so long."

My grief had just begun. "I don't want to leave you," I said. The only thing I could see for my life was dedicating myself to her people, mindlessly gathering and grinding herbs and medicines to make up for what my people had done. Even the prospect of seeing Rahula failed to move me. In my despair, I saw my desire to be with my son as selfish. He had made his choice, and my presence—especially in my current state—would only upset him.

"Your destiny is not with us," she said, keeping her eyes on the dead fire. "It's time you thought about giving up the world." She glanced at my ash-smeared arms. "What happened to Bahauk and the others is part of the world, not an aberration. Love is followed by death, now or later."

A truth I'd thought I'd known. But all this time, I'd nourished the secret hope that love and death were separate.

Stick Woman studied me, the normally sharp wrinkles around her eyes sagging as if swollen with tears of her own. "It's time to forgive your former husband—for leaving you and for the pain that made him do it."

Something huge and heavy shifted in my heart, then broke open. The full image of Siddhartha's face the day I fainted arose in my mind's eye. What I'd seen as merely horror at my appearance was his realization of ultimate and inevitable loss. "He did love me, after all," I whispered.

Stick Woman continued to watch me closely. "You need to seek him out."

I wiped my eyes with my wrist and looked out over the hills, black cutouts under the half-moon, knowing that she spoke the truth. "But what about you?" I asked Stick Woman. "Now that Bahuak is gone, who will help you?" My voice broke. I knew how much Bahauk had done.

She gave a snort, "You think these things matter to me? I was sacrificed. My life ended when I was a child."

"But you're still alive. You still help people."

She shook her head. "Think of me only in terms of yourself. For you, I'm an agent of the Tathagata." The sly sparkle returned to her eyes, and I had the uncanny feeling that this whole time she'd simply mirrored me and my needs with no interference from a self with desires of its own. "Your destiny with him needed preparation," she added.

I looked down at the mess of ashes and soil. Once again I would be leaving the dead behind. I bent over and more tears came.

I felt her hand on my back. "Bahauk chose his own destiny. He will be married to you forever in the spirit world."

I shook my head. "The spirit world is empty," I said.

"Well, yes, but that's not the end of the discussion. You'll figure all of this out after you spend some time with the Tathagata."

I'd hoped to wait for daylight, but I had barely lain down in my skins when the night noises, which I hadn't even noticed, stopped with an abruptness that jolted me awake. Stick Woman was standing over me. I scrambled to my feet. She shoved the robes and the herb packets, already bound in a cloth, into my arms. In the moonlight, she looked like a varnished effigy, her cheekbones thrusting out from her face, her eyes blank.

"Go now," she said. "If you stay, you jeopardize my life and yours."

As quickly as I could, I wrapped the bundle in a sling. I didn't even have time to change into the robes. "The villagers hate me that much, that they would kill you as well?"

"These aren't Gorge people. It's the Sakyans."

My heart froze. "They're going to raid the village after all."

Stick Woman was pushing me in the direction of the lesser known trail to the overhang. "I'll stop them."

I whipped around to face her. "You plan to sacrifice yourself. I won't let you."

"Didn't you hear anything I told you? I've already been sacrificed. Now leave, or they'll either kill me or kill us both, after raping you. Without you here, there's a chance I can talk them out of it. But not with a Sakyan traitor woman to rile them up. Now go!" She gave me one last shove.

The trail tunneled through the barely moonlit trees. I stumbled forward, looking back only once, and I saw nothing but the corridor through the black trees leading into the dark. I half-walked, half-ran, the damp forest smells rising to meet me, the echoing crickets resuming. Then all at once they went silent again. I halted, my heart jammed in my throat, listening for warriors' footsteps nearby or cries in the distance, but there was nothing. I started up again, aware of rustling in the underbrush on both sides of me. I looked around and saw what I'd never seen before in these hills: wolves. They were dim shapes, little more than shadows, perhaps a half dozen of them. Somehow I wasn't afraid, and with them near, any warriors who had found this path would soon abandon it. I kept going, and after a time the wolves disappeared.

As I reached the banyan forest, I heard them in the distance. Their cries rose into the night and echoed down the canyons, shrieks to tear the moon and stars from the sky.

8

I followed the common roads to my parents' house; Ama was the only person I could trust to tell me the truth of my brother's role in the Sakyan raid. Beyond the jungle, the fields were a full-fledged green, cinnamon-colored cows grazing peacefully, white cattle egrets foraging in the lime-colored grass and flying overhead, the smell of hay and mint hovering in the sunshine. The beauty of the post-summer season only made my grief bleaker, like a burned-up forest, desiccated and charred black. I'd exhausted all my tears. My life had once again pared down to coming to terms with the soul. My year with Stick Women had revealed facets of the truth, but every facet reflected new depths of an ignorance I hadn't known I'd possessed—and which she implied could be dispelled only by the Tathagata. There had to be some way, I told myself, to persuade him to take on women students.

On the way to Ama's, I slept in fields and begged for scraps at kitchen doors of the big teak and sal wood houses of prosperous kinsmen, not revealing who I was. Although I spoke little and in low tones, I never denied I was a woman, but everyone presumed I was a man. I wasn't surprised. I was far thinner than a year earlier, and I had knotty muscles in my calves and ropy muscles in my arms.

My robes disguised what few curves I had left; my hair was twisted up in a beggar's knot, my skin a deep mahogany from the sun, my face and hands scratched and dirty. For reasons of safety, I was glad my femininity was not recognized. But I assumed my father would know me.

I reached the house of my childhood around midday. The addition I'd seen under construction the year before was now complete, a rambling structure that seemed to enclose a courtyard, making me fear that my father now confined my mother in a woman's compound not unlike Suddhodana's. At least the area around the kitchen door, where I'd spent long seasons with Deepa and the holy men, remained the same, a patch of packed dirt in front of a door half-opened to the dark, busy kitchen. I approached slowly.

A middle-aged man in a brown paridhana was striding toward me through flickering shade of the nearby mango grove. With a mild shock, I recognized my father.

As always, the sight of Suppabuddha scrambled my emotions into a confused mix of fear, guilt, and anger, along with a kind of shamed love that I immediately swallowed. Respectfully, I put my hands together and bowed from the waist. "Father," I said. "I've come to visit."

My father peered into my eyes. "Young man, is that your new religion? That you address your elders as father? I've never heard of such a thing."

"You don't recognize me?" I was more incredulous than hurt. I'd spoken in my normal voice and he'd looked deeply into my face, and yet he saw only some anonymous beggar, not even female.

"Of course I recognize you. Like all men, you are a broken-off shard of the First Man, seeking out reunion with the eternal Soul," he said. "But I have no time to converse with you today." He nodded toward the kitchen door in the dismissive manner that he'd always had with holy seekers who struck him as lacking in power and influence. "Our servants will provide you with some repast."

Now I did feel like a hurt child, as I had years ago when my father ignored me, even when I tried to talk to him about holy matters. I prepared to plead with him, to beg him to see through my dirt and pain and acknowledge his daughter, but something stopped me. Or someone. I felt the presence of Stick Woman inside me, dry and watchful. Perhaps my visit here should be a secret one.

"Thank you, good sir," I said, straightening my spine while keeping my hands together. I waited for him to march off to wherever he was going, then I rapped on the kitchen door.

A young, sad-eyed woman appeared from the kitchen's depths. She was a stranger, for my beloved Cook had been taken by the water-fever during my time in Suddhodana's household. She looked me up and down. "I can give you some rice-pot scrapings," she said. Unlike Cook, she was slender, her stained blue sari pulled tight around her flat belly. Her hair was pulled equally tight into a flawless bun, a contrast to her sad eyes. It struck me that her nature was sad but far from resigned.

"I thank you for your generosity," I said, bowing to her. "But I would like to speak to the lady of the house."

She took a step back. "My mistress only speaks to the seekers her husband has approved."

This was something new. I was fearing more and more that my father had clamped down on his women. I had to wonder—was this taking place throughout the clan? And did my brother have anything to do with it? "Please," I said in a low voice. "I have a message from her daughter."

"Her daughters are visiting with their mother at this very moment," the woman said. "As are her grandchildren." She put her hand on the door, perhaps to close it in my face.

"Not those daughters," I said. "The one who went forth to become a seeker."

The woman's eyes darted about fearfully, as if she expected to see the seeker-daughter flitting around in the mango trees as a spirit from the realm of the dead. "We are forbidden to speak of her," she said.

My heart clenched. Had I been banished from my own family?

I reached into my robe and removed one of the packets Stick Woman had prepared for me. I held it out. "This is a particularly effective variety of turmeric," I said. "If you mix it with soapy water, it will turn bright scarlet and awaken the holy fire in your nature, banishing sorrow. Otherwise, you can simply rub the powder on your face, and it will give your skin a golden glow."

The woman stared down at the packet. "Perhaps I can hint to my mistress that a holy man wishes to speak to her briefly about an urgent family matter. But she will probably not be able to get away until after her meal."

"I'll be meditating in the mango grove," I said, handing her the packet.

I sat down and arranged my robes around me. I thought in my emotional turmoil meditation would be impossible, yet as I sat observing my terrified breath, a strong current of realization swept me up from my fears. An outrageous plan was taking shape in my mind. I only hoped I wouldn't have to follow it.

The sun had shifted toward the west when Ama arrived, standing over me. I had to stop myself from throwing my arms around her knees. "Ama," I whispered. "Do you know me?"

She stared down at me. In spite of the dark crescents of grief under her eyes, her skin was still smooth over the elegant framework of her bones. "Yasi!" she finally said. "What's happened to you?" Tears washed her cheeks, as she thrust her arms down to gather me up. After the deaths of her daughters, her movements had never regained the confident precision I remembered from my childhood. "Who did this to you?" she asked.

I held out my arms to stop her. "No, wait. Is there somewhere you can hide me?"

My mother's fish-shaped eyes widened with terror. "My daughter, what have you done?"

"No, no," I said, looking around and praying no one had seen me. "I've done nothing other than stay with the holy woman you recommended. But the Sakyans attacked us. Now I can't risk making myself known here until I find out what's happened since I've been gone."

She showed no surprise at what I'd said about the tribe being attacked. "I can try to smuggle you into the women's quarters," she said.

I had to fight panic. Once inside the women's quarters, I might never be able to leave. "Not there," I said. "What about the cow shelter? If they find me, you can always say you were just trying to put me up."

"Oh, Yasi, your father no longer allows me to consort with beggars." Her eyes, once so steady, now shifted about in a kind of apprehension, the eyes of someone who no longer trusts in her gods to look after her, yet hasn't given up on them completely. "When you're dressed this way, I'm taking a risk just talking to you."

I was beginning to see the hopelessness of it all. "I need to know what's happening here. I can only beg you as your daughter to help me."

My mother cast one last glance at the house. It stood silent, dozing in the sun, its occupants recovering from the main meal of the day. "We'll go to the cow shelter."

The shelter was a straw-roofed, clay-brick structure that housed a hundred cattle, who this time of year spent little time there, which meant, fortunately, the place smelled more of straw than cow dung. In the aisle between the stalls, we picked up a couple of milking benches and took them to the stall farthest from the door "I can't stay here long," Ama said in a low voice.

"First, tell me about my son. Is Rahula all right? Is he still a monk?"

"He's fine, as far as I know. He's with Siddhartha—a good place for him, considering."

"Considering what? What's going on here?" Although I feared I knew.

Ama flicked her gaze around the barn, as if fearing detection. "Before I say anything, I need to know the reason for your secrecy."

I related what had happened in the hills, leaving out the sexual aspect of my relationship with Bahauk. Although I longed to confess to Ama about my love and receive the balm of her comfort, I didn't dare risk her rejecting me for loving a tribesman. Not when she was in all likelihood the only person in my whole clan I could trust.

"You obviously know about the Sakyans' attack," I said. "So tell me who was in charge."

She placed her fingers on the bridge of her nose, the pained gesture of a woman used to disillusion. "Who do you think?" she said.

She confirmed my worst fears. After I'd left, Suddhodana had undergone some kind of mental breakdown, begging his son to teach him how to awaken, not as a monk but as a layperson. Instructed by the Tathagata, he retreated into meditation for a half-year, and then, according to some people, he emerged fully illuminated. The next day he died, prompting these same people to wonder whether it was possible for laypersons to awaken and remain in their secular state.

"So I take it my brother is now in control, and his greed is responsible for cutting down the Gorge tribe's trees."

My mother nodded, averting her eyes.

With all my grief, I hadn't felt any anger at the attack this entire time, but now it roared through my body as if flaming up through the floor from hell below. My improved ability to forgive had its limits. Jagdish had incited the massacre of a whole tribe, including Bahauk of the kindly brow and wide innocent smile— the man who had made me happy after the sorrow of being abandoned.

With the rage came a fantasy of taking a machete to my brother's neck.

I know you, Mara, I prayed desperately. Be gone, god of death. Killing was never a solution to killing. "What else has Jagdish done?" I asked, as calmly as possible.

My mother looked at me tentatively, as if to gauge how much I could take. She sighed. "Pajapati is a virtual prisoner; the women's quarters there are more guarded than ever before. The varnas are strictly enforced—I'm glad Rahula no longer lives in that household."

So was I. But the women would suffer more, servant women most of all. I thought of Vasa, my young servant and friend. "And what of Vasa?" I asked. "By now, I hope she's married."

Ama fingered a fold of her green sari.

I felt a flare of fear. "What is it? Has my brother killed her?"

Ama kept her eyes on her lap. "No, he took advantage of the

education you gave her and passed her off as a princess. He married her to the Kosalan king."

"What?" My mother might as well have told me that elephants could balance on their ears. As I've said, the Sakyans despised the Kosalan people as low-borns. But for our clan to deceive their king was sheer folly; the Kosalan army, with fifty thousand men and over a thousand horses and elephants, could dispatch the Sakyan warriors in a single day. "Has my brother lost his mind?"

My mother stared out at the dust-choked sunbeams, looking older, the white threads in her hair visible in the cow shelter's ocher light. "He did it to spite your husband, whom he hates for defying what your brother sees as the holy order of the universe—not to mention that Siddhartha dishonored our family by abandoning you. King Pasenadi has become a lay follower of your husband, inviting him to stay and teach at his palace. So Jagdish figures that if Pasenadi finds out, he'll either have to denounce the Tathagata and his belief in varna equality or put up with a lower-caste wife."

"Or destroy the Sakyans in revenge! Tell me, did my brother ever think of that?"

My mother grasped her elbows, huddling into herself. "The King believes in peace."

"The King, perhaps, but if other Kosalans find out..." My rage at my brother rose again. "If I were a man, I would..." I stopped. I, too, believed in peace.

Ama sighed. "Your brother has his reasons, Yasi. He truly believes in the sacred social order and condemns your husband for encouraging people to give up the world. The Tathagata has gone so far as to say he's 'against the stream,' not only of society, but of ordinary religion and life itself."

"You would defend Jagdish! He's a thief and a murderer who

indulges his personal grievances above all, and he's put our whole clan in danger."

"He's my son," she said, her voice thick with held-back tears. "Think of Rahula. Wouldn't you at least try to see his point of view?"

"I suppose," I said, temporarily off balance until I made myself remember what Jagdish had done. "But Jagdish is no longer my brother." I stood up, realizing that the plan I feared to implement was all I had left. "Ama, I can no longer live as a member of this family. I'm joining the Tathagata's Sangha."

"You know he doesn't accept women! That hasn't changed, dearest, and I don't think it ever will. Pajapati longs to join, but the Tathagata has refused even her."

"I'm not joining as a woman. I'm joining as a monk."

My mother sprang to her feet, her eyes dry with horror. "You're disguising yourself as a man? You're every bit as mad as Jagdish."

"I'm not disguising myself as anything, although I'll shave my head to indicate that I've sacrificed my sexual nature, something all monks do in any case." I had the fleeting thought: perhaps Stick Woman was right. Saving the world required sacrifice. I only wished I were surer about the nature of the world I was saving.

Ama remained distraught. "Yasi, he'll recognize you. Let alone your years of intimacy, it's said he has psychic powers."

"Of course he'll recognize me. But he can choose to see me as other than my feminine self. After all, he has preached that the soul is a fluid, with no permanent essence. Perhaps he'll see me with the eyes of Dharma, knowing I have a role to play in his life."

"And if he doesn't?"

"I'll live as a solitary wanderer," I said, not wanting to think that far ahead. "Ama, please give me your blessing. I'm doing this for all women—but especially for the women in this clan who, if the

Kosalans end up attacking, will be enslaved if not killed. Once in the Sangha, I'll try to persuade the Tathagata and the other monks that women deserve the chance for awakening. Then you, Pajapati, and all our clanswomen will have the option of escape."

My mother reached out and stroked my cheek. "My beautiful daughter. Does it have to be this way with you?"

"I fear that it does."

She took an unsteady breath. "Well, in that case, what would you have me do?"

"If anyone asks, say that your daughter Yasodhara vanished in the hills."

She closed her eyes for a moment, then studied me in that motherly way she once did to check that my shift was spotless and my hair neatly braided. "You'll need a life story. I recently heard of a remote Sakyan village where almost everyone died of the water-fever. You can say you come from that village as a seeker, and there will be no one from that place to challenge you." She stood up, brushing off her sari. "You'll also need a name, one that no one will associate with you."

"I'll take the name Ananda—bliss," I said. Then I added, "Ama, where can I shave my head?"

Book Two

ANANDA

nce again I took to the road, begging my way through the Sakyan territory. I bypassed my former father-in-law's household, now my brother's stronghold, and continued south to the kingdom of Magadha, where Ama had told me that the Tathagata was staying. The capital, Rajagaha, surrounded by big-shouldered hills that turned the valley into a fortress, was by far the largest town I'd ever seen. But I couldn't afford to look timid, lest I be suspected as feminine, apprehended as a woman traveling alone, and sent home before I even managed to reach the Tathagata's Sangha.

Fortunately, the civilized world could hardly conceive of a woman without ornaments and makeup. Even poor women outlined their eyes in kohl and adorned themselves with earrings and bangles, so to my great relief I passed unsuspected through the tall stone gates into a city consisting of thousands of timbered brick dwellings and temples, mixed with uncountable wooden shacks and little shops selling everything from dung patties to diamond rings. The smoky air teemed with noise: bells, flutes, vendors' cries, dog barks, chicken squawks, and the crashes and hammering of the construction everywhere. Carts, carriages, horses, and elephants clogged the streets where princes and merchants in silk brocade crowded up against loincloth-clad soldiers and ash-covered ascetics, and princesses and courtesans bobbed along high-headed in litters past servant girls crouching in the gutters as they scrubbed urine from the paving stones.

Like a good monk, I barely glanced at the women—or the men. In a private ritual on the night I left Ama's, I'd sacrificed my sex, burying my hair in the mango grove along with the little cloth packet I'd taken from Stick Woman's camp. It held the last of Bahauk's ashes. They were now the keepers of my womanhood.

Right away, I sought to blend in with with the holy seekers who traveled alone or in clusters like floating saffron gardens, begging from the populace and arguing with one another. Each had his own opinion of the Tathagata, most of them positive. He was praised as the Buddha of the current age whose Middle Way, as Pajapati had said, avoided the extremes of self-indulgence and self-denial and offered liberation, not to just a few priests, but to all classes. He'd already converted a famous fire-worshiping Brahmin and his thousand matted-haired followers, as well as additional thousands of Magadhan householders, including their king, Bimbisara, my husband's longtime friend. It was Bimbisara who was currently hosting the Tathagata just outside the city in a bamboo grove he had created especially for him—a pleasure park that a few detractors criticized as too luxurious for holy men, let alone monks. I largely discounted their words; at this point I desperately wanted the Tathagata to be truly enlightened. Realistically speaking, he was my last hope for a spiritual life.

"How does one get an interview with the Tathagata?" I asked a group of six or seven ocher-robed monks, possibly disciples, seated on the granite steps of a hulking brick temple in the middle of town.

I had yet to venture to Bimbisara's grove, an hour's walk from the city.

"By ascending to the Tavatimsa Heaven and petitioning his dead mother!" The monk—a round-eyed, pink-lipped boy who couldn't have been more than sixteen—burst into laughter.

"No, not enough!" His companion, equally young, grinned broadly, his freshly shaved head shining like a polished chestnut. "To get to the front of the line, you need to fly up to the heaven of streaming devas and beg the holy Brahma and his ten thousand deities to place you personally at the Master's feet."

I stared at them, my heart pitching. "Is the wait truly so long?"

"Well, let's see," said the first monk. "It probably won't take too much more time than for a mountain to wear away by brushing a feather against it once every hundred years." With that, the group dissolved into hilarity.

These monks, little more than children, were enjoying laughter at my expense, and I felt a wave of motherly affection. Then I had another thought, that with my beardless face and delicate features they probably thought I was their age—a misperception that, come to think of it, could help me maintain my disguise now and in the future. And so it came to be that the monk Ananda was always estimated to be far younger than he was.

"I want to be admitted to the Sangha," I said in a comradely way. "Does that give me any priority? Otherwise, I'm afraid I'll be ordained as a pile of dust."

"Don't listen to them." A hollow-cheeked, hook-nosed member of the group who seemed older—though still young, perhaps in his early twenties—gave his companions an astringent look. "These monks need to remember that the Blessed One frowns on superficial jesting." The teenaged monks looked in various directions of down.

No superficial jesting? How different this characterization of the Tathagata sounded from the easy humor of the man who had once been my husband. But perhaps this difference was all to the good. The less the Tathagata resembled his former self, the more I could concentrate on him as a teacher and not someone who had once shared my bed. "So," I asked the older monk, "how do I avoid the crowds?"

The round-eyed, baby-faced younger monk spoke up again. "You can't," he said in a sober, chastened voice, keeping his eye on the older monk. "But you can stand up at the end of the Dharma talk and announce your intention, though you may have to shout."

This was the last thing I wished to do, considering that inconspicuousness was a major part of my strategy. A lone seeker standing up in front of thousands—and shouting with a voice higher than most men's—could attract scrutiny, which might well make me suspect to everyone—including my son, who was probably in attendance. My hope had been to meet with the Tathagata alone and let the Dharma judge. "Surely," I said, "there must be a less... annoying way to make my desires known."

"Perhaps," the older monk said. "Try to speak to one of the Tathagata's attendants before the Dharma talk. You might find one willing to help."

Might? "I thought that the Sangha was eager to accept new members," I said.

The monk arranged his upper robe over his shoulder, preparing to leave. "Of course, but some of the monks are less encouraging than others. You may need to shout after all."

*

After five days listening to gossip and philosophy, sleeping fully clothed in temples and pavilions, and bathing after midnight at a deserted *ghat* just outside the city, I felt ready to face the future. In the dead of night I put on a fresh white robe Ama had given me, and at dawn I began the hour-long walk to King Bimbisara's Grove, accepting a stale chapati from an elderly, hunchback woman, one of the many people of all varnas eager to create conditions for a better rebirth by feeding holy men—the more varieties of holy the better to increase the likelihood you'd chosen an effective one.

It was another crystalline post-monsoon morning, with broad fields similar to those of the Sakyans but for the rocky hills towering around me. The valley itself was flatter than the Sakyan countryside, its river more leisurely, as befitting one of the most prosperous kingdoms in the land. Outside the city walls, King Bimbisara's five-tiered, glazed-brick, pink palace soared like a celestial citadel in the western distance, far bigger and more splendid than Suddhodana's establishment. I swallowed an unexpected lump in my throat. What sort of power did my former husband have, that he could convert the ruler of such a place? A single straight highway led in its direction, paved with stones so smooth one's feet didn't trudge but whispered, as if to prepare the traveler for the divinity beyond. Even at this early hour, a river of people, about half of them in holy robes, headed toward the complex.

The Tathagata was to give his talk in a bamboo grove not far from the palace. By the time I arrived, hundreds of people of all varnas had gathered, the rich seated on cushions under a white silk canopy;

the rest of the laypeople on the matted grass between clumps of jade-stemmed bamboo. The slender bamboo trunks soared as high as Bimbisara's palace, their sun-filled leaves suffusing everything with a living green light, reminding me of the palm grove where I had dissolved into the soul of the universe, an experience I was sure would not be repeated today. What if I ended up making a spectacle of myself? And what if my son was here? I longed for the sight of him, but what if it made me lose my resolve?

Around noon, King Bimbisara's servants, wearing scarlet turbans and gold livery, served rice and red lentils on banana leaves to the laypeople. As I struggled to swallow a bite or two, I spotted a pair of middle-aged monks weaving their way through the crowd. The two resembled descriptions I'd heard over the past week of the Tathagata's two main disciples, Sariputta and Mogallana, and they were heading in the direction of the dais. Abandoning my food, I hurried toward them.

"Excuse me, sirs, but I wish to speak to the Master in hopes of joining the Sangha," I said, the sentence coming out as one uninterrupted word.

Sariputta, small-featured and still-faced, smiled serenely, bowed, and headed off, leaving me to his companion, the teak-skinned Mogallana. I looked up into his deep-set brown eyes and fleshy, olive-black face, alive with a world's worth of expressions, changing every instant, yet all of them friendly in one way or another. If there was ever evidence of rebirth, Mogallana was it, carrying points of view from all his lifetimes with him, all transfigured into benevolence by his present blissful incarnation.

"And what do you call yourself?" he asked.

He had not asked my name, but rather what I called myself. He was not about to force me into a lie. *He knew.* "Ananda," I said.

"Well, Ananda—"

"Excuse me." A tall monk in a dingy, patched robe was approaching, and at the sight of his narrow face and acerbic eyes, I felt a cold fist in my throat. It was Devadatta.

Of course he would be here at the center of everything. He looked the same as I remembered, except thinner, his jaw more prominent, his skin stretched tightly across his sharp cheekbones. He'd acquired the look of an ascetic, and the hard creases bracketing his mouth made me think he lacked mercy for himself and others.

Devadatta asked Mogallana, "Is this fellow bothering you?" He nodded in my direction.

"Not at all," Mogallana said. "He simply wishes to join the Sangha. He goes by the name Ananda."

Devadatta burned his gaze into mine. "Where are you from?"

I swallowed. Like my father he'd never really looked at me; but perhaps I'd been foolish to hope he'd be unable to conceive of me as a man. "The northern part of the Sakyan territory," I said. "My father's name is Chetan." One of the few names Ama knew from the disease-decimated remote village.

"So you're a Sakyan," he said. "Then why is it I've never heard of you? I, too, am Sakyan."

"My village is far from here," I said. "And few of my people travel."

Devattta closed his eyes and seemed to enter into meditation. What was he up to? I glanced over at Mogallana, who seemed unperturbed. After a long moment, Devadatta spoke. "I must tell you, I'm renowned for my psychic powers."

I couldn't run. I could do nothing but wait for what he had to say. Cold sweat wormed down the back of my neck.

"I sense Mara's presence here," he said. "I fear you may not be speaking the truth."

"I am Sakyan," I said, barely able to breathe. "I only wish to learn from the Blessed One."

Suddenly, Mogallana intervened. "Devadatta," he said, "why are you harassing this monk, whose motives are pure?"

Devadatta bowed his head. "My apologies, Noble One, but I fear that he belongs to a lower varna, and he's concealing this fact. Otherwise I would have heard of his family."

"Is this true?" Mogallana asked me.

All at once Mara came to my aid—or so I interpreted it later—filling me with the kind of huffy righteousness that banishes fear, and in that way prevents the suspicious behavior fear can engender. I was also relieved that Devadatta's pyschic powers, such as they were, didn't include the ability to see through my robes. "The Sangha accepts all varnas," I said. "I don't see the need to recite my genealogy."

Mogallana smiled equably at us both. "This young monk is correct, Devadatta, as you well know."

"Of course," Devadatta said, "but I'm concerned that the Sangha has invited too many men of low origins into our company. Lately, we've had brawls and drunkenness, and even King Bimbisara has noticed." He addressed me. "Friend, discipline is extremely important in our Sangha, and many monks from lower varnas simply are not prepared for Mara's temptations. You would do well to return home and fulfill your class duties. In this way, you'll earn merit for a better reincarnation. If as a monk you succumb to the Evil One, you will fall much farther than a layperson—you could get yourself reborn in hell."

"I'm willing to take that risk," I said. "I imagine Mara would pose an even greater threat to upper-class monks with high opinions of themselves."

I thought I saw a glimmer of amusement in Mogallana's brown eyes, but Devadatta's narrow Sakyan face tightened. "I have only your welfare in mind, monk," he said. "I can sense Mara inside of you even as you speak."

"Enough, Devadatta," Mogallana said. "Mara has coursed through all our lifetimes and lingered in all our souls." He smiled at me. "We've all been Mara many times over." Later, I would learn that Mogallana had supposedly remembered all of his countless lives, including one where he had murdered his parents. And although he was now fully enlightened, he had stated that his past karma would cause his death to be a violent one, which turned out to be so.

"Well, then," Devadatta said to Mogallana, not looking at me at all, "I leave this monk to you." He flipped his upper robe over his shoulder and marched off.

Mogallana turned to me. "Come to the platform after the Dharma talk. The Blessed One will interview you then."

I bowed to him in gratitude, my heart soaring with relief. "I only wish to be a good monk."

"Then mark well your karma," he said in a not unkindly way. Yet I knew what he meant: my Mara self had created the karma of turning Devadatta into an enemy—and I hadn't yet even joined the Sangha.

Not long after the midday meal, King Bimbisara and his Queen— reputedly an even more devoted supporter of the Tathagata than her husband—arrived with their entourage. They both wore brocade paridhanas, he in russet and gold, she in blue and silver, yet their splendor faded into the background with the approach of the Tathagata in his simple ocher robes. I sat about two-thirds of the way back in the crowd—close enough to see that he was as physically peerless as ever; he also emanated that impersonal radiance I remembered from the last time I saw him, which now brought a hush to the crowd and compelled every gaze to follow him as he mounted the dais. Except mine. For directly behind him, his head shaved and in almost every way a smaller version of his father, was my son.

Tears burned my eyes. It was all I could do not to rush up to the stage, crying out, "My darling!" and bundling him into my arms. My sweet one! Rahula had grown taller and lost every bit of his childhood plumpness, yet he looked happy. And right next to him was Mogallana, who appeared to be one of his teachers, for which I rejoiced.

But nothing could quell my longing to be with him as his mother, and without realizing it, I'd stood up and taken a step toward him, remembering his boyish scent and the softness at the back of his neck. Then our eyes met, and the innocent curiosity in his face filled me with love, then dread. If I were found out in this public way, I would most probably be banished from my son forever. And what would Rahula think of me, his mother, in the guise of a male? He could be repulsed or horrified far beyond simply never wanting to see me again.

I sat down, my back rigid and my heart thrashing, and ordered myself to listen to the talk, about how clinging to worldly phenomena caused suffering. The Master made another point: that this clinging was always the clinging of possession and identification. Was it true that I loved Rahula only because he was *my* son? And how selfish was my craving to be with him? How much of it was my clinging to the identity of being his mother?

Selfish or not, I knew that the only way I could be with my son was to join the Sangha. And the Tathagata would discern my craving simply by looking at me.

After the talk, I stopped at the edge of the crowd around the Tathagata, who was still seated on the platform, patiently conversing with all sorts of people, from vulture-catchers to Bimbisara's queen. The cowering child-self inside me almost hoped he wouldn't notice me, that he'd go off with his attendants and I'd never see him again. But all of a sudden he stood up, engulfing me in his gaze. "Please come with me," he said, descending from the dais, and I had no doubt he was speaking directly to me, and that he'd recognized me right off. The crowd parted on either side of him. Woozy with a terror that contained a sense of momentousness of what I was about to do, I followed him into the depths of the grove. And even though I thoroughly believed that my deception was justified, I still suffered the guilt of a child who has broken her parents' rules.

We stopped in front of a shed, which housed a single room, simply constructed of varnished sal wood, with narrow scalloped windows on all sides. It had to be an interview room, I decided, and when the Tathagata ushered me inside, it seemed to contain its own silence. In here it felt as if the crowd outside had abruptly gone mute.

We sat cross-legged on low cushions, facing each other. The room was entirely of polished pale hardwood, with no adornments but for a single brass bowl containing a blue lotus, its petals edged with flame-orange. When I looked up from the flower I saw in his eyes that same compassion I remembered, which gave me hope that he wasn't going to denounce me, although his compassion could well be for the pain that such a denunciation would bring. Then, as moments passed and he didn't speak, I noticed something else in his gaze, something beyond emotion—even beyond serenity—filling me with that strange sense that I had only known once before. "Here" and "there" had disappeared, and the distinction between one mind and another no longer applied.

"Why do you wish to join the Sangha?" he said, but the words were already inside me as he spoke, as if I was posing this question to myself for the first time. At the same time, the question was posing itself to the universe.

Somewhere back in the ordinary world, I knew I needed to be as honest as I could without saying too much. Then I felt the Tathagata's will engulf me, just as his gaze had earlier. Only it wasn't his will; it was the will of the Dharma, speaking through me. "To help you liberate as many beings as possible," I said, surprising myself. Earlier I'd thought mainly in terms of helping women and my son. I looked into the Tathagata's face. Its sober expression exactly mirrored my own, as the truth of my words settled over me.

He closed his eyes, and I felt the Dharma's power fade. Had he closed his eyes out of sympathy or irritation?

The silence returned, now taking on time as well as space, stretching out until I felt compelled to speak in my own behalf. "I can memorize your teachings word for word and spread it beyond the Sangha."

He nodded very slowly, but the silence went on.

Finally, he spoke. "The Tathagata never tells an untruth."

My hopes plummeted. He was obviously saying that he couldn't participate in my deception. Yet my purpose wouldn't let me give up. I closed my eyes and willed the Dharma to reveal itself.

Instead, I felt the presence of Stick Woman, as if she were the only Dharma I was going to get just now. Then words came to me. "You have stated that there are countless leaves in a forest," I said, "but that you hold only a few in your hand."

"I have." His voice was noncommittal.

I continued, "The leaves in the forest stand for everything that you know; the leaves in your hand represent all that you teach. You don't speak of all the things you know, because they wouldn't lead to the end of suffering."

By which I meant, you don't need to say outright to anyone what sex I am.

The Tathagata's gaze intensified; I had no idea what he was thinking. "I do refrain from answering certain questions," he said, "such as whether the world is eternal, or whether a self exists forever, or whether the Tathagata persists after death. This is because any answer would only leave the listeners vexed and confused, ending up with wrong views that would lead them to more pain."

I didn't know whether to be encouraged or discouraged by his reply. I persisted, "And you also address different listeners in different ways, depending on what they are able to comprehend."

"Yes."

"And so there must be many items that people living in this age cannot understand properly, and therefore you must keep silent about them." *Such as a woman taking vows as a monk.*

Abruptly, he stood, turning toward one of the windows, and I feared he was going to say the interview was over and I had failed to convince him.

"I have a question for you," he said, looking back at me. "You've already memorized some Dharma, it seems. Have you not heard the Dharma that cherishing a loved one causes suffering? How can this be otherwise when you, your loved one, and the very nature of your love is doomed to change and eventually die? I've preached that if you have a hundred loved ones you suffer a hundred times more."

I knew he was referring to my feelings toward Rahula, which he was using to discourage me from engaging seriously with the teachings. I wouldn't let him. "I haven't heard that Dharma specifically, but it seems to follow from what you preach."

He remained standing. "There are many people who might think this teaching is cold. Mothers would fear abandoning their feelings for their children."

The windows seemed to go dim, and I felt myself sinking into the memory of the night he left, his silhouette in the doorway, the star and crescent moon in the window shining heartlessly away. Had he awakened to a Dharma that had taken away his humanity?

A thought approached me. "Perhaps some parents would not abandon their love for their offspring. Instead, they'd expand that love to include every living being—which I have also heard you preach. I gather that, if someone loves all equally, then he can't cherish any single being or group of beings over the others. Perhaps to develop this kind of love is the practice."

Could I do that? Surely, this task was impossible except perhaps for an enlightened being. Yet I was committing myself to try.

He sat down again, facing me. "You are clever, Ananda, but this practice requires more than mental agility." He gestured around the little room. "King Bimbisara has started constructing wooden *kutis* for all the monks. But currently many of them still live out in the open, in the forest, in fields, and even in charnel grounds. Before making your final decision you'll have to sleep in a charnel ground— not only to prove that you are willing to endure the hardships of the holy life but also as a matter of practice, as a way of learning to understand the earth and the body as they really are."

He knew about Deepa, of course—was this why he was sending me to such a place? I had not been in a charnel ground since I left my sister to the dogs. I dreaded the possibility that returning to such a place would undo me in ways I couldn't begin to predict.

"Meditating in charnel grounds is required of all Sangha members," he said, as if he wanted to assure me I was not being singled out.

"I'm ready to do what you ask." I hoped I could make this statement true.

I bowed and left.

That same day, after receiving instructions from Mogallana, I arrived at the city's charnel ground just before sunset, carrying only a water gourd and a sharp stick to discourage dogs and jackals. The corpse area was far larger than the one outside my village, occupying a vast trampled plateau. The evening was mild, with just enough breeze so that as I climbed the stone steps to the top, wafts of decay assailed me, each more revolting than the last. Every breath transported me to that first charnel ground, where the smell of death was a warning to flee from its presence. I readied myself to be terrified.

Instead, my righteous rage, which I was always sure I had banished forever until it came back again, heated up in my heart. Why was my former husband subjecting me to this filth? What good would it do to spend the night wading through corpses and staring into their rotted-out eyes? I already knew death too well, and the gore of strangers' bodies would certainly affect me far less than the image of Deepa's lifeless form chewed up and digested by dogs.

By now I'd reached the top of the steps overlooking the plateau, bruise-purple under the still pale sky, black hills looming in the distance. This charnel ground was better planned than the one in my village, and after walking briefly over suspicious-looking dust,

I came upon a neat row of naked corpses—ten men, women, and children lying on their backs an arm's length apart, mouths agape, ants flowing over faces and bellies. These bodies had been laid out recently, perhaps this very day. Beyond them, the rows were progressively more disorganized, flung about by dogs and wolves, noses pecked out by vultures. A black rat slithered out from under the body of a huge fat woman lying on her back, her bloated breasts and stomach half-devoured and looking like they'd exploded. I shuddered with revulsion, but the hideousness of the scene did nothing but amplify my anger about spending the night.

Where would I sleep? The stench crawled down my gullet and sank into my lungs. I had half a mind to march back to the palace grounds, where the Tathagata was lounging around with kings and nobles, and tell him exactly what I thought of his disgusting so-called test. He knew I wouldn't be terrorized by ghosts. And as for the god of death, hadn't I already met Mara and known him as a part of myself? Even now I knew my rage to be Mara within, but I didn't care. The injustice was real, that I had to spend the night in this putrid squalor for no reason, after having suffered so much from death already.

If I couldn't find a place to lie down where the odor wouldn't overwhelm me, I wouldn't stay. I looked out over the plateau. Beyond the corpse rows were scattered bones, and at the field's far end, the rotted bones had been raked into piles, the grass around them scummed with bone dust. Obviously, the corpses were rotated, perhaps according to specifications of the Sangha.

Before I had time for another bout of anger, I sensed a motion on the periphery. A dog? I peered into the twilight, the setting sun in my face, the dim shapes in front of me vague and flickering. A being was moving in my direction, wreathed in the faintest of whispers, as of incantations. No living human would move this way, make these sounds, I told myself. Could it be a corpse risen from the dead? It was too small for a man or woman. A child's corpse! Deepa. I felt the dread as a blow.

Perhaps I'd been wrong about spirits and about everything else in my life, and now Deepa had come to haunt me, to punish me for failing to find her. No, for causing her death. Or was I in some nightmare, unable to wake up?

I stood there open-mouthed, the breath sucked out of my body as the corpse, head lowered and muttering its awful prayer, continued to approach. Then I noticed its head was shaven, and it was shrouded in a monk's robe, the yellow color a dusty ocher in the twilight. The corpse wasn't Deepa, but it was definitely a child.

Oh, please, let it not be Rahula.

Had he suddenly died? Had his ghost come to warn or reproach me?

Or was he alive, and had he found me out?

My throat and lungs paralyzed, I ran toward him—blindly, instinctively, needing to know, even if it meant he would hurl me into hell.

The little monk looked up at me. I stumbled to a halt. His whispering continued. "This body is of the nature as these corpses," he said, pointing his finger into his chest. "It will become like them, it will share their fate."

The monk wasn't a ghost, nor was he my son. But he was a little boy, no older than seven, sent here to perform the same contemplation Mogallana had instructed me to do—instructions that in my righteous rage I had completely forgotten. I, who had so blithely assumed I knew all about how Mara operated inside me, had failed to see what the Evil One had been up to, which was to use anger to blind me to the fear of my own death—and thereby to prevent me from confronting the truth, such as this little monk was trying to do.

I looked into his round dilated eyes, glazed with terror. He was too young to be facing this! "Greetings, my friend," I said. "Are you a follower of the Tathagata?"

"My name is Kavi," he replied, nodding and raising his stubby little chin, perhaps to show me his courage.

"I'm Ananda," I said. "I also look to be a follower of the Awakened One. Tell me, did he send you out here?" Anger once again surged through my veins at the thought of my former husband doing such a thing.

"No, it was Venerable Devadatta."

I should have guessed! I had to keep my anger in check. By now, surely I had learned how Mara used it to cloud my judgment. For one thing, if this little monk was anything like Rahula, he might have insisted on coming out here himself. "You are very brave to be doing this," I said. "But perhaps you've meditated enough for tonight. Perhaps you and I could return to the bamboo grove and camp out there."

"No!" And now the terror in the little boy's eyes made room for suspicion as if I were Mara himself tempting him from the Path.

I took a step backward, raised my hands in a display of harmlessness. "I don't mean to interrupt your practice," I said. "But what do you think would happen if you returned to the grove?"

He glanced around as if to make sure no corpses were listening in. "The Venerable Devadatta would send me back to my father."

Another jolt of rage; I swallowed it. "And what would be so bad about that? Perhaps your parents miss you."

Kavi stared down at the trampled grass, coated in bone dust. "My

Ama's dead. I have seven brothers. There's not enough food for all of us."

So his father had left him off at the monastery. I knew that after Rahula became a monk, Suddhodana had exacted a promise from the Tathagata that all boys under eighteen would require their father's or grandfather's permission to join the Sangha. But this was the first I heard about taking in destitute children.

"Tell me," I said, "what's your father's occupation?"

Kavi sank his gaze even further into the ground. "He's a tanner."

One of the lowest varnas. I was sure this was why Devadatta sent him out here: either to teach him discipline or to have an excuse for getting rid of him if he failed. The other alternative, the possibility that he could be killed by wild animals, I could hardly bear to attribute even to Devadatta. And yet there it was. "I could stay with you here if you'd like, Kavi," I said.

He glanced up, his eyes soft with hope but quickly looked down again. "I think I'm supposed to do this alone."

There was no way I'd leave this little monk by himself. I peered down at him. "But where's your stick?"

"What stick?"

"To protect yourself against the animals. All monks are issued a stick when they come here," I lied. "Even I received one, and I've yet to be accepted into the Sangha." In fact, I'd cut my own stick.

"But how could the Venerable Devadatta have overlooked such a thing?"

I shook my head, hoping that Kavi took my gesture for one of unknowing rather than one of disgust. "He probably intended that we should meet here," I said. "Perhaps you are to instruct me in the contemplations. After all, you're a monk and I'm only an aspirant."

I gestured toward my white robes, yet to be exchanged for yellow ones.

Kavi gave me a doubtful look.

Just then the last of the sun winked out below the horizon, and the forest began to rustle with night beasts. Kavi looked out at the eastern sky, whose ink-blue stain was rapidly spreading west, then at the darkness of the trees, where a dog fight had broken out, yaps and growls spilling into the night. He looked back at me. "You need to meditate on each corpse," he said in a pedagogical voice. "And know that one day you will be the same as it is now. We all think we are our bodies and we cling to them, and this causes suffering because we refuse to accept their impermanence."

He resumed his whispering, I joined him in the chant, and we walked for awhile, studying the dead bodies. But I couldn't concentrate on the chants or the corpses, or even my repulsion, concerned as I was about Kavi. Once I got back to the grove, I'd talk to Devadatta about sending little boys out at night, especially to charnel grounds. If necessary, I'd go to the Tathagata himself.

A greenish two-thirds moon, which had been in the sky all along, was whitening quickly as if desperately absorbing the last pale dregs of daylight. It illuminated the jackals crouching at the field's edge, surveying their feasting grounds, ready to strike. Kavi walked as close to me as possible, while being careful not to touch me, and I wondered whether this was monastic fastidiousness or a result of being in a varna where touching anyone in a higher class was forbidden. Once again, I felt my anger rise that this child might consider himself so unworthy.

It was then I had the first glimmer of the course my life would take in the Sangha and why the Tathagata was considering my ordination. From what I'd seen, many of the monks were very young—teenagers, if not children. The young monks who'd teased me at the temple could all be my sons: helping them to adjust to sangha life was how I might start expanding my love for Rahula to eventually include all beings. Was this what the Tathagata wanted of me? And was it for my sake or for the sake of the monks? I also wondered how my motherly feelings would affect my own enlightenment. As I walked along, preoccupied with Kavi, my own meditations were perfunctory, sometimes fading entirely into the background.

Two or three jackals were creeping toward us. "I do remember one thing Mogallana told me," I said, hoping to distract Kavi, who kept glancing uneasily at the animals. "He said we need to keep watch on our minds. See how the mind craves for things to be different than they are, and how that craving causes suffering." Such as had happened with me, I realized, especially when I'd first arrived here. My anger had come, at least in part, from not wanting to consider the corpses' resemblance to my own condition. I'd seen them as other, as objects of disgust, and ignored the fear and the shame that came from the perception that I was indeed like them. As a result, I'd missed the opportunity to see through my fear of death and perceive the corpses as they really were, as simple matter in the same way as my body was simple matter, and not me or mine.

But I didn't have time to relish this insight. The jackals had stopped within three body-lengths of us, and more followed.

Too late, I realized that the fear I'd temporarily escaped through anger was not only of my eventual demise but also of dying this very night. All around us, the jackals straddled corpses, plunging their heads into lumps of moonlit slime, crunching bones and every so often glancing up at us, their wet snouts wrinkled, their eyes and teeth flashing moonlight. By this point the fear-Mara inside me was assailing me with memories of the dogs trying to make off with my sister's body. Yes, I was making my own fear worse, but the fear itself was no illusion.

I raised the stick.

Completely unexpectedly, Kavi jerked it away from me. "Devadatta said no harming!" he whispered and stepped back, his suspicion of me having returned. "No killing with sticks."

"Of course not," I tried to reassure him, remembering when my son had said something similar back in the woman's quarters when he'd accidentally killed a beetle. Even now, I had yet to decide how literally to take such rules. "The stick will harm the animals only if they run at us. I can hold the stick out, but I don't have to thrust it at them."

Kavi gripped the stick with both hands, his small face clenched in despair. "Devadatta said no harming. He said that a monk should be willing to die at any time, knowing that it is only a body that dies."

"Well, perhaps Devadatta should be out here, and not us," I said. *That murderer.* I couldn't help myself. My anger had broken through.

Ironically, Mara rescued me from fear once again, only to clutter up my judgment with another bevy of angry thoughts. I clutched my stick. I had no idea what to do next.

Watch the mind, I reminded myself, and I saw Mara's hatred trying to take hold, pelting me with every noxious memory I'd ever had of my cousin. Then fear reared up again, and self-reproach for my failure to find a solution.

Watch without judgment.

Then I understood. A part of my awareness, separate from the chaos, could see things as they are in themselves. This was the mindfulness put forth by the Tathagata.

My emotions, impersonal as weather, were composed of parts:

phrases, images, a squeezing in the throat, a hot crushing pressure in the heart and belly that intensified into a fiery craving for violent release, in turn requiring more thoughts of Devaddatta's villainy to keep the fire stoked.

As I saw the emotions for the hodgepodge they were, they seemed to shrink to a cluster of tiny wiggling snakes, which then faded altogether, leaving me with only one thought.

I grasped Kavi gently by the shoulders. "The point is not to *intend* harm," I said. "If we purify our intentions, we will not be abandoning the Path."

Kavi still clutched the stick. "But how?"

I looked out at the animals, innocently eating, and I remembered Bahauk and his ability to adopt animals' points of view, he said, by entering into their souls. "We need to hold all these animals in compassion," I said. "Like us, they get hungry, and right now they're enjoying their dinner. They don't want us to bother them, and if we don't, they probably won't bother us."

In a low voice, I started up the loving-kindness chant that I'd learned as a way of expanding my love to all beings. I spoke to the jackals: "May you be safe, happy, healthy, and may you achieve liberation." But I had to do more. Imitating Bahuak, I let the jackals fill my mind and heart. I saw the scars on their nappy coats, their half-starved ribs, their frightened eyes shifting around, knowing that larger carnivores, wolves and dogs, would soon arrive from the forest and take over.

My jackal soul saw a broken path leading through areas where the animals had already worked over the corpses. I took Kavi's hand and led him to the edge of the woods. "We can meditate here," I said. "We still have a good view of the bodies. And we can also wish loving kindness for whoever comes to eat them."

10

I stayed awake most of the night, although my meditation was not very successful, my mind fumbling through
a murky daze filled with worry over Kavi and my son.
Around midnight Kavi fell asleep, slumping against me and filling
me with tenderness and grief. I put my arm around him, grateful for
his warm, small presence. Tonight was the first time since I'd said
goodbye to Ama that I'd touched another human being.

I jolted into full wakefulness at dawn, and my movement woke
up Kavi, who immediately began his whispered cemetery chant.
I joined him in a rote kind of way, thinking of how I'd confront
Devadatta about his practice of sending little boys to the charnel
grounds. Once the sun was all the way up, I told Kavi it was time
to leave. "We should probably return separately," I said. "Devadatta
might want to see us meditating in solitude."

"But I thought he wanted me to teach you."

"He probably intended us to separate afterwards." I smiled in
an artificially confident way, and then l left, wanting to encounter
Devadatta without getting Kavi in trouble.

I spotted my cousin as hundreds of monks were silently lining
up to embark on their daily almsround. The morning sun dazzled

through the bamboo trunks, casting splintered light that rippled over the monks' robes, ranging from ocher to bright yellow, and a hush hung in the chilly morning air, as if the tree-dwellers were exhausted from yesterday's feast. Devadatta, in his robe that looked like it had spent its previous incarnation as a pile of cleaning rags, had yet to take his place in the still-forming line. "Venerable Devadatta," I said, "I encountered a seven-year-old monk in the charnel ground last night who'd mistakenly believed you sent him there."

Devadatta's narrow face, raw and nicked from his unmerciful razor, remained unchanged. "It was no mistake," he said. "It's a requirement for all monks, no matter what their age, to face death in this way."

"Ah, I see. He was a little confused. He didn't seem to think other monks were supposed to accompany him, but of course he would need protection from the animals."

Devadatta skimmed his gaze over my new white robe, as if pained at having to view such a pristine garment on a mendicant. "Friend," he said, "it is clear that you still live in delusion about what life and death actually are. If a monk, meditating in the forest or some other dangerous area, meets his physical demise, he is actually fortunate. His meditation will have given him the clarity of mind to understand death as a simple threshold to be crossed, and with this understanding he will pass into a better incarnation, or perhaps leave the endless round of suffering forever."

"This boy did not seem to be of an age to achieve this clarity."

Devadatta shook his head. "As I pointed out to you yesterday, many unqualified aspirants have entered the Sangha. For them, accidental death is far superior to failing as a monk, for their subsequent life will be far more benign. But outsiders, with their untrained minds, will never understand this."

A knell sounded in my heart, similar to the one that I'd felt when the Tathagata told me that women couldn't enter the Sangha. *Be mindful,* I told myself. Don't fly off into all sorts of conclusions. I had no idea whether the Tathagata condoned what Devadatta was saying. Also, I couldn't afford to turn Devadatta into an enemy, someone who might spend too much time studying me for possible flaws—and in that way begin to suspect my sex. So once again, I held my anger at him in check, not having the time to wait for it to disintegrate in the elixir of mediation.

I bowed deeply. "I didn't intend to imply that the boy was unqualified," I said. "In fact, he assumed you wished to have him teach me some Dharma, which he did. I'm beginning to understand, Venerable One! The boy demonstrated perhaps the chief requirement for a monk—the spirit of a warrior. No wonder we Sakyans are so drawn to this Sangha."

"Quite," Devadatta said, straightening as if in deference to his own warrior spirit. "Ignorant people fail to comprehend the difficulty of this path. Mara colludes with our human weakness to foil our every step. The only hope for any of us is discipline." For the first time, I noticed, Devadatta had used the first person plural, and I allowed myself to appreciate that his main battle could well be against himself. But then he added, "And as far as young boys being incapable of facing death in charnel grounds, consider the Tathagata's own son. He completed this meditation within the first six months of his arrival. Perhaps you should speak to him for inspiration."

I kept my eyes lowered, lest I betray my outrage. Had my former husband risked my child in this way? "Perhaps I will speak to both him and his father," I said. "They will no doubt enlighten me."

*

I watched the long line of alms-bowl-carrying monks file off in the winking sunlight, walking in order of seniority, which meant Devadatta headed up the line and Kavi, arriving just as the line started moving, took his place at its end. The Tathagata and his most senior disciples, I assumed, were dining with the King, making me wonder how much my former husband needed to play up to powerful leaders in order to ensure that he and his monks could spread the Dharma. I also wondered whether he still enjoyed activities such as dining in the King's palace. I hated to think he was completely indifferent to earthly pleasure, but perhaps my own unawakened nature made me feel that way. What was the word I'd heard to describe how people living in the truth viewed the world? Disenchantment. Overcoming ignorance meant becoming disenchanted with the joys one formerly lived for, whether milk sweets, landscaped gardens, battlefield triumphs, or maternal love.

Kavi beamed at me as he passed by, and he signaled me to take my place behind him where those aspiring to be monks were allowed to walk, collecting alms-food with the others. I smiled back but declined. I needed time alone to consider how I should approach the Tathagata. How much did I want to denigrate Devadatta to him? And what about Rahula? I should at least inform his father that I planned to talk to my son. I wouldn't want anyone reporting to the Tathagata that I'd gone behind his back.

As far as food was concerned, it could wait, although my stomach was hollow with hunger. My life as a monk required a balance between keeping up my strength and staying as lean as possible, which reduced not only my curves but also my monthly bleeding.

Fortunately, a monk's life included opportunities for solitary meditation that I could use to my advantage to conceal womanly functions as well as for bathing on secluded banks of rivers and streams. I'd also devised various pads and plugs and had become adept at binding the different parts of my body as necessary. Finally, I could take advantage of the monastic practice of modesty. Monks were supposed to keep their bodies to themselves and covered at all times. I would prove exemplary in this way.

The last of the monks were disappearing into the narrow passageway between the trees, the leaf shadows jiggling over their yellow robes. For now, I'd stave off my hunger with water. At the far end of the grove was a small stone well with a clay bucket where flurries of tiny blue butterflies had come for the moisture as the day heated up. I wandered over to the well and quenched my thirst, then sat down under a tree to ponder my strategy, the hum of insects around me and birdsong sparkling above.

I took a deep breath, prepared to call my mind to order, and looked up to see the Tathagata walking toward me, his yellow robe flashing in the sun. No, too early! I wanted to shout out to him. Instead, I sprang to my feet, took a couple of steps forward, put my hands together, and bowed. Had he come here deliberately to seek me out? He seemed half-dissolved in the sunlight dazzling on his robe. In the glare I couldn't focus on his face, much less enter into the otherworldly unity of the last time we spoke.

"I assumed you'd be here," he said, without explaining how or why he'd interrupted his important day to encounter me. "Now that you've meditated in the charnel grounds," he said, "do you still wish for the life of a monk?"

His voice seemed to come from everywhere at once, an impression that was perhaps a result of my dismay. I wasn't ready for this interview. "I met a little boy among the dead bodies," I said. "He seemed far too young for this sort of meditation."

"Only monks over eighteen stay in charnel grounds."

"Not according to Devadatta." I took a breath. "He mentioned Rahula"—I couldn't bring myself to say "your son," and saying "my son" or "our son" was out of the question—"also spent the night there early in his training." Simply stating this possibility out loud reawakened my outrage.

"Rahula is an exception. He will achieve enlightenment before he turns twenty-one."

"Luckily, then, the dogs didn't devour him." I did not conceal my sarcasm.

"He was watched over."

I felt some relief, but my anger had been aroused and my suspicion not fully allayed. "The little boy I saw last night was completely alone," I said. "Devadatta seemed to think that a premature death would do him good."

"That's Devadatta's view. He believes that we've all spent enough time on the samsaric wheel of life and death to fill the oceans of the world with our tears. To die meditating can reduce our misery by cutting the number of future lives we'll have to endure—or even eliminate them altogether."

"And you agree?" I fought off an attack of vertigo. Once again I was thinking that the man who had been my husband had gone beyond humanity, his mind as vast and impersonal as the winter sky.

His eyes remained steady. "It doesn't matter whether I agree with him or not. More important is the intention to do no harm. Placing children in danger is doing harm."

"But you allowed him to do it!"

"No, I didn't know."

"I thought you had psychic powers!"

"Even a Tathagata's powers are limited."

"And yet you knew I was here."

"Perhaps I was lucky." He fastened his gaze to mine. "You will not be of help to me if you need to see me as a god."

"I don't believe in gods," I reminded him.

"That's just one point of view, you know. Although I may not be a god, some of my teachings concern deities, because this is the only way some people can understand the Dharma. As my follower, you would have to memorize and spread these teachings."

"So do you believe in deities, or is this your way of talking down to humans?" I couldn't shake my mistrust.

An ordinary man would have exhibited some annoyance by now, but his voice remained smooth and soft as a river after the rains have passed. "There are many ways the unawakened mind perceives this universe," he said, "and every one of them is conditioned by ignorance. My perception, except in that it results from a human body, is no longer conditioned. I can choose to see deities or not. So you see your question concerning my beliefs is impossible to answer."

I folded my arms, realizing I had wanted him to be annoyed. Then I would have had some power in this exchange, in spite of his slippery answers and non-answers to my questions. "If you're not a god, what am I to make of you?" I asked.

"The question is, what are you to make of the Dharma? You have to see the truth for yourself. This is also one of my teachings."

Right now I wasn't sure about the Dharma or his teachings. "I need to know the truth about Devadatta," I said. "How can you let men like that remain in the Sangha, let alone grant him so much power?"

"You don't understand," he said. "I will certainly stop him from sending young boys to the cemeteries, but I can't force him to disrobe." As he stepped back out of the blinding sun, I noticed a faint network of creases under his eyes and a certain sharpness of his cheekbones, as if the resilient youthful flesh had worn away, showing the fatigue of teaching day after day for hours at a time. I had the thought that his body would have preferred to remain in the bliss of meditation for his entire lifetime, rather than trying to convince us humans to go against the raging current of our obsessions and delusions. Surely, a body would live longer bathed in eternal peace than traveling on foot from city to city, facing endless questions and controversies. But this was the choice he—or the Dharma—had made.

"If you can't force Devadatta to disrobe, I don't understand why you think you can stop him from doing anything he wishes."

"By instituting a rule. When I started, we had hardly any rules, but the behavior of some monks has made them more and more necessary." He half-smiled. "At least Devadatta likes rules, especially when he gets to enforce them."

"He could refuse to obey your rule."

"Then he'll disrobe on his own. But he won't, any more than I would force him to."

"So by saying you can't force him means that you won't."

"As I said, you don't understand." And now his eyes seemed to dim with true sadness. "This Sangha is divided. Monks quarrel about all sorts of things, particularly issues of discipline, and many agree with Devadatta. If I asked him to leave, the Sangha would not survive the division, not at this point, and the Dharma would be lost for hundreds of generations. Devadatta knows this, and he's no more willing to take the risk than I am."

"That reflects on the Dharma," I said. "If Devadatta is required to maintain it."

"The Dharma is not maintained, it unfolds." His voice was gently corrective, making me wonder if his sadness, along with his fatigue, belonged only to his flesh and not to the mystery of his being. "There's a chance that Devadatta will awaken into a great teacher," he said. "His emphasis on discipline has much to offer, especially to those monks who think meditation means lolling in the grass all day and enlightenment happens after parroting a few sentences from a Dharma talk. This case of the boy monks is an opportunity for Devadatta to learn. Perhaps I can persuade him of the moral wrongness of his point of view."

"I doubt it." Yes, I told myself, even a Tathagata's powers were limited, perhaps too limited to maintain the integrity of his Sangha.

"Doubt is permitted," he said. "But you must make a decision whether to ordain or not."

I couldn't answer. Although I feared I had nowhere else to go, how could I live in a spiritual community that not only tolerated but in some ways endorsed someone like Devadatta?

"You do have a choice," he said, and once again he seemed to have read my thoughts. "If you decide not to join the Sangha, I'll ask King Bimbisara to admit you as a member of his court. You'd have more freedom there than among the Sakyans, and as you see, I come to this grove often. You'll still have some contact with the monks."

It was almost noon, and hot white sunlight bore straight down on my bare scalp. His offer stunned me. Here was a chance to return to life as a woman without living under my brother's thumb. I could give up my current deceptive, half-starved existence, where I'd already made a powerful enemy. As a laywoman I could continue my meditation practices—granted, they would necessarily be more superficial—but did I really trust the Tathagata's Dharma? In Bimbisara's court perhaps I could unite the women around an independent spiritual life, not as extreme as what the Tathagata taught. Or—although it was almost impossible to conceive of it at this point—I might even remarry. Best of all, I'd have a chance to meet with Rahula in a way that, even if there were rules against physical contact, he'd know me as his mother.

"You can do this?" I said, a whole new future lighting up inside me.

"Bimbisara and I have been friends since boyhood."

Of course, I knew this to be true.

Just as I was about to agree to this arrangement, I heard the hollow thunk of bamboo trunks striking each other. Someone was entering the clearing. Emerging from the shadows was Kavi, holding up a banana-leaf package. "Look, Ananda! I brought you *pokaras* and cheese!"

He was smiling so happily at being able to make this offering.

My throat caught. How could I leave my little friend, let alone all the other lower-caste child monks, in Devadatta's heartless realm?

By now, Kavi had recognized the Tathagata. Still clutching the package, he dropped to his knees. "Please forgive me, Blessed One! I didn't mean to disturb you."

My former husband smiled, and his warmth confused me all the more as to what I should do. "You didn't disturb me, Kavi. In fact, you have gained merit by your practice of generosity." He nodded in my direction, in a way that told Kavi to go ahead and give me the package, warm and fragrant with cinnamon and ghee. He handed it to me, eyes lowered.

"Thank you so much!" I took the package, feeling my stomach lurch in anticipation of food in spite of everything else that was happening.

"You're welcome," Kavi whispered, and vanished as suddenly as he'd arrived.

I stood holding the package, my mind and heart in disarray. The prospect of King Bimbisara's court beckoned me like a soft breeze leading to a gentle lake, one I hadn't known existed until now. Yet such a life of ease was a temptation I could withstand. The opportunity to reunite with Rahula as his mother was a whole other matter.

I looked directly at the Tathagata. "Before I decide, I have to talk to Rahula," I said, offering no pretext.

"You'll find him here just before sunset. I trust you'll say only what's necessary."

I bowed. The truth between us felt like the clearest day in the coldest part of the year.

I returned to this secluded part of the grove late in the day, having been too agitated even to attend the afternoon's Dharma talk. The light was fading quickly and in my current mood I heard the distant peacocks' cries as edged with desperation. "Dukkha! Dukkha!"—Suffering! Suffering! I took deep breaths to calm myself, trying to feel soothed by the cool evening smells of moss and damp soil as I sat in the same spot I'd occupied earlier, near the well.

Then, there he was, my dearest son, beaming down on me. "The Blessed One said you wished to ask me some questions," he said.

For a moment I just sat still and drank in the sight of him, the glowing brown eyes and strong Sakyan cheekbones just beginning to emerge in his nearly nine-year-old face. I missed the wild softness of his thick black hair, but perhaps his shaved head—that hint of strangeness in his appearance—would keep me from being overwhelmed with the desire to clutch him to my bound-up bosom. I motioned him to sit.

"Thank you for agreeing to speak with me," I said. I tore my gaze away from him, telling myself I was relieved that he didn't recognize me—only just now realizing how much I had longed for him to do so. I steadied my breath. "I'm thinking of ordaining, but I wonder about some of the practices here. Is it true that children are sent to meditate in the charnel grounds?"

"Not that I know of," he said.

"But didn't you do this meditation yourself?"

"Yes, but I volunteered."

I wasn't surprised, but I was still worried. "Was someone there to protect you from the beasts?"

He laughed his warm, full-throated laugh, a kind of laugh he'd probably have all his life, and which I had missed so much. He was laughing as if I'd asked an obvious question. "Of course I had protection, more than I knew what to do with!"

Greatly relieved that the monks, other than Devadatta, had proved themselves responsible, I asked, "So who went with you?"

He was still smiling. "Hundreds! The same ones who are always with me, whenever I need them."

Hundreds? Reflexively, I looked around, half-expecting to see a monk behind every clump of trees. But there was nothing. "It must have been quite a sight, so many of the Tathagata's followers surrounding you as you meditated."

"Yes! And all wearing gold, or shimmering rainbows! All flooding down from the heavens and singing songs from their thousands of lives."

I stared at his bright eyes, his wide, innocent brow. But of course he must be teasing me. "Truly," I said, "how many monks were there in this amazing chorus?"

"Monks? I'm talking about devas. The ones who swarm around me when I meditate, or even when I'm just walking along! They protect me all the time."

My throat went numb. "Please, don't tease me about this. Who really protects you?"

He looked into my eyes, a quizzical expression on his face. "I'm not teasing. The Blessed One tells us never to lie, even as a joke."

I hoped he couldn't read the mixture of horrors on my face. "And so when did you start seeing these deities?" I asked.

His smile belonged to a good-natured boy who only wished to be helpful. "Not long after my mother left me."

I felt as if he had pushed me off the edge of the earth.

I had to force myself not to scream out a denial. Instead, I nodded, as if with my own knowledge. "There are many stories about you," I said, "told to inspire other monks. One is that you'd already joined the Sangha when your mother left your home, and that your willingness to live apart from her was a sign of your dedication to the monastic life. Surely, your mother didn't abandon you." No, I begged him in my mind, please don't ever have felt that way, not for a second.

His smile widened. "She did it for me! You see, otherwise I would have yielded to my worldly loneliness and returned to my grandfather's house. Because I missed her so terribly, you see." He hesitated and my heart stopped. Then he smiled again, even more widely than before, as if he gladly accepted any sadness that remained. "But my Ama knew my destiny, and she didn't want to tempt me to abandon it, because that would have been the will of Mara."

I pretended to be arranging my robes so he wouldn't see the tears that it took all my strength to keep from overflowing. A year ago, I'd berated myself for my self-centered blindness to the possibility of endangering Rahula by taking him on the road with me as a seeker, but now it seemed that this self-judgment had enabled me to hide behind another, far more pernicious, blindness. I'd never considered the chance that he'd want to return to me. And why hadn't I? Perhaps because part of me wanted an excuse to embark on a spiritual journey of my own.

"So you're saying that your mother sacrificed herself?"

"Of course. But her spirit is always with me, along with the devas."

Devas. Had loneliness driven him mad? No, I told myself. Many people saw devas. Maybe I was the mad one. What did I know about anything?

And how would I learn, living a pampered existence confined in King Bimbisara's court, squeezing meditations between formal dinners and beauty routines? And how would Rahula feel, his mother suddenly returning to his life, to tempt him back to his childhood?

"So you're happy in your life here?" I said. "And you don't regret your choice?"

"How could I? Even more than the bliss that comes down on me when I meditate, each day is clearer than the last. I'm so grateful to both my Ama and my father for allowing me to learn the Dharma in this way."

He had the same luminous skin as the Tathagata. And I thought I saw in his open face his father's clarity and joy. Yet whether this clarity and joy belonged to this world, another world, or no world at all, I couldn't say.

"Just tell me one last thing," I said, trying to keep my voice from buckling. "When you were in the charnel ground with the devas, were there also monks?"

"Oh yes, including the Tathagata."

I had to settle for relief.

"Thank you so much," I said to my son, "for showing me the benefits of ordination."

As he took his leave, smiling and bowing in the way he would to any other unrelated grownup, I was transported back to the desolation of our little room on the day he left me to become a monk—the silence, the empty windowframe, the dangling ropes. If I ordained, I would lose my son all over again, in the sense that he would never know who I really was, and no matter how often our paths crossed, never would I see a son's love for me in his eyes.

I covered my face with my hands.

The next evening, I met with the Tathagata in the little wooden hut where we'd had our first talk. The weather had turned; a slow rain ticked on the hut's thin walls, and the smell of damp sandalwood soothed my nostrils, if not my mind. For half the day I had been standing in line for the opportunity to see him in this little room where he met with everyone from senior monks to street sweepers in bad weather. Near the front of the line a woman carried her white-shrouded dead child in her arms, hoping the Tathagata would restore it to life.

Now I finally was sitting opposite him, both of us cross-legged on the polished wooden floor. "I met with Rahula," I said. "He speaks of hundreds of devas that swarm around him like so many gilded gnats—how can these devas be real?"

The Tathagata's eyes were both sympathetic and remote. "I could reassure you," he said, "but you have no more reason to trust my words than you do Rahula's. The only way is to find out for yourself. This requires faith."

"Faith in what?" Not in devas, I hoped.

"In the possibility of awakening. In the glimmers of truth that you experience as you cultivate the Way." He paused and for just a moment, we merged again into the Dharma conversing with itself, the small wooden room dissolving and simultaneously expanding—as much mental as physical and beyond both these concepts. I blinked, and this sense of truth—and the peace that went with it—evaporated. Or was it a form of madness? "Faith," I said. "But not certainty."

He nodded.

"What did you say to the woman with the dead child? I asked.

"I told her I could grant her request if she visited the houses in this city and brought me a mustard seed from a family that had never known death."

"I don't see what that will do."

"She won't find the family. But her search will teach her that everyone knows tragedy and that no one can escape death. She will begin to follow the Dharma."

Yes, but. "What if she wants to ordain? She won't have the opportunity."

He gave me a sharp look, no doubt remembering when I was his wife and he gave me his reasons why women couldn't join the Sangha. "Surely by now you know the monks would never accept such a thing."

"But with more and more monks becoming enlightened, couldn't they persuade the others?"

He shook his head. "More and more monks are also entering the Sangha. It's hard enough for these unenlightened beings to accept the lower varnas—and for monks of the lower varnas to accept the equality here. Not to mention that our supporters in the lay community would lose faith. I'd be accused of whoremongering, and the Dharma would be spurned by all."

Suddenly I was overwhelmed with my own inadequacy to the task before me, not the least of which was persuading him to change his mind about women. "I'm not sure I have the faith necessary," I said.

"The choice is yours."

"Very well," I said perfunctorily—then all at once it seemed that Mara the Evil One was making one of his all-too-frequent visits to my mind. For I had the following conceited thought: I wasn't going to let this or any other Tathagata defeat me. I winched myself forward. "I'll stay and cultivate faith—I've heard you teach that this can be done, in the same way as we talked about fostering the growth of impersonal love."

He nodded, as if this was what he'd wanted from me all along.

Which made me realize that, in my Mara-induced confidence, I'd forgotten my most crucial concern. What if he told me to speak against women's ordination? "I have one serious problem," I said. "Will I have to transmit teachings before I come to trust them? I don't mean about the supernatural—I can always begin the discourses with 'Thus have I heard,' and I won't be perjuring myself. But things that go against my sense of right and wrong are another matter."

He kept his eyes on me, his black pupils each with a single still point of reflected white light. Was this a warning look, I wondered. "I trust that as you mature in the Dharma," he said, "you will find that none of it violates your morality."

"I will assume this to be true," I said, but I wasn't going to promise anything more.

"I know that this path is difficult for you," he said softly. He glanced out the narrow window, by now gone the color of slate, then turned back to me. "I'll help you as much as I can."

I nodded, my heart clutching. Had I seen a flash of some personal concern in his eyes? I could not assume this. I was relieved, though, to observe that I wasn't hoping for any sort of husbandly love from him. No, that hope and the self that went with it would stay buried with Bahauk. Yet perhaps there was something between me and this Blessed One, some humanness that one day would let us be together in an entirely new way.

"I'm ready to ordain," I said.

Before I left, he explained some of the precepts I'd have to keep, which included eating only one meal a day and sewing and patching my own robes—we were permitted to own a maximum of three. The Sangha was completely dependent on the lay community. We weren't even allowed to serve ourselves food, let alone handle any sort of money. We simplified our lives so we could focus on awakening, but we were also responsible for teaching the Dharma to the laypeople so that everyone, monastics and otherwise, could live lives of both service and gratitude.

After we agreed on a time for my ordination, the Tathagata rose to his feet, but not with his usual single, effortless motion as if he were temporarily without weight. His one extra heave showed his body's strain as he ushered me to the door. Outside, the line remained, still waiting for him in the black fog. His conferences would continue far into the night.

I was ordained after the Dharma talk on the following afternoon, in a very simple ceremony, which was the practice in those early days of the Sangha before the community's growing popularity made it the target of, you might say, less sincere applicants. I climbed the five stairs to the Tathagata's marble pavilion and stood before him and his disciples Sariputta and Mogallana, the four of us facing out over the assembled community. The night's rain had moved on, and a white silk canopy shaded us from the damp sunshine while under the trees the rows of bowed shaven heads seemed immersed in a sun-fluttering lake of yellow robes, the monks looking like a single radiant being, the sun glorifying even Devadatta's faded garment. Soon I would be immersed in this living light, I thought, and I recited the precepts and declared three times my desire to join the Sangha as a monk.

The next day my monastic education began. After memorizing the afternoon's Dharma talk, I sat in a bamboo grove to meditate. It was windy, the tree trunks ponging one another as I practiced "guarding the sense gates," which mainly meant staying out of temptation's way. In the simple world of monastic life, made even simpler by the stillness of the mind, the merest whiff of a curry or a handful of notes from a flute (or for that matter the prospect of relieving the pain of sitting for half a day or more) had the power to set off strings of fantasies. These in turn led to longings, regrets, and recriminations I thought I'd given up long ago. Over the weeks and months that followed, the mind's Mara spewed forth empires of craving, which required selves to *have* these cravings. Some were trivial— the self craving sex or lusting after a rich pudding. Some were more profound—the mother devoted only to her son, the seeker demanding to know the origins of the cosmos, the sister crusading in the name of her sibling's soul—and the judge who condemned all these selves as selfish. I understood the Tathagata's statement that there was no enduring, essential self—but I'd had no idea there were so many temporary, non-enduring selves that in the heat of the moment I mistook for my soul. And once I did, that momentary craving self became Mara.

This was the purpose of meditation: to develop my powers of concentration so I could watch my mind without being dragged into the worlds and personal identities it conjured up. Then I would understand how the mind was creating pain and misery when it grabbed on to what inevitably will cease. Once understood—yes, this grabbing and clinging is *itself* truly suffering, then I'd let go of the whole mess, the same way I'd drop a hot coal.

But I found certain obsessions impossible to drop, especially the ones that revolved around injustice. Once they got hold of me, a sinkhole opened up in my concentration and dragged every shred of discipline into its murky depths, sometimes for days at a time. How I longed for my brother to pay for murdering Bahauk and his people! And what about the injustice when it came to women's access to the Dharma? How could these monks, and male house-holders dare call themselves enlightened when it was women who kept their holy lives free from the drudgery of cooking and cleaning up after themselves?

As I sat cross-legged in my hut, all sorts of fantasies engorged me, such as raising an army of women to demand ordination or take blood revenge on their male oppressors, starting with my brother. Fortunately, like all else, these scenarios were subject to the law of impermanence, eventually petering out until nothing remained but the outlines of their foolishness and cruelty. Have faith, the Tathagata had advised, and keep practicing until your mind is clear enough to see what truly needs to be done. Yet, as the days wore on, I feared that meditation would not be enough.

Barely a month after I'd ordained, Kavi came up to where I was meditating under a lemon tree, the faint scent of blossoms tickling the air. He was accompanied by a pinched-face boy a year or so older than himself. The boy wore a filthy dhoti and had scabs on his feet.

"This is Naveen, my new friend," Kavi told me. "I met him on almsround. He wants to join the Sangha, but we're afraid that the Venerable Devadatta will say no."

"I hear you're the Tathagata's cousin," the older boy said to me, in a man-to-man tone. He gave me a quick wavering smile, making me think of a merchant trying to sell a barrel of moldy betel nuts on the cheap.

"I'm one cousin of many, and a distant one at that," I told Naveen, while giving Kavi, who had been beaming at me with pride, an admonitory glance. He was too young to realize that if I went over Devadatta's head, it would only create more division in the Sangha— and put me under unwanted scrutiny.

Kavi looked dubious, perhaps realizing he'd presumed too much. "Naveen's family's poor like mine."

"Not exactly," Naveen said, picking at the black under his finger-nails. "I come from a better varna. My father was a scribe, but he went blind."

So even this child believed in the varna system and thought it might help his cause. "In this Sangha, we are all poor in the same way," I said, an important concept to get across, had not my feeling of righteousness tightened like a strip of leather around my chest. There it was, *dukkha*, suffering.

"So you won't help me get in?" The boy had dropped his fel-low-adult facade, his narrow little eyes filling with worry. He peered up at me. "I can teach you to write."

Write? Why would I want to learn the markings of scribes, used mainly to tally up crop totals and construction costs? Neither the Tathagata nor any of his enlightened disciples had ever written a word in their lives. Still, I supposed writing could serve the practical needs of the Sangha. Even more, this little boy reminded me of myself when I'd tried to offer my services to the Tathagata and before him, Stick Woman—all the while fearing that my services weren't worth offering.

The leather strap of my righteousness disintegrated. "Thank you for your offer," I said and, even as I spoke, realized he had indeed offered me something valuable. Not so much the writing but the idea that I might perform concrete tasks for the Sangha. Generous acts were a practice in themselves, the Tathagata taught. Not only did they provide a respite from thinking of oneself, they were satisfying on their own, engendering the contented mind-state essential for concentration.

"I'll talk to the Blessed One," I said.

"You're getting too attached to these boy monks," the Tathagata said.

We were standing in front of the King's palace, its rose pink brick tiers mirrored in the long rectangular pool in front of its arched doorways. It was after the midday meal, and most of the monks had dispersed to meditation spots deep in the forest.

I'd just told him about Naveen and his family's poverty.

"There will always be poor people," he said, glancing soberly at a small bent man with a net and a cleaning brush leaning over the pool, the knobs of his spine shining bare and brown in the sun. "But there will not always be the opportunity to learn the Dharma. In this respect, Devadatta has a point. As a Sangha, we can do only so much."

"I can train the younger monks," I said, hating to think of him and Devadatta on the same side against me. "And Naveen offered to teach me to write. This might be of use to the Sangha."

He shook his head. "What about your own training? At this point, your primary focus must be yourself."

"My meditations are clarifying my mind," I said. "And because I'm not so fogged up with old identities the way I used to be, I can see ways to conduce a better atmosphere for training everyone in the Dharma—including me."

"And the other monks, in their meditative clarity, have failed to see this?" This was the closest to sarcasm I would ever perceive in him.

"Perhaps they lacked the opportunities I had in my former life." I made sure not to give him a knowing, let alone accusing, look. "A lot of these younger monks don't know how to live on their own—and even the older ones have spent much of their lives being waited on by women." I held my neutral gaze. "And because they can't tell one end of a broom from another, their kutis look like refuges for spiders and smell like privies for mice—hardly conducive for developing a pristine consciousness."

"Certainly you would not wish to have women waiting on them again." And here, although he didn't sound sarcastic, he did sound dry.

"I'll instruct them in ways so they won't need anyone to wait on them," I said, "such as how to use a dust rag."

The Tathagata lowered his eyelids, perhaps to contemplate all these mundane chores or perhaps to enter some meditative absorption to wait for a reply to arise by itself. Behind him, a peacock fanned out his teal-eyed tail, as if he'd been waiting to display his worldly splendor when the Tathagata wouldn't see it. Or perhaps the bird's glory was merely reflecting the meditative state my former husband was currently enjoying.

"Very well," he finally said, "I'll admit Naveen." He bowed in a gesture of dismissal. "Just make sure you keep on meditating. That's my instruction to you. Life is very brief and you could die at any time. Meditate as if your head was on fire."

I looked out over the pond, with its reflected arches wavering in and out of themselves as breezes rose and fell. Although the shimmering duplicates hinted at the instability and impermanence of all things, the colors and shapes undulating on the water's shining surface seemed clearer and richer-toned than the solidities they reflected. I could enjoy them for what they were, I thought, impermanent like all else.

I tried to keep up with my meditations, but the more I meditated, the more I saw what needed to be done around the Sangha. At first this worked out well for me; even Devadatta could see my usefulness. To this end, I took up Naveen's offer to teach me to write—a strange process of trapping words on birch bark, using a wing feather to apply markings made of a mixture of soot, crushed nuts, and myrobalan dye. I was glad I hadn't engaged in this activity until now. Otherwise, I might never have bothered to learn how to keep words locked in my mind, although of course words describing the Dharma could never be written down, because they would always mean different things to different people and had to be spoken with care.

Even back then, I was beginning to worry about who would preserve the Dharma after the Tathagata was gone. I couldn't bear the thought that the likes of Devadatta would be in charge. For this reason alone, I was determined to remain in this Sangha and exert as much influence as I could when the time came.

As the years went by, I became more and more dedicated to the truth as I ascertained it. I had no idea that it might well require a personal falsehood far worse than the concealment of my sex, one that many might argue would send whatever remained of me after my death to the deepest realms of hell or at the very least, ban me from the Sangha for life. But this choice was many years in the future.

For now, I figured out a schedule for everyone's use of the wash-house (this had the added benefit of guaranteeing my privacy). With the help of writing, I communicated (sometimes through scribes) with merchants and other laypeople who supplied firewood, cleaning materials, and eating utensils, including begging bowls, and kept them informed about our actual needs, so we wouldn't end up with, as we had the year before, privy brooms enough to supply the entire Magadhan kingdom. Also, I instructed doctors and herbalists and even prescribed medicines and treated patients on my own. There were few hard-and-fast monastic rules against this yet. Finally, I kept up with my studies, getting proficient enough to lecture laypeople and the younger monks on basic Dharma.

I was also the one who asked the Tathagata questions that others were afraid to ask, often because the monks thought they should already know the answers. Many years later, my manner of asking these questions, like so much else, would be distorted to make me sound like an idiot who thought he knew all the answers in advance. "The Chain of Dependent Origination is easily understood," I've been quoted as saying, when everyone knew this doctrine was unfathomably complex, describing in minute detail how the ignorant mind creates worlds of suffering out of merely pleasant or unpleasant experiences. As the story goes, the Tathagata reprimanded me: "Never think such a thing, Ananda!" Although I'd never thought it in the first place.

But these distortions happened long after the time I'm describing. For the first few years of my life in the Sangha, things went smoothly, even with Devadatta, who spent days on end meditating in the forest—when he wasn't trying to impress King Bimbisara's family with magic tricks, which he declared were supernatural powers. The Tathagata seemed to ignore him, and I did likewise, concentrating on meditation, my Sangha duties, and refining my role as a male. Fortunately, a monk doesn't have to learn a prince's strut or a warrior's swagger, and my year in the hills had deprived me of my courtly femininity. I kept up the practice of hauling buckets for the sake of a masculine physique, carrying water from the river to the washhouse, one of the few worldly tasks that monks were still allowed to perform. My willingness to do this was favorably received by the other monks, who were thereby spared it, although occasionally I feared I saw some monk, especially among the older ones, studying me with slitted eyes, but nothing ever came of it. Except for Devadatta, the monks seemed to like me, partly, I'm sure, because I made it my business to be of use to all—much as I had learned to do in the women's compound at Suddhodana's household so long ago.

Yet as my mind became clearer as to what I needed to do, the more my sense of injustice gnawed at me, especially when it came to women's ordination. Since my one argument with the Tathagata, I had done nothing to further its cause. In my travels with the Sangha I met plenty of women who would have given anything to join us— not only aristocrats such as King Bimbisara's wife but also ordinary women and girls ground down by poverty, brutal husbands, or demanding relatives and who, unlike their male counterparts, had no hope of freedom of any sort. I began to wonder whether I'd been deceiving myself about why I joined the Sangha. Perhaps I'd done so for selfish reasons after all—out of a need to escape death rather than to help others awaken.

By then I'd been in the Sangha for five years. Rahula was almost fourteen, as tall as I was, and although I still couldn't imagine him as just another monk, I no longer wept in secret after every casual encounter. Kavi, aged eleven, had turned from a wispy to a sturdy little friend, as well as a receptacle for my motherly feelings, disguised as fatherly affection. Around this time, I made my first big mistake.

It started with the matter of the monks' robes. Most of our robes were donated by the lay community, with us responsible for hemming them and keeping them in repair. However, many of the monks—particularly the ones from higher varnas—had never picked up a needle in their lives. I decided to organize a group where monks could sit together in the evenings and learn to sew seams and patches—something the Tathagata wanted done, for he felt it important to respect the laypeople's gifts. Even so, to prevent anyone from wondering how I had such skills, I took the precaution of telling everyone that I'd learned them as a teenager, enlisting a local tailor's help as soon as I knew I wanted to ordain.

At first, everyone seemed to delight in these meetings, sitting under the trees in one of the many pleasure parks we stayed at during those times, listening to evening birdsong, smelling the jasmine, and talking of whatever the monks needed to talk about as I demonstrated sewing knots and cross stitches. It turned out many monks, young and old, missed their wives and mothers, and I was happy to give them a place to vent their feelings. Then one evening not long before the rainy season—we were currently staying in a deer park belonging to a local Sakyan leader—about fifteen of us were sitting in a circle on one of his smaller stone pavilions. We'd brought lamps burning citrus oil to discourage mosquitoes as well as to provide light for our work. It was a soft black night, with the moon nowhere to be seen.

The youngest monk in the group spoke up. He was ten, small for his age, with deep brown downturned eyes. "I miss my Ama," he said.

"I miss mine, too," said Kavi. "But it helps if you meditate on the Divine Abodes, the way Ananda teaches." He smiled at me. Over the years I'd taught this meditation to him and others, having used it myself to dissolve the pain over the superficiality of my relationship with my son.

"The loving-kindness Abode belongs to everybody and nobody," I said. "So when you enter into it by wishing every being well, you can remember that your Ama's love is part of it. By feeling love, you can know that your Ama is with you."

"And then you don't have to be sad anymore," Kavi said.

"Good, Kavi," I said, "but we also can't ignore these emotions of sadness." I looked over at the younger boy. "Only when we admit sadness is inside us are we able to let go of that feeling and watch it fly away. But if you still feel sad, you can always talk about it to me."

"Talk?" The furious voice came from behind me.

I whirled around. It was Devadatta, back from the forest and flickering like a demon in the collective lamplight, his face taut with rage. "What's going on here? A ladies' gossip fest? This is precisely the kind of chattering social group that the Tathagata abhors! Any monk who derives his happiness from this sort of insipid togetherness will never know the bliss of solitude, or of awakening.

Trivial social concerns will bog down your every meditation—you'll obsess over what others think about you rather than contemplate the Dharma. You might as well simply disrobe now and go back to your Amas and your big fat beds."

Silently the monks began to disperse, their shame thickening the air. I lacked the authority to call them back, let alone raise objections to Devadatta's views, and to some extent I shared the monks' shame. Perhaps my efforts to make our monastic life easy had damaged my solitary quest, blunted my once keen dedication to the truth.

"We were simply repairing our robes," I said.

"That's nothing to be proud of, monk," Devadatta said. "Personal vanity to go with your idle chatter! The townspeople are spoiling this Sangha by plying it with cloth suitable for princesses—you should be digging for your robe material in the trash, the way I do."

Kavi, who'd remained seated, wrinkled his nose. "At least our robes don't stink," he muttered.

Devadatta glared at him. "What did you say?"

I cleared my throat. "I think the Venerable Kavi was expressing his gratitude that his nose-consciousness is undistracted by the odor of bodily fluids and rat droppings. In this way, he can direct his attention to the Four Noble Truths, the Eightfold Path, and the contemplation of wholesome states of mind."

I couldn't help myself. Yes, this was my mind-Mara judging Devadatta. But just then my mind was tired of judging me.

Devadatta kept his hard gaze on Kavi. "Monk," he said. "You need to confront your aversions, not escape them." Devadatta switched back to me. "You are teaching these boys sentimentality, idle chatter, and cherishing the body, and I know why you're doing it."

He raised his arms and announced it to the entire grove: "*You are a woman!*"

My vision turned dark and mottled, and the ringing of a thousand insects filled my head.

I have destroyed the Sangha was all I could think. The python around my chest made it impossible to breathe, much less speak in my own defense. Not that there was anything to say.

Had he just guessed? Or had he somehow found out?

I sat paralyzed in my cross-legged position, my hands limp in my lap, the yellow robe I'd been repairing crumpled in front of me. But even if I could have moved, I wouldn't have known what to do. Try to lie my way out of it? And be publicly stripped and dragged to jail?

One of the older monks, with mole-speckled ocher skin and deep grooves in his forehead, cleared his throat. "My humblest pardon, Venerable Devadatta, but you have violated the Precept of Right Speech. You have insulted the Venerable Ananda by calling him a woman. I suggest you apologize."

I stared at him numbly. Apparently, he hadn't understood the accusation.

But then Devadatta turned in my direction. "I apologize that your unmanly behavior resulted in my wrong speech," he said, inclining his head in a bow that seemed more like a glance down at a pile of dung. "I am nonetheless going to report the unwholesome conduct of this group to the Tathagata."

I felt my ears pop. He didn't know about me, after all. I inclined my head, my relief temporarily blotting out my fear of the Tathagata's reaction. "Your apology is accepted." Even though it was no real apology at all.

"Be warned, monk," he said, marching off into the blackness.

Years later, many people claimed it was the Tathagata himself who had come upon our group. The division in our Sangha continued, you see, and perhaps the strict ascetics wanted to use the event to their advantage. By then there were many more monastics hoping to undermine me, who—ironically—had the reputation of being the monk liked by all.

And the Tathagata did order me to disband my group. We were still camped near the Sakyan clan leader's sprawling teak mansion, located on a flat plain where a ruffle of clouds on the horizon marked the distant mountain range, some of whose foothills I knew so well. Would that I could have been wandering in them, heedless and free, instead of retreating in defeat from the hut where the Tathagata had told me that although spiritual friendship was vital as a means to discuss Dharma and shore one up in times of doubt, I couldn't draw attention to myself by alienating Devadatta.

I understood his point, of course, but as I walked away it occurred to me how men always used the word "woman" as an insult, and I'd never given this a second thought, until now. But now the word flipped back on me, igniting the coal of anger I always hoped I'd meditated away. My anger had a new object: the world, samsaric or not, controlled by men. I couldn't keep living in an all-male community, no matter how holy. I had to do something, although not in my current state. I sat under a tree to let my rage disassemble itself along with my underlying nostalgia for the hills, observing my tendency to gild memories with a perfection that never was. Gradually, a new clarity dawned, as if I'd camped in the darkness and awakened outside a city that had been there all along.

And in that clear dawn, my mind presented me with an actual city: Kapilavatthu, my former home and that of my former mother-in-law, Pajapati. For the first time since I'd joined the Sangha, we were headed for Kapilavatthu—and Pajapati, I'd heard over the years, wanted enlightenment above all else. I would persuade her to plead her case with her stepson and prove to him the existence of women who wanted to live as ordained monastics. I would help her in whatever way I could, even if I had to go against the Tathagata—and my brother—to do it.

xcept for the gentle hills surrounding Suddhodana's former residences, the fields outside of Kapilavatthu were a green and yellow patchwork shimmering in the premonsoon heat and extending to a blur of the faraway mountain range. It was my first time in Kapilavatthu since I'd left for the hill country seven years earlier. In those days I'd been so caught up in my marriage and my immediate realm that I suppose I'd perceived little else. I'd never seen—as the Tathagata might say—things as they really are, least of all the terrain beyond my personal concerns. Not that I was doing much better now. At first, all I could do was lament the neglect of the gardens and groves I had so assiduously tended. They were either overgrown or desiccated, the lotus ponds clogged with weeds, the fruit trees skeletal and insect-gnawed—more reason to heap blame on my brother.

Then I caught myself. My mind, like most unenlightened minds, was exaggerating the differences between then and now to create a Mara-self of outrage. The truth was that no one, even back then, cared as much as Siddhartha and I did about creating a deva realm on earth. Why was I pumping myself full of anger at my brother when he shared most people's attitudes? He had plenty to answer to other than landscaping, and I had plenty to do other than grieve vegetation, which was impermanent in the best of circumstances. I had to find a devious way to meet with Pajapati. For, as my Ama had warned, Jagdish had all the women locked up. Only the Tathagata was allowed to visit his stepmother, and only once.

I formulated a plan. I would approach my former mother-in-law during the one time the household women had some exposure to the outside world—in the breakfast hall, where they had their meal after the men left. I remembered that the door to the dining hall at that time of day was unattended, although that custom might have changed since then. But I couldn't think of any other way to proceed than as a lone monk offering Dharma lessons to the older ladies of the household—this was before strict rules prohibited any monk to meet with any woman without another man present. In any case, I was ready to take risks, including the likelihood that Pajapati would realize who I was—or more accurately—who I once was. I just had to hope that if she recognized me, she wouldn't give me away.

The next morning, rather than go on almsrounds in Kapilavatthu, I made my way to the teakwood mansion where I had lived years ago. By this time of year, the flame trees had exploded into bloom, their scarlet flower-conflagrations massing around the residential complex and almost completely obscuring the separate kitchen building. I veered off the path, faded back into the shadows of the big trees and waited. Before I ventured anywhere, I had to make sure my brother was no longer inside the dining hall. Like Pajapati, he'd known me close up; we'd glared into each other's faces all too many times over the years. But unlike Pajapati, he would have no possible motive to keep my secret. Not only would he expose me, he would make sure that the Sangha would suffer the worst of consequences.

Finally, I saw him, in an eggplant-black paridhana and his black hair in a warrior's knot, striding off in his single-minded way toward the stables, in the opposite direction from where I stood. Relief washed through me. I headed toward the outside courtyard, where the smell of cardamom rice and the household's particular kind of tamarind-infused dahl brought a rush of memories of my former life, good and bad. In those days, though, there hadn't been nearly as many armed guards. Now they manned every entrance.

But at least the one at the dining hall door looked bribable. In late middle age, he had vast sagging cheeks, and a butternut-colored paunch poured out over his dhoti. He also had a habit of knuckling his lower back when he thought no one was looking. I offered him four sprigs of apamarga, an all-purpose herb if ever there was one, good for mitigating the effects of all kinds of bad karma, from over-indulgence in rice wine to impeding the flow of truth from monks to lay people.

"I'll let you in," the guard said, "but you can't stay long."

I entered the paneled room, draped in the same striped red and blue tapestries I remembered. A half-dozen men, mostly in dark, gold-edged paridhanas, remained at breakfast, reclining at one of the long tables, as servant women in blue-gray saris, much plainer than in my day, cleared the dishes around them, seeming to make every effort to avoid any physical contact. I shuddered and looked away. The varna system seemed far stricter now, and my brother was partly responsible.

Over the men's banter and the clatter of knives and ceramic bowls, I heard rustling and murmuring at a far door—the ladies of the household had arrived, about thirty in number. Right away I recognized Pajapati, wearing widow's white. She'd changed little. She had the same faded gray braid and patient, intelligent eyes. I also noticed that her habitual stiffness, which had melted when she'd first started practicing the Dharma, had not returned. Her movements still seemed buoyed by her faith, although perhaps with a slight tremulousness. By now she had to be over sixty. "Good morning, Madame," I said, walking toward her in a stately manner, which belied my pounding heart. "The Tathagata wished me to impart some additional Dharma to you."

Her mask of politeness hardened and her pale brown eyes grew sharp with incredulity and then briefly dimmed with embarrassment as if even to entertain such a preposterous idea—that her daughter-in-law was masquerading as a monk—was an insult to her visitor. I bowed, ordering my knees not to give way.

"I'm your cousin, Ananda, from the north," I said, my voice in the lower register that by now was second nature to me. "I've been in the Sangha for over five years." Under my robe, sweat crawled down my flanks, only partly caused by the day's rising heat. "Is there a quiet place where we can talk?"

She blinked, her mask of politeness solidifying once again as if my membership in the Sakyan clan explained my familiar appearance—or perhaps she was willing to go along with me for now. "We can use the main banquet room." She nodded toward the door I knew led to the cavernous hall, unoccupied at this time of day but with yet another guard at the door. This grand room also had a separate door that opened on a corridor that led to the women's courtyard. Even when I lived here, the courtyard had been guarded. My gut knotted. Pajapati and I would be closed in.

The room we entered, large enough for a hundred people and two or three elephants to mill about comfortably, was where my former husband and in-laws had hosted vast entertainments. I remembered the oversized metallic-threaded wall hangings depicting

225

pentagrams and other geometric patterns, the moveable pinewood stages for musicians and dancing girls, and the long banquet tables surrounded with cushions and set with goblets of silver and gold, even when they weren't being used. Unlike the gardens, this room had been well-maintained, the morning light angling through the tall windows and delineating the room's splendor, which to me had a ghostly quality, the air cool and still, every cup and cushion glinting with memories of the past. Yet now these memories belonged to a ghost of myself, a teenaged bride fluttering through a dream, having forgotten her earlier conviction that this sort of opulence had nothing to do with true happiness.

My pleasure that I could view this former self with detachment and compassion shriveled into nothing when I glanced at the windows. Covered in openwork iron filigree, they were all locked, making any kind of quick escape impossible.

Pajapati and I sat on a bench against the back wall, in the darkest part of the room. I had to resist the urge to embrace her. For all our differences, I'd come to love and respect her over my years of captivity—and how I missed female companionship! "Tell me, Madame," I said, "I have heard that you wish to enter the Sangha and establish a woman's order."

Once again suspicion flickered in her eyes, but she spoke softly, her slender, veined hands folded in her lap. "I'm afraid that's impossible. The Tathagata has expressly turned me down."

I couldn't let discouragement overcome me. "That's because he fears most of his monks will disapprove. But I think he's wrong. So many of our clansman have entered the Sangha by now. If their mothers, sisters, and grandmothers joined together and earnestly requested ordination, I think they'd convince enough monks to change the Tathagata's mind."

She smiled in the resigned way I had always disliked, then glanced around at the walls, as if to indicate her confinement. "I'm hardly in a position for such a confrontation, I fear."

"Not true," I said, depressed that I hadn't progressed spiritually enough not to be piqued at her attitude. "You can gather all the women of our clan who believe in women's ordination and meet with him outside of his quarters, all of you barefoot and in white robes. Then you can plead your case to him and the rest of the monks as well."

Her resigned smile vanished. "You're asking me to defy my stepson, who is also an awakened Master."

"I don't see it that way," I said, afraid to look her in the eye, lest I betray myself. "His main consideration is that the Sangha will break up over the issue of women monastics. But if enough women ordained, the monks who disapprove of such women would constitute a far smaller proportion of the community as a whole, and they'd no longer pose such a threat."

She raised one of her ungroomed eyebrows. "You forget. I, along with all the other women here, are locked in our quarters."

"Surely, if you all gathered at a meal and made your request to the men in the clan as a whole, your nephew would have to give in. After all, the majority of his male cousins already follow the Tathagata as laymen."

Now the suspicious glint in her eyes ignited, burning away, I feared, whatever was left of her embarrassment. "Who are you," she asked, "that you're so eager for such a thing to happen?"

I had no choice but to forge on, even if I was headed off a cliff. "I believe that all human beings deserve the chance to fully awaken in this lifetime. I've witnessed all too many women, rich and poor, trapped in beaten-down lives with no chance of freedom of any sort, let alone ultimate freedom."

"I feel for these women," she said, "but surely the Tathagata knows the best Dharma."

"The Tathagata knows that the Dharma is alive and can change. That's why scribes are forbidden to write it down," I said, and at that moment I felt a rush of what could have well been the Dharma inside me, because the words formed by themselves. "The Sangha needs women every bit as much as women need the Sangha. Without a female presence, men are like too many roosters confined in too small a cage. We peck and claw each other for dominance, and what suffers is truth and compassion. So much squabbling over minor rules and mistreating the younger members—some are mere boys! I've witnessed this firsthand."

She looked me up and down, all too knowingly, especially after I'd criticized "my" male sex. "Unfortunately," she said, "I've never believed that women are all softness and virtue."

"No, but when women and men are in each other's company as equals, they balance each other's extreme tendencies. Men become kinder, women more resilient."

The lines around her pale mouth hardened. "And you know this, too, from experience?"

Before she had the chance to name me directly or I had the chance to deny anything, the door opened, and another beam of light leapt across the vast tile floor. The guard spoke, his bass voice echoing. "Madame Pajapati, your nephew-in-law would like to speak to you."

My heart stopped.

"I can't let him see me," I whispered. These words, if my former mother-in-law had any doubts left at all, were tantamount to a full confession.

"I'll be right there," she called to the guard.

"He will meet you here." The guard left, closing the door behind him.

Pajapati whirled around and stared at me, her braid loosened by the vehemence of her motion. "Hide behind the tapestry."

In three steps I was behind the suffocating folds of heavy striped fabric that half-covered the back windows. In the scratchy darkness, my panic mixed with exaltation. Pajapati hadn't denounced me!

I heard my brother's footsteps; he spoke from in the middle of the vast room. "Aunt, what are you doing here?" he asked her.

"I was meditating. I had no appetite this morning, and I took advantage of this empty room for my practice."

There was a silence. Was Jagdish glancing around? Scrutinizing the tapestries?

His voice cut like an axe. "Some of the servants reported seeing you enter this room with a monk."

I was dizzy with terror.

Pajapati's voice was steady. "He left some time ago, Nephew. He has a new way of breath counting he was teaching. Starting backwards from one-hundred while keeping the qualities of the breath in the foreground. Would you like me to instruct you in this technique?"

"Keep it for the priests and the women."

I heard his footsteps, and they were moving in my direction. I held my breath, then realized I'd made a mistake, because now it was all I could do to keep from gasping for air, the metallic-threaded woolen textile pushing up against my face.

Just as my chest was about to burst, the footsteps stopped. "You'd best hurry," my brother said to Pajapati, "if you want any food at all. And I hope that monk left, because I've asked the guard to lock the front door."

The footsteps diminished; the door to the entrance hall opened, closed, and clicked.

The only way out was through the women's quarters.

I remained behind the tapestry, my breath hot and damp on the cloth, until Pajapati pulled it back, the gleaming room and its furnishings blinking back into existence.

"Thank you," I whispered, glancing at the door my brother had closed behind him.

Pajapati stared at me. "Are you deceiving the Tathagata?"

I shook my head.

"I can't believe that he would condone this." She flashed a skeptical look at my yellow robe and shaven head.

"He serves the Dharma. As I try to as well."

"But he always speaks the truth."

"He only speaks what needs to be said." I took a step forward, holding her in my gaze. "I'm begging you, Pajapati. Take your case to the Tathagata. For the sake of the Sangha and all the beings that suffer on this earth."

Her penetrating eyes rounded with a kind of wonder. "You sacrificed everything—your sex, your position in society—and perhaps even your own chances of awakening. Oh, my dear..." She leaned forward as if to embrace me, but I raised my hand to stop her in spite of my own desire for her human touch. Whatever my sex, I had ordained, and monks were forbidden all physical contact with women. "My name is Ananda. Believe me, if I could have done this in any other way, I would have."

She nodded. "I can try to gather the women, but I have my doubts that Jagdish can be coerced to let us go."

I breathed in. "There's a way to persuade him, but only as a last resort," I said. I was about to make use of yet another deception—so many by now, that Pajapati was in all likelihood correct that I had seriously damaged if not destroyed my own chances for enlightenment. "Tell him you know he passed off the handmaid Vasa as a princess to marry King Pasenadi. Say you met a monk who saw this crime with the eye of Dharma."

Her jaw dropped. "How could Jagdish do such a thing, and how could you have found out?"

"He told our mother," I said. "And if the other Sakyan leaders get wind of it, they'll roast him on a spit." I was referring, of course, to what Ama had said to me in confidence when I last saw her. If the elders knew that Jagdish had risked the anger of such a powerful king, my brother could be deposed, even executed.

Pajapati sighed. "The Tathagata is right. We all live like helpless puppets, jerked about by passions that we think belong to us, but which in fact are the spawn of Mara. Let's just hope that I won't have to resort to this threat, or I fear my own awakening will be greatly postponed." She half-smiled. "I'll meet with the other women and determine a strategy. It will probably take a couple of days, then we'll visit the Tathagata en masse."

"When you arrive, I'll do all I can to help," I said.

We stood facing each other, each taking the other's measure, knowing now we wanted the same thing. "I need to leave," I said, glancing at the locked door and windows. "But I'll have to do it as a woman."

"Yes, of course," she said. I didn't have to explain to her that if I got caught as a monk, it would badly compromise the Sangha, whether my sex was discovered or not. Better to be beaten as a runaway servant or even imprisoned as Yasodhara, the prodigal daughter-in-law who tried to sneak back into her old home. "But I don't know how you can escape," Pajapati said.

"If you can get me women's clothes, I can climb out a window."

Pajapati shook her head. "Since you left, the windows have all been barred."

I breathed into my fear. *Still the mind* and hope other possibilities will rise like lotuses in calm water. "Very well," I said. "Get me a wrap and a couple of shawls belonging to a woman of the lowest varna in the household—oh yes, and a rag for my head."

Pajapati's eyes bulged. "You can't! Even touching such things will pollute you far more than your acts of deception."

"That's not what the Tathagata teaches."

She nodded, suddenly haggard, as if exhausted from the struggle to understand all of what the Tathagata meant. "But why do you want them?"

"Only one kind of woman has permission to leave this building," I said. I nodded toward the door to the women's quarters. It was the time of day, when the women were downstairs at their meal, that the servants belonging to the most despised class of all emptied the chamber pots. "I need to disguise myself as a privy servant."

Pajapati pressed her fingers into her forehead. "My mind understands," she said, "but my body still recoils."

And—had it not been for my year with Stick Woman—so would have mine because, even back before the varna system solidified, everyone shared a dread of bodily impurity, which was believed to befoul and corrupt the soul as much as the worst forms of theft and murder. Of course, for the Tathagata the only real purity was purity of intention.

"Can you exchange some castoff garment of yours?" I asked Pajapati. "You could say you need to wear rags as part of your spiritual discipline."

"I'll give away one of my best saris," she said, with a sudden wild girlish smile. "You keep yourself hidden here and pray no one comes to search the room." She vanished into the hallway to the women's quarters. There would be a guard at its entrance.

In her absence, I retreated to my hiding place, mentally going over the building's exits as I remembered them, including the narrow corridor used only by those responsible to rid the women's quarters of pollution. It too was guarded, but I doubted that would present a problem.

Pajapati reappeared, holding a wad of grayish rags away from her body. The bundle, limp as a corpse, was surprisingly light, the fabric almost diaphanous with wear. As quickly as possible, I pulled off my monk's robes and rolled them into the shape of a four-months' pregnant belly and, with the help of Pajapati, used my upper robe to secure the bundle around my waist. Then I tied a rag around my shaven head and settled a thin cotton scarf over the rag and followed Pajapati through the narrow room that led to the women's courtyard. I kept my distance so the guard would rest assured I was not contaminating a woman of the upper varnas.

The guard barely looked at us as we passed. Of course he would be far more interested in anyone headed in the opposite direction, although his glance flickered over both of us to make sure we weren't amorous men in disguise. He recognized Pajapati, but he didn't bother to identify me. He was confident that no man, no matter how randy, would wear my despised garments for any reason.

The women's courtyard had changed little since I last saw it: the same ornamental pools, gilded swings, sickle-shaped orchid and chrysanthemum beds, and the same brick interior walls, the color of dusty apricots glowing a rosy gold in the morning sun. Even the ginkgo and karanja trees looked to have been pruned or replaced to remain the same size, and a faint smell of floral incense hung in the air—a way of dispelling the cow-dung and woodsmoke odors from beyond the wall. The thought came to me that here was a stunted paradise for interchangeable princesses—an observation that reminded me that I hadn't emptied myself completely of my old bitterness. Alas, even though these emotions from my past evaporated in the luminosity of meditative consciousness, they all too easily sprouted again in the fertile muck of worldly experience. Still, for now I had to trust I had trained myself to rise above my old aversions before they took on the power of a Mara-self and used me for their own purposes.

Barefoot, I padded toward a recessed corner of the courtyard, where, in a large covered wooden box hidden by clumps of ill-tended kamini, the privy buckets were stored, eight of them, along with two wooden yokes. As I lifted the cover, the box exhaled the faint stench of feces and musty urine—yet another opportunity for a monk to practice detachment. I instructed myself to allow these disagreeable sensations to come and go, along with the thoughts and emotions that inevitably crowded in into my awareness, every-thing from petulant resistance to the chore ahead to a shuddering revulsion for the intimacy of these smells, inhabiting my nostrils and lungs as if they were my true self. I had to stop elaborating on these mental phenomena; if they stopped feeding on each other, they'd dissipate. Besides, I didn't actually have to empty the cham-ber pots. All I needed to do was to carry the buckets outside the courtyard door before anyone returned from the dining hall.

I took up one of the wooden yokes and attached four buckets, and the familiar framework eased onto my shoulders in an almost friendly way, rich in associations with my life in the monastery and earlier in the hills. I also enjoyed some satisfaction in my ability to balance all four buckets easily as I stepped out into the main courtyard.

I was practicing well, I told myself. I even remembered to notice the pleasant along with the unpleasant, to see how quickly they changed places, underscoring their impermanence. Allowing myself to savor the enjoyable aspects of bucket hauling acted as ballast against disgust.

A high-pitched shriek cut through my self-congratulation. "Why is my room still full of filth!" Standing behind me was a girl I didn't recognize from my former life here, although perhaps I had known her as a child. About fourteen years old, she wore a rose-colored sari, her face imperfectly beautiful with thin arching eyebrows, a narrow hooked nose, and the kind of black hair that flashed blue in a tangle all the way down her back. Her raging black eyes dazzled with tears of frustration. "Where are the rest of you!" she demanded, meaning the other servants.

"Everyone is still at breakfast, mistress," I said, averting my eyes. I turned in the direction that I needed to go and started off.

Suddenly the air cracked open and searing pain tore through my back, then another blow, driving me to my knees. The girl had got her hands on a whip.

"How dare you walk away from your betters!" screamed the girl, raising the leather whip, about the length of a man's arm.

Rage deprived me of all thought. I grabbed the whip and jerked it, but she held on, flying forward as if holding the reins of a runaway chariot and landing on her chest in a heap of pink silk and glossy black hair. I glared down at her. In that moment, I was no longer

Ananda, or Yasodhara. I had been drawn entirely into the identity of a slave. And this arrogant girl was regarding me in the same way as she did the stunted donkeys forced to haul mounds of bricks many times their weight until they keeled over to be fed to the dogs.

I yanked the whip out of her hands, barely stopping myself from slashing it across her face. Instead, I raised it over her head.

"I'll have you killed!" she screamed.

I dropped the whip, now terrified. How could I have let rage take over yet again, jeopardizing everything I was trying to do?

"Esha. Stop this immediately." It was Pajapati. She seized the girl by one of her shoulders, and the girl, surprisingly, collapsed in her arms. "I won't marry him!" she sobbed. Then even more surprisingly, she turned her head and addressed me. "He's fifty years old and his breath smells like pig shit and he has three other wives and now you can just kill me along with yourself!" Her face was a tragedy of tears. "I'm no better than any other slave." She pressed her face into Pajapati's collarbone and wept.

I should have realized earlier that her anger had nothing to do with me. She was like a trapped sand fox hurling herself against the bars of her cage, and I was simply one of those bars. My anger melted into a heavy sorrow, which apprehension quickly replaced. The other servant women would be back any minute, and they'd recognize me as a stranger. I only hoped no one had heard the commotion.

"You should take the buckets out to the privy. Now!" Pajapati gave me a significant look.

But I still was sealed into the perspective of a slave, even as my spine stung and throbbed from the lash across my back. As a slave I knew that if the buckets were discovered at the latrine with none of the chamber pots emptied, one or more of my fellow slaves would get flogged, or worse. I hadn't thought of this. "I need to do the chamber pots first," I said.

Pajapati stared at me. "The women will soon return from breakfast," she said.

"I'll work as quickly as possible." I headed toward the first arched doorway.

Pajapati stood in silence for the time it took me to reach the half-open door. "I'll help you," she said.

The girl, still kneeling on the tiles, looked up in horror. "Auntie! You can't!"

Pajapati smoothed her boney hands along the sides of her white sari. "Remember what we've learned of the Dharma, my dear," she said. "Of all freedoms, there is none greater than from your own hatred and disgust. The only way to obtain this freedom is to face those things. Running away from them, or making others suffer them for you, only increases your slavery."

I never loved Pajapati more than at that moment.

"But you'll be contaminated!" the girl said.

Pajapati actually smiled. "I'm training myself not to worry about that."

The two of us hurried from room to room, reaching under the carved beds and children's cots and pushing aside bright patterned coverlets to find the white ceramic chamber pots, generally about two to a room. We worked in silence, the stench breathing into our faces, as urine foamed and slurped, and feces of all shapes and sizes plopped and slithered into one bucket after another, the odors intensifying with the day's increasing heat. At first I fought to swallow a dizzying nausea, my throat clutching and seizing at a sudden tang of fresh urine; then I reminded myself that I had been trained to look upon these human wastes as simply one more manifestation of earth, made glorious or horrendous as a result of my ignorance of its true nature. As I continued pouring and lifting, the nausea subsided, my movements coalescing into a rhythm, blending in with the shapes and shadows around me, the smell just another texture in the air.

As we worked in the fourth room, we heard a stirring at the door. The girl Esha stood there, her shoulders tense, her black hair twisted back. She nodded as if to herself and stepped forward to help us with our task.

The three of us continued, all the while listening for noise in the outside rooms. At the first footstep or murmur, Pajapati and Esha would need to stop working immediately. Then, hopefully, Pajapati could come up with some explanation, perhaps passing me off for a servant borrowed from one of her male relatives for the day. I doubted the servants would object very much to someone who had taken on a good portion of their work.

Meanwhile, the women were conveniently slow in returning. It didn't occur to me that there might be a reason for that.

Finally, the buckets were full. We attached them to the yoke and I was just about to raise it to my shoulders when heavy male footsteps sounded outside the door. Jagdish stamped into the courtyard, followed by two guards. He bore down on us, looking directly at me, his face deep russet with fury, his gaze pouring over me like flaming oil.

"This is an abomination."

I felt more despair than terror. It almost didn't matter whether or not he knew about Ananda. At best I would be imprisoned here forever, at worst, sold as a slave or even killed for disgracing my clan. I lowered my eyes, so he would not see me weep.

"What are you doing here, Nephew?" Pajapati's voice was metallic.

"Originally, I came to make sure that the monk you were chatting with wasn't lurking on the premises. No one ever saw him leave the dining room. But I never thought I'd see you defiling yourself in this way, Aunt."

"This is my spiritual practice." Pajapati said.

Jagdish turned his head and spat onto the tile. "And you would corrupt the children of this compound as well?"

"I'm not a child," Esha said.

I glanced up, not daring to speak. It was still unclear whether he'd recognized me as disguised as a monk or simply as his wayward sister performing a spiritual exercise in the clothes of a slave. If the latter, then at least the Sangha would be spared the embarrassment. The male Sangha, closed to women forever.

Jagdish turned around and addressed the two guards, both in late middle age and bleak-faced. "Search the rooms." Then he turned back to me.

"What are you still doing here!" he demanded. "My aunt is finished with you. She will now spend the rest of the day performing the purification rituals."

Even as had happened with Devadatta, it took awhile for me to glean that perhaps I hadn't been recognized after all. Could it be true that he'd stared at my face and seen only a slave? How was this possible?

I stood up under the yoke, the wooden bars bearing down on my shoulder bones much harder now that the buckets were full. My legs quaked, fear and incredulity jolting through me. I'd lost my meditative detachment. The foul stew in the buckets gurgled and sloshed.

"Get that shit to the privy, now!" my brother ordered.

I nodded, then risked one last glance at Pajapati. One that said:

don't forget what we agreed on. Then I started walking, the buckets swaying and clunking together with each deliberate step. I would not allow myself to feel any relief until they were safely in the privy and I was on the path back to the summer palace.

The cobweb-draped brick passageway that led to the exit nearest the privy was barely wide enough for the yoke to fit, and it went on much farther than I'd estimated. I finally reached the door to the outside, the opening concealed by tall oleander bushes, hidden like an anus—which in a way it was, with only one class of humans meant to pass through it. Meanwhile, Pajapati would spend the rest of this day scrubbing her face with cow dung and taking a ritual bath in milk to purify herself from the pollution brought on by contact with her slaves. What folly! I refused to believe that these practices were the natural order of the universe, whether decreed by powerful kings, personal karma, or prettified gods lazing in pampered eternities. And even though the Tathagata never spoke on such metaphysical subjects, I was sure he would agree.

I understood now why my brother failed to recognize me, even though I was sure he would have done so had I been in my monk's robes. His eyes examined men's faces as a matter of course, but he'd never get that far with a slave. From a single glance, his mind had fashioned an all-purpose slave-face, created from his need to justify his own image in the silver mirror of his upper-class life.

By now I'd followed the path leading from the concealed door and reached the privy, a wooden shed about half the size of the palace kitchen, in a grove of acacia trees not far from the river, doves cooing in the branches, rust-colored chickens pecking in the dirt. I planned to change into my monk's robes here, then return to the dry-season residence, where the monks were staying. I wasn't worried about being late; the Dharma talk I was supposed to memorize wasn't until the late afternoon, and I wasn't scheduled to teach the younger monks until after sunset.

I didn't realize I had more to learn about being a slave.

Just as I opened the warped balsa wood door into dimness and privy-reek, I heard behind me a chicken's panicked cackling, followed by a young man's heavy laughter and a sudden flutter of wings. I froze, cursing my luck. I couldn't risk having anyone see a slave woman walk in and a monk walk out. I'd have to find somewhere else to change my garments. As quickly as possible, I dumped the torrent of waste down the privy hole, hung the buckets on a wooden peg, and returned to the tangled sunlight of the acacia grove, the pollen-scented air all the sweeter for the contrast with the privy smell. The young man had disappeared and the chickens had fled into the underbrush, but I secured the bundle around my waist and retied the scarf on my head, pulling it tightly against my brow to minimize the danger of it falling off, in case I needed to run.

I took the privy path back to where it branched off to a main road leading away from the summer residence. Almost as soon as I'd passed the oleander-concealed doorway, I heard the young man's laughter again, just behind me. Before I could even turn around, the man, bare-chested and in a worker's dhoti, grabbed me around the shoulders, still laughing. "You're not allowed on this path!" he said. "You're fair game!"

Once again terror whirled inside me. I couldn't afford to struggle and risk him tearing the rag off my head or discovering the robes under my wrap. "Please," I said. "I need to get back to work."

"This won't take long!" Digging his fingers into my shoulders, he shoved me against a tree, a strip of pain igniting my whipped back as he ground his pelvis against mine. In horror, I stared into his grimacing long-chinned face with its bent nose and missing front tooth. One of his eyes floated off to one corner, giving him the look of a panicked horse, despite his high humor. His rotten-meat breath enveloped my face. "Lie down," he said, pressing down on my shoulders and forcing me to my knees.

"Stop!" A tall man in a gold-edged lapis blue paridhana was striding toward us. My heart gave a little leap. Was he coming to my rescue?

"I get her first," he said, shoving the first man aside, crushing all hope. This second man was in his thirties, his oily face hard-seamed, his heavy-lidded eyes swimming in scarlet, strands of black hair smeared over his forehead. He stank of perfumed sweat and stale wine, and his garment was wrinkled and stained, as if he'd been up all night, but now he'd seen fit to exercise his aristocratic privilege. Casually, he pulled out his sword and touched the point to my chest. "On your back," he said, pressing his sword until I had no choice but to lie down.

How was it that I was too polluted to touch, yet not exempt from being used for sex?

Now both men were holding me down, but it was fear that was overwhelming me, a Mara-self paralyzing my reason and plunging me into its own terrifying thoughts. At the very least, my attackers would expose me. They'd impregnate me or kill me, and living or dead, I would disgrace the Sangha and destroy the lives of those I loved most, including my son. At best I would live out my life as a slave.

Unless I got free of this fear, I had no chance to save myself at all. Taking a breath, I turned my attention toward my emotion—as I had done so many times in practice—and slowed down time.

Mara was far stronger than usual. I understood now why the Tathagata used the words "Mara's army" to describe the thoughts and sensations assailing me: confusion tumbling behind my eyes, a sense of danger stabbing in my heart, a deadly weakness clawing my abdomen, a craving to run away from my own life pounding in my throat.

These are only sensations, not me or mine. Even thoughts are sensations, coming and going. And as I watched them, they dissipated, receding in all directions.

But Mara hadn't finished with me.

"Open your legs or you'll die right here on your back!" the aristocratic man said, straddling me and waving his sword. The fear returned.

I had to expand my awareness further, beyond time and body. I inhaled again, and suddenly I was watching countless emotions arising and all sorts of beings grabbing onto them, taking them for the truth.

My fear had never held me. I had been holding it. And it was not truth, only an emotion. Breathing out, I let it go.

In the space it had vacated were all the possibilities that had been there all along.

I let out an unearthly howl, opening my throat to the demon-wolf voices in my lungs, arching my back and jerking rhythmically, my fingers bending into claws. *"Owwoooooooooh!"* cried the wolf. Then I called forth the serpent from the Gorge, hissing and writhing, rolling my eyes back in my head, not in terror but in the ecstatic throes of a demon-possessed corpse, even as I made sure to writhe about in a way that wouldn't tear off my scarf. I whooped and shrieked, foaming at the mouth, a living celebration of death.

The men recoiled, their grip slackened. "She's possessed!" said the walleyed man, stumbling backwards. "The *asuras* are rising out of hell."

If only for a moment, they released me.

I surged to my feet and streaked toward the river. Behind me I sensed the men gathering up their thoughts, starting after me. In front of me the river flowed past like a glittering milky brown goddess proceeding to some distant sea, happy to carry me if only I could swim.

I had no time to worry whether I'd remember what Bahauk had tried to teach me over that last summer. I plunged into the current, ordering myself to keep my head above water. As my feet lifted out from under me, my arms panicked, they had nothing to hold on to. *I know you, fear. I know you, Mara.* I moved my arms and legs the way I remembered and took a gulp of the rivery air. The water was not nearly as cold as the Gorge River; it was a pleasant contrast to the earth's hot, dry breath. The current eased me along, spinning me out into the river's middle, trees and fields flowing by, my waterlogged clothes dragging me down but not yet so much as to pull me under. My head scarf unraveled and the knotted rag around my head floated off like a hat, exposing my baldness but too far away from my assailants for them to see. The river goddess held me in all her splendor. Now all I had to do was somehow steer myself to a deserted beach.

The river carried me past Kapilavatthu, where I couldn't have beached myself in any case, and finally turned sharply into a wild jungle of mostly palms half-sunk in tangled vines and other shrubbery. Aiming myself toward the small bay formed by the bend in the river, I kicked and paddled with all my strength until I could reach down and grasp the black river stones, tumbling over themselves in the water as I clawed my way to where the surface was nearly still and I could float to shore. Still prone in the water, I checked for people, but all I saw were black and white shelducks bobbing in the shallows, and all I heard were the ducks quacking and the loud murmur of the river. Crouching in the knee-deep water, with the stones bruising my feet, I untangled my sopping monk's garments, fought my way into them, and staggered forward. As I stood up, my yellow robes adhering to me like an oversized, wrinkled second skin, I finally allowed myself to celebrate. I'd persuaded Pajapati to confront the Tathagata. A bolt of joy shot through me even as I realized I was much farther from the monks' residence than I'd expected. I probably wouldn't get back until late afternoon, but at least the day was sunny, good for drying my robes in the now welcome heat.

A narrow path led through the jungle patch to the hard clay road heading back to Kapilavatthu. As I walked along, passing amber barley fields rippling in the wind, I realized that my practice made it possible to see my attackers not as evil but as asleep, and slaves to their own suffering, and that to view them in this compassionate way was to be free of them forever.

But I couldn't have gained this freedom without faith in the possibility of awakening, where my body was other than some essential self that would be irreparably damaged by forced sex. This was the faith the Tathagata had bestowed on me by allowing me to become a monk. Not that all women needed to turn themselves into monastics, but I truly believed that nothing other than the existence of fellow women seeking full enlightenment could give them the confidence that they, too, were other than their bodies; they were part of the mystery that all beings shared. How could the Tathagata talk of faith and yet be blind to this truth?

As it turned out, I didn't get back until almost the time for the Dharma talk. Although my robes were wrinkled and smelled of the river, I judged myself presentable and made my way straight to the pavilion where the talk was to be held. In spite of fatigue and the stinging of my wounded back, my optimistic mood continued, until I noticed that everything was strangely quiet except for a rising breeze and the far off hollow knocking of a woodpecker.

All at once Kavi emerged from the trees. "Ananda! Where have you been?"

"I tried to visit householders and got waylaid." As much as possible, I always told the truth, but the stricken look on Kavi's bright little face made me pause. "Where is everyone?"

"You didn't hear? The Tathagata decided that we all needed to leave for the Vesali forest dwellings at once. Master Jagdish complained that the monks were disturbing his women."

His worried look deepened. "We need to leave right now, Ananda. We have to catch up before midnight."

He'd covered for me. I looked back at the pavilion, occupied only by the small hunched form of a wizen-faced monkey, scratching its belly and muttering to itself. There was nothing for me here but desolation.

12

On that long walk to Vesali, made grueling by the heat, I had no opportunity to broach the topic of female ordination with the Tathagata, but I was determined to try again once we reached our destination. Of course I worried about Pajapati. Had anyone even told her that we'd left? What if she'd shown up at the Tathagata's lodgings, only to find them empty? I feared she'd give up on ordination altogether.

The hundred or so monks in our company bypassed the actual city of Vesali, which was as large as Bimbisara's capital and reputedly even more friendly to the Tathagata—and settled down in a nearby monastery consisting of a gabled, all-purpose wooden building and scattered one-person huts in the adjoining forest. The canopy of heavy-crowned sal and elm trees offered relief from the heat, though I feared it would bring gloom—at least for me—when the rains arrived. I missed Rahula, currently in temporary seclusion with his teachers and several younger monks reportedly on the brink of awakening, but at least I could be glad for his ongoing happiness. What distressed me far more was what had happened with Pajapati.

On the second day after our arrival, following almsrounds to the wealthy suburbs surrounding the city, I saw a chance to speak to the Tathagata about her desire to ordain. By now I'd located the well and taken up my practice of carrying buckets of water to the washhouse for the monks to rinse their bowls. Kavi, Naveen, and several of the other younger monks always helped me—something I encouraged as a way of developing their arm and back strength. I hated to see young boys weak and vulnerable—especially when they went out on the road to teach the Dharma on their own. Many muscle-developing activities—such as chopping wood or any kind of digging—were denied monks, both to encourage the mutual dependence of monks and laypeople and also to help the monks avoid directly harming living beings, such as trees and their inhabitants, as well as creatures who lived underground. So I had no qualms about letting the boys take over carrying water while I waited for the Tathagata in the shade. Around me, darts of white sunlight flickered shyly over the undergrowth, as if knowing they intruded on an alien domain; far above, the treetops rustled with the usual crowds of birds and monkeys, their complaints and scoldings forming yet another canopy, one of sound.

Soon enough I spotted the Tathagata entering and then leaving the wash house after cleaning his bowl and storing it with everyone else's. But no sooner had I started walking in his direction when Devadatta flashed in front of me, blocking my way.

"Blessed One," he addressed the Tathagata. "I know what this monk has come to tell you."

"I had no idea your psychic powers were so advanced," I said. "But perhaps the Tathagata would like me to use actual words to confirm them."

The Tathagata raised an eyebrow at me, just as I was tasting that nasty satisfaction that comes with sarcasm and the bitterness that follows, and I realized for the thousandth time how such remarks create suffering in the speaker as well as in the listener. Once again, instead of first meditating myself into a state of equanimity before taking action, I had allowed all sorts of attachments and emotions to accompany me here, including my dislike of Devadatta.

Devadatta, of course, saw his opportunity. "The monk Ananda can decide for himself the adequacy of my psychic abilities. I believe he wishes to discuss the preposterous topic of whether women should be allowed to ordain."

All I could think was that someone had seen me approaching Pajapati and reported this to Devadatta. But who?

Devadatta continued. "However, most of us agree that the presence of female monastics would affect our community in the way of hail falling on a ripening wheat field: the field will not flourish but come to ruin."

I was determined to stay polite. "Although your image is striking," I said, "I fear it has no real meaning."

"Does it not?" Devadatta's narrow face seemed to become even narrower. "Well, then, consider a household with many women and few men—would it be productive? Of course it wouldn't."

I felt my politeness disintegrating. "One could say that households overstocked with men present every bit as much of a problem," I said. "Even our revered Sangha seems to suffer from its members treating each other harshly and fighting over doctrinal minutiae—so much that, if you remember, last year the Tathagata left us for three months so he could meditate in peace apart from quarreling monks. It's my humble view that our community might well be helped by the presence of women."

The Tathagata raised his eyebrow again, but said nothing.

Devadatta tightened his upper robe across his body. "The holy life would not last," he said. "The Dharma would soon be forgotten."

"That's nothing more than an opinion," I said. "I hope you're not attached to it."

"It's no mere opinion. Women, with their scant wisdom and preoccupation with love, can have only a negative effect on the Dharma. This is self-evident."

"Is it?" I asked. "According to whom, the bulls in the fields?"

Devadatta turned to the Tathagata. "Are you going to let this monk get away with such a heinous example of wrong speech?"

"Enough," the Tathagata said, addressing us like quarreling children. "Devadatta, allow me to speak in private to this monk as to why his view is incorrect. This show of animosity is only creating suffering for all involved."

"Certainly not me," Devadatta said. "I have gone beyond all suffering."

The Tathagata said nothing.

"Allow me to add one more observation," Devadatta said. "Beware of this overly handsome monk, Master. He's always gathering the girls around him, supposedly to learn the Dharma, but who knows? Our cousin Jagdish saw him lurking around the women of his household more than once. He was even worried that he'd sneaked into their private quarters."

"That's a lie!" I said, even though I thought I saw the smallest hint of a smile on the Tathagata's face, and I myself had to appreciate the irony that my former suitor was now accusing me of womanizing. But then a realization darker than the forest shade filled me: It was Jagdish who'd reported me to Devadatta. The thought of the two of them joining forces to undermine social freedom, women, and me in particular turned my dark realization into an even darker foreboding. "I spoke only to Pajapati, who is sixty-five years old."

"You spoke to my stepmother?" the Tathagata said. "What of the Dharma could you have said to her that I had not expressed?" He spoke this as a simple question, but the animals' clamor in the trees overhead seemed to underscore his disapproval.

"I would like to reply to you in private," I said, my throat tight. "As you suggested."

"Come with me," the Tathagata said, nodding a dismissal to Devadatta, and I followed him into the woods. Devadatta stalked off in the opposite direction.

I never would have guessed that in later years, many of Devadatta's words would be attributed to the Tathagata, particularly those against women. No matter, I would have made the same replies to whoever spoke such nonsense. And I still would, although without the sarcasm. But back then I had little compassion for Devadatta, whose deluded fears about women endangering the discipline crucial for enlightenment no doubt caused him great suffering.

The Tathagata and I ended up out of earshot of even the most far-flung hut, in not so much a clearing as a gap between huge trees where two moss-covered logs lay in the half-light. Everything was damper here, with a mossy smell and a small stream making salivary sounds in the near distance. We'd entered the deepest part of the forest where even the dry season couldn't wholly penetrate.

We sat down on the logs. They were shockingly green, as if they had absorbed the color from somewhere else. "Pajapati wants to ordain," I said, and I presented my arguments for women's ordination.

The Tathagata smiled as I finished speaking but not in an encouraging way. "Consider how much my stepmother's accomplished without ordination!" Strangely, his face seemed to shine with his preenlightenment innocence, the pride of a child for a parent. "Why should she have to subject herself to monastic life?"

"The overwhelming majority of people, men and women, are unable to attain enlightenment in isolation." I was aware of sounding pedantic, but in my urgency I felt I needed to cut through my former husband's inexplicable innocence. "Not to mention that most women lack Pajapati's advantages," I said. "And that women need female examples to make them truly understand their potential to penetrate the deepest truths of the universe."

The Tathagata's innocent look sharpened into an intent search of my face, as if to find a way into it and fill me with his own understanding. "There's another problem," he said. "I had the premonition that if women ordain, Dharma would cease to be taught on earth far earlier in this epoch than otherwise."

In spite of the heat, a chill passed through my bones. "I don't see how you can blame women for the future failure of the teachings."

"I don't at all," he said. "But the danger comes when the sexes live in proximity and play the same roles." He was silent for a moment, long enough for memories of our marriage to arise. Siddhartha and I had shared many tasks, living together with a mutual regard almost unknown to householder couples, and our marriage had ended in pain.

My former husband continued. "If the two sexes lived together in full respect and understanding, they would discover whole new ways to delight in each other—as I did in my marriage." His face wore the slightest of sad smiles, as if to remind me of the knowledge we shared—or perhaps he'd arranged this sadness on his face to arouse a similar resigned emotion in me. "Soon they'd begin to wonder whether some of the rules could be changed, starting with the rule of celibacy. They'd abandon the discipline needed for full enlightenment. Instead, they'd settle for just enough Dharma to improve their daily lives, convincing themselves that they could find paradise on earth."

I stared down at the green-glowing dead log I was sitting on, a heretical thought taking root. "Maybe that would be all right," I said. "Maybe just that little bit of Dharma would suffice to make life worth living."

"How can you say that! Surely you remember how it was with me before I went forth, when I thought I could remake the world into a heaven on earth? Then I came upon the truth of impermanence. Not only of our lives but of contentment itself. I saw how my desires multiplied whenever one of them was satisfied, causing even more discontent. And the fear and then the pain of loss made everything worse." Now his level eyes under his perfectly arced eyebrows were aimed directly into me, and for that moment he was my husband again, explaining himself.

I replied accordingly, a righteousness in my tone. "Yes, of course you suffered, but maybe if you'd had that little bit of Dharma, you needn't have gone to such extremes." *And we might have a good life together, with more children and...* I stopped myself and watched my thoughts proliferate—memories, regrets, images of idyllic lives both with him and with Bahauk. Along with thoughts came more emotions, stampeding through body, mind, and heart.

He shook his head as if he actually saw my mental tumult hovering in front of him. "Unless there are practitioners dedicated completely to the Dharma and demonstrating its truth, your so-called 'little bit' of Dharma will die out. Even the most well-meaning people will do what I did, try to make a deva realm on earth, and they'll cling to their notions of what that heaven is and how to create it—and eventually cause great harm to all who disagree with them. Wars, murder, torture, starvation in times of plenty—the world as we know it." He leaned forward, his eyes softening. "Maintaining the monastic discipline means keeping the Dharma alive, with its promise of a far greater happiness than worldly joy. Please tell me that you remember that happiness."

As if by the sheer power of his mind, I remembered those rare times when the universe sprang open inside my heart, of being freed from time and loneliness. A state beyond any happiness that the sensual world could provide.

Although these experiences had faded like all else, I remembered being awake.

"But why do women have to be left behind? It's not fair!"

"Because not enough women want enlightenment." He shook his head gravely, as if this was an unarguable fact. "If they were the sex chosen to ordain, the Sangha would die out."

"You don't know that, and you haven't proven that proximity of the sexes alone will destroy the discipline. Men and women would still live in separate dwellings. The idea that sexual attraction would take over is just a view, as you yourself would say."

He nodded. "But my views belong to someone who's free of the distortions of craving. Whereas you can't deny that you, like all unawakened people, are still under the sway of afflictive emotions."

As he spoke, my anger, which I might have expected, failed to arise; I was coming to fear that something hidden, even to him, was determining his arguments. "Your view may be impartial," I said, "but it's limited by what we've believed our entire lives. As you always say, you're not a god and you don't look down from an objective heaven."

"I can only judge from my own experience," he said, and I had to admit that in the flickering darkness, the light in his eyes seemed to come from pure concern for the welfare of all beings. "I've known the suffering of women, starting with my own mother, and I've experienced firsthand the deprivations of the holy life. Women would suffer from its demands much more than men."

This time I met his intense gaze with my own. Using my ability to detach myself at least temporarily from my own needs and wishes, I opened myself to whatever truth I could find in his face. All at once I was transported back into my marriage, to that day I fainted and he changed forever, but this time I experienced it from Siddhartha's point of view. Until this moment, I could not have imagined the sharp knife of purest terror that had cut through his viscera at the sight of me—it was beyond the simple terror of death. It was as if he could not bear the slightest hint of female suffering. Was it because he'd experienced the death of his mother at such a young age? In any case, I saw that in that moment, Siddhartha determined never to subject women to any kind of physical pain.

I blinked, and I was back to the present with one new conviction: Siddhartha had felt that terror but not the Tathagata. At the time of his awakening my former husband let go of his fear of and grief over female pain, transforming them into a compassion that was their equal in size and power. This compassion, I was convinced, was blinding the Tathagata to reality.

He uncrossed his legs and made as if to stand. "Look at it this way," he said. "Everyone can awaken eventually. Women aspirants will be reborn as males, or in the deva realms."

A grayness settled over me. "I have no experience of rebirth," I said, my voice dry and desolate. "You know that."

"And you know that rebirth and deva realms are ways of speaking." He stood up. "Of expressing the truth that our self-centered lives are an illusion. For the unawakened, this spiritual path requires faith. Remember when you first joined the Sangha. You promised to cultivate faith."

I looked down at my hands. At this point, faith seemed like another form of blindness.

"I'm so sorry," he said. "If I could end your suffering, I would." When I didn't look up, he vanished into the forest.

I remained sitting in that grove until darkness had swallowed every glint of light. Then I lay down in the mulch, with only insects' voices and my own desperation as a cover. How could I ever pit my views and opinions against a system of beliefs about the female sex that even a Buddha couldn't escape?

The all-engulfing blackness of the forest prevented me from leaving before dawn. I alternated between meditation and sleep, Mara's armies charging through both of these states. In the invisible undergrowth, mental and physical, all my old regrets and recriminations lurked, and as the night wore on, Mara's most powerful commander took over: what the monks called the Hindrance of Doubt.

Doubt's main strategy was to snare me with questions. What had meditation ever done for me, really? Was I better off now than in those days and weeks after Siddhartha left, my mind in chaos, my heart and body enslaved to one agony after another? What about my original quest to seek out my sister's spirit? Had the practice helped me or just supplied me with delusion?

All night long I tried to avoid these snares by simply being aware of them, like dodging rope-traps in the jungle. But every snare was baited with the false promise of certainty, that all I had to do was give myself completely to doubt and I'd come up with some absolute truth, which however terrible, would either lead to disrobing or not. Of course the possibility of making this decision—condemning either myself, the Dharma, or the universe—was the supreme bait of all, because it promised a sense of being in control.

Finally, dawn arrived, and as the forest fed on light and took on color and form, I made my way back to the Sangha's encampment. At the sight of the younger monks hauling water to the washhouse, I saw that I wasn't ready to disrobe. They needed me to impart the Dharma, however imperfectly, to them and to laywomen. Also, in the morning light I realized that even when doubt swept me up and had its way with me, my awareness returned faster than it had before I joined the Sangha, enabling me to observe doubt's false-ness—its flimsiness and the confusion that substitutes for thought. I had some freedom, after all.

But the thought hammered me—I had left Pajapati stranded. At this point, what could I do? Teach the Dharma to as many women as possible in hopes that their sheer numbers would persuade the Tathagata that the female sex was not as repulsed by the monas-tic life as he believed? But Devadatta had already decided I was a womanizer, and flocks of women students would only confirm his delusion.

To counter Mara's other general, Despair, I spent the day making myself useful, inspecting all the huts and main buildings to make sure everything was ready for the approaching monsoon. My writ-ing skills continued to prove valuable. I wrote on a piece of birch bark what repairs needed to be made and handed the list to the King's messenger, who in turn gave it to an agent with reading abil-ity who could assign laypeople to do the work. Writing saved time, sparing me not only having to help the messenger memorize the order but also from having to memorize it myself. So I had more room in my mind for Dharma talks, such as the one from Sariputta, who spoke that evening on the importance of developing tranquility as a prerequisite for meditation.

I took his talk to heart. I had already decided to devote a good part of the following day to meditating in hopes that a way to change the Tathagata's mind would emerge. But shortly after breakfast, my forest meditation was interrupted by monks' voices.

"It's an insult to their clan," came the voice I recognized as belonging to one of Devadatta's most loyal devotees, an emaciated monk in his mid-thirties. "How can they degrade themselves in such a way?"

"Mara has infected them with unnatural cravings," came the reply.

I stepped forward through the trees. "What's going on?" I asked.

The gaunt monk bowed. "I apologize for my idle talk, which has produced this troublesome curiosity in your mind." He mouthed a smile that had nothing to do with his sunken cheeks and blazing eyes, and I tried not to dismiss him as a typical Devadatta follower. "I will most certainly confess my speech transgression at the next *Upasaka* ceremony," he said.

"Rest assured," I said. "What has arisen in my mind is not curiosity, but concern. It sounds like these beings are in the grip of suffering, which as I remember, we have a responsibility to alleviate."

"They're just some beggars on the road," the gaunt monk's portly companion said. He was the opposite of the first monk, with trembling cheeks and frightened eyes, someone who most likely hoped the Discipline would change him into someone other than he was. "Hopefully," he said, "they have not worsened their karma by continuing to create a disturbance."

"Do they need teachings?" I asked, "or perhaps physical assistance?"

A third monk, oldest of the three, with mottled mud-gray skin and about as deep a voice as a human can possess, approached, raising his hand in an ambiguous blessing. "The Tathagata has provided for them. Please, monk, spare yourself the karmic consequences of further frivolous talk." He nodded to himself, seeming to savor the authority of his bass rumble, and the three monks walked off, each in a different direction.

I headed for the road.

The main thoroughfare was at the bottom of the slope where forested foothills rose from the valley. On an expanse of pounded dirt wide enough for four tandem chariots, I spotted a group of at least fifty shaven-headed beggars in brownish gray rags, some kneeling and others stretched out in exhaustion under the roadside trees. They were surrounded by half a dozen yellow-robed monks and fifteen or so laypersons in bright-hued paridhanas, some carrying water jugs. The deep-voiced monk had been right; these people were being tended to. At this point I began to doubt the wisdom of risking Devadatta's ire by snooping around and asking questions.

A young layman, his face the color of bright copper, waved to me. "Do you know where we can get some ointment? These women have come a long way."

Women?

A tiny girl in a crimson paridhana and carrying a bowl of rice approached. "They walked barefoot here all the way from Kapilavatthu!" she breathed.

I broke into a run.

The robes weren't brown; they were white cloth coated with road dust. "Pajapati?" I said, trying to recognize her among the shaven heads. I was joyful, shocked, and terrified at the same time. Here were my clanswomen, exhausted, their feet blistered, a few of the younger ones weeping, others murmuring, "We take refuge in the Buddha, the Dharma, and the Sangha."

"Ananda." Pajapati spoke from behind, her voice amazingly firm, considering. She limped toward me, bowing her head to the little girl and waving the bowl away. "Give it to Esha," she said, gesturing toward a bald young woman whom I recognized as the angry girl who'd whipped me.

I motioned Pajapati to sit down. "How...? Did you...?" What had she sacrificed to do this? Obviously, she'd started with her own body, which had spent the past sixty-some years confined in an area one could walk around in a matter of minutes. How had she managed to escape?

Underneath the streaks of dust on her face, her skin looked like scorched brick. "Don't worry. I didn't blackmail Jagdish," she said in a low voice, looking around to make sure no one overheard.

"Even if you had," I said, "it's mostly my karma, since it was I who suggested it." Not that I'd had much hope that she'd take me up on it, given her strict principles.

"However," she said, "when I asked my nephew Mahanama where you'd gone, I did let drop the rumor I'd heard about Jagdish marrying off one of our servants to King Pasenadi."

"What?" She'd succeeded in surprising me. Certainly here was a sign of her desperation—even more than the arduous walk she and the others had just completed.

"I didn't implicate you or anyone else," Pajapati said. "Many of our clansmen have been unhappy with Jagdish trying to take over. He was in no position to go against my request. In fact, Mahanama not only told me where you'd gone, he offered to accompany us with an entourage of litters, servants, and elephants, which of course, I rejected."

Jagdish deprived of his power? I couldn't speak. If our cousin Mahanama took over as clan leader, this could benefit not only the confined women but the Sangha as well, as he was a known follower of the Tathagata. At the same time, the thought of a vengeful Jagdish thrust a cold sword through my vitals.

I recovered myself. "Have you spoken to the Tathagata?" Surely this show of dedication would have proven to him that women did not dread the holy life.

She was silent for a moment, long enough for me to guess what I should have seen at once. She had not smiled this whole time, and the posture of the entire worn-out, sun-blasted group was that of hopelessness.

Pajapati gazed out over the yellow-stubbled fields. "He will not meet with us."

I stood dumbly, dazed by defeat. I couldn't believe it. "But he has too much compassion to leave you out in this desiccating heat."

Pajapati nodded. "Of course he has. But it took awhile for the message to get to him. As soon as he found out, he sent his monks to help us." She finally smiled, albeit ironically. "He's arranged for Vesali's oligarch to prepare just the sort of entourage to take us home that we refused when we traveled here. I know he cares for us, and I'm sure he intends his refusal as a way to help me let go of selfish desires."

A tremendous outrage roared through my blood, not so much against the Tathagata but against the male tyranny that deformed the minds of everyone, even those of enlightened beings. And even that of Pajapati, who was now using a distorted notion of the Dharma to rationalize abandoning her quest. "What about the desires of your kinswomen here?" I said. "Are they equally selfish?"

Pajapati's age-hooded eyes met mine. "It's possible to say that all desires are selfish. Anyway, we can go home full of resentment, or we can treat this defeat as an opportunity for personal purification."

I would never be as pure as Pajapati—the proof arising right here as I felt myself once again chafing against the chains she insisted on viewing as ribbons. "Perhaps the Dharma itself needs to be purified," I said.

Pajapati shook her head. "Be careful, Ananda. You may have gone too far."

"Too far! He claims he won't ordain women out of compassion for them. What a convenient compassion it is, allowing him to preserve his precious Sangha full of woman-hating monks. Someone needs to break through his blindness."

"Yas—Ananda!" Pajapati raised her hand, stopping herself from grabbing my arm, that of a monk forbidden all physical contact with women. "We have to trust he knows what he's doing."

"He always says he's not a god." Yet I paused in the center of my anger, which my training had taught me not to obey blindly but to observe while it changed. And so it did, filling my heart and body with a sense of purpose, which immediately expanded into the purpose of my life. Or so it seemed. Was this delusion?

No answer came, but the feeling remained.

"Let me speak to him," I said. "After all, I got you into this."

"That doesn't matter—I'm grateful for your guidance. You've done enough. Don't risk your own position." Her sunburned face darkened with concern, probably because she suspected what I was going to do.

"He will talk with you," I said and headed off. "Just don't leave."

Eyes straight ahead, I started down the clay road, nodding curtly at the clutch of yellow robes standing at the turnoff, presumably to protect their peers from female pollution. I wound up at the gabled *agama* where the Tathagata and other senior monks were staying. There was a porch on the second floor with a view of the road below where he would have been able to see the women, but he occupied a tiny oak-paneled room in the back, isolated so he could meet with individual aspirants in private. I entered without asking. The room barely had space for a sleeping pallet, a shelf for his sewing utensils, and a couple of cushions, used for the many interviews he so generously conducted when he might have spent his time in holy bliss. I made myself remember that fact.

Otherwise, I was past thinking, except for the sense that I was acting out a role determined in a distant past and encompassing far more than my own life. I bowed, placing my *kasaya* respectably over my shoulder and ignoring my pounding heart. "I talked to Pajapati," I said, "who traveled all this way on foot to meet with you. What sort of Dharma has you turn away the woman who brought you up—and loved you—as her own?"

He looked at me once again with eyes as innocent as my former husband's—or so was my perception in that dim little room. "I can feel how much she suffered on this journey," he said. "Can't you? Think how much more she would suffer if she took up the arduous life we live here—so much that she would learn nothing."

"That's your view. Not mine. I'm here to ask you for the third time—*allow women to be ordained.*" Such was the protocol: important requests were to be repeated three times. The tradition was that they then had to be granted, but of course this was not always the case. My legs were shaking.

The Tathagata closed his eyes, then opened them. "I'm very sorry to say no."

I looked into the eyes of my former husband, my beloved teacher, most likely my last hope for ever awakening in this lifetime, the only time on earth I was certain I had. "If you refuse your stepmother," I said. "I will disrobe." I must have known all along I was going to say this, along with what followed.

"You have this choice," the Tathagata said, his body as still as a corpse.

"I will disrobe and let everyone know who I am."

His stillness took possession of the little room, changing it into an eternal twilight where I was utterly alone. Cut off from all love, I had only my memory of it and my sense of justice to keep me from contracting into nothingness. I would not abjure the words that had come out of me.

The Tathagata finally spoke, his voice as impersonal as an edict. "You realize the consequences of harming a Buddha, not to mention the Dharma."

"I hope my intentions are pure." Yet now, in this gray nonplace I sensed the hell realms, not so much opening up below me as spreading through my void of a self. I foresaw the hell of never knowing my motives' purity and the far worse hell of looking into the eyes of Kavi and my other young students, once they found out that I had made them live a lie. And Rahula! How would he ever forgive me? How would anyone? I would end up isolated from everyone I loved for lifetimes to come.

On their own, my fists clenched.

The Tathagata continued, his voice both soft and clear as if he wanted to make sure I knew what I was doing. "The Sangha could be lost forever."

"I trust that the Dharma would allow the true Sangha to survive."

"Have you not worried that I could try to discredit you? And what if I succeeded? You could spend eons in the hell realms for jeopardizing the Dharma—and all for nothing."

I nodded. Please, Stick Woman, be with me now. *I am already dead.*

"You're willing to suffer all this."

"It seems to be my destiny."

"Oh, Yasi,"

There were tears in his eyes. Or at least so I would remember this impossibility—impossible because enlightened persons feel no grief, only compassion.

He fell silent, and I have no idea how much time passed. Perhaps none. Or perhaps an infinity of time, as of that between one eon and the next. I had no power over the silence; I had said all I could.

Finally, he spoke. "We're lucky that all is impermanent," he said, in a warm, dry tone that strangely resembled Stick Woman, "and that eternal truth continually gives birth to itself."

It was then the gray twilight seemed to shift to dawn.

Not that I ever became certain of my moral correctness, but all at once he and I were together again in that undifferentiated state of peace, in a new way, as two halves of the same whole. Beyond male or female, we were the Dharma seeking and expressing itself. *Awakening awakens.*

Perhaps the Tathagata's tears were mine.

"I'll talk to Pajapati," he said. "Women have proven their determination. I now understand we will all benefit if they enter this holy life."

There was a price to pay. Although the Sangha managed to remain one body, the Tathagata had to make concessions to appease Devadatta and his allies. These days, everyone has heard of these compromises: although women can take full ordination, all male monastics, even the smallest boys, are senior to them, standing in front of them in every line and authorized to admonish and reprimand them. Ultimately, men would have two hundred and twenty-seven rules, women over six hundred, many about restricting them in the vicinity of males—although nuns were expected, as were all Sangha members, to teach the Dharma to those who requested.

In the early days, these rules rested lightly on most of us, especially in the presence of nuns who had attained full liberation. As soon as Pajapati announced she was founding a women's order, women from all varnas poured into the parks and groves where the Sangha stayed—aristocrats and prostitutes, street vendors and farm wives. An astonishing number of nuns awakened over the next few years, starting with Pajapati. To my great joy, they began to teach the Dharma, and I memorized and passed along their teachings, some of which I could only wonder at. One nun (who wished to remain anonymous) compared her defeated worldly passions to a pot of pickled greens boiled dry; another described attaining freedom from grief (inconceivable to me) over the death of her child ("What is there to lament?"). And then there was the famous story of the Venerable Subha, who to discourage a libertine trying to seduce her by praising her beautiful eyes, yanked out one of them and handed it to him. Such stories made me realize how far I had to go on my own spiritual journey.

Well, my failures to swim against the worldly stream were part of the price paid for my lack of purity, perhaps the most severe consequence of my life of deception. No matter how many times I glimpsed enlightenment, no matter how many Dharma teachings I memorized and hours I meditated, I couldn't shake the uncontrollable desires that these enlightened women had apparently left behind. My cravings often took the form of worry. I worried about my young charges' safety, about the survival of the Dharma, about Devadatta's sullen retreat to the forest where these days he spent much of his time meditating and (I feared) plotting revenge. I worried about the Sakyans' secret—that they'd passed off a slave to marry a king—and one day the king would find out. And I of course worried about my son, now praised for his own precocious enlightenment. As someone who had not awakened, I could never know for sure. Was he truly in bliss or lost in a trance?

I also worried about my own lack of enlightenment, but all I could do was work hard to train my mind and not create new karma. Fortunately, I remained ignorant of the future—and the transgressions that I might face if I wanted to prevent what I regarded as the true teachings, including those of the nuns, from falling into oblivion. For now, in spite of everything, I felt content.

13

O ver the next fifteen years, the Sangha grew. We monastics traveled and taught in pairs or larger groups except during the monsoon, when most of the Sangha would gather in some king or merchant's pleasure park or settle down in an ever-growing number of monastic *viharas.* During the rest of the year, we walked from town to town through every kind of weather, on wide roads next to fields breathing sweet pollen and sun-baked dung, or on narrow paths through jungles where everything seemed to sprout out of everything else, and the sharp scent of fresh greenery trilled over base notes of mold and decay. We slept on bare pallets on the ground or in palaces, one day swallowing down gluey rice mucked at the bottom of our begging bowls, the next day savoring lotus root and spiced peaches from China served on golden plates. Treat everything equally, the Tathagata reminded us, for the goal was to cultivate disenchantment with it all. Take only what was freely given, and cultivate compassion for all beings.

As I said, I counted myself happy. And even though I knew happiness can never last, I made one of the most common mistakes of an unenlightened being. I forgot that impermanence applied not only to happiness as a generalized whole, but to each of its components, every one of which happiness relies on to exist.

*

One of my greatest joys back then was being in the presence of my son. As fellow monks, Rahula and I saw each other often, and even though I still at times longed for him to love me as his mother, I'd learned to use this craving as grist for my meditation's mill. I was grateful for the kind of love we did share. He seemed eager to hear me recite his father's Dharma, and often he helped me and the younger monks carry water from well to wash house. I was most grateful that he seemed happy in his life, reflected in his kindness toward everyone around him, including his grandmother—my dear Ama—whom he visited at least once a year. Ama was now a widow; my father had died under the wheels of a chariot while wandering the streets of Kapilavatthu in a drunken stupor not long after Jagdish was replaced as head of the Sakyans.

Rumor has it that my father was never the same after Siddhartha dishonored our family by abandoning me, but I knew better. According to Ama, he was hardly bothered by Siddhartha's leaving, especially when Jagdish used his absence to advance his own ambitions. But when Jagdish returned home in disgust, if not disgrace, my father took to strong wine in ever greater amounts. Did I grieve him? The way you grieve a hole that will never be filled. My main concern was Ama, whom I couldn't visit—because there was no reason for Ananda to visit his unknown cousins. I could only hope that Ama knew she could always join the nuns' Sangha. Perhaps Rahula could persuade her, although I never wanted him to do so by resorting to his thousands of protective deities, a subject I never discussed with him.

By now I was in my mid-forties, although I was often taken for much younger, thanks not only to the delicacy of my features but also to a youthful appearance in general, similar to my mother's. (I didn't disabuse people about my age—better to be taken for young than for female.) We were back at Bimbisara's bamboo grove in the middle of a pernicious monsoon season, reminding me of the one after Deepa's death. Every day, storms galloped through our encampment, and even on rare sunny days, thunderheads promenaded across the sky like an emperor's army parading through conquered lands just to remind us of its power. One couldn't escape the sounds of pounding, rushing, slashing water, rivaled only by the moans and howls of the wind. When the wind calmed, it was replaced by fog, hulking over fields and swallowing jungles, themselves exhaling the mounting odor of rot. Even the green bamboo trunks were slick with moisture that never had time to dry. Disease stalked us all.

The possibility of sickness was a perennial concern for me, for I could allow no one to take care of me lest I be found out. Luckily, the three humors of my body—phlegm, bile, and wind—almost always remained in balance. Fainting during my pregnancy was the sickest I'd ever been. But I still took precautions. Wherever we stayed, I'd acquaint myself with the local doctors and herbalists who doled out medicine to the monks in the same way as almsfood, as monks were forbidden to procure them on their own. Since I knew herbs, I could make recommendations and give advice, welcomed for the most part, and I always made sure that the basic medicines—ginger, fenugreek, coriander, rice starch, tulsi leaves, holy basil, and other herbs—were easily available. My efforts were supported by the Venerable Sariputta, who also concerned himself with the health of the monks. He stressed cleanliness and—like me—was known for taking up mops and brooms whenever necessary, much to Devadatta's disdain.

But now we'd heard that people in town were succumbing to the worst sort of swamp fever, the kind that boiled the blood and voided the bowels, leaving many corpses behind. The Sangha could do little other than keep the quarters clean and make sure our suppliers among the laypeople had the correct herbs on hand. Then one morning I awoke to a headache and a heavy chill shuddering through my body. I had a fever, but, steadying my mind in meditation, I became convinced I could wait it out. For now, I needn't put on the white robe I kept hidden under my folded-up yellow ones. It was not yet time to crawl off to the charnel ground to die as an anonymous widow and be devoured by beasts. Ananda was not ready to disappear.

A week later, except for residual stiffness, I was back to nearly complete health. It was morning; the weak sun pushed half-heartedly though sagging clouds as I opened the flimsy pine door of my hut into a green world of stems and leaves, which struck me as wildly intricate after days of having white muslin's opacity as my only view. I made my way through the bamboo grove to its main clearing where the monks were lining up for almsrounds. The group was smaller than the week before.

Something dark tore through me. In my illness, I hadn't thought much of who else might be sick. I glanced around, catching sight of Kavi, Naveen, and most of the younger monks. Most.

Where was Rahula?

I took several deep breaths. Rahula could be with his father and his chief disciples dining with the king, and even if he had fever, he was young and strong enough to fend it off, as I had done. Nonetheless, my feet carried me directly to Devadatta, who headed up the line. "I notice many monks are absent this morning," I said, trying to prevent myself from swaying on my still quavery legs, suddenly much more unstable. "If you tell me who is ill, I can collect medicine for them."

Devadatta raised his long chin, an almost triumphant expression on his face, like that of a soldier full of lust for a battle he'd been long awaiting. "The fever is taking many," he said. "There are so many clutching fingers, which now finally have to let go of this delusion we call health."

"And who has been taken?" My throat was throbbing.

Devadatta told me the names of five or six monks, mostly elderly, and I allowed myself a breath of relief along with my sadness for the loss of these venerable ones. "And others—are there monks who are seriously ill?" I asked.

Devadatta's expression hadn't changed. "Illness is a concept," he said. "One of our finest awakened brothers is about to enter his *parinirvana*," the word for the death of an enlightened being.

"And who is this, that I might honor him?" *Not Rahula. It can't be.*

"The Tathagata's own son has chosen to be an example to us all."

I did my best not to run until I was out of sight.

I knew he would be in his hut; he was never ostentatious, not even in dying. By the time I arrived there, I was possessed by a blinding terror. Even now, as I record this, I can't remember who was standing outside—Sariputta or Mogallana or the Tathagata himself, or all three of them—when I pushed my way through the door.

Rahula lay on his mat, skeletal and with a fiery yellowish glow, his skin like glazed terra cotta, as if no longer alive. A young monk I didn't know attended him.

My son looked directly into my eyes and smiled. "I waited for you."

"You need medications," I said, glancing at the young monk, who I was sure had neglected him, caused his death, murdered him. "I can get them to you by noon."

Rahula nodded at his caretaker. "Please leave us now," he whispered to the young man, and I had the feeling he was protecting him from my anger.

As the monk left, I knelt over my son, desperate. He was still so beautiful. He looked like his father but slenderer even when healthy, with larger eyes and longer eyelashes. But now his eyes were sunken and his jaundiced face was glazed with sweat. A fecal atmosphere filled the tiny room. "I know the kind of fever you have," I said, trying to tamp down my terror for his life. "You need cinnamon and sweet wormwood, and I can boil some grapefruit. These will bring down the fever and restore the balance you need—"

"No," he said, raising a trembling hand, yet smiling, and I realized he had been smiling all the while. "I'm done with this body. I am in bliss and love fills my every breath."

"Your deities! They're deluding you!" I was filled with a vision of Mara's hallucinatory legions glimmering in the costumes of angels, plotting the death of my son. All these years they'd deceived him! "You're needed here in the Sangha, where you teach and inspire." I was gasping for air. "Only Mara would deny this."

His voice, barely above a whisper, remained calm in the way of his father. "I wasn't meant to teach in that way. There are people here, in this city and in this sangha, who will awaken because of my passing. You can be one of them."

His peacefulness only added to my despair. "What do I care about awakening if you die?" I had given up all pretense of concealment, but I at least had the presence of mind to stop talking at this point and plead only with my eyes.

He raised his hand and closed his icy fingers around my wrist, sending a jolt through my heart. We had not touched since the day he left for his father's Sangha when he was seven years old. His grip tightened. "Don't let your love for me overwhelm all you have learned."

My face was drenched with tears. "You know."

"Ever since I awakened. How could I not?" And now his still shining dark eyes softened with deep gratitude and great concern. Enlightened or not, they held the love of a son for his mother.

I longed to clutch him in the embrace I had been denied for years, but even now the fear of someone seeing us ruled me. I did my best to bury my sobs deep in my chest. "Don't leave me. Please. Please."

"Look at me," he said. He had not released his grip. "All things pass away."

And for that moment, I saw. He and I reflected each other, our bodies and minds temporary manifestations of a splendor only suggested by the whorl of golden light that seemed to engulf us. No reason to mourn these manifestations, any more than grieving the ripples in the sea.

I couldn't let this insight go, not this one. I needed to hold on to this gift of eternity.

But of course grasping after it threw me back into the nightmare of myself. I stared down at my son's empty corpse.

It was only my love of and ultimate belief in the Dharma that prevented me from howling in agony and tearing the brick and straw room apart with my hands and teeth. But Ananda composed himself. I spent some moments with the body waiting for the certainty to enter me. This cooling lump of clay was not my son.

When I was ready, the monk Ananda opened the door and let in the others. "Rahula has become his nonbecoming," I said. Later, the other monks and I washed the corpse and prepared it for cremation, a practice that was slowly replacing the charnel grounds. Locked away in my heart, Rahula's mother screamed without ceasing.

For weeks, although my mind accepted the death of my son, my body—the body of a mother—did not. It remained clenched into itself, assailed by typhoons of grief that made the storms outside seem merely a drizzle. Eating and sleeping were memories from another life; they made no sense now. I could barely drink enough water to keep going. Ananda's mind was dedicated to teaching the Dharma. The mother's body wished only to die.

Yet I continued with my practice, remembering Rahula's gift of faith.

Most of all, I remembered my promise to the Tathagata when I first joined the Sangha, that I would expand my love for my son to include all beings. I intensified my efforts to create harmony in our community, comforting the little boy monks who missed their Amas, making sure the older monks received the medicines they needed, and reminding all the monastics that class distinctions had no place in our community. I also kept up with the routine tasks of keeping records, noting where repairs were needed, and hauling water to the wash house. Slowly, the feeling of walking around with my heart and throat torn out subsided into a quiet determination to keep busy.

Not long after the monsoon ended, the Tathagata called a meeting of about sixty senior monks at Bimbisara's pavilion, the place where I'd heard my first Dharma talk. The forest around us and the fields beyond radiated an intense green in the aftermath of the rainy season, and the freshness of revived vegetation filled the air, which even I could enjoy. It was early afternoon just before the daily

Dharma talk, doves cooing in the branches, their liquid voices seeming to cool the breeze and fill the atmosphere with a tranquility at odds with the monks' uneasy anticipation. The Tathagata stood at the edge of the pavilion, accompanied by Nagita, who sometimes served as his personal attendant and was now frail and elderly, his bent shoulders huddled together, the knobby fingers of both hands clamped shakily around a wooden staff. The rest of the monks were seated crosslegged in the clearing in front of the two men.

"Nagita has been an invaluable companion to me for many years," the Tathagata said. "But he needs time for his own practice at this point in his life." The Tathagata looked out over the yellow-robed group of his followers. "Today I'm seeking a new attendant."

My first impulse was to retreat into the bamboo forest. Already, I could see some of my friends from the Sangha nodding and smiling at me, thinking that I deserved this great honor. But the last thing I wanted was to draw attention to myself. Fortunately, my former husband would agree, I was certain.

Already, monks were stepping forward to volunteer, but the Tathagata held up his hand. "I have already made my choice. My new attendant will be Ananda."

This couldn't be.

Surely, as was the case with his earlier views about women, something in his former nature was blinding him to the present reality. Or else he had to be testing me, expecting me to refuse. I stepped forward, prepared to turn down his offer.

"I am deeply honored, Master," I began. "But—"

There was a stirring among Devadatta's cohorts on the other side of the group. Not that Devadatta, who hadn't even come to this gathering, would ever deign to be the Tathagata's attendant, but I had a sudden fear that Devadatta would want control over whoever would serve in that way. Although he continued to spend most of his time in the forest these days, I never could shake the fear that one day he hoped to undermine his master. One way to do this would be to make himself privy to the Tathagata's intimate life by receiving regular reports from a close ally. Which would not be me.

My refusal died in my mouth.

"But I can only accept this kind offer," I continued, "if you will agree to the following provisions." It was then I spoke the conditions that by now have become famous. The Master wasn't to pass on any gifts to me or include me in any dinner invitations. I also made more positive requests, such as asking for the right to discuss any questions I had about the Dharma with him, and to make sure that he would let me memorize all of his discourses, including ones he might give in my absence.

In this way, I hoped to stave off criticism, especially from Devadatta and his followers, that I was accepting the Tathagata's offer for the sake of material comfort, and for awhile I thought I'd succeeded. As for why the Tathagata chose me as his attendant, I made a point of asking him as soon as we were alone together. We stood at the door of his hut, the first crickets testing out their songs of night.

His face seemed to fade into the twilight. "For many reasons. I trust they'll all become clear." He refused to say any more.

I believed that at least in part his choice had to do with Rahula's death. Although I assumed he was beyond ordinary grief, perhaps his body experienced the loss in the same way as he still felt physical pain during times when he was unable to seclude himself from it by entering meditative absorption. Perhaps he saw our new relationship as some kind of compensation, a way of redirecting love. Or at least my love. Certainly, we would be far more intimate than before, although I knew that there was nothing sexual in it for either of us. For better or worse, I had sacrificed that part of me. Beyond my motherly feelings, I hardly even thought of myself as a woman anymore. And I now remembered Stick Woman's words, that saving the world required sacrifice, and I asked myself again: Was that what I was doing? Trying to save the world? Yet the Tathagata himself characterized the world as a dream, a mirage, a magic show, no more substantial than foam on a river.

Then I thought again about Devadatta and his cohorts wearing dingy unwashed robes to express their utter hatred of the world. Perhaps the Tathagata needed me, who still believed in the world, to save it.

14

*Y*ou can't untangle karma, the Tathagata always maintained. It's far too complex to explain in simple terms although easy enough to conceive of as the law of the universe, where every cause has its effect. But you never know when causative events, so complicated and multifarious, will come to fruition. All you know is that their effects cannot be escaped. In the Buddha's seventy-first year, karma ripened for our Sakya clan in the worst way possible, which would eventually put the survival of the Tathagata's teachings in peril.

By then I was almost sixty, and I'd been his attendant for twenty years. During that time, my life resembled my previous years with the Sangha although with more duties. In spite of them, my contentment grew as my grief for my son, while never leaving me, slowly transformed itself in the way of shadows giving shape and beauty to my life, blended as they were with my gratitude for his time on earth. I may not have been enlightened, but along with the other monastics, I periodically caught sight of a truth that sparkled through the sludge of ignorance, sometimes unexpectedly, in the ordinary course of living. This glimpse of the infinite came from the power of the Dharma, which shattered the cramped prisons of habit and stripped away the self-concepts smothering our hearts and minds.

My time to meditate was limited, though, what with teaching every sort of student, from fellow monks to kings and courtesans; plus, I was still in charge of the day-to-day sangha business of coordinating Dharma talks and public meals and reporting the likes of privy leaks and rat infestations to the appropriate lay volunteers. I also now had the Tathagata's personal schedule to manage, along with his health and general well-being. I enjoyed caring for him—simple, loving tasks, such as rubbing his back after he'd spent an entire day and a large part of the night teaching and doling out advice. Was this my femininity expressing itself? It didn't matter what I called it—by this time I had been posing for over half my life as a man. But perhaps the simple acts of one being caring for another is actually what the deepest joy of a marriage comes down to, whether or not the partners abdicate their sex.

The conflicts we had were mainly over my tendency to worry and grieve. Those years saw the deaths of many beloved monks and nuns, and most devastating to me, that of Pajapati, who I missed almost as much as my son. I also worried about the Tathagata. His unremitting life of teaching and running the Sangha was wearing out his body, a process that all too many of his monks—who wanted to maintain their illusion of an all-powerful leader—tended to overlook. But his back pained him after years of wandering from town to town, sitting on hard platforms giving lectures, and conducting interviews until he went hoarse and every one of his monks had fallen asleep. I of course was old too, but I seemed to have inherited my mother's youthful vigor (at almost ninety, she lived on), people continuing to take me for far younger than I was. And even though I worked hard, the Tathagata toiled harder, for he also had to juggle

the politics of his supporters, which got messier and more dangerous as the years went by.

Shortly after his seventieth birthday, when we were once again
staying in Jeta's grove, our clan's karma bore the first of its poisonous fruit. It began with a panicked visit to the Sangha by King
Pasenadi, who had remained a faithful follower even as his kingdom expanded. The king had always counted the Sakyans among
his vassals, so for him to visit our private part of Jeta's grove, instead
of having the Tathagata come to his palace, was unusual, especially
considering he had brought his queen, none other than my former
servant Vasa. That day her round, once-bright face was lusterless
and frightened, and as soon as I saw her, the fear I'd lived with for
so many years awakened in my heart. It seemed very likely that the
king had discovered that my brother had passed her off as a noble-
woman for him to marry.

The Tathagata seated himself on a raised dais on the main pavilion, the royal couple sitting in front of him, with a half-dozen senior
monks—including Devadatta, unfortunately—standing at the
pavilion's edge. It was a hot, white-skied day, and the mango leaves
stood unmoving, lightly scummed with ocher dust. Beyond them
flies buzzed, and the late-season roses were faded and shriveled.
Had I not been trying to quell my uneasiness over this visit, the day
would have been a good one to spend reflecting on impermanence,
all the more so at the sight of the king. I'd always thought of him
as the picture of heedless confidence, an amateur Dharma student
happy to debate abstract matters over wine and roast peacock, surrounded by bright tapestries, beautiful women, and loyal retainers
armed to the teeth. But today he averted his eyes, his thinning black
hair pulled back awkwardly on his bare head. He'd left his turban

and sword—symbols of his royalty—back at his palace, obeying the protocol for visiting a spiritual teacher.

Gently, the Tathagata asked Pasenadi the purpose of his visit.

"Such treachery is not to be borne!" King Pasenadi's thick, beardless cheeks quivered as if he was about to cry. Then came his story of how my brother, Jagdish, partly out of Sakyan arrogance and partly to spite the Tathagata, had misrepresented Vasa when Pasenadi—who, even though he ruled over the Sakyans, came from a lower varna—had requested a bride. I had always hoped against hope that no one in Pasenadi's Kosalyan kingdom would ever find out. But now that karma had come round.

"Far worse than anything that happened to me," Pasenadi said, "my son was humiliated." He clutched his wide belly, clothed in crimson silk, and gave his wife a doleful look. Both he and Vasa were on the portly side, their faces soft with benign sensuality. Although the king considered himself a loyal student of the Dharma, he was too much in love with the life of the senses to make much progress on the Path—an example, the Tathagata sometimes pointed out to me, of how "a little bit of Dharma" failed to work.

The king, periodically swiping his plump face with an embroidered red and yellow handkerchief, explained how his and Vasa's son, Prince Vidudabbha, had visited the Sakyan home he assumed belonged to his maternal grandparents, only to find that none of the elders would receive him. Even worse, after his departure the servants washed every chair he and his retinue had occupied with a ritual solution of water and milk—something he discovered by accident when an attendant returned to the Sakyan residence to recover a lost sword. In this way, Vidudabbha understood that he had been treated as a member of a despised lower caste. He concluded that his mother had deceived his father's whole kingdom.

Pasenadi made his miserable conclusion: "I'll be forced to cast my beloved wife into prison."

Although appalled, I was at least gratified that, in spite of everything, the king had loved Vasa over the years. "None of this is your wife's fault," I said, not meeting Vasa's eyes, although at this stage in our lives I had very little fear she'd recognize me. Both of us had changed so much. Dear, lovely little sparkly-eyed Vasa, who had once reminded me so much of my sister Deepa! Now, no likeness remained at all in this puffy-faced, sad-eyed woman. Yet perhaps my sister would have come to resemble her, had she been the one to share Pasenadi's gluttonous life.

"The Sakyan leaders forced the deception on this woman," I reminded him. "She deserves no punishment."

Devadatta intervened, as I should have known he would. "The Blessed One's attendant is expressing only his views, which unfortunately are suffused with his well-known weakness regarding the inferior sex. One woman seems a small price to pay for your kingdom's peace."

All my years of mindfully managing my distaste for Devadatta evaporated even before he'd finished his reply. "Since when did the Sangha institute a policy of human sacrifice?" I demanded. "Non-harming, if I remember, is Precept Number One."

The Tathagata gave me a sharp look the likes of which I hadn't received from him for over a decade. I had demonstrated the critical difference between the enlightened and the unenlightened: Awakened beings have destroyed every seed of greed, hatred, and delusion inside themselves, whereas the unawakened still carry these seeds in their hearts, ready to sprout as soon as conducive conditions arise. Devadatta provided a rich source of water and fertilizer, at least for the seeds dwelling in me.

Nonetheless, the Tathagata did not disagree with me. He addressed the king: "You have duties to your wife, no matter what her varna. She's still your queen. Assert yourself with the authority of the Dharma, which so many of your subjects follow."

Pasenadi's heavy face slackened with a look of shame for his lack of decisiveness—mixed with relief to have his true desires sanctioned by his teacher. But soon enough his tense grimace returned. "I will gratefully follow the Dharma. But my son is another matter. He wants revenge."

"Persuade him otherwise. A father needs to guide his son." The Tathagata's habitual equanimous tone edged toward warning. "Revenge can only lead to an endless cycle of death and suffering."

As the royal couple descended from their dais, the monks all standing at attention, Vasa turned to me. "I thank you," she said softly, and I bowed, filled with sadness. I had a premonition I'd never see her again, and a sharp regret cut into my heart at the thought of a friendship that never had the chance to blossom beyond the promising buds of youth. But considering the varna system, with me as a noble woman and Vasa as my servant, any love between us would have always been stunted, and at its center a falsehood far greater than the deceptive roles both of us had played in our lives.

When the king and queen had gone, Devadatta spoke out. "Master," he said to the Tathagata, and the condescending way he said "master" stirred the hairs on the back of my neck. "Why do you shirk from using your superhuman powers to counter the threats of the Prince?"

The Tathagata spoke with the patience he usually reserved for seven-year-old novices. "Liberation takes place in the human realm, where karma must be faced. Not in magic shows that blind the ignorant to the truth of life."

Devadatta's cold gaze followed the path that the royal couple had taken through the trees. "You overestimate the human realm, I fear. People need to awaken to the authority of something larger then their piddling little lives." He cast me an unenlightened look of sheer hatred and walked off.

He was right, though. King Pasenadi never succeeded in persuading his son to abandon revenge. Within the year, word came back that Prince Vidudabbha had sworn to wash every chair that the Sakyans had cleaned with milk with the blood of their slit throats, a revenge that would eventually destroy our clan. Although the karma didn't belong solely to my brother, he had initiated the tragedy. And, sadly, my own karma with my brother was far from over.

For years I'd heard little about him, other than that after our father's death he'd left the family farm to my sisters' husbands and hired himself out as a mercenary soldier, fighting mainly for Sakyans who wanted to uphold their warrior caste against those who would deny its supremacy—people such as the hill tribes. As a monastic living the holy life, I sought to forgive him for what he had done to Bahauk and his people, although I would have been happier to forget my brother had ever lived. Because this was impossible, I refused to arouse my memories of him by ever asking of his whereabouts.

For years, I knew nothing of his dealings with Devadatta. I never forgot, however, that Jagdish had informed him that I'd visited Pajapati back when I was trying to persuade her to request ordination. And I still suspected that my brother and Devadatta were in collusion to keep the current regime as rigid as possible.

I also became more and more convinced Devadatta was planning to take over the Sangha. Ever since King Pasenadi's plea, he had taken every opportunity to complain to any monk who would listen that the Tathagata had done too little to squelch Prince Vidudabbha's threats. But Devadatta's dealings with another prince worried me more. This prince was none other than Ajatasattu, the son of the Tathagata's other main supporter, King Bimbisara, the owner of the bamboo grove where we so often stayed. Devadatta had initiated a friendship with Prince Ajatasattu when the prince was a child, impressing him with his magical powers, turning himself into a boy clad in snakes and sitting on the prince's lap—or so the story went. This was nonsense, of course; the so-called psychic powers had been a matter of puppets and ventriloquism. I knew this for a fact, because over the years I'd made an effort to learn some of these tricks myself as a way of teaching children and other gullible people not to believe in every demonstration of the supernatural they saw. Nonetheless, back then I'd dismissed Devadatta's performances as nothing more than his need to show off in front of royalty; in fact, I even saw them as a hopeful sign that Devadatta was easing up on his asceticism. Now, though, with Ajatasattu nineteen years old and often in Devadatta's company, a foreboding similar to my feelings about Devadatta and Jagdish spread through me.

My fears proved true. The Sangha was staying in Bimbisara's kingdom, and the monks, along with King Bimbisara and his court, had gathered in a mango grove for a Dharma talk. Three hundred or so people sat or stood around the main pavilion, the king and queen up front, servants fanning them with glittering palm leaves. Like Pasenadi and his queen, the royal couple provided an opportunity to observe the impermanence of all beings, however privileged. King Bimbisara's beard, now white, stood forth from his chin stiff as a shovel, vibrating with a slight palsy. His wife's shoulders, draped with a silvery shawl, were frail and hunched. Prince Ajatasattu stood off to one side, conspicuously resplendent in royal purple, surrounded by warriors from the King's army.

Devadatta stood up and said he wanted to make an announcement.

He nodded to the prince, then looked at the elderly king and queen pointedly, and at the Tathagata as if to include him in an assessment of old age. He took a step forward and spoke, hands together in the formal way. "Venerable One, you have worked so hard these many years. Surely, you deserve to dwell in ease here and hand over the Sangha to me."

The crowd shifted and stared in shock. As for myself, I remember that my panic was mixed with a feeling of justification. I'd never trusted the man and said so often enough.

But the Tathagata—in my opinion—looked mainly amused.

"I thank you for your concern," he said. "But I'm not ready to retire, not to mention that you are very close to my own age."

"Perhaps I am," Devadatta said. "And perhaps the Sangha needs new leadership." He gestured in the direction of the assembled yellow-robes. "A large portion of our monastics have been lolling about in a very unseemly kind of luxury." At this point, he switched his gaze to the lay audience, many in silk and with fan-waving servants. "Of course, this luxury is perfectly suitable for high-varna worldlings. But ordained monks, besides hastening their own enlightenment, should set an example for how laypeople might spend their future lives." He started in reciting what he felt the required practices should be for the Sangha, rules he'd been trying to institute since he'd joined and which we'd heard hundreds of times. These rules forbade monastics to live under any sort of roof and to wear anything other than discarded rags; we were also supposed to abstain from all meat or fish and to spend our entire lives in the forest.

The Tathagata stopped him mid-list. "Enough," he said. "Our monastics already can choose to live this way if they please. But such asceticism isn't necessary for awakening and often acts as an impediment, either overwhelming aspirants with unnecessary physical pain or filling them with spiritual pride for so-called accomplishments in self-denial. We've discussed this before, Devadatta. The Dharma has always been about teaching a Middle Way."

"It is my belief that the Middle Way is the Mistaken Way," Devadatta said. "As the new leader of our rejuvenated Sangha, I will myself serve as supreme example of what we monks all must aspire to—the life of spiritual warriors."

The word "monks" was not lost on me, any more than "warriors." I dreaded to think that Devadatta's proposed new sangha would exclude nuns. "I think the Tathagata has made his position clear," I said. "He is not about to retire."

This time the Tathagata didn't give me any sort of admonishing look. "Indeed I am not," he said. "And when I do, I trust that the Sangha is perfectly capable of self-government. I've never even considered relinquishing the Sangha to Sariputta or Mogallana, my oldest and most venerated disciples." His voice remained serene. "So how in the world, Devadatta, could you ever think I would hand it over to a lick-spittle such as yourself?"

The crowd gasped. The Tathagata never sullied his speech with direct insults. But when I looked over at his face, it was firm, not angry, as if the insult had been the only way he could get through to Devadatta.

Devadatta just stood there, his face gone dark as iron. "You yourself have called me one of your most accomplished monks, praising my psychic abilities."

The Tathagata's face was without expression. "Perhaps you've changed, Devadatta. In any case, beware above all of falsifying your accomplishments. You of all people should know the consequences of such lies."

Everyone, monastics and laity alike, knew the terrible karma of lying about one's spiritual abilities. For monastics it was nearly on a par with killing, because the delusions it created had the power to do such great harm. Any monastic caught uttering such untruths was immediately expelled from the Sangha, followed, it was said, by many lifetimes in hell.

In a silence heavier than a thousand elephants, Devadatta marched off.

With Devadatta gone, the Tathagata began the Dharma talk. He didn't seem to notice that Prince Ajatasattu left before he started speaking.

Later, alone with the Tathagata in the damp hush of the empty mango grove, I tried to explain my fear: Devadatta, considering the company he kept, could very well resort to violence, especially after such a humiliation.

"He'll do what he'll do, Ananda," the Tathagata said. "I spoke to him in the rough way I did solely for his own good, the way you might have to pry open a child's mouth to remove a pebble that he's about to swallow. I've done all I could. Now it's up to him to save himself."

I took a breath and asked the question that until now I had dreaded even formulating in my mind. "Should you die," I asked, "who will guide us?"

"I most certainly will die," he replied. "And your guide will be the Dharma."

And in his all-too-familiar way, he fell amiably silent, refusing to speak anymore. I tried to concentrate on the present moment, where he would remain alive forever.

With the rains ending, I began to overhear talk among the younger monks that mercenaries were in town. We were still in Bimbisara's grove, having spent the season there, and now dark rumors slithered about concerning Prince Ajatasattu, who supposedly wanted his father to abdicate, as Devadatta continued to hint that the Tathagata should do likewise. I often spotted Devadatta conferring with Ajatasattu and members of his retinue, and each time I approached all talk stopped. When I mentioned this to the Tathagata, he refused to involve himself in this intrigue, reminding me that the rains retreat was almost over, and we would soon be going on the road to teach. Then, on an overcast morning in Rajagaha, where about fifty monks and I had gone on foot to collect our alms food, I caught sight of my brother.

We had just entered the city gates of reinforced teak that ascended high above us, dark and glowering, especially in cloudy weather. But the atmosphere was brightened by the usual colorful crowd: bronze-skinned construction workers with clay-splattered dhotis, glittering nobles with crimson turbans and bronze scimitars, barefoot dancers with jangling silver bells around their ankles, and holy seekers of all kinds, along with animals from elephants and war horses to tiny yellow finches twittering in gilded cages. The air smelled of wood smoke, frying spices, and a mixture of human and animal pong.

Our line of monks let itself be carried by the crowd's motion as we made our way to the side streets where householders stood waiting to fill our bowls. Turning a corner, we eddied around a half dozen soldiers in black paridhanas fitted out with bronze daggers and iron swords. The tallest of them appeared to be their leader. I stared at the cleft in his chin, the set of his jaw, the righteous flare in his eyes. A deadly chill closed around my heart. The man had to be Jagdish.

He looked almost the same as I remembered him, older of course, but he, too, had our family's youthful appearance—his hair still mainly black, his shaven jaw almost as firm as a thirty-year-old's. The skin sagged around his eyes, but they retained their almond shape. I kept walking. I wasn't terribly worried at this point in my life that he'd recognize me, an aged monk among other monks, but I took no chances even as my mind thrashed about, frantic to know what he was doing here of all places. I thought of the hushed conversations in the Sangha and the suspicious meetings between Devadatta and Prince Ajatasattu, which excluded the King, loyal follower of the Tathagata that he was. I also thought of Jagdish reporting my "womanizing" to Devadatta so many years earlier. All my suspicions about the two of them conspiring returned. They could well be plotting against the Tathagata himself.

I spent the afternoon in the city questioning laypeople, mainly innkeepers and shop owners, about the military presence in town. No one knew exactly what these mercenaries wanted, but one word kept coming up: assassins. Finally, I convinced the local *paan* seller, a notorious gossip, that to supply me with information would gain him much needed karmic merit with the Tathagata, who he believed could fly to the deva realms and walk through walls. The paan seller confirmed my suspicions; Devadatta had been seen several times conversing with certain Brahmins known to oppose the Tathagata, who had in turn been seen with Jagdish.

I thanked him and returned to the bamboo grove, reflecting that I had my own karma to worry about. Once again, I'd broken my monk's precepts and engaged in deception, which I'd done by omitting the fact that I'd never witnessed the Tathagata's supernatural powers. I vowed this violation of the truth would be my last, never imagining, as it turned out, that I'd break this vow in less than two days.

That evening, I attempted once again to convince the Tathagata that he was in danger. He was in his wattled hut, meditating between interviews. "Ananda," he said, "there are two people in the world that you have yet to forgive. Devadatta and Jagdish. Don't you find it strange that these are the same two you now accuse of threatening my life?"

"I have evidence, not the least of which is that Jagdish has come to this city! Why can't you see this?"

He smiled wearily, as if to encourage a child who once again has gotten his lesson wrong. "Don't worry," he said. "I'll make sure to remain mindful of my immediate surroundings. And you be mindful of your emotions, for only if people think you're sufficiently enlightened will they give you the authority you'll need to recite the Dharma once I'm gone."

"I don't want you to die prematurely," I said, and with these words my fears burgeoned, even as the Tathagata dismissed me with a kind but firm nod.

By the time I reached my own hut, I was convinced that only I could save him from the mercinaries, although I had enough presence of mind to ask, was this Mara's doing, this self-importance clothed in mounting torment? Not to mention that I was virtually helpless, an elderly woman disguised as a monk committed to never harming another living being.

But I had to do something.

The following morning I made a private alms visit to Bimbisara's physician, which I often did to procure medications for the monks. Long ago I'd used some of these substances as cosmetics; now I needed them to transform my face into that of the demon who would visit my brother. The day was bright and sunny, making it reasonable for me to request some kohl to protect some of the older monks' sensitive eyes; I also asked for turmeric powder, my old friend, to help with the digestive problems that had lingered on since the monsoon. In my hut, I mixed the turmeric into a soapy red paste and blended the kohl with seed oil. Yes, I was already involved in unwholesome acts of deception. Surely they were justified if they saved the Tathagata's life! That is, if my intentions were pure.

Yet how could I know? What I was about to do was hardly suitable for a person of my age—monk or woman. But no one else had seen fit to stop my brother, killer of my lover and countless others, most likely even our sister, and he was now seeking to destroy the opportunity for all beings to end their suffering forever.

A desire shuddered through me to see Jagdish in hell.

Involuntarily, I gasped. Had I really had such an evil thought? Apparently, by plotting against my brother, I had prepared the soil for hatred and delusion to sprout and flourish in my heart. Oh, so quickly!

Whatever I did tonight, I had to do mindfully and take no pleasure in feelings of revenge.

As soon as I finished my chores, I headed for the outer forest, ostensibly to meditate but actually to change into my widows' white clothes, the ones I still kept hidden in whatever cave or hut I occupied for when I had to crawl away to die. I took with me the medicine vials, as well as a hand-sized oil lamp, a half-dozen cleaning rags, and a little clay jar containing a mixture of lard, ash, and lye for washing my face afterwards. In a tangled grove of palms and ivy, I buried my yellow robes and placed a rock over the spot. Then I started out for Rajagaha, draping my head in a thin white scarf.

I'd learned from various shopkeepers where my brother was staying, at a courtesan's brick mansion that also functioned as an inn. It stood on a side street, not far from the main road. By the time I arrived, the city was glimmering with oil lamps and smelling heavily of their smoke, the air vibrating with the human din of shouts, conversational chatter, flute warbles, and—as I reached the house's voluptuously carved wooden gate—the moans and shrieks of love.

In spite of my nervousness, I had little trouble entering the courtyard—brown brick and dripping with jasmine—I passed myself off as a servant, a hunched-over widow who begged for rice and stray coins as payment for any sweeping and scrubbing I could do. Here was yet one more example of impermanence to ponder—that women are the most visible of beings in youth, only to fade away with our beauty until in age we are as close to invisible as a being can get. Tonight I took advantage of this invisibility, an anonymous crone peeking into boudoirs and banquet rooms. Jagdish was in one of the latter, seated at a table with a dozen of his cohorts, the group wreathed by spangled women undulating their hips, caressing the men's muscled bare arms, and murmuring as many flattering lies as they needed to create the illusion that they were the source of supreme happiness. My brother merely scowled even as he pinched breasts and bottoms between swigs of wine. A woman-hater, resenting his dependence on them for physical relief.

I returned to the courtyard, which was empty but for three bejeweled women lolling in wrought-iron swings. I bowed and spoke in my most elderly and obsequious voice. "I have a digestive potion that Jagdish Gotama wishes me to deliver to his room."

The oldest of the women, about forty and wrapped in crimson silk, shrugged. "Second floor, right-hand corner. But don't expect him there anytime soon." With this remark, she glanced at her companions, and the three of them shared a titter at the idea of an old widow waiting in a virile man's bedroom. I thanked them, smiling at the humor that helped them forget that they shared the old widow's fate.

The balcony overlooking the courtyard was dark and narrow, lit only by wall sconces. Earlier I'd spotted a couple of empty bed chambers, doors ajar, where now I stopped to borrow a mirror, my throat tight with guilt—*Second Precept: Never take what is not freely given.* I whispered a plea for forgiveness, then made my way to the room where my brother was staying. It was a corner chamber hung with striped tapestries and furnished with a table, a stool, a stand-alone closet the height of a man, and a canopied bed large enough for two or three people to engage in many kinds of imaginative copulation. If I knew my brother, he wouldn't bring a woman to this room, preferring to sleep alone after having degraded himself with the female sex. But if he brought someone, so be it.

I needed to prepare my face. Daubing on the kohl and turmeric pastes, I thought of Bahauk's war paint, the night he almost converted me to demon belief. My demon face would be far worse: a glossy fire-red skull and face with black-smeared teeth, eyes sunk into hell-black hollows. Pale, wormy tongue writhing in the darkness of its mouth-pit below black-rimmed nostrils. Black neck, and hands and arms saturated in blood-scarlet. I rearranged my widow's robes, fraying the sleeves with quick jerks to the thin white fabric. I wound the long scarf around my waist to give form to my figure, then threw the ends over my shoulders to be used later to drift veils of mystery through the air. I hid behind the closet, extinguished my lamp, and waited.

Downstairs, it took a long time for the noises of rutting and revelry to subside. Now I was glad for my practice, because in the growing silence my mind dredged up all kinds of fears. My brother would see through me, he'd have me arrested, he'd panic and kill me. I was only partly successful at calming myself. All my subterfuges and breaking of precepts, not to mention my rekindled anger, had greatly agitated my mind. There's good reason that the prerequisite for meditation practice is a moral life. A quiet conscience forms the major part of a quiet mind.

It was the absolute bottom of the night when my brother finally tramped through the door, a cursing, sweat-stinking presence but alone. Muttering an incantation to whatever gods he was worshiping these days, he slumped into bed. He lay on his back, fully clothed, snoring, a change from the Jagdish who always took pride in discipline. Another example of impermanence, I told myself. It seemed the anger and greed in his heart had finally triumphed over his pride.

I waited for his breathing to even out and sink him into the farthest depths of sleep, for I wanted his rise to the surface to be as disorienting as possible. I could only hope that my own thundering heart wouldn't wake him, especially when I took his sword off its hook and cast it into the bushes outside the window. It was then my second treacherous fantasy burst in on me, passing away almost immediately but filling me with horror. I saw myself plunging the blade into my brother's breast.

Forgive me, I prayed to all beings. May my motivations be pure.

But it was time to act. The sword disposed of, I tiptoed out the door and lit my lamp on the nearest sconce. Back inside, I placed the lamp on the floor and crept over to the bed, where I poked my brother hard in his still firm belly. Then I rushed back to the room's opposite side and climbed up on the stool, my robes drifting down as if I were floating. As he stirred, I hissed as loud as I could. His eyes blinked open. "Who?"

I hissed again, just as loud. *"We know what you did."*

He sat bolt upright and stared ahead, not entirely awake. Then his gaze flew to the room's upper corner where the sound was coming from. My black teeth were bared, but they remained closed together, thanks to my ability, inspired by Devadatta's magic tricks, to throw my voice. *"We know what you did,"* I repeated.

He half-scrambled, half-fell out of bed, then lunged for the wall, grappling the bare brick for his sword.

"There are no manmade weapons in hell," I hissed, then treated him to a performance of my writhing tongue.

"What are you!" His demand, loud as it was, cracked with fear.

I cast my voice to the room's other side, and spoke in the lowest register of the low voice I had cultivated over decades. *"Those who kill a Buddha will live in hell forever."*

"What are you talking about!"

I spoke through my demon teeth. *"We have seen you and the monk Devadatta plotting against his life."*

"You have the wrong man!"

I doubted this; otherwise he would name someone. But I had another test for him.

As he glared at me, shaking his head in feigned denial, I projected an imitation of our sister Kisa's voice into the room's opposite corner: *"Brother, why did you poison me?"*

From my own corner, I hissed again. *"We know what you did."*

A sharp pungence almost knocked me backwards. My brother had urinated. "I did nothing!" he sobbed. "It was the gods! I prayed to them and they chose that mushroom! I just put it on her plate to test whether she had offended them!"

My viscera contracted, squeezing out my breath. So he had poisoned our sister, after all.

And now my Mara-self whispered to me outright: You shouldn't have thrown his sword in the bushes. You have every right to cut out his liver and feed it to the crows.

I had no time to repent this thought, only to cast it aside. I had to keep going, speaking as Kisa: *"Call off your men and confess to the Buddha or I will send you to hell before the first bird calls at dawn."* I picked up one of the cleaning rags and held it to the lamp's flame. As it flared up, I let it drop to the floor. *"Go, now! Purify yourself in the river, then go to the Buddha and beg forgiveness. Leave this place and speak to no one until you've made your confession. Or this whole building burns to white ash and you are lost forever."*

He crawled to his feet, trembling.

I made my voice ricochet all over the room, hisses and curses and threats. *"Go! Now! Or die forever!"* I lit up another rag and held it out.

My brother had all but liquified in terror. Smelling of excrement, he stumbled out the door.

I heard his clamor on the stair, heard the outside gate creak open and swing shut. Then came Mara's final visit.

It took the form of a wild triumph somersaulting through me, making me want to tip over the table and tear the tapestries off the walls in sheer exhilaration. I'd done it!

I only had time to mutter a generalized forgiveness plea, no time to concentrate on remorse. I stamped out the burning rags, gathered my equipment, and rushed out the door.

After rearranging my white garments and veiling my face with my scarf, I hurried through the streets to the nearest well, deserted at this time of night. As quickly as possible, I washed off as much of the kohl and turmeric as I could, using my rags and the contents of the soap vial.

Once outside the city gates, I had my lamp to see my way through the nearly absolute blackness of the cloudy night, paying attention to every step. It was only when I reached the Bamboo Grove that I realized how often my higher motivations that night had been engulfed by the black ignorant ocean of anger and pride.

I sank to my knees in the cold sedge grass. I knew then that I'd have to confess to the Tathagata and beg his forgiveness. And that he might likely expel me from the Sangha.

If so, along with losing everyone I loved, I would fail in my life's original purpose. I would let Deepa down. I would never awaken to her soul or find a way back to her, beyond mere glimpses on the path. And these glimpses were only memories, fading by the second even as the dawn seeped into the sky.

I opened my eyes in my stuffy little hut, the air smelling of straw heated by the midday sun. Panicked, I jolted to a sitting position. It had to be past noon. In spite of all my fears and regrets, I'd fallen asleep as soon as I reached shelter. My feat had exhausted me: I was no longer a twenty-year-old.

By now the Tathagata would be meditating on the small teak

platform in the grove's depths, a place restricted to private interviews for monks. With the rain's retreat nearly over, he'd probably
be alone—unless the assassins had visited, either with an apology
or an attack. I hurried to the platform, stopping at the washhouse
to scrub off any last traces of my demonic identity.

The sight of his solitary presence sitting cross-legged on the varnished floor made me want to weep with relief. I paused at the platform's edge. Sun and shadow danced through the trees and over the
Tathagata's head and shoulders, now gaunt with age but still alive.

"I'm here to ask forgiveness," I said, falling to my knees. I confessed everything, including my feelings of triumph and hate.

The Tathagata folded his hands, as equable as could be. "They
have been here," he said. "The whole Sangha is reverberating with
the wondrous story of how the Tathagata stymied his would-be
assassins by the power of a single enlightened glance. It seems I
have you to thank."

I dared not look up

"How could I not be grateful?" he asked. When I looked at him, he
was smiling. "Don't forget, gratitude is one of an awakened being's
favorite emotions."

"So you forgive me?" I asked, as perplexed as I was relieved.

"My forgiveness is a given," he replied. "You now have to forgive
yourself. Your remorse and regret are your karma; self-forgiveness
is your practice." He stood up, slowly, favoring his back. "When
motives are mixed, so is the karma, but you did well to save Jagdish
and his men from serious consequences."

I felt compelled to ask. "Did he confess that Devadatta hired
him?"

The Tathagata shrugged. "He confirmed your story about a third party. I questioned Devadatta, who replied by declaring that he was leaving the Sangha and teaching on his own."

My rush of relief plummeted, as though struck by an arrow. "So he's not disrobing. And we don't know for sure if he tried to have you killed."

The Tathagata merely smiled. "A good example of uncertainty, one of the primary characteristics of reality. But our Sangha will survive. For now."

"For now?"

"Impermanence. The most primary characteristic of all."

I closed my eyes, concentrated on my breath, and observed the stream of sensations arising and disappearing in my body. In this way I prevented the fear gnawing inside me from swallowing my mind.

That was how I learned that Devadatta created the schism in the Sangha that he'd threatened all along. With several hundred fanatical monks—and to my surprise, a dozen or so nuns—he'd already left for Gaya Hill, never to return. Yet the Tathagata never uttered another word against him other than a general announcement to the public that Devadatta, who had failed to uphold the principles of the Sangha, was no longer to be considered a part of it. There were rumors later that Devadatta regretted his actions and wanted to apologize to the Buddha, but I never saw him again to find out. Many of his monastics did rejoin our Sangha eventually. But I never knew for certain if Devadatta actually hired Jagdish or merely suggested the deed to Prince Ajatasattu, who we soon found out was already scheming against his father.

My joy at Devadatta's departure made my efforts to forgive him— for whatever he had done—much easier, but, oh, the stories that have flapped about ever since and come to roost in minds that should have known better. Tales that Devadatta not only hired assassins but also tried to crush the Tathagata with a giant rock and later used a mad elephant to attack him—all these attempts failing, according to the storytellers, thanks to the Tathagata's superhuman powers. Unfortunately, I was implicated in some of these tales, probably by monks who'd observed my concern about the danger to his life and drew their own conclusions. In a few stories, I actually saved the Tathagata; others portrayed me as a fool, throwing myself in front of the rocks and elephant, trying to rescue a superhuman Tathagata who never needed saving. Jagdish might very well have heard many of these tales, which may have caused him to suspect that somehow Ananda had set the demon up. At any rate, my karma with him was not finished.

But my personal karma formed only a minuscule part of the catastrophes in the years that followed.

15

*T*o relate the historical events that eventually led to me ending up disgraced and contemplating leaving the Sangha forever would take far more time than is left to me, so I'll say little more than that both sons of the Tathagata's devoted kings betrayed their fathers in terrible ways. The Tathagata called it the karma of monarchy, which even at its best was imbued with violence and greed.

In short, the princes Vidudabbha and Ajatasattu staged coups and both kings wound up dead. And that wasn't the worst of it. In the Tathagata's seventy-eighth year, Vidudabbha carried out his revenge, sending his army to raze our capital and massacre nearly all of the Sakyan clan. The Tathagata tried to negotiate a peace, but he managed only to buy time, for which I thank him, as most of my family escaped (my beloved Ama had recently died), including one of my sisters, who joined the Sangha. (Since then, the rumor has arisen that she's me, the Tathagata's estranged wife who finally made amends by ordaining as a nun. However many times she denies this, such rumors have a way of persisting.)

There were so many deaths! That decade also saw the end of the Tathagata's beloved chief disciples, Sariputta and Mogallana. When we received the news, the Tathagata's eyes seemed to mirror the loss itself, and I felt my heart tearing open. "To the Sangha, they were like the largest branches of a mighty tree," he said. "And now they've broken off." Yet as I continued to weep, the Tathagata's face clarified into purest compassion—and even joy. "How can you sit there and cry?" he asked me. "They have both attained parinirvana, complete freedom from the prisons of space, time, and emotion."

We were once again in King Bimbisara's—now King Ajatasattu's—bamboo grove, seated in a small pavilion not far from the three-story sal-wood residence hall Bimbisara completed for us shortly before his abdication. We'd returned to Magadha, after traveling from town to town, mostly among the Mallans and Vajjins. They were clan-republics, much like the Sakyans had been, their governments a far better reflection of our Sangha's organization than the region's ever more tyrannical monarchies, such as the one presently hosting us. Although the king's grove was green and shimmery as ever in the late monsoon morning sunshine, it echoed with shouts, grunts, thudding hooves, crashing metal, and all the other noises of warriors training in the fields nearby. Prince Ajatasattu may have knelt at the Tathagata's feet and sobbed his repentance for, as he put it, his "negligence" toward his father, but it was clear to me that he mostly hoped to glean information from his itinerant spiritual teacher as to how easily the clan-republics we had visited could be subdued, in case he felt like invading them.

"I can't help but grieve," I said, weeping anew at the sight of Sariputta's neatly folded yellow robe and worn acacia begging bowl, returned to us by one of his companions.

The Tathagata folded his arms, gaunt with age, and shook his head at me, the hopeless case. "Consider this," he said. "Your refusal to embrace the full truth of impermanence is prolonging your suffering in the same way that resistance to pain causes more pain."

Suddenly, I felt I could no longer bear his calm ability to savor the colors and textures of his life, light and dark, without attachment. "I know, I know," I said. "Like all beings, I'll be separated from my body and all that I love. Meanwhile, we're staying here with a king who's using you for his own selfish purposes, wasting your energy, and compromising your health when the Sangha needs you. The Order's future, especially without your chief disciples, is far from certain."

"What do you expect of me? I've taught you monastics everything I know. There are no secret doctrines in the Dharma I teach to be passed along to a select few. As I told Devadatta, the Sangha is perfectly capable of governing itself after I die."

"The Sangha is not ready for you to die!" I said, my voice jagged with desperation. "And you don't have to—if you only stopped working so hard and took seriously the tonics I make for you." I worried particularly about his attacks of dysentery, which seemed to be worsening.

"Oh, I take your tonics seriously, I just don't take them orally."

"This isn't a joke." Once again, I'd descended into huffiness. I couldn't help noticing that in his old age, the Tathagata was reminding me more and more of Stick Woman in his offhand comments about his personal survival, and I was reverting to a petulance I thought I'd outgrown years ago.

The Tathagata leaned his chin on his mottled fist, and for the first time I noticed a definite tremor. "So you yourself are not ready for me to die. But how long would you have me live? A thousand years?"

I concentrated on my breathing, trying to return to a reasonable state where the Tathagata wouldn't need to mock me. "You know how I feel about supernatural feats," I said. "I truly believe that the best way to gain enlightenment is with the help of a teacher with human limitations, not a god with special powers. Otherwise, one just ends up worshiping the god."

"Very well, then I won't choose an unnatural life span," he said cheerfully. I had no notion of the future consequences of our little exchange. I'd simply tried to disguise my personal distress by stating an intellectual argument. Nor did I particularly notice the novice, a pale, spindly twenty-year-old with a premature furrow between his eyes, who suddenly appeared in front of us and heard our conversation, or at least the last part of it.

The young monk cleared his throat. "The Venerable Kassapa the Great will give the Dharma talk tonight." Kassapa had joined the Sangha several years before, boasting of his spiritual knowledge and hinting that he was being groomed as the Tathagata's successor. I'd been too caught up with the recent tragedies to worry about whether he would turn out to be yet another Devadatta, poisoning the Sangha with elitist views.

The Tathagata cocked an eyebrow. "Kassapa *will* give the talk?"

The novice looked down. "Requests to."

The Tathagata stood. "Fine, if the other monks agree. But I'll be presenting the talk tomorrow." He smiled at me. "It will be my last one here. We'll be leaving Magadha within the week."

As the novice bowed and took his leave, I stared at the Tathagata, my surprise mixed with a new apprehension. Kassapa would remain in this area along with most of the other monks. Was the Tathagata departing from here to be with followers he could trust? How much influence did this great kassapa have, anyway? Surely the Sangha had not rid itself of Devadatta only to face another threat from within. "Why are we leaving so abruptly?" I asked.

"You were right. I need to make some preparations before I die, and I can't do it here. We'll spend the next rains retreat in Vesali."

"Why Vesali?" My feeling of danger was in no way assuaged by his choice. During our last stay in the republic of Vesali, a former member of the Sangha had denounced the Tathagata in front of the Vajjin parliament for promising nothing to his adherents except to teach them how to end their suffering. The Tathagata merely chuckled and thanked his denouncer for the compliment, but there were now those in Vesali who had become disillusioned with the Tathagata for failing to reassure them that he would use supernatural powers to save Vajji from military attack.

For the first time, I felt, like the sudden stab of a needle, the possibility that everything the Tathagata had tried to do in his life could fall apart.

At the very least, in Vesali our selections of lodgings would be limited. "Do you care nothing for your safety?" I asked him.

"Safety?" He gestured, the loose skin on his arm's underside swaying, toward the sunny fields beyond the trees, where metal clunked against metal and the warriors' cursing and laughter filled the air. Again he smiled. "One of the greatest sources of suffering is the craving for safety."

"Very well," I said. "I'll suffer for us both."

The next day the Tathagata gave the last talk he would ever give in the Magadha Kingdom, on the hunched gray shoulder of Vulture Peak, speaking to the Sangha from the granite cave that had been carved years before into a vast cube-shaped enclosure able to accommodate a hundred monks. "Be a lamp unto yourselves," he said. "Live with the Dharma as your only refuge."

His Dharma talk made clear, as I remember it, that we were to make the teachings part of ourselves and not seek an authoritarian leader to rule over us. After his death, we were to govern ourselves in a democratic way, similar to the Mallan and Vajjin republics, where we were headed. But not everyone agreed with my interpretation, and even then I wanted a more definitive statement from him, explicitly forbidding anyone from taking his place.

But now we were on the road again, wandering from town to town with a company of forty other monks, including my old friends Kavi and Naveen, my little-boy students who now were nearly fifty. At first everything seemed to go well. The Tathagata's health stabilized, and even though we were no longer staying with kings, our hosts owned estates that allayed my fears that we would end up sleeping on rock piles and eating cow fodder. The Tathagata still had plenty of followers among the Vajjins, who were a cheerful if decadent lot, dancing and singing at the slightest pretext and decorating everything in sight—sewing spangles on their clothes, artificially gilding the spokes of their carts' wheels, and even painting pink or blue polka-dots on their cattle. "We don't need to visit the deva realms!" the Tathagata joked. "We have them all around us."

For a couple of months, it almost seemed like old times, the Tathagata teaching in pleasure parks or dining with some, if not all, of the town's notables and discussing the Dharma, always encouraging the servants to listen in. He spoke often about how mindfulness and virtuous behavior fortified each other, teachings that suited the Vajjins, who lacked the discipline to pursue deep meditation.

Then one morning, under a sky packed with ominous purple clouds, the Tathagata announced to the monks that they were on their own for the rains retreat. He and I were leaving for the tiny nearby village of Beluva for an indefinite time. When I asked him why the change of plans, he replied that Beluva was a good source of lemons and water.

My fear for his life reawakened, clawing through me and shredding the foolish complacency that had lulled me over the past months. Lemon juice and water were treatments for dysentery. The Tathagata was predicting that his illness would return.

Beluva was a dank little hamlet of fewer than five hundred people. In the rainy season it seemed to generate its own darkness full of miserable little teakwood cottages black with rain and cringing under banyans and huge oaks that creaked and shuddered in the constant wind. But lemon trees flourished on the hillsides, and rivers and streams skipped and glittered everywhere. The Tathagata's lay followers procured a cottage for us—two dim little rooms next to a private wash house—and set about supplying us with curries and rice.

Almost immediately, the Tathagata fell ill.

As he had in the past when sick, he spent much of the time in deep meditative absorption, far from whatever pain his body might otherwise have suffered. But this time, his body seemed far more tortured, either rigid or quaking, moans echoing out of his dry and cracked mouth as if with a life of their own. Yet even when his mind was not absorbed, his words remained calm. "It would be good if you recited some Dharma," he said, his face a gray cadaver's but for the foul breath that hovered over it. "It will help me meditate."

A sick dread dragged through my body day after day as I performed the necessary tasks to keep the Tathagata alive, reciting whatever of his teachings came to mind while supplying him with water and dosing him with lemon, ginger, yogurt, and alkaline drinks, most of which he refused. For hours he just lay there, dry and shaking. My meditation practice barely kept me from caving in to the increasing terror that the Sangha would not survive.

Then one morning the Tathagata arose from his bed and went to the wash house. He returned in a fresh robe, emaciated but with the light back in his eyes. I was not shocked at his quick recovery—it was always so when the Tathagata was ill. Once the illness passed, he didn't prolong the symptoms by telling himself stories that he was still sick.

At the sight of his revived self, I wept with relief, telling him how terrible I had felt and how grateful I was for his revival.

"Not again!" he said. "This respite is temporary. How many lessons do you need to understand impermanence?"

But I wasn't going to hang my head. "I fear for the Sangha. Without your guidance it could very well fall to the Devadatta surrogates—such as Kassapa—who think that the heart of your teachings is to practice spiritual acrobatics."

He smiled. "That's where you come in. You know all my teachings. It will be up to you to ensure they survive."

Now I did hang my head. "I haven't even awakened."

"Well, then, awake! You have the power. You're loving and kind, and you've done so much for the Sangha over the years. Everyone delights in your presence and benefits from your recitations."

Flattered though I was at his praise, hopelessness weighed me down. So often in my life anger had ruled me. "I've never thought of myself as kind."

"That's because you don't cling to your kindness to define yourself. This is all to the good."

"I've practiced deception, I've indulged in grief," I said. "I've meditated all these years but don't seem able to get beyond this karma."

The Tathagata was silent for a moment, and our little hut seemed to open to the cries of the cuckoos and the wind in the trees. "Perhaps you need to confess."

I blinked, completely perplexed. "To whom? I already confessed to you."

"Maybe you need to confess to the world." In the dimness of the hut, I couldn't read his eyes. Was this more of the cryptic mischief of a man who considered himself beyond death?

"How could I tell the world the truth? The Sangha would be completely discredited; the teachings would be mocked." I studied the shadows gathered in his face. Maybe his illness had deranged his mind.

"Not that sort of confession," he said. "Write it down. There must have been some reason why you learned this skill."

"What would I do with such an account?"

He shrugged. "Perhaps you'll burn it. Perhaps you'll give it to a trusted friend. Have faith that the Dharma will guide you."

I still feared for the condition of his mind. "I need to know something of why you would have me do this."

The Tathagata sat down on the clean bamboo mat I had put out for him when he was in the wash house. He may have recovered, but he was still weak. "You yourself once quoted me comparing my knowledge to the innumerable leaves in a forest and my teachings to only a handful of them. For that handful is all that's necessary to end human suffering."

I nodded.

"Beyond that handful, I know some of the future—not what will come but what may come—knowledge that would not benefit an unawakened being. So you must have faith in the Dharma and ask me no more." Just then the sun came out, whitening the muslin screens over the windows and suffusing the room with feeble light. Now I could see his eyes, serene and compassionate as ever.

"I'll need something to write on."

"Palm leaves last longer than birch bark, I've heard."

It was then, in that sad little black-walled hut, that I first conceived of this confession, which you now have in your hands. But I had no idea that I might have to commit the most difficult crime of all to confess, one I wasn't sure even the Tathagata could forgive.

We spent the remaining two months of the rains retreat in Beluva, the Tathagata regaining some strength, meditating in the dank little hut or, on sunny days, under the oak trees. Then, on the day we were to rejoin the monks and go back on the road, the Tathagata turned to me, as if to make some pronouncement. We stood outside our hut, carrying our bowls. It was early morning, sun plashing through the greenery and birdsong embroidering the soft summery air. In a sling on my back I had my growing collection of marked-on palm leaves and all of our spare robes, including my white death robe, patched and repaired since I'd used it as a demon's costume.

"When I was ill," the Tathagata said, "I spoke with Mara."

This disturbed me. "You know I don't think of Mara as a separate person."

"You know I don't think of anyone as a separate person." His gaze focused and for a flicker of an instant I slipped out of time, merging with him into a single flow of purpose. Almost immediately, this experience faded into abstract memory, as it always did.

"What did Mara say to you?" I asked.

"He tried to convince me to die on the spot. Enter my parinirvana there and then. But I refused."

I knew not to feel relief but rather to feel the opposite. His health hadn't improved all that much. "And?"

"I told him he didn't have to wait long. Three months. Now we have two months left."

Along with the expected shard of dread, I felt a jolt of anger, as if Mara indeed were standing there, dangling the Tathagata's remaining time in front of me, daring me to look away. But more accurately, Mara was inside me, directing my anger at the Tathagata, who had presented me with this prophecy without my asking. "Why did you even listen to him?" I demanded. "Why didn't you just send him away?"

"Mara doesn't upset me," he said. "But it seems that because you're resisting him, he is always with you."

I had to swallow the corrosive mix of my feelings; the monks were arriving, the usual yellow procession flickering through the trees. As they lined up before us and bowed, I noticed that several of the younger ones carried poles and heavy cloth, which could be made into a litter if the Tathagata needed it.

An awful memory overtook me, of the donkey cart transporting my sister's body to the charnel ground.

In our travels we were accompanied by fewer monks than before (perhaps twenty-five), and most of the time we stayed in villages not much larger than Beluva. Why was the Tathagata taking us into these remote places? He refused to say. At the same time, I was heartened by the villagers' enthusiasm for the Dharma. "We have waited years for your presence, Blessed One!" The cry went out, a welcome relief from the jaded, quarreling adherents we had left behind in Ajatasattu's kingdom.

Our group reached the little village of Pava perilously close to

the time that the Tathagata had predicted he would die. We settled down in yet another mango grove, belonging to perhaps the
most enthusiastic villager of them all, a goldsmith named Cunda,
a name that even now many followers of the Tathagata refuse to
speak aloud. At the time, Cunda hardly seemed the type whose
name was headed for such an unfortunate future. He was a plump
man with delicate fingers and secretly pleading eyes. That day he
wore a big purple paridhana and couldn't stop smiling and bowing.
"I'm so honored to have you, Blessed One!" he kept repeating as he
conducted our saffron-robed procession through the fruitless trees
to our lodging, individual kutis of bricks painted red and yellow in
the Vajjin-Mallan fashion. Cunda gave us one last bow and invited
us all to dinner the next day. At the time, I thought nothing of it. I
was just grateful to be settled and, for the Tathagata's sake, hopeful
that we wouldn't have to move soon.

The next morning Cunda led us to an open pavilion in the
grove where a long table awaited us, ablaze with scarlet hibiscus
arrangements and Cunda's handcrafted gold plates and goblets.
The air smelled of frying yams and cumin, and peacocks strolled
about, only occasionally disconcerting me with their ragged cries.
Servants in red and green striped turbans were setting out breads,
yogurt, and lentil dishes, but the main course, Cunda told us, was
yet to come.

Once we were seated on the pavilion's many silk cushions, he
disappeared into the nearby brick kitchen and reappeared carrying a huge covered bowl, all gold. "Allow me to present to you
our supreme dish—pigs' delight, made with mushrooms, bamboo
shoots, and soft truffles. It's a speciality of the region."

I ordered myself not to jump to silly conclusions at the mere
mention of mushrooms. Surely Jagdish could be nowhere near

here—if he still even lived, considering he was almost the age of the Tathagata. Still, I couldn't help myself. I was seated next to the Tathagata. "You shouldn't be eating such rich food," I said.

"Nonsense," the Tathagata said, as Cunda spooned out the ocher-colored mush on his golden plate. When our host garnished the dish with chopped brown mushrooms, terror ripped through me.

"No!" I whispered, leaning toward the Tathagata, preparing to push his plate away.

"Stop that." His voice froze me. He had never given me so direct an order.

I stared down at my hands, my heart and gut churning with confusion and shame. The Tathagata tasted the dish, and pronounced it delicious. "But this is food that only a Tathagata can digest," he said. "Serve the rest of the monks more of your excellent dahl." He ate six or seven more bites, then pushed his plate away. "Bury the remainder of this dish," he said. "And I thank you very much for it."

I sat there stunned, thinking that Cunda must have believed that the Tathagata was carrying out some unknown ritual. In any case, he obeyed, his worried eyes only a little more dubious than usual, and then sat down to hear the Tathagata's Dharma talk, tailored especially for him, comparing the training of the mind to the refining of gold. "One practices with the goal of making the mind malleable by removing all impurities," he said. "Then, as with gold, it will have many excellent uses. Eventually, it will lead you to liberation."

I just stared at my golden plate, barely able to listen, unable to eat.

Two hours later, the Tathagata and I were meditating not far from our kutis when he fell over. He lay on his back, agony having its way with his face, while his voice remained serene. "I need you to do a few things," he whispered.

The dread and despair of the past year crashed over me. "They poisoned you!"

He actually smiled. "No, I skipped the mushrooms."

I had no time to think of the implications of this now. It was all I had to do to ignore my fear and desperation, as I turned him over in the grass and looked down at the back of his robe, which looked like he'd sat in a black swamp, spreading foulness through the yellow cloth. "As soon as this bleeding lets up," he said, panting a little, "we need to go to Kusinara."

"Why?" My voice buckled in my throat. Only if he were planning his funeral would it make sense to go to Kusinara, the largest town in the area and a place where he had many followers. Was this his destination all along? "You're too sick to move."

"Don't worry. I'm mindful of what I'm doing." With that he crawled to his feet and staggered to the river to bathe, waving away my help. As he emerged, I covered the wreckage of his body with a soft sheet, determined to concentrate only on caring for him. He smiled his thanks and sat down, his back against a tree. "Before we go, we need to make sure that Cunda hasn't blamed himself for my death. He had no idea about the poison, and he needs to be reassured that to serve a Buddha his last meal is a great honor."

Now outrage joined all my other emotions. "If he didn't poison you, who did?"

"No one poisoned me. As you well know, this blood is a recurrence of my earlier illness."

He was right, of course. I knew the symptoms of food poisoning, and they didn't include bloody diarrhea, especially so soon after the poison was consumed. "Then why did you skip the mushrooms? And why did you have the food buried?"

"Ananda," he said softly, "they were trying to poison you."

It was as if a warhorse had kicked me in the chest. "Why?" I managed to ask. I was too shocked at first to be frightened.

"You alone have memorized my teachings. It seems there are persons who don't want your version passed along."

"Who?" Now I was frightened, but also angry. "Could my brother somehow have done this?" I shook my head, trying to order my thoughts. "I thought I'd scared him away."

"You stopped him from assassinating me. But perhaps not from targeting the monk who's been praised for saving my life and perhaps conjuring up a demon to humiliate him."

I clutched my elbows, thinning skin sliding over aging joints and tendons. "I don't know what to do."

"Forgive your brother, if indeed he advised the poisoners." He looked beyond me, in the direction of Cunda's stately brick house. "Our host will make sure that those responsible will be brought to justice. This I know with the Dharma's eye. They will not live past tomorrow, but this karma does not belong to you." He turned his face to me, and it seemed cleared of all pain and illness. "My dear Ananda, it's time for me to die."

I had no time to forgive Jagdish, not then. I had to enter the same mentality that had got me through the death of my son, a state of complete concentration on my duties. The next day, I and the twenty-five other monks accompanied the Tathagata to the outskirts of Kusinara, carrying him on the litter, although he insisted on walking part of the way. At this point my focus was so intense I almost believed the miracles some of the monks were exclaiming about:

that the clouded river water had cleared so the Tathagata could drink it, that his skin had turned to the gold of the heavenly realms, that swarms of deities packed every point in the surrounding atmosphere. (The less enlightened devas supposedly protested his death, the more aware ones celebrated his parinirvana.) I do remember a golden clarity in the atmosphere as the monks wept and chanted, but perhaps this was the result of my concentration. The real miracle was how calm and mindful the Tathagata remained. Even his body had abandoned overt symptoms of illness; it didn't appear to be suffering in the way it had in the village of Beluva. Finally, in the late afternoon we reached our destination, the monks climbing the low hill to the sal grove where he ordered a bed made up for him between twin sal trees. Sal trees, considered sacred by so many peoples, were a logical choice, but I couldn't help remembering their role in the massacre of Bahauk's tribe. From now on, I would always associate these trees with death.

The thatched and wattled roofs of Kusinara lay below us already in shadow when the Tathagata motioned me to his side. It was then he told me that I shouldn't preoccupy myself with venerating his remains, and that after his death the Sangha should abolish those of its rules that were trivial or irrelevant, most of which had arisen on a case-by-case basis.

I glanced up at the swallows ducking through the deepening sky. I had a premonition that these directives would never be carried out.

My discipline gave way. I covered my face with my hands. "I've failed you. I've not awakened."

"You will," he said. He called the monks to gather around him as the sun buried itself in the forest beyond the city. "All past Buddhas have had an attendant like Ananda. These attendants embody kindness. They are also wise. Ananda will direct my funeral proceedings, which will be held in the way of the clan-republics, with celebrating and singing. Ananda will now go into the city and instruct the people how they may view my body. I will reach parinirvana on the final watch of the night."

My concentration returned, fortified by a sense of enormous responsibility and the power of his will, which seemed to have fused with my own. For now, I had gone beyond personal emotions and did as he asked.

By midnight, hundreds of white-clad mourners were milling around the hillside, their skin the silver of fish scales in the moonlight, their oil lamps bobbing in a stream that led from the town. They kept on arriving, in a din of chanting and weeping that—if one believed in that sort of thing—must have reached up to the realms of the gods. A smell of lamp oil, marigolds, and distressed humanity vied with the damp night air, all overlaid with drifts of frankincense. Still, the Tathagata lived on, answering questions from the monks while I tried to organize the mourners by household, so everyone could pay their respects, especially the women, some of whom were offering their jewels to be burned up along with their teacher. I longed to be at his side, but my duties kept me apart until the monks waved me over. He lay on his side in the lion's pose, and I would have knelt beside him, but I didn't want to block anyone's access to his presence. His voice came out, ageless and pure—or so it sounded to me. "Everyone, I say this to you. It's the nature of all formations to dissolve. Work for your freedom with diligence. Tread the path with care."

He entered absorption, then died.

As his final breath left his body, I remembered two other pre-dawns in my life, that of Siddhartha's desertion and that of Bahauk's death, where both times I thought I'd never felt so completely alone. Oh, but nothing like this. Then, as I knelt between the sal trees, the crowd all around me, the moon about to set, I thought I heard a sound discernible through all the prayers and weeping. Far off, it seemed, I heard the howling of a wolf.

16

In the days that followed, I submerged my despair in action. Above all, there was the body to prepare—that inert object that had once contained my husband, my teacher, my dearest friend, and what I mistakenly—or not mistakenly—called my soul and the spirit of everyone I had ever loved. I had no inner visions to gild or animate this corpse; to me it looked as dead as any cadaver dumped into a charnel ground. The sight of that gray husk, now lying on its back, eyes already dull as dried bone, transformed my grief into a paralyzing fear. What would our Sangha do now that our leader and teacher was so completely gone? What would I do?

I couldn't give in to that fear; I could tell by the shrieks and sobbing that too many others, especially those far from awakening, were on the point of doing just that. I pushed through my emotions, turned the body over, closed its eyes and mouth, and addressed the crowd of a thousand, now restrained by a half-dozen monks. "We will prepare the Blessed One's remains as those of a Universal Monarch who turns the wheel of righteousness," I said, because I knew this is what the senior monks of the Sangha—and almost everyone else, for that matter—expected, even though the Tathagata had not seemed all that concerned. I then informed the people of the city that the Tathagata had requested to be cremated according to their funeral practices, with flowers and song.

I realized I wanted the ceremony too. I needed some great observance with bells, drums, clouds of incense, and—most of all—towering golden flames that illuminated as well as consumed, transforming the deflated corpse from a thing into an event—a cosmic display inspiring awe even in those who'd never heard of the Tathagata's teachings. In no way did I see this fire as feeding a corpse to some deity, as Bahauk's tribe had done with my dead lover, leaving me with a handful of ashes to bury in secret. The flames that incinerated the Buddha had to live in the memory of the world, give form to countless human lives, and reach to heaven, whether gods lived there or not.

I ordered an iron vessel filled with oil and aromatic herbs to contain and preserve the wrapped body, and I arranged for the construction of a pyre. Meanwhile, monks from nearby kingdoms and republics staked out sleeping patches among the tall brown columns of the tree trunks, and whole families of laypeople wandered through the woods on their way to the city, hoping for lodgings with relatives, however distant. The crowds needed direction, and someone (me) to assign the monks who'd been traveling with the Tathagata to help organize the newcomers. And so I did, filled with an ever-increasing unease. Now was the perfect time for some ambitious monk to take over the Sangha. At least Kassapa was far away—too far, I hoped, to show up here and take advantage of everyone's confusion and grief.

The formal ceremonies began as soon as the body was moved to the city's center. With the bells and drums came harps, flutes, and conch trumpets, their cacophony somersaulting through the scented air. Laypersons of both sexes adorned the pyre as well as themselves with garlands of all colors, and in a matter of hours the whole city—roads, paths, parks, and even the trash heaps—was strewn with fist-sized mandarava flowers. Their color was the vermillion of blood and sunsets, and they had delicate curving stamens, each blossom like some strange creature with multiple antennae clawing the air.

The precremation ceremonies lasted seven days, after which we monks and the city elders agreed, to my relief, we could wait no longer for monastics and other devotees traveling from distant places. It was time to light the pyre, especially in view of the layered wall of gray clouds in the far west forecasting rain soon if not today. For now, the cool morning air was thick with incense and the sounds of drumming, which, as word spread that the burning was about to begin, were almost drowned out by the crowd's collective wail. The head of the town council, a gentle-appearing gray-haired man with rounded shoulders, picked up the unlit flare. I was about to nod to him to light the fire when a loud clang shattered the atmosphere and every sound in it, leaving the crowd in stunned silence, our bodies quaking with the bell's vibration.

Unseen in the incense smoke and masses of people, a hundred new monks had arrived, led by Kassapa. Here was the monk I'd feared above all, the one who could very well replace Devadatta, striding in my direction. He had a vast blade of a nose and eyes like polished zinc, his steps twice the length of an average man's—despite his age, which had to be at least seventy, the same as mine. He extended a long arm out over the crowd. "What is this outrage!" he demanded.

Mutely, the council headman handed him the flare, yet to be ignited.

I struggled to resume breathing, at this point not so much

terrified as horrified that Kassapa had interrupted the Tathagata's funeral in such a way. "The Blessed One ordered that the ceremony be conducted according to the customs of this town," I said as calmly as possible.

"With all these women? They have defiled the Tathagata's body with their tears."

My horror sharpened into anger. At that point I was convinced he was no better than Devadatta. But I knew enough not to indulge my unenlightened emotions at this sacred moment.

By now the crowd, men and women, had backed away from him, leaving plenty of room for Kassapa and his monks—all in patched and shabby yellow robes, their eyes scummed with disapproval of the people's flower-wreathed garments—to surround the pyre. Kassapa arranged his robe over his shoulder in the formal way, and the monks followed suit. Then he put his hands together, raised them and circumambulated the body three times, touching his head to the corpse's feet, his monks all doing the same, walking so close together that none of the crowd, including me, could see who lit the flare.

An enormous orange flame sprang up and spread out into space, as if to tear down the top of the sky. The crowd gasped and fell to its knees. Most of them believed that Kassapa's mere presence had brought the fire to life.

The Buddha's body burned until only the bones remained. I could do nothing but watch, hoping that somehow this great flame would burn away my own ignorance and delusion, so I would know what to do next.

Not long after the fire started, Kassapa approached me. "I hold you primarily responsible for the desecrations that I've witnessed," he said. His black eyebrows were sharply peaked as if in permanent outrage, although his voice was calm as stone. "As the Tathagata's chosen successor, I will now take over."

"The Tathagata never mentioned that you were to succeed him," I said, my chest tightening as if to contain a wrathful Mara baring his fangs in my heart.

"The Buddha and I exchanged robes shortly after we met," he said. "And I attained enlightenment in one week's time. If one could say that any man was his true son, he would say it of me."

I found myself wanting to tear down his presumption and remind him that the Tathagata's true son was Rahula, who had awakened long before Kassapa and at a far younger age. But such a remark would only feed Mara. "The Tathagata has spoken little of you to me," I said.

Kassapa raised his eyebrows. "Why would the Perfect One speak to you of me? You're not even enlightened."

"And you claim to be?" Alas, my personal anger at this man who had so insulted women proved my lack of enlightenment yet again. But I couldn't believe his assertions—had he really let go of his attachment to his sense of a separate self?

Kassapa turned toward the crowd and addressed them in his bass voice. "I have attained the direct knowledge of things as they really are. Anyone not completely mired in delusion can see this in me. One might just as well think that a bull elephant seven cubits high could be concealed by a palm leaf as think that my direct knowledge could be hidden."

I was about to demand some kind of proof for this assertion when the crowd's murmurs changed into shouts of amazement. "Look!" a man cried out. "The Devas are coming to earth! They're surrounding Kassapa the Great!" "They're blessing him!" came another voice. And another: "Rainbows pouring out of heaven!"

I saw none of this. Although I may not have been alone in my blindness, it seemed as though more and more people were peering upward and agreeing that Kassapa's power had spangled the air with divine beings. Then almost simultaneously, as if under a spell, they all knelt, pressing their foreheads into the earth. "You may lead us," came the shouts and murmurs. "Kassapa the Great!"

Were these people's visions a sign of his enlightenment? The crowd obviously believed it, but I wondered: The Tathagata's followers had been cast into the same darkness that I occupied, and here came some powerful monk vesting great authority in himself to offer them a way forward on their path. Could their longing for miracles actually produce them? I didn't know.

Kassapa continued. "In Rajagaha in two month's time, I will hold a council to decide on who will transmit the Blessed One's teachings from now on and what exactly will be taught." And now he directed his zinc gaze back on me. "Only monks who have attained full enlightenment will be allowed to attend."

My despair returned, leaping up like a panther and closing its jaws around my throat.

Over those next weeks I redoubled my efforts to awaken, using my grief as the object of my meditation. This feeling of utter loss remained with me, as if a scimitar had swooped through my chest, cutting out my heart and then continuing on to sever the ground from under my feet. I tried to open myself to this state and perceive its deeper reality, investigating its movements, patterns, and qualities within my body and mind, knowing that if I could observe it from outside itself, it would pass in the way of all mind states, once I detached from them. The feeling did disperse at times, until I remembered my last look at the Tathagata's dead face. Then it seemed I'd made no progress at all.

Yet I persisted. For if I was unable to attend the Council, Kassapa's version of the Dharma would prevail—with its emphasis on severe asceticism and supernatural feats, along with its view of women as little more than an impediment on the path. Not that I had any hope of obliterating his influence, but at least I could state the Dharma as I knew it and perhaps even slip in alternatives to his one-sided stories. Most importantly, I could make sure that the nuns' discourses were preserved. Although at least Kassapa never suggested abolishing the nuns' order, there were far too many monks who felt that the first duty of all women was silence and who would conveniently "forget" the nuns' wisdom unless someone explicitly included it for memorization. If I couldn't get into the Council, my only hope—a very slim one—was that the Sangha itself, especially the nuns and younger monks, could resist caving in to Kassapa's authoritarianism and preserve the Dharma as they remembered it originally spoken.

Then one day this hope all but died. By now I was back in Rajagaha, site of the Great Council and realm of the treacherous King Ajatasattu who'd imprisoned and starved his father, our old friend Bimbisara, to death and who Kassapa now praised as a true follower of the Dharma. As a result, I was no longer comfortable staying in the Bamboo Grove. I'd made myself a little sleeping shelter under a rock outcropping in one of the surrounding hills, which reminded me of where I'd once stayed with Stick Woman, sleeping on straw among bats and eagles—at least Kassapa couldn't fault me for my bedding.

The dry season was underway, though not yet oppressive. I was doing my early morning walking meditation on a barren hillside with a path winding through wispy bleached grass and slanting gray boulders as big as a procession of elephants when I spotted a yellow-robed flock of mostly younger Sangha members climbing a gravel slope and calling out to me. My old and beloved friend Kavi, the former boy monk, still round-eyed and stubby-chinned at fifty, headed up the group, followed by Naveen, my other boy-monk friend, who had taught me to write so many decades ago. From the pinched-face urchin I'd persuaded the Tathagata to ordain, Naveen had become quite the handsome monk, with long dimples under his cheeks giving a dramatic shape to his face.

"May we walk with you?" Kavi asked.

"Of course," I said, warmed by the presence of so many monastics who were dear to me. Included in the group were four nuns, careful to obey the precept of remaining at the end of the line as it took form on the path—a sight that always produced a little twist inside me along with a hope that someday this rule would change.

The group walked awhile in silence but for the wind thrumming in my ears and the calls of raptors bouncing off the boulders. Below us stretched the flat valley, checkered yellow and green, the silver strand of its river glittering with morning sun. From this distance everything seemed so small, the trees like humps of moss encroaching on the miniature city and the tiny pink confection of King Ajatasattu's palace, which had once so overwhelmed me with its size.

As the path dipped down into the oak forest, Kavi cleared his throat. "Ananda?" he said, "we wish to request something of you." As he spoke, the line of monastics disintegrated and the group reformed around me.

A nun called Thullananda spoke out. "It's more than a wish. It's an absolute necessity." She was about forty, of average height but with a wide stance and fierce brown eyes.

I nodded in a neutral reply. Thullananda was known as a brilliant and powerful teacher who had taught the Dharma to King Pasenadi, among others. However, as a woman of strong opinions she had made enemies in the Sangha, not the least of whom was Kassapa.

Kavi cleared his throat again. "Many of us think you need to press your case for being on the Council. After all, you alone have memorized all of the Tathagata's discourses."

"Kassapa knows this," I said, "but he's afraid that if he invites one unawakened monk, all the other unrealized ones will complain of injustice." Which was true, but what Kavi didn't understand was that for me to go up against Kassapa and his fellow Council members would put me under the scrutiny of over a hundred presumably enlightened masters, directing their attention to my mental and physical being, in all likelihood resulting in my exposure. Although I had assumed over the years that the truly awakened would accept me for who I am, as had the Tathagata, how could I know what awakened people would do until I achieved enlightenment myself? Also, the Sangha contained highly aware individuals who had not necessarily taken the final step of wiping out their personal desires completely. And these desires could well take the form of condemning the Sangha and even the Tathagata for allowing a woman to do what I had done. At the very least, I would be expelled from the Sangha for all time.

Thullananda threw her robe over her shoulder. "I can't believe Kassapa is worried about injustice. That grandiose hypocrite! There are plenty of enlightened nuns—but do you see any invited to the council? I think not."

"He's worried about the Sangha's unity," I said, cringing at my memory of when I excoriated the Tathagata for using the same argument to exclude women. "A majority of monks would still be unable to accept the idea of women in the Council."

"None of us here feel that way," Kavi said, the others murmuring their agreement.

"On the contrary," Naveen said, "everyone here would vote to include nuns in the Council in at least the same proportion as they are in the Sangha. But not getting that, we need you in the Council—you, who have been such a great support for women over the years."

In other circumstances, I might have been able to appreciate the irony here, but now I felt only dismay. "There's nothing I can say to Kassapa to influence him, I'm afraid. He's never liked me—and even less after I allowed women to play such a major part in the funeral." I attempted a smile. "But I still have ten days left, and I mean to go into absolute seclusion in hopes of liberating myself at last. The Tathagata assured me that this would happen."

"Not enough," Thullananda said. "We need you to talk to Kassapa now. Some of us will go with you."

"I fear we'll only confirm his doubts about me," I said.

"Ananda," Kavi said in his soft voice, making me remember him once again as a little boy. "It's like this. If you don't attend the Council, hundreds of monks and nuns are planning to disrobe. Some have already done so, and only an assurance that you have a real chance to be accepted will stop the others."

I stumbled on the dirt path, almost falling into the underbrush. I had not expected this. The Tathagata—and I, too, for that matter—had always worried that the Sangha would fall apart because the ascetics and authoritarians would leave, disapproving of his supposedly lax rules and ways of living. But now, much to my dismay, it was the spectrum's other side who threatened to depart—the very supporters I depended on to preserve the Dharma and balance out Kassapa's extreme views.

I addressed the group: "You would abandon your chances for liberation—not to mention the opportunity to teach the Dharma—just because a single monk has been excluded from this Council? You would destroy the Sangha for this?"

"What Sangha? What Dharma?" Thullananda shook her head, as if some insect had invaded her ear. "Groveling to some pompous monk just because he claims he's enlightened? If I remember, the Tathagata told us, 'Be a lamp unto yourselves.'"

"He also spoke of respect for authority," I said.

"Fine," Thullananda said. "If your great respect for this despot prevents you from speaking with him, we'll all go and speak on your behalf."

I expected the others to protest this, but instead they all murmured in what sounded like agreement.

"Good idea!" Naveen said. "We shouldn't expect Ananda to risk his position, much less interrupt his meditation, but the rest of us have nothing to lose."

I was surrounded by cries of "Correct!" "Let's tell him what we think!" "We'll disrobe right in front of him!"

That truly frightened me: disrobing in such a way was tantamount to stripping naked in public, resulting in extremely bad karma, at least according to the Sangha. "Wait," I said. "I don't want you doing what you can't undo. You in fact have much to lose, even if you don't see it."

"That's your view, Ananda," Thullananda said. "But it's no longer ours."

I met her eyes, wedge-shaped and narrowed at the corners with her habitual determination. "If you insist on this protest," I said, "I'll speak with him myself. I'll take some of you with me."

"The nuns need to be represented," Thullananda said.

"Well, choose someone from among you," I said, hoping against hope they wouldn't decide on Thullananda, whose defiant attitude embodied all too many monks' fears of women's power.

The other nuns were younger, smooth-skinned girls of various shades of delicate brown, uniformly gentle in their manner. "We choose Thullananda," they said almost in unison.

Our group—which included Kavi, Naveen, Thullananda, and five other monks—visited the bamboo grove late that afternoon. In spite of the clangs and whoops of Ajatasattu's soldiers just beyond the trees, the grove was as beautiful as ever, each bamboo clump a fountain of long green curving trunks culminating in an ocean of lime-green leaves overhead. Kassapa, in a robe so faded it had almost lost its yellow color, sat in meditation on the grass, flanked by two other older monks in equally faded robes. As we approached, Kassapa's black eyes snapped open.

I barely had time to bow to him before he spoke. "Ananda, why did the Blessed One forbid more than three monks from traveling together?"

"To avoid trampling young plants, to prevent factions from forming, and to spare families from having to feed large numbers of people," I said, having no idea what he was getting at. I glanced over at my group, who stood at a respectful distance, hands together in formal obeisance.

"You and at least thirty of your followers were seen wandering the hills," Kassapa said, eyeing my group. "You could very well have been destroying crops and ruining families."

"We weren't 'traveling together,' Venerable One," I said. A Mara voice spoke inside me: *The old coot has spies, that's for certain.* "Nor were we wandering. We were performing walking meditation on a barren hill."

Kassapa flared his long nostrils. "The point is, you broke a rule, and you did it with untrained monks over whom you have little or no control." He glanced at his two companions, then poked his chin in my direction. "This boy has no idea of his limitations."

There was a whisper of fabric as my group of younger monastics shifted and stirred, apparently outraged at this insult to me.

I gave my friends a warning glance and addressed Kassapa politely. "I wonder what these gray hairs are doing on my head. Perhaps the Venerable One in his mindfulness of underlying reality has not noticed my age?"

Thullananda stepped forward, eyes blazing. Oh, no, I thought. "How dare you call the Lord Ananda a boy?" she demanded. "He's kept the Sangha and the Tathagata going for all these years. And he's taught us not only the formal Dharma, which he knows better than anyone in the Sangha, but also how to love and care for each other."

Kassapa replied to her with the emotion of a chunk of granite. "Your rudeness proves my point." He looked away from Thullananda and over at me, his gaze steady under the black tents of his eyebrows. "You've lost all control over your followers."

Naveen, the dimples in his cheeks hardening into deep creases, spoke up. "We're not the Venerable Ananda's followers. We're members of this Sangha. But if you don't let the Buddha's most loyal attendant—and the only person with complete knowledge of his talks—be a member of your Council, we and many others are prepared to disrobe."

I fully expected Kassapa to tell them to go off and do so. Instead his dry lips tightened almost imperceptively. "You need to have more concern for your karma," he said. "Abandoning the Blessed One's teachings, especially in these precarious times, would bring great harm to many beings, including yourselves."

I actually felt some relief at this point. Considering that the martial noises nearby were symptoms of these unfortunate times, I allowed myself to entertain a perhaps foolish hope that Kassapa cared for these monks and his autocratic manner came out of his sincere belief in the need for a strong leader to protect the Sangha from increasingly tyrannical kings. "Please listen to me, Venerable One," I said. "I speak the Blessed One's words strictly out of memory, unchanged by my views. For the sake of Sangha unity, I humbly request that you invite me."

Kassapa kept his eyes forward. "Very well," he said. "But in this Council, the Blessed One's words will pass only through lips that have been fully awakened. Since yours fail to qualify, you'll have to attend as a water carrier. I hear you've had much practice at this task."

My friends' outrage came forth in an audible gasp. I took the insult less personally—at least all my years of meditation had some effect—but I feared that Mara was on the point of taking over this group. "I've never found supplying people with water a degrading task," I said. "But I still have ten days to achieve liberation. The Tathagata expressed confidence that this will happen."

"I sincerely hope your practice goes well," Kassapa said. "But you have one more requirement, if you are to attend the Council in any capacity at all. You will have to answer certain charges against you. On the day before the Council, you will come into the Hall and meet with a committee of monks whom I will select."

I felt a plummeting in my chest.

Tullananda was glaring at Kassapa. "Who are you to order such a thing!"

Did I see a flash of anger in Kassapa's eyes? But this was impossible for an awakened Master. "You seem to have forgotten that the Blessed One and I exchanged robes shortly after we met," he said. He went on to repeat other details of their meeting, ending with him once again comparing his direct knowledge to a bull elephant seven cubits high.

"That's enough, Kassapa," Thullananda said, her failure to use his formal titles making his two subordinate monks gape. Thullananda ignored them, keeping her hard glare on their leader. "You've failed to convince me of anything," she said. "Out of respect for the Venerable Ananda and my fellow monastics, I won't disrobe on the spot. But I'm leaving this Sangha. I no longer can conceive of it as conducive to the holy life." She threw her robe over her shoulder and prepared to head off through the trees. She gave me one last glance, her eyes shining with tears.

Her sadness reverberated through me long after she'd disappeared into the trees. I knew then, whether or not I ended up accepted into the Council, I would never be able to salvage her reputation.

That evening I returned to the hills for my planned seclusion. Near my sleeping place under the rocky overhang was a granite cave the brownish maroon of raw meat, its walls polished and hewn to a size just large enough to stand up in, with a window-opening to let in light. I planned to spend the next ten days here, meditating with an emphasis on mindfulness of the body, as the Tathagata had advised me to do. The body, which never wanders into past or future the way the mind does, would tell me the truth of what was really happening—and hopefully, finally, I would awaken to things as they really were. If only the mind wouldn't interfere.

Sadly, it did. In the midst of the deepest bodily contemplations, where sensations of skin, muscles, and viscera sparkled and fizzed in and out of existence, revealing the body's composite and temporary nature, the thought would intrude: *What if I fail?* If I failed to achieve liberation, what would happen to the monastics I loved? Would they all disrobe? Would the Dharma be lost to everyone—or at least to women? When thoughts like this arose, I would switch my awareness to the clenched fist of fear behind my solar plexus. If I could keep my attention on it, the fist would loosen, for nothing stays the same, but all too often the embodied fear maintained its hold, recruiting emotions and other thoughts to kidnap my awareness—until another question took over my entire being: *What if the Council's examination revealed my gender?*

If I were to reach enlightenment, at least I'd know what to do about the problem of my sex. But if I didn't awaken in time, I couldn't bear to think of what might happen.

The more I struggled with these thoughts, the more my meditation stumbled.

The days hurled themselves past me, each night a reminder that the Council was to take place on the morning of the full moon. The moon was fattening all too rapidly, its growing light shrinking the stars and turning the rocks to chalk as I did my walking meditation on the high ledge. Day and night the winds shifted and moaned like the underlying restlessness that was one of the last fetters of the human mind to dissolve before awakening. Or so I'd been taught.

The day of my interrogation arrived. I would have to undergo it as an unenlightened monk.

*

The Council was to take place in the vast Sattapani cave on the north side of the Webhara Mountain, one of the biggest hills in the area. After an hour's sleep, I got up in darkness and reached my destination shortly after dawn, in time to get my bearings before the other monks arrived. Even though the hillside was still in shadow, I could make out the opulence inside—soon the cave's floor would be glowing with its patterned carpets of all colors, and the sun through the cave's overhead apertures would reveal polished stone walls bright with red and yellow banners. The cave had seven compartments and a wide outside ledge that extended far enough in front of it to fit the entire Council. At the center of the inside meeting hall gleamed a gilded throne, backed by a wheel of Dharma that looked to be solid gold. Kassapa might have espoused the most severe asceticism, but apparently his patron Ajatasattu had other ideas. Or perhaps Kassapa had approved of all of this in the same way I'd approved of the cremation, out of a need to add as much significance as possible to the Buddha's life and death. On the other hand, he may have set this all up to intimidate the ignorant and confirm his power.

I sat cross-legged at the mouth of the cave, waiting, as the rocks and scrub on the opposite hill warmed with the colors of the day. The winds had stilled completely, and the smell of rock dust and stale incense enveloped me along with a hush so profound that the bird notes inside it seemed like silver droplets reflecting the stillness rather than interrupting it. In this silence I heard the whispering slaps of multiple sandaled footsteps several moments before I spotted the line of monks, at least fifty of them, making its way up the hill. I felt a wave of dread as I imagined them focusing the precise attention of fully awakened beings on my minute facial expressions, the subtle textures of my voice, and the complete lack of beard on my unshaven jaw.

It didn't take long for them to settle in the cave, sitting cross-legged in their yellow robes, their shaven heads gleaming faintly in hues from pale mushroom to darkest teak, with Kassapa on the main throne and a pair of elders on lesser thrones on the opposite walls. I faced the assembly, sitting cross-legged in front of Kassapa's raised dais.

Kassapa's voice boomed forth. "I will now interrogate this monk before me on his infractions of rules." He turned to me, raising one black-peaked eyebrow and lowering the other. "You stepped on the Blessed One's rain-robe when you were sewing it."

What? I couldn't believe the pettiness of this accusation. Shocked out of my fear of exposure, I said, "Venerable Ones, not long before the Blessed One passed into his final nirvana, he told me that the Sangha, once he was gone, was free to abolish its minor and circumstantially based rules."

"And did you inquire which rules they were?" Kassapa's voice echoed through the chambers.

Again, I was shocked. "No, Lord Kassapa. The Blessed One was extremely ill at the time. It would have been a terrible strain on him, and besides, he said the Sangha could decide."

Kassapa shook his head. "Obviously, it was through a lack of mindfulness on your part that you failed to ask him. For he wouldn't have told you this unless he meant to enumerate the rules in question. What would people think of us—or of the Blessed One—if we abolished whatever rules we pleased as soon as his ashes were cold? As a result of your wrongdoing, I now decree that every rule will remain in place for as long as the Sangha persists."

The elders murmured their assent. I was too dumbfounded to feel outrage. Since when were we supposed to base our conduct on what people thought of us?

"Furthermore," Kassapa said, "for this interrogation to proceed, you must admit that treading on the Blessed One's robe and failing to ask him further about the abolishment of rules are both wrongdoings on your part."

Now I had to choose. For me to attempt further to defend myself could well stimulate the kind of scrutiny I needed to avoid. Even worse, Kassapa was now saying that if I didn't admit to his charges, he would expel me from the Council immediately and I'd lose all chance of saving what I believed was the true Dharma. I took a breath.

"I don't see my actions as wrongdoings," I said. "However, out of faith that my future enlightenment will reveal to me the truth, I will acknowledge them as such."

Kassapa nodded curtly, affording me some relief that he, too, had faith in my enlightenment. Of course, at this point our views of my future enlightenment differed greatly.

Kassapa cleared his throat. "Now we come to the question of women."

My insides went cold.

"You and I have already spoken about the funeral," Kassapa said. "Women, weeping over and fouling the Blessed One's sacred remains—you allowed this. Acknowledge that as a wrongdoing."

I allowed myself one breath of relief in spite of my extreme repugnance for what I now had to say. "I do not see my behavior as wrongdoing, but out of faith in my future enlightenment I will acknowledge it as such." At least, I reminded myself, I was able to maintain my integrity by registering my disagreement, although this was cold comfort indeed.

Kassapa wasn't finished. "Then there is the matter of women's ordination. You involved yourself in this matter."

Was he implying more than he said? Did he know how I had resorted to something close to blackmail?

His eyebrows revealed their usual amount of moral outrage, nothing more.

"I do not see what I did as wrongdoing," I repeated. "I was thinking particularly of Pajapati, who had cared for the Blessed One when his own mother died. She deserved ordination, and indeed, she has become liberated. As have many other nuns since then."

"Still, you must acknowledge your actions as wrongdoing."

"I cannot see them that way. But if this is what is required of me to join the Council, I will formally acknowledge them as such." I put my hands together and inclined my head.

By now my fear was passing into bewilderment. Nuns, including Kassapa's former wife, had been part of the Sangha for years. Were these men truly enlightened?

Kassapa cleared his throat. "Now we come to quite a serious offense, one that has repercussions on the entire age."

My heart lurched. All I could think was that the previous accusations had simply been a prelude to my exposure. Surely, there were no serious formal rules I'd broken other than my disguise.

"If not for you," Kassapa said, "the Blessed One would be alive today."

I was beyond bewilderment, black flecks swirled before my eyes. "I have no idea what you're talking about."

"Do you not remember that the Blessed One asked you how long you would like him to live? He even suggested a number—a thousand years—and he would have lived out the age had you begged him, which he expected you to do. Needless to say, this would have benefitted countless beings, who will now be deprived of his living presence."

It was then that I remembered the conversation I'd had with the Tathagata right before we left Rajagaha for the last time, when he'd asked me, jokingly, how long would I have him live, and I'd replied with some theoretical remark about the importance of having a human teacher and not a divine one. I now also remembered the spindly young novice, apparently one of Kassapa's spies, who'd overheard us. "That was a theoretical conversation!" I said. "The Blessed One was in no way hinting for me to beg him to live to an impossible age! Surely, if he'd wanted to live that long, he would have simply done so."

"You can't know that," Kassapa said. "Obviously, your mind was under the influence of Mara. You must acknowledge what you did was a wrongdoing."

"I don't see it as such. But for the sake of Sangha unity I will acknowledge it."

My interrogation was over.

"Go, now," said Kassapa in a flat voice. "You still have time for practice. Think of this session as a lesson in humility and detaching from the self."

It was all I could do not to storm out of the cave, much as Thullananda had the bamboo grove. At this point, I was certain that Kassapa planned to discredit all I stood for. Which was all the more reason to stay. But after these attacks I was in no state to meditate, much less achieve any sort of enlightenment.

The sun hit me full in the face as I pulled back the white cloth covering the Sattapani cave's entrance, and suddenly I was struck by a thought that nearly knocked me off the ledge: What if awakening transformed me entirely? What if I ended up on their side?

The way back to my personal cave was a winding gravel path lined with disorderly scrub and hut-sized, rust-streaked boulders; I walked in the day's mounting heat until the high noon sun became too much. By now I'd reached the notch between the hill I'd been descending and the one where I was headed, and the vegetation had burgeoned into jungle. A huge banyan stood not far from the path, its hundreds of aerial roots streaming down from horizontal branches and flowing out over the ground, as if the tree craved to possess the whole of earth and sky. It reminded me of the banyans I'd encountered when I'd first gone forth as a seeker, and I gratefully stepped into its haven of damp green aromas and glimmering shade. A good place to meditate, I decided, seating myself in an enclosure formed by a circle of vertical aerial roots, almost as good as a cave for darkness and isolation. I hoped that my lack of sleep would help weaken my self-constructed reality, allowing the truth to manifest at last.

But even before I lowered my eyelids, an all-too-familiar question attacked me. How would I know when and if I was truly liberated? People like Kassapa maintained that unless I recalled my thousands of past lives, traveled through multiple heavens, and acquired superhuman powers, I could never make such a claim. But in all my years of practice, I had failed to enter any of these unworldly states. Did I actually believe I could meditate my way into them in less than a day? The mere thought of it overwhelmed me with fatigue.

Before I knew it, I was asleep and dreaming.

The banyan had changed; its tangles and cascades expanded into a green dusk without limit where dim streaks of sunlight trembled up and down a ragged infinity of roots and tendrils. "Is *this* ultimate reality?" my dreaming self asked, "nothing but temporary shreds and fragments?" Then, on the other side of the tree's vast, braided trunk I spotted Kassapa and four or five other monks, standing in a circle and shouting. They seemed to be berating a man, a householder, in their center; then Kassapa raised a whip as if to strike him across the face. I ran to defend the man, stumbling and ducking around the tree's tentacles. "Stop!" I shouted.

Kassapa shouted back, "This boy tried to kill you!"

All at once I saw the householder's face, suddenly intimate, as if I were staring at my own reflection transformed into a male's. But the face wasn't mine. It belonged to Jagdish.

Not as a boy. It was his face the last time I saw him, when I'd tricked him into believing I was a demon. Then, in the way of dreams, the realm of the banyan tree vanished and my brother stood alone at night in a charnel ground, lumpy with corpses everywhere I looked. "Go home!" I shouted, my dream-self fearing for his life. "They shouldn't have left you here!"

I woke up, disoriented. The sun had set, and the trees's appendages looped and twisted in floods of darkness, the hanging roots surrounding me like the bars of a cage. My heart pounding with guilt for having slept so long, I scrambled to my feet, thrust aside branches and tendrils, and staggered out to the twilit path beyond. I had no time to ponder this or any other dream, and so I cast it from my mind.

The full moon was rising, a huge pumpkin over the eastern valley. I had less than a night to awaken after sixty years of effort. I decided not to waste time returning to my cave. I sat down on a rock and resumed my meditation.

I couldn't locate my breath. Instead, my awareness fell into a memory.

I was very young, four or five, and I'd been playing in the mud puddles outside of the kitchen door of my parents' home. All of a sudden Jagdish appeared, aged ten, shirtless and bleeding from a gash on his cheek, his face strangely dark as if flushed with some incomprehensible shame. I knew without having to be told that our father had beaten him, and not for the first time. A great dread crept through me. "Don't tell anyone!" he said.

"Why did he hit you?" I'd asked.

"He wants me to be a man."

At the time, I had no idea what this could mean, so in a child's way I accepted it at face value: Boys turned into men by being beaten. By the time Deepa was old enough to be my playmate, I had forgotten about these beatings, or perhaps I assumed that the beatings had in fact transformed my brother into a man. I remembered my older sisters teasing him, which still, I thought, did not excuse his behavior.

Now, age seventy, I forgave him everything, and the iron shackle that had been around my heart for so many years fell open. My brother's whole life had been driven by a terror too terrifying to acknowledge. I saw that now—and I was not just seeing it. I felt it as my own, the terror and helplessness shared by all beings, all needing salvation from the violent uncontrollable universe we'd landed in, the domain of Mara, lord of death. But there were many different notions of salvation. For my brother and so many men it required superiority to other beings, starting with women and children, which meant the ability to conquer and subdue them—as if treating beings like mere things somehow prevented you from turning into a thing yourself, a chunk of rotting meat in a charnel ground. Even Siddhartha had once believed this, although the only being he'd tried to conquer and subdue by extreme asceticism had been his own.

He'd changed, of course. After his awakening, he repeatedly warned against judging oneself as superior, inferior, or even equal to another being. To do that was to create a false sense of self.

I thought again about my dream, how Kassapa had called my brother a boy, the same as he had me. Did Kassapa still believe in his superiority and require it for his salvation? Whatever he had done, I needed to forgive him, too, and allow for the possibility that I really didn't understand the underpinning of his motivations.

I squeezed my eyes shut in a grotesque last effort to gain enlightenment so I wouldn't fail all those beings who, instead of aspiring to awaken, would despise themselves as women or boys who could never become men, doomed to decay into meaningless fragments. Desperately, I drilled my attention into my breath—but of course this was the absolute worst thing to do. Awakening meant opening my mind and heart to the present moment, not forcing my awareness into an image of what I supposed it to be.

I slowed my breathing, and finally calmed my body. But I could feel that some deep part of me was still holding on to self and world. Or, more accurately, I felt myself letting go, only to grab on once again. My feeling of total defeat returned. All I could offer the Council was the care I had for this world and the beings in it. At best you could call it love, which the Council recognized only as a means to that ultimate end, the final cessation of all suffering. This cessation was beyond words. Human love, compared to this non-state, was just another attachment.

I closed my eyes again, but this time I didn't meditate. I prayed.

In my thoughts I addressed the Tathagata, who not long ago had maintained that someone like me had served all the Buddhas of all the ages because the Sangha required someone who embodied kindness. The Tathagata had wanted me to serve on the Council.

Please tell me what to do, I said to him now.

But the voice that came into my thoughts wasn't the Tathagata's; it sounded like Stick Woman.

You know what to do, she said. Like the priests and the shamans, make your sacrifice to save the world.

I don't believe in sacrificing innocent beings, you know that.

Forget beings. All true sacrifice is of the self.

What "self"? What do I sacrifice?

What else? Your highest self's most precious possession. Your aspiration.

I still don't understand.

Fake your enlightenment.

My eyes opened on their own. I was staring at the white moon, which made me blink. I couldn't perpetrate such a deception. There was no way of justifying it—not to myself and not to the Council. Kassapa and the others had no interest in saving the world. The whole point of the practice was giving it up.

And you? came the question. What do you think?

I don't know.

But I realized I could form an intention to relinquish, one moment at a time, my attachment to the way I wanted the world to be.

I could also walk into the Council and let them draw their own conclusions about my enlightenment.

And if they declare you unawakened?

Perhaps I'll deserve whatever they do to me. If I end up in the hell realms—well, I've risked that before, haven't I?

I stared up at the rising moon, constricting into a white light pitiless as a judgment. At this point I wasn't all that far from my cave, where I could meditate in a welcoming darkness. I stood up. I could make it there by the time the moon was directly overhead.

I stepped onto the path up the dry hill, its gravel almost as white as the moon. For the first time that night, I noticed the crickets' chorus, shrill and quivering. I let the sounds penetrate me as I walked. In my cave I could resume practicing mindfulness of the body and wait out the night. I'd still have a few hours left to let go of everything for all time. If such a thing was possible.

Forgive yourself for not-knowing, came the inner message. And ask all beings to forgive you for any harm you have done or will cause.

And so I did. And I do.

Here ends my confession.

May all beings find the path to liberation.

Epilogue

Three Hundred Years Later, Mauryan Empire

Mercy, mercy, mercy, whatever am I to do with this strange "confession," passed along from monastic to monastic over the generations, ending with my eldest brother handing it over to me? I'm his far younger half-sister, a Sangha member like him and already fifty years old, my seventy-year-old brother not wanting to die with this wooden box full of inscribed palm leaves still in his possession. But am I to believe these written words? My brother told me the Venerable Ananda, Second Patriarch of the Sangha, bestowed this document to his closest friends, the venerables Kavi and Naveen, and told them to do with it whatever they thought best. So far, the decision has been to keep handing it down, recopying it over the years when the script becomes worn. Still, I'm probably not the first monastic to ask, "Should I throw it in the fire?"

This confession certainly casts new light—or maybe it's better to think of it as shadow—on the Blessed One's discourses. They're still not written down, although writing is becoming more and more common—look at our King Asoka, who works so tirelessly to spread the Dharma throughout the Empire. He's inscribed every boulder, pillar, and statue he can get his hands on with his own version of Dharma, even while the spoken word remains the only proper vehicle for the Buddha's teachings. By this time in my life my ears have received most of them, including the one where he warns of a counterfeit Dharma as the only thing that could bring the true Dharma to an end. Is this what I now hold in my hands?

Or is the counterfeit Dharma to be found among the spoken discourses themselves? Contradictions lurk in so many of them, although the basic tenets—descriptions of suffering's true nature, its causes, and the way out of it—seem clear enough. But sometimes the teachings appear to imply that godlike powers necessarily accompany awakening—and other times not. The judgments of women and stories about Ananda and others living back then are even less consistent. Yet it's clear that we women were accepted into the Sangha in the Buddha's day and that many became enlightened. Were the stories of these first nuns Ananda's contribution to these original discourses? Did he provide the balance he spoke of between his view and Kassapa's? (I use the male term only because of my own perplexity. Until reading Ananda's purported confession, of course I assumed he was male.) And what should I make of his eventually taking over the leadership of the Sangha? According to the history we've been told, it was handed over to him by Kassapa himself, designating Ananda as his true successor.

Maybe this document is a forgery, but surely if a forger wanted to discredit Ananda or the teachings, he would have made certain that as many people as possible read it and not just hand it to Ananda's friends with no instructions whatsoever—and without really finishing it. Also, consider this: Ananda lived an extremely long life—some claimed he reached the age of 120—and after his death, his body was burned on an island between two rivers as a way of avoiding favoritism of one group of followers over another. As a result, few people viewed the cremation and even fewer saw the unwrapped body. Perhaps the then-holder of this document was the only witness.

Still, I've thought about burning these pages. Even if they're true, their appearance in all likelihood would only stir controversy and cause division. With women's position in society continuing to erode, despite the Dharma's success this so-called confession could discredit Ananda, not to mention the Buddha himself, even more than in the time it was written. On the other hand, the admonition not to cling to any aspect of oneself—including one's sex—as an essential identity remains crucial to the teachings. Perhaps one day this distinct feature of the Dharma will be taken seriously enough for attitudes to change.

No, I cannot destroy these pages. The story of Ananda is such a mystery, and this confession might one day illuminate it in a way that helps people find the true Dharma. Especially considering that Ananda's enlightenment is perhaps the greatest mystery of all.

The official account is that he decided to spend the night in the contemplation of the body—which the confession relates as well. But, needless to say, the oral tradition has nothing about him feigning enlightenment. Instead, the monks relate how, near dawn, he decided to lie down after meditating all night. In accordance with proper practice, he'd been mindful of his body in the positions of standing, sitting, and lying down. Yet his enlightenment—when he finally abandoned all clinging—occurred in none of these positions. It happened "before his head touched the pillow and his feet touched the ground."

How could this be? He seems to have awakened in mid-air.

HISTORICAL NOTE

*"The Pali Canon served as the bricks, and characters like Svasti
the buffalo boy were the mortar. Although a boy named Svasti was
mentioned in the early scriptures, I embellished his character to help
tell the Buddha's story."*

— THICH NHAT HANH,

describing writing a biography of the Buddha*

In *Bride of the Buddha*, I portray a Buddha who is both a historical being and an evolving, collective creation of the human imagination. Both types of material—historical and imaginary—have advantages and disadvantages when it comes to depicting a figure who has guided millions of lives for twenty-five centuries. Factual evidence has the advantage of creating credibility, but even carefully documented earthly lives are always being reinterpreted, with some facts included and others left out—and the facts themselves are constantly being recast as well. The danger of demanding total conformity of a particular story to history is that we can become attached to facts as defined in any given era, confusing them with unchanging truth and closing ourselves off from other viewpoints. In hopes of pointing to possibilities beyond the strictures of our

---

* Thich Nhat Hanh speaking to a small group of students in 1988 about *Old Path, White Clouds: Walking in the Footsteps of the Buddha* (Berkeley, CA: Parallax Press, 1991), recalled by the book's editor, Arnie Kotler.

time and culture, I've also made use of some imaginary material, with its power to symbolize truths beyond words.

I wrote the life story of Yasodhara, wife of the Buddha, to explore the relationship between love and the quest for awakening; I also wanted to address the contentious questions surrounding the Buddha's abandonment of his wife and infant son to pursue his quest for enlightenment. My preparations included several visits to India, combined with an examination of the earliest Buddhist discourses, as found in the Pali Canon, and other early written documentation of the Buddha's life and teachings. Ultimately, I felt I had to treat both Yasodhara and the Buddha as historical individuals and imagined creations. Thus I mixed fact and fiction, taking advantage of modern scholarship while at the same time weaving in myths and symbolic narratives to express truths beyond words. Above all, the material I included, whether fact or myth, had to serve the story.

Many of the book's characters and scenes are based on canonical writings, but when the traditional tales, canonical or not, veer far from historical accuracy as currently understood, I toned down or discarded them, keeping only what seemed to me to have important symbolic value. Legend has it that the Buddha was a prince who lived in three palaces, for example, while scholars today believe he was the son of an elected clan leader in an oligarchy. To me, the palace legend demonstrates how even a life of power and splendor is subject to suffering, so I present Siddhartha as the son of a clan leader (rather than a king), while retaining the symbolic element of the story by depicting his residences as more opulent than they probably were. Another example: I portray characters witnessing paranormal events that Yasodhara or others present cannot perceive, leaving readers to decide for themselves whether these events were supernatural or hallucinatory (or both).

The ancient texts also contain certain anomalies about Yasodhara and Ananda. One is the failure of the Pali narratives to mention the Buddha's wife after she gives over her son to his father's Sangha, even though the same scriptures make much of Pajapati, his stepmother, the first woman to ordain. Two other, more striking, incongruities have to do with Ananda: Why did the Buddha need Ananda to persuade him to ordain women? Ananda hadn't even achieved enlightenment, and he used arguments that must have already occurred to the Buddha. The other inconsistency about Ananda is that in spite of his privileged relationship to the Buddha, he was the only close associate of the Buddha who failed to awaken in his teacher's lifetime.

My fictional solution was, as you've seen, to merge Yasodhara with Ananda, a strategy I hope will work well in our current age, with its openness to gender fluidity. (A monastic I know has referred to himself as belonging to a "third gender.") In any case, Yasi's joining the Sangha in disguise could explain her absence in the texts, while her life of deception, which violated the Buddha's fundamental precept that all speech must be truthful, could account for Ananda's difficulties attaining enlightenment. Also, her threat to the Buddha to make her female identity public *could* serve to explain why the Buddha was persuaded to reverse his objections. The texts themselves give some support for my choice to make Ananda and Yasodhara the same person. Both were cousins of the Buddha; both were known for their physical attractiveness; and Ananda is often depicted as devoted to women and their causes, even beyond his plea for their inclusion in the Sangha.

I also had to choose from among contradictory accounts of the same events. To resolve these inconsistencies, I had Yasi/Ananda treat many of them as inaccurate gossip. Non-canonical sources offer several versions of Yasodhara's life after the Buddha abandoned her, for example. There are stories of Yasodhara fending off suitors, others of her joining the Sangha as a nun, and one rendition of her being pregnant with Rahula for the full six years it took the Buddha to become enlightened. In *Bride of the Buddha*, Yasi denies these accounts, which strike me as apologetics for her absence in the earlier texts.

I also changed both Yasodhara's and Ananda's ages relative to the Buddha, not only because they're presented inconsistently, but because the numbers don't add up. The accounts that have Yasodhara and the Buddha born on the same day are legends, not historic truth. For one thing, in the ancient world men usually married women far younger then themselves. Also, if Yasi and Siddhartha were sixteen when they were married, as some stories tell, they would have been childless for nearly thirteen years, as Rahula was born when Siddhartha was twenty-nine in all the accounts. Thirteen years of infertility would have caused Siddhartha's father, if not Siddhartha himself, to arrange for him to take a second wife for childbearing. Even more important, his ongoing failure to sire children—an essential husbandly duty, especially for a clan chief-to-be—flies in the face of the problem-free life portrayed by the legend, which in my view demonstrates symbolically that even the most perfect life entails suffering. Finally, there is a tradition in ancient literature in which friends and associates were said to be born on the same day, suggesting that birthdays in common symbolized entwined destinies.

The problem of Ananda's age is even more complex. According to some sources, he too shared the Buddha's birthday, which would have made his job as the Buddha's attendant difficult in later years. Some scholars say the Buddha must have been thirty-five or more years older than Ananda, which raises its own set of problems. Ananda would have been a child and in no position to argue for nuns' ordination at the time Pajapati was struggling for women to be accepted in the Sangha. I chose a compromise, where Yasodhara/ Ananda is ten years younger than the Buddha but comes from a family known for its youthful qualities.

Finally, the texts portray many historical figures inconsistently. A primary example is Devadatta, the monk who in the Pali Canon tries to kill the Buddha, while another oral tradition portrays him as saintly and devout. The breakaway Sangha that Devadatta founded survived for many centuries, so the Devadatta in the scriptures might in some instances have been a representative of the Sangha's factions that promoted an extreme form of asceticism. In any case, Devadatta is sometimes identified as Ananda's brother, other times as Yasodhara's, and many scholars now believe he was just another cousin in the sense of being a member of the Buddha's clan. I chose the latter, more scholarly view. Another inconsistent account of a historical figure is that of Thullananda, the defiant nun who defends Ananda in the sutras as well as in my novel: She appears in the Pali Canon and other places as both a formidable teacher *and* a "bad nun." The bad nun moniker won out, and the novel hints at why.

Kings Bimbisara and Pasenadi both appear frequently in the Pali Canon, as do their treacherous sons, and much of what I present is true to both history and scripture. I did take liberties with the non-canonical story of Pasenadi's disastrous marriage to a servant by making her Yasodhara's personal maid before marrying Pasenadi, and I made Yasi's brother the perpetrator of the deceit.

I also added characters who are wholly fictional: Stick Woman and her assistant Bahauk, Yasi's brothers and sisters (although she doubtless had siblings), and Ananda's two boy-monk friends. Although Stick Woman is fictional, I created her in view of contemporary studies that claim women shamans were more common than formerly believed. The Sakyan clan did have relationships with the hill tribes of Northern India, although very few specifics are known, and the Gorge tribe, while fictional, is loosely based on the Khond people who may have resided in the hills near where Yasodhara grew up and reportedly practiced human sacrifice.

In some stories, I mix fact with fiction. Rahula is portrayed consistently in the texts, but the exact time and cause of his death are unknown. The texts agree, however, that he died relatively young and definitely before his father. His death in the novel from malaria is fictional, but entirely possible. Many of the novel's scenes between the Buddha and Ananda are told in the scriptures, including Ananda's attempt to persuade the Buddha to ordain women, the Buddha admonishing him for worrying about the Buddha's health, Ananda grieving over Sariputta's death, and Ananda expressing concern for the Sangha's future. The orders and advice the Buddha gives shortly before his death are almost all direct from scripture, including the famous quote, "Be a light unto yourselves."

Regrettably, some of Devadatta's sexist remarks in this novel were actually spoken in the texts by the Buddha. It's my (and not only my) belief that these attributions, which seem to contradict other statements, could be the result of later redactions and reflect misogynist inclinations in Sangha leadership, a backlash against the Buddha's allowing women to practice more or less equally with men. When feasible, I have Yasi/Ananda refer to Devadatta's remarks as wrongfully attributed to the Buddha by Devadatta's camp in an effort to make its bigoted views respectable. On the other hand, the sexist and self-serving speeches of Mahakassapa (Kassapa), as quoted or paraphrased in the novel, belong to him and him alone. Although the tradition respects him as the First Patriarch of the Sangha, some modern evaluations of his characters are considerably more negative. I didn't wish to make him and out-and-out villain—he was a man of his time—but I let the readers form their own judgments. As for his and the Council's interrogation of Ananda, this also appears in the Pali texts, with the same basic questions and replies as in the novel, although I do take some liberties with Ananda's replies, making them more qualified.

The facts around the Buddha's death are much debated. Lately, many scholars have concluded that he died of dysentery complicated by an intestinal aneurysm, as he does in the novel. But the stories about the Buddha being poisoned persist. My depiction of the Buddha's last meal comes from the Pali texts, where he tells Cunda to bury the "pigs' delight" after he samples it. Stephen Bachelor has suggested that the intended victim was Ananda, whose extensive and intimate knowledge of the Buddha's discourses was a threat to those who wished to distort them. Ananda's visit in disguise to threaten Jagdish, whom (s)he fears was hired by Devadatta to kill the Buddha, is fiction. Ananda's writing skills are also fictional, but when the nun in the epilogue describes his enlightenment, the quote she uses is directly from the Pali Canon.

A Note on Language

The Buddha probably spoke a regional dialect called Ardhamāgadhā, or Māgadhī Prakrit. His teachings were transmitted orally for about four hundred years before being committed to writing in present-day Sri Lanka in the Pali language. I used the Pali names for most of the novel's people and places, but because some Sanskrit words—namely, Dharma, karma, and Siddhartha—are already known to Western readers, I used them instead of their Pali equivalents.

ACKNOWLEDGMENTS

I owe an enormous debt of gratitude to my teachers over the years, both spiritual and intellectual. I thank the many teachers at Spirit Rock Meditation Center in Northern California, who instructed me in the Dharma, and especially Phillip Moffitt, whose wisdom over the past twenty years has informed my daily life as well as my writing. I am also grateful for the scholars and teachers whose work has inspired and informed me about the life and times of Yasodhara. (These include Karen Armstrong, Bhikkhu Ñanamoli, Bhikkhu Bodhi, Richard Gombrich, and many others.)

For helping me learn the craft of fiction, I thank my mentor James Frey, a great taskmaster as well as a good friend. I owe an equal debt to my critique group—Dorothy Edwards, Heather King, Max Tomlinson, and Eric Seder—for their incisive comments and the overall encouragement they gave me while writing this novel. I also am grateful to Jim Frey's many students who helped me hone my skills during workshops over the years. Jan Gurley, thank you so much for reading my first draft. I also want to thank my agent, Arnie Kotler, for guiding me through the publication process, as well as for his excellent editing of my final draft.

Thanks also to Paul Cohen, founder of Monkfish Book Publishing Company, for organizing his talented staff to produce *Bride of the*

Buddha: Susan Piperato for her meticulous final edits, Lisa Carta for her beautiful cover design, and Colin Rolfe for his overall creation of an elegant final product. And finally, I thank LuAnn Ostergaard for her original painting, which Lisa used to such great effect.

Most of all, I am grateful to my wonderful husband, Bill Coffin, without whose support—emotional, financial, and technical—this book never would have been possible.

About the Author

Barbara McHugh is a published poet with many years of experience editing fiction, newsletters, and technical documents. She has a Master of Arts in English literature from New York University and a PhD in religion and literature from the University of California at Berkeley and the Graduate Theological Union. A Buddhist practitioner for more than twenty years, she teaches courses in Buddhism and coleads a meditation group with her husband, William Coffin, a drummer and computer scientist. She is also on the board of directors of the Marin Sangha, founded by Phillip Moffitt, author and a guiding teacher of Spirit Rock Meditation Center. She lives with her husband in the San Francisco Bay Area.